D0204941

LOIS McMASTER BUJOLD

and

THE HALLOWED HUNT

"A thoughtful and skillful author."
Cleveland Plain Dealer

"A good writer who now seems to be writing
at the top of her powers."
Diana Wynne Jones

"Political intrigue, shamanic marriage, and dynastic
drama . . . Topnotch."
Library Journal

"An unusual kind of ghost story that transcends the usual
intimate form by several degrees of magnitude."
Locus

"Bujold [is] adept at slipping out of preconceived patterns
and delivering a story with strong characters and a
full quota of surprises."
Asimov's Science Fiction Magazine

"Talent and the pure pleasure of her voice hold a spot
for Bujold right where she should be: among the heights
of the master storytellers."
SF Site

Books by Lois McMaster Bujold

THE HALLOWED HUNT

LOIS McMASTER BUJOLD

An Imprint of HarperCollins*Publishers*

This is a work of fiction. Names, characters, places, and incidents are products of the author's imagination or are used fictitiously and are not to be construed as real. Any resemblance to actual events, locales, organizations, or persons, living or dead, is entirely coincidental.

EOS
An Imprint of HarperCollins*Publishers*
10 East 53rd Street
New York, New York 10022-5299

ISBN-13: 978-0-06-057474-1
ISBN-10: 0-06-057474-7
www.eosbooks.com

First Eos paperback printing: June 2006
First Eos hardcover printing: June 2005

10 9 8 7 6 5 4 3 2

THE HALLOWED HUNT

I

THE PRINCE WAS DEAD.

Since the king was not, no unseemly rejoicing dared show in the faces of the men atop the castle gate. Merely, Ingrey thought, a furtive relief. Even that was extinguished as they watched Ingrey's troop of riders clatter under the gate's vaulting into the narrow courtyard. They recognized who he was—and, therefore, who must have sent him.

Ingrey's sweat grew clammy under his leather jerkin in the damp dullness of the autumn morning. The chill seemed cupped within the cobbled yard, funneled down by the whitewashed walls. The lightly armed courier bearing the news had raced from the prince's hunting seat here at Boar's Head Castle to the hallow king's hall at Easthome in just two days. Ingrey and his men, though more heavily equipped, had made the return journey in scarcely more time. As a castle groom scurried to take his horse's bridle, Ingrey swung down and straightened his scabbard, fingers lingering only briefly on the reassuring coolness of his sword hilt.

The late Prince Boleso's housemaster, Rider Ulkra, appeared around the keep from wherever he'd been lurking when Ingrey's troop had been spied climbing the road.

Stout, usually stolid, he was breathless now with apprehension and hurry. He bowed. "Lord Ingrey. Welcome. Will you take drink and meat?"

"I've no need. See to these, though." He gestured to the half dozen men who followed him. The troop's lieutenant, Rider Gesca, gave him an acknowledging nod of thanks, and Ulkra delivered men and horses into the hands of the castle servants.

Ingrey followed Ulkra up the short flight of steps to the thick-planked main doors. "What have you done so far?"

Ulkra lowered his voice. "Waited for instructions." Worry scored his face; the men in Boleso's service were not long on initiative at the best of times. "Well, we moved the body into the cool. We could not leave it where it was. And we secured the prisoner."

What sequence, for this unpleasant inspection? "I'll see the body first," Ingrey decided.

"Yes, my lord. This way. We cleared one of the butteries."

They passed through the cluttered hall, the fire in its cavernous fieldstone fireplace allowed to burn low, the few red coals half-hidden in the ashes doing nothing to improve the discomfort of the chamber. A shaggy deerhound, gnawing a bone on the hearth, growled at them from the shadows. Down a staircase, through a kitchen where a cook and scullions fell silent and made themselves small as they passed, down again into a chilly chamber ill lit by two small windows high in the rocky walls.

The little room was presently unfurnished but for two trestles, the boards laid across them, and the sheeted shape that lay silently upon the boards. Reflexively, Ingrey signed himself, touching forehead, lip, navel, groin, and heart, spreading his hand over his heart: one theological point for each of the five gods. *Daughter-Bastard-Mother-Father-Son. And where were all of You when this happened?*

As Ingrey waited for his eyes to adjust to the shadows, Ulkra swallowed, and said, "The hallow king—how did he take the news?"

"It is hard to say," said Ingrey, with politic vagueness. "Sealmaster Lord Hetwar sent me."

"Of course."

Ingrey could read little in the housemaster's reaction, except the obvious, that Ulkra was glad to be handing responsibility for this on to someone else. Uneasily, Ulkra folded back the pale cloth covering his dead master. Ingrey frowned at the body.

Prince Boleso kin Stagthorne had been the youngest of the hallow king's surviving—of the hallow king's sons, Ingrey corrected his thought in flight. Boleso was still a young man, for all he had come to his full growth and strength some years ago. Tall, muscular, he shared the long jaw of his family, masked with a short brown beard. The darker brown hair of his head was tangled now, and matted with blood. His booming energy was stilled; drained of it, his face lost its former fascination, and left Ingrey wondering how he had once been fooled into thinking it handsome. He moved forward, hands cradling the skull, probing the wound. Wounds. The shattered bone beneath the scalp gave beneath his thumbs' pressure on either side of a pair of deep lacerations, blackened with dried gore.

"What weapon did this?"

"The prince's own war hammer. It was on the stand with his armor, in his bedchamber."

"How very . . . unexpected. To him as well." Grimly, Ingrey considered the fates of princes. All his short life, according to Hetwar, Boleso had been alternately petted and neglected by parents and servants both, the natural arrogance of his blood tainted with a precarious hunger for honor, fame, reward. The arrogance—or was it the anxiety?—had bloated of late to something overweening, desperately out of balance. *And that which is out of balance . . . falls.*

The prince wore a short open robe of worked wool, lined with fur, blood-splashed. He must have been wearing it when he'd died. Nothing more. No other recent wounds marked his pale skin. When the housemaster said they had waited for instructions, Ingrey decided, he had understated the case. The prince's retainers had evidently been so benumbed by the shocking event, they had not even dared wash or garb the corpse. Grime darkened the folds of Boleso's body . . . no, not grime. Ingrey ran a finger along a groove of chill flesh, and stared warily at the smear of color, dull blue and stamen yellow and, where they blended, a sickly green. Dye, paint, some colored powder? The dark fur of the inner robe, too, showed faint smears.

Ingrey straightened, and his eye fell on what he had at first taken for a bundle of furs laid along the far wall. He stepped closer and knelt.

It was a dead leopard. Leopardess, he amended, turning the beast partly over. The fur was fine and soft, fascinating beneath his hands. He traced the cold, curving ears, the stiff white whiskers, the pattern of dark whorls upon golden silk. He picked up one heavy paw, feeling the leathery pads, the thick ivory claws. The claws had been clipped. A red silk cord was bound tightly around the neck, biting deeply into the fur. Its end was cut off. Ingrey's hairs prickled, a reaction he quelled.

Ingrey glanced up. Ulkra, watching him, looked even more bleakly blank than before.

"This is no creature of *our* woods. Where in the world did it come from?"

Ulkra cleared his throat. "The prince obtained it from some Darthacan merchants. He proposed to start a menagerie here at the castle. Or possibly train it for hunting. He said."

"How long ago was this?"

"A few weeks. Just before his lady sister stopped here."

Ingrey fingered the red cord, letting his brows rise. He nodded at the dead animal. "And how did this happen?"

"We found it hanging from a beam in the prince's bedroom. When we, um, went in."

Ingrey sat back on his heels. He was beginning to see why no Temple divine had yet been called up to take charge of the funeral rites. The daubing, the red cord, the oak beam, hinted of an animal not merely slain but sacrificed, of someone dabbling in the old heresies, the forbidden forest magics. Had the sealmaster known of this, when he'd sent Ingrey? If so, he'd given no sign. "Who hung it?"

With the relief of a man telling a truth that could not hurt him, Ulkra said, "I did not see. I could not say. It was alive, leashed up in the corner and lying perfectly placidly, when we brought the girl in. We none of us heard or saw any more after that. Until the screams."

"Whose screams?"

"Well . . . the girl's."

"What was she crying? Or were they . . ." Ingrey cut short the *just cries*. He'd a shrewd suspicion Ulkra would be a little too glad of the suggestion. "What were her words?"

"She cried for help."

Ingrey stood up from the exotic, spotted carcass, his riding leathers creaking in the quiet, and let the weight of his stare fall on Ulkra. "And you responded—how?"

Ulkra turned his head away. "We had our orders to guard the prince's repose. My lord."

"Who heard the cries? Yourself, and . . . ?"

"Two of the prince's guards, who had been told to wait his pleasure."

"Three strong men, sworn to the prince's protection. Who stood—where?"

Ulkra's face might have been carved from rock. "In the corridor. Near his door."

"Who stood in the corridor not ten feet from his murder, and did nothing."

"We dared not. My lord. For *he* did not call. And anyway, the screams . . . stopped. We assumed, um, that the girl had yielded herself. She went in willingly enough."

Willingly? Or despairingly? "She was no servant wench. She was a retainer of Prince Boleso's own lady sister, a dowered maiden of her household. Entrusted to her service by kin Badgerbank, no less."

"Princess Fara herself yielded her up to her brother, my lord, when he begged the girl of her."

Pressured, was how Ingrey had heard the gossip. "Which made her a retainer of *this* house. Did it not?"

Ulkra flinched.

"Even a menial deserves better protection of his masters."

"Any lord in his cups might strike a servant, and misjudge the force of the blow," said Ulkra sturdily. The cadences sounded rehearsed, to Ingrey's ear. How often had Ulkra repeated that excuse to himself in the depths of the night, these past six months?

The ugly incident with the murdered manservant was the reason Prince Boleso had suffered his internal exile to this remote crag. His known love of hunting made it a dubious punishment, but it had got the Temple out of the royal seal-master's thinning hair. Too little payment for a crime, too much for an accident; Ingrey, who had observed the shambles next morning for Lord Hetwar before it had all been cleaned away, had judged it neither.

"*Any lord* would not then go on to skin and butcher his kill, Ulkra. There was more than drink behind that wild act. It was madness, and we all knew it." And when the king and his retainers had let their judgment be swayed, after that night's fury, by an appeal to loyalty—not to the prince's own soul's need, but to the appearance, the reputation of his high house—this disaster had been laid in train.

Boleso would have been expected to reappear at court in another half year, duly chastened, or at least duly pretending to be. But Fara had broken her journey here from her earl-ordainer husband's holdings to her father's sickbed, and so her—Ingrey presumed, pretty—lady-in-waiting had fallen under the bored prince's eye. One could take one's pick of tales from the princess's retinue, arriving barely before the bad news at the king's hall in Easthome, whether the cursed girl had yielded her virtue in terror to the prince's importunate lusts, or in calculation to her own vaulting ambition.

If it had been calculation, it had gone badly awry. Ingrey sighed. "Take me to the prince's bedchamber."

The late prince's room lay high in the central keep. The corridor outside was short and dim. Ingrey pictured Boleso's retainers huddled at the far end in the wavering candlelight, waiting for the screams to stop, then had to unset his teeth. The room's solid door featured a wooden bar on the inside, as well as an iron lock.

The appointments were few and countrified: a bed with hangings, barely long enough for the prince's height, chests, the stand with his second-best armor in one corner. A scattering of rugs on the wide floorboards. One was soaked with a dark stain. The sparse furnishings left just room enough for a quarry to dodge and run, a gasping chase. To turn at bay and swing . . .

The windows to the right of the armor stand were narrow, with thick wavery circles of glass set in their leads. Ingrey pulled the casements inward, swung wide the shutters, and gazed out upon the green-forested folds of countryside falling away from the crag. In the watery light, wisps of mist rose from the ravines like the ghosts of streams. At the bottom of the valley, a small farming village hacked out of the woods pushed back the tide of trees: source, no doubt, of food, servants, firewood for the castle, all crude and simple.

The fall from the sill to the stones below was lethal, the jump to the walls beyond quite impossible even for anyone slim enough to wriggle out the opening. In the dark and the rain. No escape by that route, except to death. A half turn from the window, the armor stand would be under a panicked prey's groping hands. A battle-ax, its handle inlaid with gold and ruddy copper, still rested there.

The matching war hammer lay tossed upon the rumpled bed. Its claw-rimmed iron head—very like an animal's paw—was smeared with dried gore like the blotch on the rug. Ingrey measured it against his palm, noted the congruity with the wounds he had just seen. The hammer had been swung two-handed, with all the strength that terror might lend. But only a woman's strength, after all. The prince, half-stunned—half-mad?—had apparently kept coming. The second blow had been harder.

Ingrey strolled the length of the room, looking all around and then up at the beams. Ulkra, hands clutching one another, backed out of his way. Just above the bed dangled a frayed length of red cord. Ingrey stepped up on the bed frame, drew his belt knife, stretched upward, cut it through, and tucked the coil away in his jerkin.

He jumped down and turned to the hovering Ulkra. "Boleso is to be buried at Easthome. Have his wounds and his body washed—more thoroughly—and pack him in salt for transport. Find a cart, a team—better hitch two pairs, with the mud on the roads—and a competent driver. Set the prince's guards as outriders; their ineptitude can do him no more harm now. Clean this room, set the keep to rights, appoint a caretaker, and follow on with the rest of his household and valuables." Ingrey's gaze drifted around the chamber. Nothing else here . . . "Burn the leopard. Scatter its ashes."

Ulkra gulped and nodded. "When do you wish to depart, my lord? Will you stay the night?"

Should he and his captive travel with the slow cortege, or push on ahead? He wanted to be away from this place as swiftly as he could—it made his neck muscles ache—but the light was shortening with autumn's advent, and the day was half-spent already. "I must speak to the prisoner before I decide. Take me to her."

It was a brief step, down one floor to a windowless, but dry, storeroom. Not dungeon, certainly not guest room, the choice of prisons bespoke a deep uncertainty over the status of its occupant. Ulkra rapped on the door, called, "My lady? You have a visitor," unlocked it, and swung it wide. Ingrey stepped forward.

From the darkness, a pair of glowing eyes flashed up at him like some great cat's from a covert, in a forest that whispered. Ingrey recoiled, hand flying to his hilt. His blade had rasped halfway out when his elbow struck the jamb, pain tingling hotly from shoulder to fingertips; he backed farther to gain turning room, to lunge and strike.

Ulkra's startled grip fell on his forearm. The housemaster was staring at him in astonishment.

Ingrey froze, then jerked away so that Ulkra might not feel his trembling. His first concern was to quell the violent impulse blaring through his limbs, cursing his legacy anew—he had not been caught by surprise by it since . . . for a long time. *I deny you, wolf-within. You shall not ascend.* He slid his blade back into its sheath, snicked it firmly home, slowly unwrapped his fingers, and placed his palm flat against his leather-clad thigh.

He stared again into the little room, forcing sense upon his mind. In the shadows, the ghostly shape of a young woman was rising from a straw pallet on the floor. There seemed to be bedding enough, a down-stuffed quilt, tray and pitcher, a covered chamber pot, necessities decently addressed. This prison secured; it did not, yet, punish.

Ingrey licked dry lips. "I cannot see you in that den." *And what I saw, I disavow.* "Step into the light."

The lift of a chin, the toss of a dark mane; she padded forward. She wore a fine linen dress dyed pale yellow, embroidered with flowers along the curving neckline; if not court dress, then certainly clothing of a maiden of rank. A dark brown spatter crossed it in a diagonal. In the light, her tumbling black hair grew reddish. Brilliant hazel eyes looked not up, but across, at Ingrey. Ingrey was of middle height for a man, compactly built; the girl was well grown for her sex, to match him so.

Hazel eyes, almost amber in this light, circled in black at the iris rim. Not glowing green. Not . . .

With a wary glance at him, Ulkra began speaking, performing the introduction as formally as if he were playing Boleso's housemaster at some festal feast. "Lady Ijada, this is Lord Ingrey kin Wolfcliff, who is Sealmaster Lord Hetwar's man. He is come to take you in charge. Lord Ingrey,

Lady Ijada dy Castos, by her mother's blood kin Badger-bank."

Ingrey blinked. Hetwar had named her only, *Lady Ijada, some minor heiress in the Badgerbank tangle, five gods help us*. "That is an Ibran patronymic, surely."

"Chalionese," she corrected coolly. "My father was a lord dedicat of the Son's Order, and captain of a Temple fort on the western marches of the Weald, when I was a child. He married a Wealding lady of kin Badgerbank."

"And they are . . . dead?" Ingrey hazarded.

She tilted her head in cold irony. "I should have been better protected, else."

She was not distraught, not weeping, or at least, not recently. Not, apparently, deranged. Four days in that closet to sort through her thoughts had left her composed, but for a certain tightness in her voice, a faint vibrato of fear or anger. Ingrey looked around the bare hall, glanced at Ulkra. "Take us to where we may sit and speak. Some place apart. In the light."

"Um . . . um . . ." After a moment's thought, Ulkra gestured them to follow. He did not, Ingrey noticed, hesitate to turn his back upon the girl. This prisoner did not fight or bite or scratch her jailers, it seemed. Her pace, following him, was steady. At the end of the next passage, Ulkra waved to a window seat overlooking the back side of the keep. "Will this do, my lord?"

"Yes." Ingrey hesitated, as Lady Ijada gracefully swept her skirts aside and seated herself on the polished boards. Should he retain Ulkra, for corroboration, or dismiss him, to encourage frankness? Was the girl likely to become violent again? The unbidden picture of Ulkra crouching in the corridor above this one, waiting in the dark for screams to stop, troubled his mind. "You may go about your tasks, housemaster. Return in half an hour."

Ulkra frowned uncertainly at the girl, but bowed himself out. Boleso's men, Ingrey was reminded, were out of the habit of questioning the sense of their superiors' orders. Or perhaps it was that any who dared were got rid of, one way or another; and these were the remainder. Residue. *Scum.*

A little awkwardly, for the short length of the seat forced them uncomfortably close together, Ingrey sat beside her. His presumption of prettiness, he decided, had been inadequate. The girl was luminous. Unless Boleso had gone blind as well as mad, she must have arrested his eye the moment it fell upon her. Wide brow, straight nose, sculpted chin . . . a livid blotch darkened one cheek, and others ringed her fair neck, a pattern of plum-colored bruises. Ingrey lifted his hands to lie lightly over them; she flinched a little, but then bore his probing touch. Boleso's hands were somewhat larger than his own, it appeared. Her skin was warm under his fingers, fascinating, transporting. A golden haze seemed to cloud his vision. His strangling grip tightened—he whipped his hands away, his gasp masked by hers, and clenched them on his knees. *What was that . . . ?*

To cover his confusion he bit out, "I am an officer of the Royal Sealmaster. I am charged to report to him all I see and hear. You must tell me the truth of all that happened here. Begin at the beginning."

She sat back, her startled glance altering to a piercing regard. He caught her scent, neither perfume nor blood but grown woman, and, targeted by that gaze, for the first time wondered what he looked like—and smelled like—to her. Riding reek, cold iron and sweat-stained leather, chin dark-stubbled, tired. Weighed with sword and knife and dangerous duties. Why did she not recoil altogether?

"Which beginning?" she asked.

He stared at her for a blank and stupid instant. "From your arrival here at Boar's Head, I suppose." Was there another? He must remember to return to that question.

She swallowed, possessed herself, began: "The princess had started out in haste for her father's hall, with only a small retinue, but she was overtaken by illness on the road. Nothing out of the usual, but her monthly time brings her dire headaches, and if she doesn't rest quietly through them, she becomes very sick. We turned aside to this place, for it was as close as anything, and besides, Princess Fara wished to see her brother. I think she remembered him from when he was younger and less . . . difficult."

How very tactful. Ingrey could not decide if the turn of phrase was diplomacy or dry wit. *Caution*, he concluded, studying her closed and careful expression. Wits, not wittiness, kept close about her.

"We were made welcome, if not to her custom, then to this place's ability."

"Had you ever met Prince Boleso before?"

"No. I've only been a few months in Princess Fara's service. My stepfather placed me there. He said—" She stopped, began again. "Everything seemed usual at first. I mean, for a lord's hunting lodge. The days were quiet, because the prince invited her guardsmen out to the hunt. Prince Boleso and his men were very boisterous in the evenings, and drank a great deal, but the princess did not attend, being laid down in her chambers. I took down complaints from her of the noise twice, but I was little heeded. They set the dogs on a wild boar they'd caught alive, out in the courtyard beneath her window, and made bets on the fight. Boleso's huntsman was very distressed for his hounds. I wished Earl Horseriver had been there—he could have quelled them with a word. He has a deadly tongue, when he wishes. We bided here three days, until the princess was ready to travel again."

"Did Prince Boleso court you?"

Her lips thinned. "Not that I could tell. He was equally obnoxious to all his sister's ladies. I knew nothing of his . . . regard, supposed regard, until the morning we were to leave."

She swallowed again. "My lady—Princess Fara—told me then I was to stay. That this might not have been my first choice, but that it would do me no harm in the long run. Another husband would be found for me, after. I begged her not to leave me here. She would not meet my eye. She said it was no worse a barter than any, and better than most, and that I should look to my own future. That it was just the woman's version of the same loyalty due from a man to his prince. I said I did not think most men would . . . well, I'm afraid I said something rude. She refused to speak with me after that. They rode away and left me. I would not beg at her stirrup, for fear the prince's men would mock me." Her arms crossed, as if to clutch a tattered dignity about her anew.

"I told myself . . . maybe she was right. That it would be no worse than any other fate. Boleso wasn't ugly, or deformed, or old. Or diseased."

Ingrey couldn't help checking himself against that list. At least he did not match any of the named categories, he trusted. Though there were others. *Defiled* sprang to mind.

"I did not realize how mad he'd grown until they'd left, and then it was too late."

"Then what happened?"

"At nightfall, they brought me to his chamber and thrust me within. He was waiting for me. He wore a robe, but under it his body was naked and all covered over with signs drawn in woad and madder and crocus. Old symbols, the sort you sometimes still see carved on ancient wooden foundations, or in the forest where the shrines once stood. He had his leopard tied up in a corner, drugged. He said—it turned out—it seemed he had not fallen in love with me after all. It wasn't even lust. He wanted a virgin for some rite he had—found, made up, I am not sure, he seemed very confused by this time—and I was the only one, his sister's other two ladies being one a wife and the other a widow. I tried to dissuade him, I told him it was heresy, dire sin and against his father's own laws, I said I would run away, that I would tell. He said he'd hunt me down with his dogs. That they would tear me apart as they had the pig. I said I would go to the Temple divine in the village. He said the man was only an acolyte, and a coward. And that he would kill anyone there who took me in. Even the acolyte. He was not afraid of the Temple, it was practically the property of kin Stagthorne and he could buy divines for a pittance.

"The rite was meant to catch the spirit of the leopard, as the old kin warriors were supposed to do. I said, it could not possibly work, nowadays. He said, he'd done it before, several times—that he meant to capture the spirits of every wisdom animal of the greater kinships. He thought it was going to give him some sort of power over the Weald."

Ingrey, startled, said, "The Old Weald warriors only took one animal spirit to themselves, one in a lifetime. And even that risked madness. Miscarriage. Worse." *As I know to my everlasting cost.*

Her velvety voice was growing faster, breathless. "He hauled the leopard up by its strangling cord. He hit me and threw me down on the bed. I fought him. He was muttering under his breath, spells or raving or both, I don't know. I believed him, that he had done this before—his very mind was a menagerie, howling. The leopard distracted him in its death throes, and I wrenched out from under him. I tried to run, but there was nowhere to go. The door was locked. He'd put the key in his robe."

"Did you scream for help?"

"I suppose so. I scarcely know. My throat was raw, after, so I suppose I must have. The window was hopeless. The forest beyond seemed to go on forever, in the night. I called on my father's spirit, on his god, for my aid, out of the dark."

Ingrey couldn't help thinking that in such an extremity Lady Ijada would call on her proper patroness, the Daughter of Spring, the goddess to Whom virginity was sacred. It seemed very strange for a woman to call on Her Brother of Autumn. *Though this is His season.* The Lord of Autumn was the god of young men, harvest, the hunt, comradeship— and war. And the weapons of war?

"You turned," said Ingrey, "and found the hammer handle under your hand."

The hazel eyes widened. "How did you know?"

"I saw the chamber."

"Oh." She moistened her lips. "I struck him. He lunged at me, or . . . or lurched. I struck him again. He stopped. Fell, and did not rise. He wasn't dead yet—his body spasmed, when I was groping in his robe for the key, and I nearly fainted. I fell to the floor on my hands and knees, anyway, and the room darkened. I . . . it . . . Finally, I got the door unbarred and called his men in."

"Were they—what? Angry?"

"More frightened than angry, I think. They argued forever, and blamed each other, and me, and whatever they could think of. Even Boleso. It took them ages to decide to lock me up and send a courier."

"What did you do?"

"I sat on the floor, mostly. I was feeling very unwell. They asked me such stupid questions. *Had I killed him?* Did they imagine he'd bludgeoned himself? I was glad for my cell, when they finally put me in it. I don't think Ulkra ever noticed I could bar its door from the inside."

Ingrey wondered. In the most neutral voice he could muster, he said, "Did Prince Boleso complete his rape?"

Her face lifted; her eyes glinted. "No."

Truth rang in that voice, and a kind of rocky triumph. In the uttermost extremity, abandoned by all who should have protected her, she'd found that she need not abandon herself. A powerful lesson. *A dangerous lesson.*

In an equally flat tone he asked, "Did he complete his rite?"

This time, she hesitated. "I don't know. I am not sure . . . what his intent was." She gazed down into her lap; her hands gripped each other. "What will happen next? Rider Ulkra said you would take me in charge. Where to?"

"Easthome."

"Good," she said, with unexpected fervor. "The Temple there will surely help me."

"You do not fear your trial?"

"Trial? I defended myself! I was betrayed into this horror!"

"It is possible," he said, still very level-voiced, "that some powerful people will not care to hear you proclaim so.

Think. You cannot prove attempted rape, for one thing. A half dozen men could testify that you appeared to go to Boleso willingly."

"Compared to fleeing into the woods to be eaten by the wild beasts, willing, yes. Compared to bringing a brutal death on anyone who tried to help me, willingly." She stared at him in sudden incredulity. "Do you not believe me?"

"Oh, yes." *Oh, yes.* "But I am not your judge."

She frowned, a glint of white teeth pressing into a lower lip gone pale. In a moment, her spine straightened again. "In any case, if the rape was not witnessed, the unlawful rite was. They all saw the leopard. They saw the secret drawings on the prince's body. Not assertions, but material things, that any man might reach out and touch."

Not anymore. If not innocent, she was *an* innocent, Ingrey had no doubt. *Lady Ijada, you have no idea what you are pitting yourself against.*

A step sounded on the floorboards; Ingrey looked up to see Ulkra approaching, seeming to loom and crouch simultaneously. "Your pleasure, my lord?" he inquired nervously.

To be anywhere but here, doing anything but this.

He'd been over two days in the saddle. He was, he decided abruptly, too mortally tired to ride another mile today. Boleso could be in no hurry to gallop to his funeral, and divine judgment. And Ingrey had no burning desire to rush this accursed naïve girl to her earthly judgment, either. She was not afraid of the right things. Five gods help him, she seemed not afraid of anything.

"Will you," he said to her, "give me your word, if I order your guard lightened, that you will not attempt to escape?"

"Of course," she said. As if surprised he even felt a need to ask.

He gestured to the housemaster. "Put her in a proper room. Give her her things back. Find a decent maid, if any is to be found in this place, to attend her and help her pack. We'll leave for Easthome with Boleso's body at first light tomorrow."

"Yes, my lord," said Ulkra, ducking his head in relieved assent.

Ingrey added as an afterthought, "Have any men of the household fled, since Boleso's death?"

"No, my lord. Why do you ask?"

Ingrey gave a vague gesture, indicating no reason that he cared to share. Ulkra did not pursue the question.

Ingrey creaked to his feet. He felt as if his muscles squeaked louder protest than his damp leathers. Lady Ijada gave him a grateful curtsey, and turned to follow the housemaster. She looked back over her shoulder at him as she turned onto the staircase, a grave, trusting glance.

His duty was to deliver her to Easthome. Nothing more. Into the hands of . . . no one friendly to her cause. His fingers clenched and unclenched on his hilt.

Nothing more.

2

THE CORTEGE, SUCH AS IT WAS, LUMBERED OUT THE CAS-
tle gate in the dawn fog. Ingrey set six of Boleso's guards
riding before and six behind what might charitably be described as a farm wagon. The wagon was burdened with a
hastily cobbled-together oblong box, heavy with Boleso's
body and the coarse salt, meant to preserve game, which
made his last bed. In some sad effort at proper ceremony,
Rider Ulkra had found a stag hide to cover the coffin, and funereal cloths to wrap the posts at the corners of the wagon
bed, in lieu of draperies unlikely to survive the local roads.
Whatever attempts the guardsmen had made to furbish up
their gear for this somber duty were lost from view in the
clinging mists. Ingrey's eye was more concerned for the se-
curity of the ropes that bound the box in place.

The teamster that Ulkra had drafted was a local yeoman,
owner of both wagon and team, and he kept his sturdy
horses well in hand during the first precarious turns and
bumps of the narrow road. By his side, his wife hung on
grimly but expertly to the wooden brake, which shrieked
against the wheel as the wagon descended. She was a staid
older woman, a better female chaperone for his prisoner, In-

grey thought, than the slatternly and frightened young servant girl Ulkra had first offered, and she would be guarded in turn by her husband. Ingrey trusted his own men, but remembered that inner bar on the prisoner's chamber door; whatever Lady Ijada had supposed, Ingrey was quite sure that obstacle hadn't been an oversight on Ulkra's part.

The whitewashed walls and conical green slate tower caps of the castle disappeared dreamlike among the smoke-gray trees, and the road widened and straightened for a short stretch. Ingrey gave a quiet salute to the two of his own escort bringing up the rear, which was as silently returned, and urged his horse forward around the wagon and its outriders. In the lead, the other two pairs of Ingrey's guards bracketed Lady Ijada.

The prisoner rode her own horse. Ingrey did not know whether Earl Horseriver's stables or Lady Ijada's own family had furnished her mount, but it was a fine showy chestnut, well fleshed and supple in action. It sidled and snorted in its freshness, its ears flicking nervously. If she should clap her heels to the beast's sides and attempt some cross-country escape, it would not be easy to ride her down. She showed no signs of doing so just yet, however; she sat the mare lightly, with an occasional touch on the reins to keep it from outpacing the other horses. This morning Lady Ijada wore a riding habit suitable to a noblewoman's hunting party, with a jacket dyed burnt-brown traced with copper thread, a polished gleam of boots peeping from the hems of her split skirts. Her dark hair was tied back severely and bundled in a crocheted net at her nape. Her creamy neckcloth just hid Boleso's purplish finger marks.

Ingrey had no intention of making idle conversation with his charge, so merely favored her with a polite nod and pushed on to the head of the column. He rode in silence for a time. The dripping of water from high branches in the steep woods and the gurgling of freshets, running melodiously beneath the road through hollowed-log culverts, sounded loud in his ears despite the creaking of gear, groan-

ing of the wagon wheels, and plodding of hooves behind
him. They rounded a last dropping curve, the road leveled,
and they emerged from beneath the leafy canopy into an unexpected well of light.

The sun had broken through a gap in the ridges to the
east, turning the moist air to floating gold and the far slopes
to a fiery green. Only one trickle of smoke, probably from a
party of charcoal burners, marked any human occupation in
the dense carpet of woods rising beyond the hamlet and its
fields. The sight did not lift Ingrey's spirits. He frowned
down at the mud of the road instead, then reined his horse
aside to check that the tail of the cortege cleared the trees
without incident. He turned back to find himself riding beside Lady Ijada.

She was staring around with muted pleasure in her eyes,
which appeared bright hazel-gold in this new light. "How
the hills glow! I love these forests between the bitter heights
and the tilled lands."

"It's difficult and dangerous country," said Ingrey, "but
the roads will improve once we descend from the wastes."

She tilted her head at his sour expression. "This place
does not please you? My dower lands are a like waste, then,
west of here in the marches where the mountains dwindle."
She hesitated. "My stepfather is of your mind about such
silent tracts—but then he is a town-man bred, a master of
works for the Temple in Badgerbridge, and likes trees best
in the form of rafters and gates and trestles. He says it were
better I made my face my dower than those haunted woods."
She grimaced abruptly, the light fading in her eyes. "He was
so pleased for me when one of my Badgerbank aunts found
me the place in the Horserivers' high household. And now
this."

"Did he imagine you would snare a husband, under the
princess's eye?"

"Something like that. It was to be my great chance." She
shrugged. "I've since learned that high lords get to be such
by being more concerned, not less, with dowers than other

men. I should have anticipated . . ." Her mouth firmed. "I might have anticipated some seducer, arrogant in his rank. It was the heretical sorcery and howling madness that took me by surprise."

For the first time, Ingrey wondered if the husband whose eye Ijada had snared might have been Earl Horseriver. Four years he had been married to the hallow king's daughter, and no children yet; was there anything more to the delay than ill luck? Reason indeed for the princess to barter her hand-maiden out of her household at the first opportunity—and if jealous enough of her lovely rival, to a fate Fara must have known would not be pleasant . . . ? *Had* the princess known of her brother's perilous plans? *Aside from the rape, you mean?*

Which beginning? Lady Ijada had asked, yesterday. As though there were a dozen to choose among.

"What did you think of Earl Horseriver?" Ingrey inquired, in a neutral voice. The earl was landed, of an ancient kin, but his most arresting power at present was doubtless his ordainer's vote, one of the thirteen needed to confirm a new hallow king. Yet such political concerns seemed quite over this young woman's head, however level it might be.

Now the lips pursed in a thoughtful frown. But not in dismay, Ingrey noted, nor in any flush of embarrassment. "I'm not sure. He's a strange . . . man. I almost said *young man,* but really, he scarcely seems young. I suppose it's partly the untimely gray in his hair. He's very sharp of wit, uncomfortably so at times. And moody. Sometimes he goes about for days in silence, as if lost in his own thoughts, and no one dares speak to him, not even the princess. At first I thought it was because of his little, you know, deformities, the spine and the oddly shaped face, but truly, he seems not to care about his body at all. It certainly doesn't impede him." She glanced at Ingrey with belated wariness. "Do you know him well?"

"Not since we are grown," said Ingrey. "I have a near tie to him by blood through his late mother. I met him a few times when we were both children." Ingrey remembered the young Lord Wencel kin Horseriver as an undersized, clumsy boy, seeming slow of wit, with a rather wet mouth. Perhaps shyness had rendered Wencel tongue-tied; but the boy-Ingrey had lacked sympathy for a smaller cousin who did not keep up, and had made no effort to include him. Fortunately, in retrospect, Ingrey had made no effort to torment him, either. "His father and mine died within a few months of each other."

Though the aged Earl Horseriver had died quietly and decently, of an ordinary stroke. Not in his prime, baying and foaming, his feverish screams echoing through the castle corridors as though rising from some pit of agony beneath the earth . . . Ingrey bit back the memory, hard.

Her eyes flicked toward him. "What was your father like?"

"He was castlemaster of Birchgrove, under the lordship of old Earl Kasgut kin Wolfcliff." *And I am not.* Would her rather too-quick wits notice, or would she merely assume him a younger son? "Birchgrove commands the valley of the Birchbeck, where it runs into the Lure." Which did not, precisely, answer the question she'd asked. How had they drifted onto this dire subject? Her tone, he realized, had been as tensely neutral as his leading question about Horseriver.

"So Rider Ulkra told me." She drew a long breath, staring ahead between her horse's ears. "He also said, it was rumored that your father died from the bite of a rabid wolf, that he'd tried to steal the spirit from, and that he gave you a wolf spirit, too, but it turned out to be crippled, and only made you very sick. And your life and wits were despaired of, which is why your uncle succeeded to Birchgrove and not you, but later your family sent you on pilgrimage, and you grew better. I wondered if all this was true, and why your father committed so reckless an act." Only when she had spat out all this hurried chain of tattle did she turn her face to his, her eyes anxious and searching.

Ingrey's horse snorted and tossed its head at his jerk on the reins. Ingrey loosened his fist, and, a moment later, unclenched his teeth. He finally managed to growl, "Ulkra gossips. It is a fault."

"He is afraid of you."

"Not enough, it seems." He yanked his horse away and pretended to inspect the cortege, returning up the other side to the head of the column. Alone. She looked after him as he passed, her mouth opening as if to speak, but he ignored her.

Forcing the cortege up the muddy road out of the valley diverted his mind enough to regain his calm, or at least replace his fuming with other irritations. On a steep incline, with the blowing team's hooves slipping, the wagon began to slide sideways toward a precipitous edge; the teamster's wife screeched alarm. Ingrey flung himself off his horse and led the quicker-witted among the guards to brace themselves and strain against the wagon's side and rear, pushing it away from the dizzying drop and up through the mire.

It cost him a strained shoulder and a good deal of filth on his riding leathers, and he was almost tempted to let the load go into the ravine. He imagined it falling, breaking up, the coffin bouncing on the boulders and splitting open and Boleso's nude corpse plunging to its just doom in a shower of salt. But the wagon must needs pull the struggling loyal horses after it, and they did not deserve the prince's fate. And, given that he stood between the wagon and the drop, Ingrey himself would have been swept over, crushed underneath the first impact. They'd have had to use his good riding leathers as a bag for his remains, after that. The gruesome thought amused him enough that he remounted his horse afterward in a restored, if winded, humor.

They paused at noon at a wide clearing just off the road, home to an ancient spring. His men unpacked the bread and cold meats provided by the castle cook, but Ingrey, calculating distances and hours of light, was more concerned for the horses. The team was mud-crusted and sweaty, so he set Boleso's surly retinue to assisting the teamster in unharnessing and rubbing them down before they were fed. The worst of the gradients were behind them now; with a suitable rest, he judged the beasts would last till nightfall, by which time he hoped to reach the Temple town of Reedmere, commandeer some more fitting conveyance, and send the rustic rig home.

More princely conveyance, Ingrey revised his thought. A former manure wagon seemed to him all too fitting. Closer to Easthome, he decided, he would send a rider ahead to guide a relief cortege to him, and hand off Boleso's body to more gaudy and noble ceremony, provided by those who cared for the prince. Or at least, cared for Boleso's rank and the show they made to each other. Maybe he'd send the rider tonight.

He washed his hands in the spring's outlet and accepted a slab of venison wrapped in bread from his lieutenant, Gesca. Gnawing, he looked around for his prisoner and her attendant. The teamster's wife was busy about the food baskets by the unhitched wagon. Lady Ijada was walking about the clearing—in that costume, she might whisk into the woods and disappear among the tall tree boles in a moment. Instead, she pried up a stone from the crumbled foundation above the spring and picked her way over to where Ingrey rested on a big fallen log.

"Look," she said, holding out the glittery gray block.

Ingrey looked. On one side of the stone a spiral pattern was incised into the weathered surface.

"It's the same as one of the symbols Boleso had drawn on his body. In red madder, centered on his navel. Did you see it there?"

"No," Ingrey admitted. "His body had been washed off already."

"Oh," she said, looking a little taken aback. "Well, it was."

"I do not doubt you." *Though others will be free to.* Had she realized this yet?

She stared around the clearing. "Do you think this place was a forest shrine, once?"

"Very possibly." He followed her glance, studying the stumps and the sizes of the trees. Whatever holy or unholy purposes the original possessors had held, the latest ax work had been done by humble itinerant woodcutters, by the evidence. "The spring suggests it. This place has been cleared, abandoned, and recleared more than once, if so." Following, perhaps, the ebb and flow of the Darthacan Quintarian war against the forest heresies that had so disrupted the kin lands, four centuries ago when Audar the Great had first conquered the Weald.

"I wonder what the old ceremonies were *really* like," she mused. "The divines scorn the animal sacrifice, but really . . . When I was a child at my father's Temple fort, I went a few times with . . . with a friend to the marsh people's autumn rites. The fen folk aren't of the same race or language as the Old Wealdings, but I could almost have imagined myself going back to those days. It was more like a grand party and outdoor roast than anything. I mean, they made some songs and rituals over the creatures before they slaughtered them, but what's the difference if we pray over our meat after it's cooked instead of before?" She added with an air of fairness, "Or so my friend said. The fort's divine disagreed, but then, the two of them disagreed a lot. I think my friend enjoyed baiting him."

It hadn't been the menu that the Quintarian divines had objected to, for it wasn't just meat that the Old Weald kin had taken from their hallowed beasts. The tribal sorcerers had defiled the souls of their battle lords with the ghosts of animals, making their leaders' spirits fierce—but also unfit to offer, at the ends of their lives, to the gods. Ingrey doubted any festival this young woman would have been permitted to see involved any consumption beyond meat, though. "It is said the fen men paint themselves with blood."

"Well," she said thoughtfully, "that's true. Or at any rate, everyone ran about splashing each other and screaming with laughter. It was all very messy and silly, and rather smelly, but it was hard to see any evil in it. Of course, this tribe didn't sacrifice *people*." She looked around the clearing as if imagining the ghostly image of some such evil slaying here.

"Indeed," said Ingrey dryly. "That was the sticking point, between the Darthacan Quintarians and the Old Wealdings." For all that both sides had worshipped the same five gods. "So when Audar the so-called Great slaughtered four thousand Wealding prisoners of war at Bloodfield, it's said he didn't pray at all. That made it a proper Quintarian act, I suppose, and not heresy. Some other crime, perhaps, but not human sacrifice. One of those theological fine points."

That massacre of a generation of young spirit warriors had broken the back of the Wealding resistance to their eastern invaders, in any case. For the next hundred and fifty years, the Weald's lands, ceremonies, and people had been forcibly rearranged into Darthacan patterns, until Audar's vast empire broke apart in the bloody squabbles of his much less great descendants. Orthodox Quintarianism survived the empire that had fostered it, however. The suppressed animal practices and wisdom songs of the forest tribes had been lost and all but forgotten in the renewed Weald, except for rural superstitions, children's rhymes, and the odd ghost tale.

Or . . . not quite forgotten, not by everyone. *Father, what were you thinking? Why did you burden me with this bestial blasphemy? What were you trying to do?* The old, painful, unanswered question . . . Ingrey thrust it from his mind.

"I suppose we are all New Wealdings, now," mused Ijada. She touched her Darthacan-dark hair, and nodded to Ingrey's own. "Almost every Wealding kin that survived has Darthacan forebears, too. Mongrels, to a man. Or to a lord, anyway. So we inherit Audar's sins *and* the tribes'. For all I know my Chalionese father had some Darthacan blood. The nobles there are a very mixed lot, really, he always said, for all that they carry on about their pedigrees."

Ingrey bit, chewed, did not answer.

"When your father gave you your wolf," she began, "how—"

"You should go eat," he interrupted her, around a mouthful of cold roast. "It's going to be a long ride yet." He rose and strode away from her, toward the wagon and its baskets. He did not want more food, but he did not want more of her chatter, either. He selected a not-too-wormy apple and nibbled it slowly while walking about. He stayed on the other side of the clearing from her, during the remainder of their rest.

As the cortege rumbled on through the afternoon, the rugged angles of the hills grew gentler and hamlets more frequent, their fields more extensive. The sun was slanting toward the treetops when they came to an unanticipated check. A rocky ford, hock deep on the ride in, had risen with the rains and was now in full and muddy flood.

Ingrey halted his horse and looked over the problem. Boleso's wagon had not been made watertight with skins or tar, so the chance of its floating away at an awkward angle and yanking the horses off their feet was slight. The chance of its shipping water and bogging down, however, was good. He set mounted men at the wagon's four corners with ropes to help warp it through the hazard, and waved the yeoman onward with what speed he could muster from his tired team. The water came up past the horses' bellies, pushing the wagon off its wheels, but the outriders held it on course, and the whole assemblage struggled safely up the far bank. Only then did Ingrey motion Lady Ijada ahead of him into the water.

His gaze lifted to mark the wagon's progress, then jerked back as the chestnut horse missed its footing, wallowed, and went down over its head. Lady Ijada was swept off into the torrent too quickly to cry out. Ingrey swore, spurring his horse forward into the flood. His head swiveled frantically, looking for dark hair, a flash of brown fabric in the turbid foam—her clothing would surely hold water, skirts dragging her down—there!

The cold water tugged at his knees as he urged his horse downstream. The dark head bobbed up by a trio of smooth rocks that stuck out of the spate boiling around them. An arm reached, caught . . .

"Hang on!" yelled Ingrey. "I'm coming to get you—!"

Two arms. Lady Ijada heaved herself upward, belly over the rock, wriggled and scrambled; by the time Ingrey brought his snorting horse close, she was standing upright, dripping and gasping. Out of the corner of his eye, he saw her horse make it to the bank farther downstream, where it surged up, stumbled through the mud, and bolted into the woods. Ingrey spared it an unvoiced curse and waved one of his men after it.

He did not look to see if he was obeyed, for now he was within arm's reach of Lady Ijada. He leaned toward her, she leaned toward him . . .

A dark red fog seemed to come up over his brain, clouding his vision. Gripping her arms, he toppled into the stream, pulling her from her perch. Down, if he held her *down* . . . water filled his mouth. He spat, gasped, and went under again. He was blinded and tumbling. Some distant part of his mind, far, far off, was screaming at him: *What are you doing, you fool!* He must hold her *down*—

The force of the water clubbed his head into something hard, and starry green sparks overflowed the red fog. All thought fled.

❧

Sensation returned in panicked choking. Cold air slapped his face, somehow held up out of the water, and he drew enough breath to cough out both air and water. His limbs flailed, feeling desperately weak and heavy, as though trapped in oil.

"Stop fighting me!" Lady Ijada's voice snapped in his ear. Something circling his neck tightened; he realized after a dizzy moment that it must be her arm. He must save her, *drown her*, save her—

She can swim. The belated realization slowed his flailing, if only in shock. Well, he could swim, too, after a fashion. He'd stayed alive through a shipwreck, once, admittedly mostly by hanging on to things that floated. The only thing floating here seemed to be Lady Ijada. Surely the weight of his blades and boots must drag them both down—his feet struck something. The current spat them into a back eddy, the river bottom flattened out, then *she* was dragging *him* up onto some welcome, blessed shore.

He twisted around out of her arm's grip, crawling up on hands and knees over the rocks onto the moss-covered bank. Pink water flowed from his hair, growing redder. He dashed it from his eyes and blinked around. The woods here were thick and tangled. He was not sure how far downstream they had come, but the ford, the wagon, and his men were nowhere in sight. He was shivering in shock from the head blow.

She stood up, water streaming from her clothes, and staggered out of the river toward him, her hand reaching. He cried out, a wordless bellow, and recoiled, wrapping his arms around a small tree, in part to hold himself upright, in part to hold . . . "Don't touch me!"

"What? Lord Ingrey, you're bleeding—"

"Don't come any nearer!"

"Lord Ingrey, if you will just—"

His voice cracked. "My wolf is trying to kill you! It is coming unbound! Stay away!"

She stopped, stared. Her hair had come partly undone, and water trickled from it in sparkling drops, plashing silently into the moss at her feet, steady and fascinating as some strange water clock.

"Three times," he gasped hoarsely. "That was the third time. Don't you realize, I tried to drown you just now? It's tried twice before. The first time I saw you, when I drew my steel, I meant to run you through on the spot. Then when we were sitting, I almost tried to strangle you."

She was pale, thoughtful, intent. Not running away

screaming. He wanted her to run, whether screaming or not made no matter to him. As long as she could outrun him . . .

"Run!"

Instead, maddeningly, she leaned against a tree bole and began to remove her squelching boots. It wasn't until she had tipped out the second one that she said, "It wasn't your wolf."

His head was still ringing from the blow against the boulder. By the unpleasant rumbling in his gut, he was due to vomit some river water soon. He didn't comprehend her. "What?"

"It wasn't your wolf." She set the boot down next to its mate and added in a tight, even voice, "I can smell your wolf, in a sense. Not smell really, but I don't know any other way to describe it."

"It—I tried to kill you!"

"It wasn't your wolf. It wasn't you, either. It was the *other* smell. All three times."

Now he merely stared, all words deserting him.

"Lord Ingrey—you never asked where the ghost of Boleso's leopard went."

It wasn't a stare anymore, he feared. It was a gape.

"It came to *me*." Her hazel eyes met his for one level, intent moment.

"I . . . it . . . excuse me," said Ingrey hoarsely. "I have to throw up now."

He retreated around his too-narrow tree, for what little privacy it could render him. He wished he could say the spasm gave him a moment to gather his wits, but they seemed scattered for a mile behind him up the river valley. Drowned, they were, without benefit of wine. All of the punishment, none of the reward.

He stumbled back around the tree to find her calmly wringing out her jacket. He gave up and sat down with a thump upon a mossy log. It was damp, but he was damper, his wet leathers sliding and squeaking unpleasantly.

She looked no different, to his eye. Well, wet, yes, sodden and wild, but still caressed by the slanting light as if the sun were her lover. He saw no cat shape in her shadow. He smelled nothing but himself, a sickly mix of wet leather, oil, sweat, and horse.

"I don't know if it was Boleso's intent that I should have it," she continued in that same flat tone, undaunted by the repulsive interruption. "It came to me when I touched his dying body, looking for the key. The other animals stayed bound, and went with him. He had held them longer, or perhaps the rite hadn't been finished. The leopard's spirit was very frightened and frantic. It hid itself in my mind, but I could feel it.

"I did not know what to do, or what *it* might do. Boleso's men were fools. I said nothing about it, and no one asked."

"Your defense—that could be your defense!" he said in sudden eagerness. "The leopard spirit killed the prince, in its frenzy. Not you. You were possessed by it. It was an accident."

She blinked at him. "No," she said in a voice of reason, "I just *told* you. The leopard did not come to me till Boleso lay dying."

"Yes, but you could *say* otherwise. There is none to gainsay you."

Her stare grew offended.

We must return to this argument, I think. Ingrey waved a weak hand. "Well. And then . . . ?"

"That night, in my cell, I had vivid dreams. Warm forests, cool glens. Tumbling in golden grasses with other young cats, spotted and soft, but with sharp bites. Strange men. Nets, cages, chains, collars. A ship journey, a cart journey. More men, cruel and kind. Loneliness. There were no words in these dreams. It was all feelings, and flashes of vision, and strong smells. A torrent of smells, a new continent of odors.

"I first thought that I was going mad, but then I decided not. That closet was just like a cage, in a way; cruel and kind men brought food and cleaned it out. It was familiar. Calming.

"On the second night, I dreamed the leopard's dreams

again. But this time . . ." Her voice faltered. Steadied. "This time, there came a Presence. There was nothing to see, in that black wood, but the smells were wonderful, beyond any perfume. Every good scent of the forest and field in the fall. Apples and wine, roast meat, crisp leaves and sharp blue air. I smelled the autumn stars, and cried out for their beauty. The leopard's spirit leapt in ecstasy, like a dog greeting its master or a cat rubbing around the skirts of its mistress. It purred, and writhed, and made eager noises.

"After that, the leopard's ghost seemed pacified. No longer frightened or wild. It just . . . lies there contentedly, waiting. No, more than contentedly. Joyfully. I don't know what it waits for."

"A presence," echoed Ingrey. *No—she said, a Presence.* "Did a—do you think—was it a god? That came to you, there in the dark?"

Did he doubt it? Luminous, Ingrey had called her, with a perception beyond sight, however denied. And even in those first confused moments, he had not mistaken it for mere physical beauty.

Her face grew suddenly fierce; she said through her teeth, "It didn't come to *me,* it came to the accursed *cat.* I wept for it to come to me. But it did not." Her voice slowed. "Perhaps it could not. I am no saint, fit to have a god inhabit me."

Ingrey grubbed in the moss with nervous fingers. His split scalp had stopped dripping blood into his eyebrows, finally. "It was also said—though not by the Quintarian divines— that the Old Wealdings used animal spirits to commune with the gods."

Her lovely jaw clenched; her eyes turned a ferocious light upon him, so that he nearly recoiled. Only then, and only for that brief instant, did he see how much seething terror she concealed—had from the first been concealing—beneath her composed surface. "Ingrey, curse you, you *have* to tell me, you *must* talk, or I shall go mad in truth—*how did you come by your wolf?*"

Hers was not some idle curiosity, spurred by gossip. It was a most desperate need to know. And how much would he, in his first confusion so long ago, have given for some experienced mentor to tell him how to go on? Or even for a companion as confused as he, but sharing his experience, matching his confidences instead of denying them and naming him demented, defiled, and damned? And all the things he could never have explained even to a sympathetic ear, she had just experienced.

It still felt like hauling buckets from a well of memory with a rope that burned his hands. He gritted his teeth; began.

"I was but fourteen. It all came upon me without warning. I was brought to the ceremony uninstructed. My father had been for some days—or weeks—distraught about something that he would confide to no one. He suborned a Temple sorcerer to accomplish the rite. I do not know who caught the wolves, or how. The sorcerer disappeared immediately after—whether in fear of having botched the rite, or because he had deliberately betrayed us, I never found out. I was not fit to inquire, just then."

"A sorcerer?" she echoed, leaning against a tree bole. "I saw no sorcerer with Boleso. Unless he had one hidden in disguise. If Boleso himself was demon-ridden, I saw no sign, not that I would. Well, you can't, unless you are god-sighted or a sorcerer yourself."

"No, the Temple would have . . ." Ingrey hesitated. "In Easthome, some sensitive from the Temple must have detected it, if Boleso had caught a demon. If he'd caught it more recently, since his exile . . . he might not have encountered anyone with the gift to discern it." But whatever had been wrong with Boleso had surely been going on since before he'd slain his manservant.

"I cannot guess what powers his menagerie might have given him," said Ijada. "I know things now that I do not see with my eyes. The leopard seems to give me a kind of knowledge or perception, but"—her hand clenched in frustration—"not in words. Why doesn't your wolf help you so?"

Because I have worked for a decade and more to cripple it, bind it down tight. And I thought I was safe, and now your questions frighten me worse than the wolf-within. "You said there was a thing, another . . . smell, not me or my wolf. A third thing."

She stared at him unhappily, her brows drawing in, as though she grappled for a description of something that had no relation to language. "It is as if I can smell souls. Or the leopard does, and leaks it to me in patches. I can smell Ulkra, and know he is not to fear. Another few men in the retinue—I know to stay out of their reach. Your soul seems doubled: you, and something underneath, something dark and old and musty. It does not stir."

"My wolf?" But his wolf had been a young one.

"I . . . maybe. But there is a third smell. It is wound about you like some parasitic vine, pulsing with blood, that has put tendrils and roots into your spirit to maintain itself. It *whispers*. I think it is some spell or geas."

Ingrey was silent for a long moment, staring down at himself. How could she guess which was which? His wolf spirit was surely a kind of parasite. "Is it still there?"

"Yes."

His voice tightened. "Then in my next inattentive moment, I might try to kill you again."

"Perhaps." Her eyes narrowed and nostrils flared, as if seeking a sensation that had nothing to do with the senses of the body. As futile as trying to see with her hands, or taste with her ears. "Till it is rooted out."

His voice went smaller still. "Why don't you run away? You should run away."

"Don't you see? I must get to the Temple at Easthome. I must find help. And you are taking me there as fast as may be."

"The divines were never much help to *me*," he said bitterly. "Or I would not still be afflicted. I tried for years—

consulting theologians, sorcerers, even saints. I traveled all the way to Darthaca to find a saint of the Bastard who was reputed to banish demons from men's souls, to destroy illicit sorcerers. Even he could not disentangle my wolf spirit. Because, he told me, it was of *this* world, not of the other; even the Bastard, who commands a legion of demons of disorder and can summon or dismiss them at His will, had no power over it. If even saints cannot help, the ordinary Temple authorities will be useless. Worse than useless—a danger. In Easthome, the Temple is the tool of the powerful, and it seems you have offended the powerful."

Her gaze sharpened. "Who put the geas on you? *Must* it have been someone powerful?"

His lips parted, closed again. "I am not sure. I cannot say. It all slips away from me. Unless I am reminded, I don't even remember, between one time and the next, trying to kill you. A moment's distraction on my part could be deadly to you!"

"Then I will undertake to remind you," she said. "It should be easier, now that we both know."

As he opened his mouth to protest, he heard a distant crashing in the woods. A man called, "Lord Ingrey?" and another, "I heard voices toward the river—over that way . . . !"

"They're coming!" He struggled to his feet, swaying dizzily, his hands extending to her in pleading. "Before they find us. Flee!"

"Like *this*?" she said indignantly, sweeping a hand down her damp costume, her bare feet. "Soaking wet, no money, no weapons, no help, I am to run off into the woods and— what? Be eaten by bears?" Her jaw set. "No. Boleso came from Easthome. Your geas came from Easthome. It is there that the source of this evil must be stalked. I will not be diverted."

"Someone there would kill you to keep you silent. They've already tried. They might kill *me*."

"Then you'd better not babble about this to anyone."

"*I* don't babble—" he began in outrage, but then their rescuers were upon them, two of Ingrey's men on horseback hacking through the undergrowth. Now *he* wanted to talk to *her,* and could not.

"My lord!" cried Rider Gesca in gladness. "You have saved her!"

Since Ijada did not correct this misperception, neither did Ingrey. Evading her gaze, he climbed to his feet.

3

WHEN THEY ARRIVED BACK AT THE WAGON WAITING ON the far bank, the sun had slipped behind the treetops. A level orange glint shone through the tangled branches by the time Ingrey and his prisoner had traded off for dry clothes and mounted their recaptured horses. Ingrey's head, wrapped in a makeshift strip of cloth, was pounding, and his shoulder was stiffening, but he refused even to contemplate the idea of sitting in the wagon atop Boleso's box. The cortege clambered out of the wooded valley and on into the gathering twilight.

A chill mist began to arise from the ditches and fields. Ingrey was just about to order his lead riders to light torches to guide them when a distant glow on the road resolved into a string of bobbing lanterns. A few minutes later, an anxious *Halloo* sounded above trotting hoofbeats. The man Ingrey had sent ahead that morning to ready Reedmere for Boleso spurred forward to greet them. He brought with him not only Temple servants with lights, but a fresh team of horses already harnessed, together with a wheelwright and his tools. Ingrey gave the prudent guardsman a heartfelt commendation, the teams were exchanged, and the procession started up again at a faster pace. In a few more miles, the lights above the walls of Reedmere shone to guide them to the gate held open for them.

Reedmere was no hamlet, but a town of several thousand souls, and the local center of Temple administration. Its temple on the town square, though large, was still very much in the old rural style: a five-sided wooden hall decorated outside and in with elaborate twining carvings of plants and beasts and scenes from saints' tales. The roof was wood shingle, doubtless lately replacing rustic thatch. In any case, it made a fit enough barn to store Boleso's coffin for the night. Reedmere's anxious ruling lord-divine, assisted by most of the lay stewards of his civic council, hastened to oversee the prince's placement therein and intone prayers. A gaggle of curious townsfolk had dressed up and assembled into a passable choir. More superior citizens mustered to make loyal obeisance at the bier; Ingrey sensed a slight disappointment that the coffin was closed. Ingrey let his bandages excuse him from the ceremonies.

The temple's outbuildings seemed mostly to consist of nearby houses recommissioned to new duties. The divine's residence was in a building with the Temple notary's office; the library and scriptorium shared quarters with the Daughter of Spring's Lady-school for the town's children; the Temple infirmary, dedicated to the Mother of Summer, occupied the back rooms of the local apothecary's shop. Ingrey saw his prisoner turned over to some stern-looking female Temple servants, gave a few coins to the wheelwright for his time, made sure the horses were stabled and his men housed, paid off the yeoman-teamster and his wife and found them and their horses lodgings in the town for the night, and, finally, reported to the infirmary to have his head stitched.

To his relief, Ingrey found that the Mother's practitioner here was more than just a local seamstress or midwife; she wore the braid of a school dedicat on the shoulder of her green robe. With briskly efficient hands she lit wax candles, washed his head with strong soap, and sutured his scalp.

Sitting on her bench staring at his knees and trying not to wince at every needle poke or tug of the threads, he inquired, "Tell me, does Reedmere harbor any Temple sorcerers? Or saints? Or petty saints? Or . . . or even scholars?"

She laughed. "Oh, not here, my lord! Three years ago, a Temple inquirer from the Father's Order brought a sorcerer with him to investigate a charge of demon magic against a local woman, but nothing was found. The inquirer gave her accusers a pretty scorching lecture, after, and they were fined his travel costs. I must say, the sorcerer was not what I expected—sour old fellow in Bastard's whites, not much amused, I gathered, to be dragged out onto the roads in winter. There was a petty saint of the Mother at my old school"—she sighed in memory—"I wished I'd had the half of his plain ordinary skill, as well as his holy sight and touch. As for scholars, Maraya who runs the Lady-school is about the best we can do, apart from the lord-divine himself."

Ingrey was disappointed, but not surprised. But sorcerer or saint or *someone* Sighted, he must find, to confirm or deny Lady Ijada's disturbing assertions. *And soon.*

"There," added the dedicat in satisfaction, giving a tug to her last knot. Ingrey turned a small yelp into a grunt. A snip of scissors told him this little ordeal was over, and, with difficulty, he straightened up again.

Voices and footsteps sounded at the back door of the shop, and the Mother's dedicat looked around. The pair of female Temple servants, one of the lay stewards, Lady Ijada, and Rider Gesca trooped in. The servants were carrying piles of bedding.

"What's this?" said the dedicat, with a suspicious glance at Lady Ijada.

"By your leave, Dedicat," said the steward, "this woman will be housed here tonight, as there are no sick in your chambers. Her attendants will sleep in the room with her, and I will sleep outside the door. This man"—he nodded toward Ingrey's lieutenant—"will post a night sentry to check from time to time."

The dedicat looked anything but pleased with this prospect; the women servants were downright grim.

Ingrey glanced around. The place was clean enough, certainly, but . . . "Here?"

Lady Ijada favored him with an ironical lift of her eyebrows. "By your order, I am not to be housed in the town lockup, for which I thank you. The divine's spare room is reserved for you. The inn is full of your men, and the temple hall is full of Boleso's retainers. More sleeping their vigil than standing it, I suppose, though some are drinking it. For some reason, no goodwife of Reedmere has volunteered to invite me into her home. So I am fallen back on the goddess's hospitality." Her smile was rigid.

"Oh," said Ingrey after a moment. "I see."

To people who knew Boleso only as a rumor of a golden prince, she must appear . . . well, scarcely a heroine. Not merely a dangerous murderess in herself, but leaking a taint of treason on any who might be seen to aid her. *And it will get worse the closer we get to Easthome.* With no better solution to offer, Ingrey could only exchange an awkward nod of good night with her, and let the medical dedicat usher him to the door.

"Off to sleep with you, now, my lord," the dedicat went on, standing on tiptoe to take one last look at her work and recovering her cheer. "With that knock to the head, you should stay in bed for a day or two."

"My duties will not permit, alas." He gave her a stiff bow, and went off across the square to fill at least the first half of her prescription.

The divine, finished with praying over Boleso, was waiting up for him. The man wanted to talk of further ceremonies, and after that, hear news from the capital. He was anxious for the hallow king's failing health; Ingrey, himself four days out of touch, elected to be reassuringly vague. Ingrey judged the Reedmere man an unlordly lord-divine, a sincere soul-shepherd, backbone of the rural Temple, but neither learned nor subtle. Not a man in whom to confide Lady

Ijada's current spiritual situation. *Or my own.* Ingrey turned him firmly to the needs of tomorrow's travel, made excusing references to his injuries, and escaped to his bedchamber.

It was a small but blessedly private room on the second floor. Ingrey opened its window onto the night chill only long enough to glance at the feeble oil lamps on an iron stand in the black square below, and at the stars burning more brightly above, then crawled into one of the divine's nightshirts laid out for him. He lowered his head gingerly to his pillow. For all his pains and churning worries, he did not lie awake long.

Ingrey dreamed of wolves . . .

He would have thought black midnight to be the time for the rite, but his father summoned him to the castle hall in the middle of the afternoon. A cool shadowless light penetrated from the window slits that overlooked the gurgling Birch-beck sixty feet below. Good beeswax candles burned in sconces on the walls, their warm honeyed flicker mixing with the grayness.

Lord Ingalef kin Wolfcliff appeared calm, if grave with the strain that had ridden him of late, and he greeted his son with a reassuring nod and a brief, rare smile. Young Ingrey's throat was tight with nervous excitement and fear. The Temple sorcerer, Cumril, made known to Ingrey only the night before, stood at the ready, naked but for a breech-cloth, bare skin daubed about with archaic signs. The sorcerer had looked old to Ingrey then, but through his dream-eyes he saw that Cumril had actually been a young man. With the foresight of his nightmare state, Ingrey searched Cumril's face for some intimation or mark—did he plot the betrayal to come? Or was he just in over his head—not in control, unlucky, incompetent? The worry in his shifting eyes could have betokened either—or, indeed, all.

Then young Ingrey's gaze locked upon the animals, the

beautiful, dangerous animals, and he could scarcely thereafter look away. The grizzled huntsman who handled them would die of rabies three days before Ingrey's father.

The old wolf was huge, savage, and powerful. Muscles rippled beneath its thick gray pelt, marred with old scars and new cuts. The fur was crusted with blood in a few places. The animal was restless, whining, resistant to the huntsman's leash. Feverish, though no one here knew that. In a few days, the foaming would have begun, revealing its sickness, but now it merely tried to lick itself in its discomfort, impeded by the leather straps muzzling its jaws. It snarled thickly in its bonds.

The young wolf, barely more than a pup, scrabbled away from its larger comrade in evident fear, claws scratching on the floorboards. The huntsman took it for cowardly, but later Ingrey would come to believe it had known of the contagion. Otherwise, it was startlingly docile, attentive as a well-trained dog. Its fur was dark and wonderfully dense, its silver-gilt eyes clear, and it responded at once to Ingrey's arrival, straining toward him and sniffing, staring up in evident adoration. Ingrey loved it instantly, his hands aching to run through the pewter-black pelt.

The sorcerer directed Ingrey and his father to strip to the waist and kneel on the cold floor a few paces apart, facing each other. He intoned some phrases in the old tongue of the Weald, pronouncing them carefully with many a side glance at a piece of wrinkled paper plucked from his belt. The language seemed to hover maddeningly just on the edge of Ingrey's understanding.

At Cumril's sign, the huntsman dragged the old wolf to Lord Ingalef's arms. He let go of the young wolf's leash to do so, and the animal scampered to Ingrey's lap. Ingrey held its soft warmth close, and it wriggled around to eagerly lick his face. His hands buried themselves in its fur, petting and stroking; the creature emitted small, happy whines and tried to wash Ingrey's ear. The rough tongue tickled, and Ingrey had to choke down a reflexive, unfitting laugh.

Muttering briefly over the blade, the sorcerer delivered the sacred knife to Lord Ingalef's waiting hand, then stepped back hastily as the disturbed wolf snapped at him. The beast began to struggle as Lord Ingalef's grip tightened. The struggle redoubled as he grasped it by the muzzle and tried to tilt its head back. He lost his hold, the jaw straps slipped loose, and the animal sank its teeth in his left forearm, shaking its head and snarling, worrying the flesh. Muffling a curse, he regained a partial purchase with knees and the weight of his strong body. The blade flashed, sank into fur and flesh. Red blood spurted. The snarls died, the jaws loosed, and the furry bundle subsided limply; then, a moment later, into a more profound stillness.

Lord Ingalef sat up and back, releasing knife and carcass. The knife clattered on the stones.

"Oh," he said, eyes wide and strange. "It worked. How very . . . odd that feels . . ."

Cumril cast him a worried look; the huntsman hastened to bind his savaged arm.

"My lord, should you not . . . ?" Cumril began.

Lord Ingalef shook his head sharply and raised his sound hand in a unsteady *Continue!* gesture. "It worked! Go on!"

The sorcerer picked up the second blade, gleaming new-forged, from the cushion on which it rested, and trod forward mumbling again. He pressed the knife into Ingrey's hand and stepped back once more.

Ingrey's hand closed unhappily on the hilt, and he looked into the bright eyes of his wolf. *I don't want to kill you. You are too beautiful. I want to keep you.* The clean jaws opened, showing fine white teeth, and Cumril's breath drew in, but the young wolf only lolled out its pink tongue and licked Ingrey's hand. The cool black nose nudged his knife-clutching fist, and Ingrey blinked back tears. The wolf sat up between Ingrey's knees, raised its head, and twisted around to gaze into its killer's face with perfect trust.

He must not botch this, must not inflict unnecessary torment with repeated strikes. His hands felt the neck, traced the firm muscles and the soft ripple of artery and vein. The room was a silvered blur. The young wolf leaned into him as Ingrey laid the blade close. He drew back, struck, yanked with all his strength. Felt the flesh part, the hot blood spurt over his hands, wetting the fur. Felt the body relax in his arms.

The dark flow struck his mind like a torrent of blood. Wolf lives, life upon life, huts and fires, castles and battles, stables and steeds, iron and fire, hunts; hunt upon hunt, kill upon kill, but always with men, never with a wolf pack; back still farther beyond even the memory of fire, into endless forests crusted with snow in the moonlight. There was too much, too much, too many years . . . his eyes rolled back.

Shouts of alarm: his father's voice, "Something's gone wrong! Curse you, Cumril, catch him!"

"He's gone all shaking—he's bitten his tongue, my lord—"

A shift of time and space, and his wolf was bound—no, *he* was bound—red-silk cords whispered and muttered around him, writhing, rooting in him like vines. His wolf snapped at them, white teeth closing, tearing, but the cords regrew with frightening speed. They wrapped his head, tightening painfully.

Unfamiliar voices invaded his delirium then, irritatingly. His wolf fled. The memory of his evil dream spattered and ran away like water.

"He can't be asleep; his eyes are half-open, see them gleam?"

"No, don't wake him up! I know what you're supposed to do. You're supposed to lead them back to bed quietly, or, I don't know, they go all wild, or something."

"Then I'm not touching him with that sword in his hand!"

"Well, how else?"

"Get more light, woman. Oh, five gods be thanked, here's his own man."

A hesitation; then, "Lord Ingrey? Lord Ingrey!"

Candlelight doubled, doubled again. Ingrey blinked,

gasped, surged to wakefulness. His head ached abominably. He was standing up. Shock brought him fully alert.

He was standing once more in the temple infirmary, if the room in back of the apothecary's could be so designated. He wore the divine's nightshirt half-tucked into his trousers, but his feet were bare on the board floor. His right hand gripped his naked sword.

He was surrounded by the steward, one of Ijada's woman attendants, and the guardsman that Gesca had designated for the night watch. Well, not surrounded, exactly; the first two were plastered against the walls, staring at him with wide and terrified eyes, and the third-named hovered in the back doorway of the shop.

"I'm"—he had to stop, swallow, moisten his lips—"I'm awake." *What am I doing here? How did I get over here?*

He'd been sleepwalking, presumably. He had heard of such things. He'd never done it before. And it had been more than just blundering about in the dark. He'd partly dressed, found his weapon, somehow made his way in unobserved silence down a stairway, through a door—which surely must have been locked, so he must have turned the key—across the cobbled square, and into this other building.

Where Lady Ijada lies asleep. Five gods, let her go on sleeping. The door to the bedchamber was closed—now. In sudden horror, he glanced at his blade, but it was still gleaming and dry. No dripping gore stained it. *Yet.*

His guardsman, with a wary glance at his sword, came to him and took him by his left arm. "Are you all right, my lord?"

"Hurt my head today," Ingrey mumbled. "The dedicat's medicines gave me strange dreams. Dizzy. Sorry . . ."

"Should I . . . um . . . take you back to bed, my lord?"

"Yes," said Ingrey gratefully. "Yes"—the seldom-used phrase forced itself from his cold lips—"please you." He was shivering now. It wasn't wholly from the chill.

He suffered the guardsman to guide him out the door, around the shop, back across the silent, dark square. Back into the divine's house. A servant who had slept through Ingrey's exit was awakened by their return and came out into the hall in sleepy alarm. Ingrey mumbled more excuses about the dedicat's potions, which served well enough given the porter's own muzzy state. Ingrey let his guardsman guide him all the way to his bed and even pull his covers up, sergeantly maternal. The man retreated in a clanking, board-creaking sort of tiptoe, pulling the door shut behind him.

Ingrey waited until the footsteps had faded away in the square before he crawled out from his quilts, groped for his tinderbox, and lit a candle, flint and striker uncooperative in his shaking hands. He sat on the edge of the bed recovering for a few minutes, then arose and made a survey of his room. He could only lock the door from the inside, which meant he could unlock it as easily, unless he then threw the key out the window or shoved it under the door, which would create awkward delays and explanations in the morning. He briefly regretted not having had his guardsman lock it as he'd left, although that, too, would have entailed awkward explanations. Or clever lies, and Ingrey was feeling singularly stupid just now. At length, he set his sword and belt knife in a chest that held spare linens, and balanced several potentially noisy objects, capped with the tin basin from his washstand, atop the lid in a deliberately precarious tower.

He blew out the candle, went back to bed, lay stiffly for a time, then got up again and felt in the dark in his saddle-bags for a length of rope. He tied a loop tightly around his ankle, played out a length, and tied another loop around a lower bedpost. Clumsily, he wrapped himself in his covers again.

His head throbbed, and his strained shoulder pulsed like a knot of fire under his skin. He tossed, turned, came up short against his rope. Well, at least it *worked*. He started to doze in sheer exhaustion, turned, and came up short again. He wallowed onto his back once more and lay staring up into the dark, teeth clenched. His eyes felt coated in sand.

Better than dreaming. He'd had the wolf dream again, for

the first time in months, though it was now only slippery fragments in his memory. He had more than one reason to fear sleep, it seemed.

How did I get into this position? A week ago, he had been a happy man, or at least, contented enough. He had a comfortable chamber in Lord Hetwar's palace, a manservant, horse and clothing and arms by his lord's grace, a stipend sufficient for his amusements. The bustle of the hallow king's capital city at his feet. Better, he had an engagingly irregular but solid rank in the sealmaster's household, and. a reputation as a trusted aide—not quite bravo, not quite clerk, but a man to be relied upon for unusual tasks discreetly done. As Hetwar's high courier, he delivered rewards intact, and threats suitably nuanced. He was not, he thought, proudly honest, as some men; perhaps he'd simply lost too much already to be tempted by trumpery. Indifference served him quite as well as integrity, and sometimes served Hetwar even better. His most pleasurable reward had usually been to have his curiosity satisfied.

Bastard's hell, three *days* ago he'd been an untroubled man. He had figured the retrieval of Boleso's body and killer to be a joyless but perfectly straightforward task. Well within his capabilities as an experienced, tough-minded, shrewd, and above all, not in the *least* wolf-haunted or in any other way whatsoever uncanny royal servant.

The rope yanked his ankle again. His right hand clenched in the memory of his sword hilt. *Curse* that leopard girl! If she'd just lain down under Boleso like any other self-interested wench, spread her legs and thought of the jewelry and fine clothing she would undoubtedly have earned, all this could have been avoided. And Ingrey wouldn't be lying here with a line of bloody embroidery itching in his hair, half the muscles in his body twitching in agony, tied to his own bed, waiting for a leaden dawn.

Wondering if he was still sane.

4

THEY ESCAPED REEDMERE LATER IN THE MORNING THAN Ingrey had desired, owing to the insistence of the lord-divine in making a ceremony, with more choirs, out of loading Boleso's coffin aboard its new carrier. The wagon at least was tolerable—very well made, with somber draperies disguising its bright paint, if not the distinct smell of beer lingering about it. The six horses that came with it were grand tawny beasts, massive of shoulder, haunch, and hoof, with orange and black ribbons braided in manes and bound-up tails. The bells on their glossy harness were muffled with black flannel, for which Ingrey, head still throbbing from yesterday's blow, was grateful. Compared to their usual load, Ingrey imagined, the team would tow Boleso up hills and through mire as effortlessly as a child's sled.

Rider Gesca recoiled at the close view of Ingrey when helping him to mount up, then intercepted Ingrey's glower and swallowed any comment. Ingrey *had* shaved, and the divine's servants had returned his riding leathers dry, supple, and buffed; but there was nothing he could do about the squinting, bloodshot eyes and gray, puffy face. He clenched his teeth, settling his aching body into his saddle, and endured the slow procession to the town gate through the clamor of bells and chants and billows of incense that Reedmere thought becoming to the prince's send-off. Ingrey waited till the town had passed out of sight behind them before waving the new teamster to chirp his beasts into a lumbering trot. The dray horses seemed the only cheerful members of the party, fresh and ponderously frisky and apparently regarding the jaunt as some horse holiday.

Lady Ijada appeared as trim as she had yesterday morning, now in an even more elegant riding habit of gray-blue trimmed with silver thread. Clearly, *she* had slept through the night. Ingrey wavered between resentful and relieved, as his headache waxed and waned. An hour into the bright morning, he began to feel about as recovered as he was likely to get. *Almost human.* He gritted his teeth at the bitter joke and rode up and down the column taking stock.

Ijada's new female attendant, one of the middle-aged Temple servants on loan from Reedmere, rode in the wagon. She was wary of her ward, much more frigid than the rural wife from Boar's Head who had known more of Boleso. She seemed even more wary of Ingrey. He wondered if the woman had told Ijada of his sleepwalking episode.

Boleso's retainers, too, seemed edgier today, as they drew closer to Easthome and whatever chastisement awaited them for their failure to keep their banished prince alive. More than one cast glances of dark resentment at Boleso's victim-and-slayer, and Ingrey resolved to keep them from both drink and his prisoner until he could turn the whole lot *and* their dead leader over to someone, anyone, else. Ingrey had dispatched a Temple courier last night to Sealmaster Hetwar with the cortege's projected itinerary. If Hetwar left it to *his* discretion, Ingrey decided, Boleso was going to be galloped to his burial in record time.

If not at a gallop, the great horses moved them briskly and steadily through a countryside growing kinder, with wider roads mostly in better repair. Narrow pastures surrounded by vast precipitous forests gave way to tracts of merely hilly woodlands surrounded by broad fields. The eye might see more than one hamlet on the horizon at a time. They began to pass other traffic—not just farm wagons, but well-clad riders and petty merchants with pack mules—all of whom hastened to give way. An exception was a drove of lean black pigs encountered in an oak woods. The swineherd and his boy, not expecting to encounter such a royal procession on their road, lost control of their half-wild beasts, and Ingrey's and Boleso's men, variously amused and annoyed, had to assist in clearing the path, hooting, swearing, and swinging the flats of their sheathed swords.

Ingrey checked himself; this squealing prey did not seem to attract or excite him unduly, which was as well. He sat his horse in grim silence till the pigs had been driven again into the tangled verge. Lady Ijada, he noted, also sat her horse quietly, waiting, although with a curious inward expression on her face.

He did not attempt speech with her on the ride. His guards, by his order, kept close to her while she was mounted, and the servant woman dutifully dogged her steps during the stops to rest the horses. But his eye returned to her constantly. All too often he crossed her grave glance at *him*: not a frown of fear, more a look of concern. As though *he* were *her* charge. It was most irritating, as though they were tied to each other by a tugging leash, like a pair of coupled hounds. Not looking at or speaking with her seemed to consume all his energy and attention, and left him exhausted.

It had been a long and wearisome day when they rumbled at last into the royal free town of Red Dike. The town's proud status left it subject neither to local earl nor Temple lord-divine, but ruled by its own town council under a king's charter. Alas, this did not result in any diminution of ceremony, and Ingrey was trapped for some time as his hosts carried Boleso's coffin into the temple—stone-built in the Darthacan style, its five lobes rounded and domed—for the night.

The town's superior size, however, meant it had not merely a larger inn, but three of them, and Ingrey had mustered the wit that morning to instruct his advance scout to bespeak rooms. The middle hostelry had also proved the cleanest. Ingrey himself escorted Lady Ijada and her warden up to its second floor, and the bedchamber and private parlor his man had secured. He inspected the portals. The windows overlooked the street, were small, and could not be readily accessed from the ground. The door bars were sound solid oak. *Good.*

He dug the rooms' keys from his belt pouch and handed them to Lady Ijada. The woman warden frowned curiously at him, but did not dare demur.

"Keep your doors locked at all times, tonight," Ingrey told Lady Ijada. "And barred."

Her brows rose a little, and she glanced around the peaceful chamber. "Is there anything special to fear, here?"

Nothing but what we brought with us. "I walked in my sleep last night," he admitted with reluctance. "I was outside your door before anyone woke me."

She gave him a slow nod, and another of those *looks*. He unset his teeth, and said, "I will be staying at one of the other inns. I know you gave me your word, but I want you to stay close in here, out of sight. You'll wish to eat privately. I'll have your dinner brought up."

She said only, "Thank you, Lord Ingrey."

With a short return nod, he took himself out.

Ingrey went down to the taproom, lying off a short passage, to give orders for his prisoner's meal. A couple of Boleso's retainers and one of Ingrey's men were already there, raising tankards.

Ingrey glanced at the retainers. "You're housed here?"

"We're housed everywhere, my lord," said the man. "We've filled the other inns."

"Better than bedrolls on the temple floor," said Ingrey's man.

"Oh, aye," said the first, and took a long swallow. His burlier comrade grunted something that might have been agreement.

A commotion and a small shriek outside drew Ingrey to

the taproom's curtained window, which looked out into the street. An open wagon pulled by a pair of stubby, sweaty horses had drawn up outside in the dusk, and one of its front wheels had just parted company with its axle and fallen onto the cobbles, leaving the wagon tilted at a drunken angle. Its lanterns swayed on their front posts, casting wavering shadows. A woman's brisk voice said, "Never mind, love, Bernan will fix it. That's why I—"

"Had me bring my toolbox, yes," finished a weary male voice from the back of the wagon. "I'll get to it. Next."

The manservant hopped out and set some wooden steps beside the now-sloping driver's box, and he and a woman servant helped a stout, short, cloaked figure to descend.

Ingrey turned away, thinking only that the late-arriving party might find rooms hard to come by in Red Dike tonight. The burly retainer drained his tankard, belched, and asked the tapster for directions to the privy. He lurched out of the taproom ahead of Ingrey and turned into the passageway.

The bulky cloaked woman had arrived therein; her maidservant was bent to the floor behind her, muttering imprecations and blocking the way. The voluminous cloak was grubby and tattered, and had clearly seen better days.

The burly retainer vented a curse, and growled, "Out of my way, you fat sow."

An indignant "Huh!" sounded from the recesses of the cloak, and the woman threw back her hood and glared up at the man. She was neither young nor old, but matronly; her curling sand-colored hair escaped from falling braids to create a faint ferocious aureole around her breathless face, pink from either the insult, the evening's chill, or both. Ingrey, looking around the retainer's shoulder, came alert; Boleso's men were not the sort whom lesser folk dared casually defy. But the foolish woman seemed oblivious to the man's sword and mail. And size and dubious sobriety, for that matter.

The woman unhooked the clasp at her throat and let the cloak fall away; she was dressed in robes of Mother's green, and was not fat, but very pregnant. If some midwife-dedicat, she would shortly be in need of her own services, Ingrey thought bemusedly. The woman reached over her jutting belly to tap her left shoulder, and cleared her throat portentously. "See this, young man? Or are you too drunk to focus your eyes?"

"See what?" said the burly retainer, unimpressed by a midwife, still less if she were some gravid poor woman.

She followed his gaze to her frayed green-clad shoulder, and pursed her lips in annoyance. "Oh, dratsab. Hergi"—she twisted around to her maid, now rising to her feet—"they've fallen off again. I hope I haven't lost them on the road—"

"I have them right here, my lady," wheezed the harried maid. "Here, I'll pin them back. Again."

She came up from the floor with not one but two sets of Temple school braids clutched in her hands, and, tongue pinched between her teeth, began to affix them in their proper place of honor. The first loop was the dark green, straw-yellow, and metallic gold of a physician-divine of the Mother's Order. The second was the white, cream, and metallic silver of a sorceress-divine of the Bastard's Order. The first brought even Boleso's retainer into an attitude of, if not greater respect, at least less careless contempt; but it was the second that drained his face of blood.

Ingrey's lips curled in the first smile he'd had all day. He tapped the man on the shoulder. "Best apologize to the learned lady, I think. And then get out of her way."

The retainer scowled. "Those can't be yours!"

The blood had drained from his brain, too, evidently. *Those who are unwilling to admit error are fated to repeat it?* Prudently, Ingrey backed a few paces down the passage; also because it gave him a better view of the proceedings.

"I do not have *time* for you," said the sorceress in aggravation. "If you insist on behaving as though you were in a sty, a pig you shall be, until you learn better manners." She waved a hand in the retainer's general direction, and Ingrey quelled an impulse to duck. He was entirely unsurprised when the man fell to all fours and his yelp turned into a grunt. The sorceress sniffed, gathered up her robes, and stepped daintily around him. Her head-shaking maid, toting a leather case, scooped up the cloak in passing. Ingrey bowed the women politely into the taproom and turned to follow after, ignoring an agonized snuffle from the floor. His other two men edged around the taproom and peered worriedly into the passageway.

"Apologies, Learned," said Ingrey smoothly, "but will your most salutary lesson last long? I only inquire because the man must be fit to ride tomorrow."

The blond woman turned to frown at him, her floating strands of hair seeming now to be trying to escape in all directions. "Is he yours?"

"Not precisely. But though I am not responsible for his behavior, I am responsible for his arrival."

"Oh. Well. I will doubtless restore him before I leave. Else the delusion will wear off on its own in a few hours. Meanwhile, the encouragement of others and all that. But I am in the greatest haste. There was a grand cortege that arrived in Red Dike tonight, of Prince Boleso who they say was murdered. Have you witnessed it? I seek its commander."

Ingrey half bowed again. "You have found him. Ingrey kin Wolfcliff at your service and your gods', Learned."

She stared at him for a long, disturbing moment. "Indeed you are," she finally said. "Well. That young woman, Ijada dy Castos. Do you know what has become of her?"

"She is in my charge."

"*Is* she." The stare sharpened. "Where?"

"She has chambers upstairs in this inn."

The maidservant huffed in relief; the sorceress cast her a look of cheery triumph. "Third time is the charm," murmured the sorceress. "Did I not say so?"

"This town only *has* three inns," the maidservant pointed out.

"Are you," Ingrey added hopefully, "sent by the Temple to take her into your hands?" *And off mine?*

"Not . . . precisely, no. But I must see her."

Ingrey hesitated. "What is she to you?" *Or you to her?*

"An old friend, if she remembers me. I'm Learned Hallana. I heard of her plight when the news of the prince came to my seminary in Suttleaf. That is, we heard of Boleso's murder, and who had supposedly done the deed, and I presumed it for a plight." Her stare at Ingrey did not grow less disconcerting. "We were sure the cortege must come by this road, but I feared I would have to chase after it."

The seminary of the Mother's Order at Suttleaf, a town some twenty-five miles to the south of Red Dike, was well-known in the region for its training of physicians and other healing artisans—the dedicat who had stitched Ingrey's head last night had likely learned her craft there. Ingrey might have searched the surrounding three earldoms for a Temple sorcerer and never thought of looking at Suttleaf. Instead, she had found him . . .

Could she sense his wolf? A Temple sorcerer had inflicted it upon him; later, a Temple divine had helped him learn to bind it. Might this woman have been sent—by whom or what, Ingrey did not wish to guess—to help bind Ijada's leopard? Incomprehensible as the sorceress's presence here was, it seemed not to be a coincidence. The notion raised all the hackles of his neck and spine. On the whole, Ingrey thought he would prefer coincidence.

He drew a long breath. "I think Lady Ijada has few friends at present. She should be glad of you. May I escort you up to her, Learned?"

The woman favored him with a brief, approving nod. "Yes, please, Lord Ingrey."

He preceded the women into the passageway and indicated the stairs to the left. In the opposite direction, the be-pigged retainer was still down on the floor, shoving his head against the door and grunting.

"My lord, what should we do with him?" asked his unnerved comrade.

Ingrey turned to observe the scene for a moment. "Watch over him. See he comes to no harm till his lesson passes off."

The comrade glanced past Ingrey at the retreating sorceress and swallowed. "Yes, my lord. Um . . . anything else?"

"You could feed him some bran mash."

The sorceress, making her way up the stairs with hand to the rail and her maid close behind, glanced back at this, her lips twitching. She lumbered on upward, and Ingrey hastened after.

To his satisfaction, he found the door to Lady Ijada's parlor locked. He rapped upon it.

"Who is there?" came her voice.

"Ingrey."

A slight pause. "Are you awake?"

He grimaced. "Yes. You have a visitor."

Puzzled silence for a moment, then the clink of the key in the lock and the scrape of the bar being withdrawn. The warden drew the door wide, blinking in astonishment as the sorceress and her maid swept within. Ingrey followed.

Lady Ijada, standing across the room, stared a moment in bafflement.

"Ijada?" said the sorceress, sounding taken aback. "My word, child, how tall you've grown!"

Then Ijada's face was swept by such joy as Ingrey had never yet seen illuminate it. "Hallana!" she cried, and hurried forward.

The two women fell into each other's arms with feminine shrieks of recognition and pleasure. At length, Lady Ijada stood back with her hands upon the shorter woman's shoulders. "How ever did you *come* here?"

"The news of your misadventure came to the Mother's seminary at Suttleaf. I teach there now, you know. And then there were the dreams, of course."

"And how came you *there*—you must tell me everything that has happened with you since—oh, Lord Ingrey." Ijada turned to him, her face glowing. "*This* is my friend I told you of. She was a medical missioner at my father's fort on the west marches, and a student in the Bastard's Order as well, pursuing both her callings—learning the fen folk's wisdom songs, and treating what of their sicknesses she could, to draw them to the fort and our divine's Quintarian preachings. When she was younger, of course. And me—I was the most gangling awkward child. Hallana, I still don't know why you let me tail around after you all day long, but I adored you for it."

"Well, aside from my not being immune to worship—makes me wonder about the gods, indeed it does—you did make yourself quite useful. You were not afraid of the marsh, or the woods, or the animals, or the fen folk, or of getting thoroughly muddy and scratched or of being scolded for it."

Ijada laughed. "I still remember how you and that dreadfully priggish divine used to argue theology over the meal trestles—Learned Oswin would grow so furious, he would positively stamp out afterward. I should have worried for his digestion, if I had been older and less self-absorbed. Poor skinny fellow."

The sorceress smirked. "It was good for him. Oswin was the most perfect servant of the Father, always so concerned for figuring out the exact rules and getting himself on the right side of them. Or them on the left side of him. It always stung him when I pointed that out."

"Oh, but *look* at you—here, you must sit down—" Lady Ijada and the maid Hergi joined forces briefly to find the best chair, pad it with cushions, and urge Learned Hallana into it. She sank down gratefully, blowing out her breath with a whoosh, and adjusted her belly in her lap. The maid scurried to prop her mistress's feet on a stool. Lady Ijada pulled a chair to the table opposite her friend, and Ingrey retreated to the window seat, no great distance away in the tiny room, where he could watch both women. The warden hung back, cautious and respectful.

"Your double scholarship is a most unusual combination, Learned," said Ingrey, nodding to the woman's shoulder braids. Their pin was working loose again, and they hung precariously on their perch.

"Oh, yes. It came about by accident, if accident it was."

She shrugged, dislodging the braids; her maid sighed and wordlessly retrieved and reinstalled them. "I had started out to be a physician, like my mother and grandmother before me. My apprenticeship was quite complete, and I had begun to practice at the Temple hospital in Helmharbor. There I was called to attend upon a dying sorcerer." She paused and glanced shrewdly at Ingrey. "What do you know about how Temple sorcerers are made, Lord Ingrey? Or illicit sorcerers, for that matter?"

His brows rose. "A person comes into possession of a demon of disorder, which has somehow escaped from the grip of the Bastard into the world of matter. The sorcerer takes it into his soul—or hers," he added hastily. "And nourishes it there. In return, the demon lends its powers. The acquisition of a demon makes one a sorcerer much as the acquisition of a horse makes one a rider, or so I was taught."

"Very correct." Hallana nodded approval. "It does not, of course, necessarily make one a *good* rider. That must be learned. Well. What is less well known, is that Temple sorcerers sometimes bequeath their demons to their Order, to be passed along to the next generation, with all that they have learned. Since, when a sorcerer dies, if she—or he— does not bear the demon back to the gods, it will jump away to the next living thing nearby that may sustain it in the world of matter. It is not a good thing to lose a powerful demon into a stray dog. Don't smile, it has happened. But done *properly,* a trained demon may be directed into one's chosen successor without ripping one's soul to pieces in the process."

Ijada leaned forward to listen, her hands clasped in fascination. "You know, I never thought to ask you how you came to be what you were. I just took you for granted."

"You were ten. All the world is an equal mystery then." She shifted in her chair, not without difficulty, evidently seeking a more comfortable position. "The Bastard's Order in Helmharbor had groomed this divine, a very scholarly young fellow, to receive his mentor's powers. All seemed to

go as planned. The old sorcerer—my word, but he was a
frail thing by then—breathed his last quite peacefully, all
things considered. His successor held his hand and prayed.
And the stupid demon jumped right over him and into *me*.
No one was expecting it, least of all that lofty young divine.
He was livid. *I* was distraught. How could I practice the
healing arts when plagued with a demon of disorder itself? I
tried for some time to be rid of it—even made pilgrimage to
a saint reputed to have the Bastard's own power over His
strayed elementals."

"In Darthaca?" inquired Ingrey.

Her brows rose. "How did you know?"

"Fortunate guess."

The flare of her nostril expressed her dim opinion of that
quip. "Well, so. We made the rite together. But the god
would not take His demon back!"

"Darthaca," confirmed Ingrey glumly. "I believe I once
met the same fellow. Remarkably useless."

"Indeed?" Her gaze grew sharp again. "Well. Since I was
saddled with the creature, I needed to learn how to ride if I
was not to *be* ridden, so I apprenticed myself all over again
to the fifth god. I went to the border during a time of great
frustration, thinking to try a simpler life for a while, and to
search again for that sense of calling I had lost. Oh, Ijada, I
was so sorry, later, to hear of the death of your father. He
was a noble man in all senses."

Lady Ijada bowed her head, a shadow crossing her face.
"Ours was not a high-walled fort for no cause. Angry, foolish men, an imprudent ride out to attempt reason at a time
when tempers were running too high . . . I had seen only the
lovely side of the marsh country, and the kindness of its people. But they were only people after all."

"What happened to you and your lady mother, after he was
slain?"

"She went back to her own kin—my own kin—in the
north of the Weald. In a year, she married again—another
Temple-man, though not a soldier—her brother made little

jokes about that. She did not love my stepfather in the way she had loved my father, but he was fond and she was ready to be comfortable. But she died—um." Ijada stopped, glanced at Learned Hallana's belly, and bit her lip.

"I am a physician, too," Hallana reminded her. "Childbed?"

"About four days after. She took a fever."

The warden, listening in all too much fascination, signed herself in sympathy, caught Ingrey's eye upon her, and subsided.

"Hm," said Hallana. "I wonder if—no, never mind. All too late. And your—?"

"Little brother. He lived. My stepfather dotes on him. But he was the reason my stepfather remarried so very quickly."

It was the first Ingrey had heard Lady Ijada had living siblings. *I hadn't thought to ask.*

"And so you found yourself living with . . . no one you'd ever planned to," Learned Hallana mused. "And vice versa. Was your stepfamily comfortable?"

Ijada shrugged. "They were not unkind. My stepmother is good with my brother."

"And she's, ah, how many years older than you?"

A dry smile fleeted across Ijada's face. "Three."

Hallana snorted. "And so when your chance came to go, she bade you farewell with right goodwill?"

"Well, it *was* goodwill. My Badgerbank uncle's wife actually found me the position with Princess Fara. She thought my stepfamily dreadfully common, and that I should be raised up out of it before yeomanry became a habit with me."

Hallana's snort was more caustic, this time. The very learned divine, Ingrey realized, had not introduced herself as *kin* anyone.

"But Hallana," Ijada continued, "physician or not, I do not understand how you may safely bear a demon and a baby at once. I thought demons were terribly dangerous, in that state."

"They are." Learned Hallana grimaced. "Disorder flows naturally from demons; it is the very spring of their power in matter. The creation of a child, wherein matter grows an entirely new soul, is the highest and most complex form of ordering known, apart from the gods themselves. Given all that can go wrong with the process *without* a demon, keeping the two apart becomes rather urgent. And difficult. The difficulty is why some divines discourage female sorcerers from becoming mothers, or women from seeking that power until they are grown old. Well, and some of them are just self-satisfied fools, but that's another subject. It's all very well, you know, but I saw no reason to stop my life for other people's theories. My risks are no greater—or different—than any other woman's, if my skills match them. Oh, apart from the danger of the demon entering the baby during the distractions of birth. Ordinary infants are demonic enough! The secret of safety turns out to be to, ah . . . how shall I put it. *Shed* excess disorder. By cascading small amounts of chaos continually, I keep my demon passive, and my baby safe." A fond maternal smile lit her eyes. "Alas, it's a trifle hard on everyone *around* me for those months. I have a little hermitage on the edge of the seminary grounds that I move into."

"Oh. Isn't it lonely?"

"Not at all. My dear husband brings the two older children to visit me every day. And some evenings without the children, too. I catch up on my reading and my studies—it makes the most wonderful retreat imaginable. I should be quite too inclined to repeat it, but I imagine a dozen babies would be a mistake, and anyway, I think my husband would draw the line well before then."

The maid Hergi, who had made herself small and quiet near her mistress's feet, giggled in a remarkably unservile fashion.

"It is not, you know, different in kind from the sort of thoughtful self-discipline any Temple sorcerer must keep. To use disorder alone, never trying to reverse the flow of its nature, but in good cause . . . calm, careful, never yielding to the temptation of shortcuts. That was the salvation of my calling—when a certain brilliant logician pointed out that surgery destroys to heal. And I saw how to correctly use the powers that had been granted me in the direction my heart desired. I was so overjoyed, I married him."

Ijada laughed. "I am so happy for you! You deserve all good things."

"Ah, what we may deserve, well, the Father alone knows that, in the balance of His justice." The sorceress's face grew solemn again. "So tell me, love, what truly happened out in that cold castle?"

5

IJADA'S LAUGHTER WAS ABRUPTLY EXTINGUISHED. INGREY quietly rose and sent the warden out for the meal that he had been diverted from ordering, increasing the servings. This also removed her interested ear from the proceedings. She looked disappointed, but dared not disobey.

He slipped back to his seat as quietly, so as not to distract Lady Ijada from her halting confession to her friend. Who was so obviously, at least to Ingrey's mind, here for subtler reasons than friendship.

He was alert for discrepancies, but the tale Ijada told Learned Hallana was much the same as what she had—finally—told Ingrey, though this time all in order with nothing left out. Except that she revealed much more to Hallana of her suffocating fears. Hallana's expression grew so intent as to be stony during Ijada's account of her leopard dreams. Ijada brought her story up to her nearly disastrous fall at the ford, yesterday, and hesitated, glancing across at Ingrey. "I think the next part should be Lord Ingrey's to tell."

Ingrey jerked in his seat, flushing. For an instant it almost seemed like the red fog returning, and his hand spasmed on the edge of the sill on which he sat. He became uncomfortably aware that he had grown careless again, on some dim assumption that the sorceress could protect both herself and Ijada. But sorcerers were not proof against steel, not once it closed on them. He'd allowed himself to be alone with the women while still armed. And now his direst secrets were challenged . . .

He blurted, "I tried to drown her. I've tried three other times to kill her, that I know of. I swear it is not my desire. She thinks it is some spell or geas."

The sorceress pursed her lips and vented a long, thoughtful stream of breath. Then she sat back and closed her eyes, her face growing very still. When she opened them again, her expression was enigmatic.

"No sorcerer has currently bespelled you. You bear no sustaining link—no spirit-threads wind to or from you. No elemental from the fifth god lies within your soul. But something else does. It seems very dark."

He looked away. "I know. It is my wolf."

"If that's a wolf's soul, I'm the queen of Darthaca."

"It always was a strange wolf. But it is bound!"

"Huh. May I touch you?"

"I don't know if I am . . . safe."

Her brows twitched up; she looked him over, and he grew acutely conscious of his road stains and brigand's beard stubble. "I think I shall not argue with that. Ijada, what do you see in him?"

"I don't *see* anything," she replied unhappily. "It is as though the leopard smells him, and I overhear . . . oversmell? Howsoever, I am lent these unfamiliar sensations. There's the dark wolf-thing you see—at least, it *smells* dark, like old leaf mold and campfire ashes and forest shadows— and a third thing. Whispering around him like a rumor. It has a most strange perfume. Acrid."

Hallana tilted her head back and forth. "I see his soul, with my soul's eye. I see the dark thing. I do not see *or* hear the third thing. It is not of the Bastard in any way, not lent from the world of spirit that the gods rule. Yet—his soul has strange convolutions. A clear glass that one cannot see with the eyes, one might still touch with the fingers. I must risk a deeper touch."

"Don't!" said Ingrey, panicked.

"Lady, ought you . . . ?" murmured the maid, her face crimped with alarm. "Now?"

Hallana's lips moved on what might have been, *Dratsab, dratsab, dratsab.* "Let us think."

A knock sounded at the door; the warden had returned, flanked by some inn servants with trays and the man Hallana had called Bernan, who lugged a large chest. He was a wiry, middle-aged fellow with an alert eye; his green-leather jerkin was spattered with old burn spots, like a smith's. He inhaled with deep appreciation as the trays were borne past him. The delectable odors of vinegared beef and onions seeping from under the crockery covers forcibly reminded Ingrey that he was both ravenous and exhausted.

Hallana brightened. "Better still, let us eat, then think."

The inn servants set the table in the little parlor, but after that the sorceress sent them away, saying she preferred to be served by her own folk. She whispered aside to Ingrey, "Actually, I make such a mess, just now, I don't dare eat in public." Ingrey, warily circumspect, sent the warden downstairs to eat in the common room and tarry there until called for. She cast a curious look back as she reluctantly withdrew.

The manservant Bernan reported Hallana's horses safely stabled at the local temple's mews, the wagon wheel repaired, and arrangements made for her night's rest with a certain Mother's physician in Red Dike, who was evidently a former Suttleaf student. Ingrey found himself, without having intended any such thing, joining the two women for a meal at the small table. The manservant presented the basin for hand washing, and the double-divine intoned a perfunctory blessing.

Hergi whipped a napkin the size of a tablecloth around her mistress and helped her to her food, deftly catching tilting glasses, skidding jugs, and sliding stew, often before they spilled, but sometimes not. "Drink up your wine," the sorceress recommended. "It will go sour in half an hour. I should take myself off before the innkeeper discovers the trouble with his beer. Well, his store of fleas, lice, and bedbugs will not survive me, either, so I hope it is a fair exchange. If I linger, I may have to start in on the mice, poor things."

Lady Ijada seemed as famished as Ingrey, and the conversation waned for a time. Hallana reopened it with a blunt inquiry of the origin of Ingrey's wolf-affliction. His stomach knotted despite his hunger, but he mumbled through an explanation rather fuller than he had yet confided to Ijada, as well as he could remember the confusing old events. Both women listened raptly. Ingrey was uneasily aware that Bernan, who had taken his plate to a seat on his wooden chest, and Hergi, who snitched bites standing between mopping up after her mistress, were listening, too. But a Temple sorceress's servants must surely be among the most discreet.

"Had your father had a previous interest in the animal magic of our Old Wealding forebears?" Hallana inquired, when he had finished describing the rite.

"None known to me," Ingrey said. "It all seemed very sudden."

"Why attempt such a thing *then*?" said Ijada.

Ingrey shrugged. "All who knew died or fled. There were none left to tell by the time I recovered enough to ask." His mind shrank from the fragmented memories of those dark, bewildered weeks. Some things were better forgotten.

Hallana chewed, swallowed, and asked, "How came you to learn to bind your wolf?"

Things like that, for example. Ingrey rubbed his tense neck, without relief. "Audar's ancient law, that those defiled by animal ghosts should be burned alive, had not been carried out within living memory at Birchbeck. Our local divine, who had known me all my life, was anxious that it not be invoked. As it turned out, the Temple inquirer sent to examine the case ruled that since the crime was not of my making, but imposed upon me by persons whose authority I was bound to obey, it would be tantamount to cutting off a man's hand for *being* robbed. So I was formally pardoned, my life spared."

Ijada looked up with keen attention at the news of this precedent, her lips parting as if to speak, but then just shook her head.

Ingrey gave her an acknowledging nod, and continued, "Still I could not be left to wander freely. Sometimes I was lucid, you see, but sometimes . . . I could not well remember the other times. So our divine set about trying to cure me."

"How?" asked the sorceress.

"Prayer first, of course. Then rituals, what old ones he could find. Some I think he made up new out of bits. None worked. Then he tried exhortations, lectures and sermons, he and his acolytes taking turns for days together. That was the most wearisome part. Then we tried to drive it out by force."

"We?" Hallana cocked an eyebrow.

"It was not . . . not done *against* my will. I was desperate by then."

"Mm. Yes, I can . . ." She pressed her lips together for a long moment, then said, "What form did these wolf-wardings take?"

"We tried everything we could think of that wouldn't out-right cripple me. Starvation, beatings, fire and threats of fire, water. It did not drive out the wolf, but at least I learned to gain ascendance, and my periods of confusion grew shorter."

"Under those conditions, I should imagine you learned rather quickly."

He glanced up defensively at her dry tone. "It was clearly working. Anyway, better to be shoved under the Birchbeck till my lungs burst than listen to more sermons all day and night. Our divine held everyone steadfast through the task, though it was hard. It was the last thing he could do for my father, whom he felt he had failed."

Ingrey took a swallow of wine. "After some months, I was pronounced well enough to be let out. Castle Birchgrove had been settled on my uncle by then. I was sent on pilgrimage, in hopes of finding some more permanent cure. I was glad enough to go; though as hope failed, and I grew to man size and shed my keepers, my search turned into mere wanderings. When I ran out of money, I'd take what odd tasks came to hand." Anything had seemed better than turning his steps toward home. And then . . . one day, it hadn't, anymore.

"I met Lord Hetwar when he was on an embassy to the king of Darthaca." His desperate contrivances to win access to the sealmaster, he didn't think worth recounting. "He was curious how a Wealding kinsman should be serving strangers so far from home, so I told him my tale. He was not daunted by my wolf and gave me a place in his guard that I might work my way back to my own country. I made myself useful during some incidents on the road, and he was pleased to make my place permanent. I rose in his household thereafter." Ingrey's mouth firmed in tight pride. "By my merits."

He applied himself to his spiced meat, sopping up the last of its gingery gravy with the inn's good bread. Ijada had stopped eating a little while ago and sat solemn with thought, running her finger around the rim of her empty wine beaker. When she looked up and caught his eye, she managed a wan smile. Hallana waved away her maid's attempt to feed her a second apple tart, and Hergi rolled up the stained napkin and bundled it away.

The sorceress eyed Ingrey. "Feeling better now?"

"Yes," he admitted reluctantly.

"Do you have any idea who laid this bridle on you?"

"No. It's hard to think about it. It almost bothers me more that I cannot feel it, between fits. I begin to mistrust everything in my mind. As if straining to see the insides of my own eyeballs." He hesitated, marshaled his nerve. "Can you take it off me, Learned?"

She huffed uncertainly, while the manservant, behind her, made an urgent negative gesture to Ingrey, and Hergi squeaked protest.

"The one thing I might safely do right now," said Hallana, "is add to the disorder in your spirit. Whether this would break or disrupt the hold of this strange thing Ijada smells upon you, I do not know. I dare attempt nothing more complex. If I were not pregnant, I might try—well, never mind. Yes, yes, I see you, Bernan, please refrain from bursting," she added to the agitated manservant. "If I do not vent disorder into Lord Ingrey, here, I shall just have to kill some mice, and I *like* mice."

Ingrey rubbed his tired face. "I am willing to have you try, but . . . fetter me, first."

Her brows climbed. "You think it necessary?"

"Prudent."

The sorceress's servants, at least, seemed greatly in favor of prudence in any form. While Ingrey laid his sword and belt knife against the wall by the door, Bernan opened what proved to be a well-stocked toolbox and rummaged within, producing a couple of lengths of sturdy chain. In consultation with Ingrey, he fitted loops tightly around Ingrey's booted ankles, and secured them with an iron staple and hasp. Ingrey crossed his hands at the wrists and suffered a similar arrangement there, then tested both bindings, twisting and straining. They seemed solid enough. Then he sat on the floor with his back to the window seat and had Bernan bolt the wrist chains to the ankle chains. He felt an utter fool, sitting crouched with his knees up halfway to his ears. His audience looked extremely bemused, but no one demurred.

Learned Hallana heaved herself up out of her seat and waddled over to him. Ijada stood anxiously by her on one side, and Hergi on the other. Hallana shot back her cuffs and laced her fingers together, stretching her hands with a faint crackling pop of the joints. "Very good," she said, in a medically brisk voice all the more sinister for its good cheer, "tell me if this hurts . . ." She laid a warm palm across Ingrey's forehead.

The sense of heat flowing from her touch was pleasant for the first few seconds, and he leaned into her hand. But then it grew uncomfortably warm. A disturbing haze clouded his vision. Abruptly, the heat was roaring like a smithy's furnace across his mind, and he was seeing double. The second image parted from the first: twisted, altered.

The room was still present to his physical senses. But equally present was another *place*. In it . . .

In it, he was standing nude. Above his heart, his pale flesh puckered, then swelled. The skin burst. From it, a vine, no, a vein, sprouted, and began to wind and twist around him, climbing. He felt a second hot bulge burst on his forehead, and saw the vine-vein wind down from it, blurred by its proximity. Another from his navel, another from his genitals. Their moving tips muttered and dripped blood. His tongue, too, was transformed, pushing out from his mouth, forming into a pulsing tube.

In the material room, his body began to writhe and yank against his chains. Harder. His eyes half rolled back, but still he could see the Learned Hallana leaning near—she scrambled back as he opened his mouth to howl. But between her two glowing hands, held apart, violet fire still roared, spiraling into his horribly transformed mouth.

The long tentacle growing from his tongue flapped and jerked in agony, its unintelligible whisper speeding into a hiss, yet seemed to devour the heat. The other four, mirroring its excitement, continued to mutter and thicken, splashing him with blood. The hot metallic smell and slippery feel of it drove him to distraction. His real body bucked and arched with near bone-cracking force, straining against his chains. His hair rippled, and his genitals engorged and stiffened. He fell sideways, convulsed, began to try to roll and rock himself across the room toward the wall where his sheathed sword leaned.

Ijada had fallen to her knees, mouth open, eyes wide. In the second reality, the leopardess appeared . . .

Its fur was a silken ripple over moving muscle, its claws carved ivory; its brilliant amber eyes flashed with golden lights. It fell upon the writhing veins for all the world like a kitten upon a mess of cords, paws patting, then clawing, then pulling the hissing things toward it to bite at them with its great teeth. The veins lashed like whips of acid, leaving black burns across the elegant, spotted coat, and the leopardess snarled, a rich sound that shook the air, that shook Ingrey to his heart. From somewhere deep inside him, an answering growl arose.

His jaw began to lengthen . . .

No. No! I deny you, wolf-within! He bit down, clenched his teeth. Fought wolf, fought tentacles, fought his body, fought his mind, rocked nearer to his sword. *Fight. Kill . . . something . . . everything . . .*

The tortured chain twisted, an iron link snapping like a stick. His wrists and ankles were still bound, but freed from each other. His body straightened, and then he could writhe and roll, arch and turn. His sword was very close. Panicked feet trampled about him.

His real hands were as slippery with real blood as his second body now was with the strange red spew that flowed out of himself, onto himself. To his utter horror, he began to feel the links slip from his bleeding wrists, over his yanking hands. If he freed his right hand, reached his sword . . . surely none would leave this room alive. Perhaps not even himself.

He would take the yammering manservant's head first, with a single stroke. Then turn upon the screaming women. Ijada was already on her knees like an executioner's victim, strands of loosened hair falling forward veiling her face. The whipping sword edge, the pregnant one . . . his mind shied, denied.

Then howled denial, so fiercely that it turned itself inside out and transmuted to assent. *Help them, save her, uphold me, wolf-within! Take of me, take . . .*

His jaw lengthened, his teeth grew into sharp white knives. He began to bite and rip at the veins, snarling and shaking his head as a wolf shakes a rabbit to break its back. The hot blood spurted in his mouth, and he felt the pain of his own bites. He gripped, ripped. Pulled the things out of his body by their gory roots. Then it was no longer inside him, but in front of him, wriggling like some malevolent sea creature brought to the lethal air. He kicked at it with naked, clawed feet. The leopardess pounced, batted, rolled the shrieking red thing across the floor. It was, briefly, alive. Dying.

Then it was gone.

The second vision vanished, or rejoined the first, melting one into another, the leopardess into Ijada, his wolf-jaw— where?

His body sagged. He was lying on his back near the door, ankles still bound, bloody hands free. Bernan was standing over him, his face pale as parchment, a short iron crowbar gripped in his shaking hands.

A little silence fell.

"*Well*," said Hallana's bright, strained voice. "Let us not do *that* again . . ."

A rumble of footsteps sounded from the corridor outside the chamber. An urgent thumping on the door: Ingrey's soldier called in alarm, "Hello? Is everyone all right in there? Lord Ingrey?"

The warden's frightened voice: "Was that really *him*, screaming like that? Oh, hurry, break it down!"

A third man: "If you break my door, you'll pay for it! Hey in there! Open up!"

Ingrey stretched his jaw, his normal human jaw, not a muzzle, and croaked, "I'm all right!"

Hallana was standing with feet braced, breathing rapidly, staring at him with very wide eyes. "Yes," she called out. "Lord Ingrey . . . tripped and upset the table. It's a bit of a mess in here just now. We'll see to it. Don't concern yourselves."

"You don't sound all right."

Ingrey swallowed, cleared his raw throat, adjusted his voice. "I'll come down to the taproom in a while. The divine's servants will deal with the . . . with the . . . mess. Go away."

"We will take care of his injuries," added Hallana.

A baffled silence, a mumble of argument: then the footsteps retreated.

A sigh seemed to go through everyone in the room but Bernan, who still brandished his crowbar. Ingrey lay back limply on the floorboards, feeling as though his bones were turned to porridge. He was sick to his stomach. After a moment, he raised his hands. The chains dangled heavily from his left wrist; his right, lubricated with blood, was free. He stared at it, barely comprehending the torn skin and throbbing pain. By the unpleasant trickle in his hair, his furious thumping around had ripped apart some of his new stitches, as well.

At this rate, I'm going to be dead before I ever get to Easthome, whether Lady Ijada survives me or not.

Ijada . . . He twisted around in feverish concern. Bernan made a warning noise and raised his crowbar higher. Ijada was still on her knees a pace or two away, her face very pale, her eyes huge and dark.

"No, Bernan!" she said. "He's all right now. It's gone."

"I have seen a man afflicted with the falling sickness," said Hallana in a distant tone. "This most assuredly wasn't *that*." She ventured near Ingrey again and walked around him, peering down searchingly over her belly.

With an eye to the crowbar, Ingrey rolled very slowly and cautiously onto his side for a better look at Ijada. The movement made the room turn in slow jerks, and his grunt came out sounding more like a moan, or perhaps a whimper. Ijada wasn't leaping to her feet, either. She sat limply, her hands on the floor propping her; she caught his gaze, took a breath, and pushed upright. "I'm all right," she said, although no one had inquired. All eyes had been on Ingrey's far more spectacular performance.

Hallana's head came round. "What did *you* just experience?"

"I fell to my knees—I was still on my knees, in this room, but at the same time, I was suddenly in the leopard's body.

The leopard's spirit body—I did not mistake it for flesh. But oh, it was strong! Glorious. My senses were terribly acute. I could see! But I was mute—no, beyond mute. Wordless. We were in some bigger space, or other space—it was as big as it needed to be, anyway. You"—her gaze swung to Ingrey—"were in the place before me. Your body was sprouting scarlet horrors. They seemed to be of you, yet attacking you. I pounced on them and tried to bite them off you. They burned my jaws. Then you started to turn into a wolf, or a man-wolf, some strange hybrid—it was as if your body couldn't make up its mind. You grew a wolf's head, at least, and started tearing at the red horrors, too." She looked at him sideways, in a fresh fascination.

Ingrey wondered, but dared not ask, if she'd hallucinated a loincloth for him as well. The wild arousal of his frenzied state was only now passing off, damped by confusion and pain.

"When we had ripped the burning, clutching things all out of you, they could be seen to be not many, but all one thing. For a moment it looked like a ball of mating snakes, raked from under a ledge in the springtime. Then it went silent and vanished, and I was back here. In *this* body." She held up one long-fingered hand before her eyes as if still expecting to see pads and claws. "If that was anything like what the Old Weald warriors experienced . . . I think I begin to see why they desired this. Except not the part about the bleeding things. Yet even that . . . we *won*." The pulsing dilation of her eyes was not just fear, Ingrey thought, but also a vast, astonished exhilaration. She added to Hallana, "Did you *see* my leopard? The bleeding things, the wolf's head?"

"No." Hallana huffed in frustration. "Your spirits were very disturbed, but I hardly needed second sight to tell *that*. Do you think you could return to that place where you were? At will?"

Ingrey started to shake his head, discovered that his brain felt as though it had come loose, and mumbled, "No!"

"I'm not sure," said Ijada. "The leopard took me there—

I didn't go myself. And it wasn't exactly a *there*. We were still here."

Hallana's expression grew, if possible, more intent. "Did you sense any of the gods' presences, in that space?"

"No," said Ijada. "None. There was a time I might not have known for sure, but after the leopard dream . . . no. I would have known, if *He* were back." Despite her distress, a smile softened her lips. The smile was not for him, Ingrey knew. It still made him want to crawl toward her. Now, *that* was madness by any measure.

Hallana stretched her shoulders, which had alarming effects given her current girth, and grimaced. "Bernan, help Lord Ingrey up. Take off those bolts."

"Are you sure, Learned?" the manservant said doubtfully. His eyes flicked toward Ingrey's sword, now lying in the room's corner; he had apparently kicked it out of Ingrey's rolling reach during his scramble to get into striking position with his crowbar.

"Lord Ingrey? What is your opinion? You were certainly correct before."

"I don't think . . . I *can* move." The oak floor was hard and chilly, but by the swimming of Ingrey's head, horizontal seemed vastly preferable to vertical.

He was forced to the vertical despite himself, dragged up and placed in the divine's vacated chair by the two servants. Bernan tapped off the bolts with a hammer and Hergi, clucking, collected a basin of fresh water, soap, towels, and the leather case of what proved to be medical instruments and supplies that she had brought in with her. She tended expertly to Ingrey's injuries, new and old, under the divine's eye, and it occurred to Ingrey belatedly that of *course* the sorceress would travel with her own midwife-dedicat, in her present state. He wondered if Hergi was married to the smith, if that was Bernan's real calling.

Ijada levered herself up as far as her own chair and watched Hergi's mending in apparent fascination, pinching her lips at the needle pokes. The flap of flesh on the back of

Ingrey's hand was neatly reaffixed and covered with a white-linen bandage, the lesser lacerations on the other wrist cleaned and wrapped. His hand did not hurt nearly as much as the burning muscles in his back, or his throbbing ankles; or perhaps each pain served as distraction from the next. He wondered if he ought to pull off his boots while he still could, and if he didn't, if they would have to be cut off later. They were good boots; he hated to risk them. The chains had left deep scorings in the leather.

"In that *place* you found yourselves," Hallana began again.

"It wasn't real," mumbled Ingrey.

"Mm, well, yes. But while you were in that, um, state, what did you perceive of me, if anything?"

"Colored fire flowed from your hands. Into my mouth. It drove the vein growing there into a frenzy, which it passed on to the others. Its other parts, I suppose. It was as though your fire flushed them from their hiding places." He ran his tongue around his mouth now, to reassure himself that the hideous distortion was truly gone. More disturbingly, he found his face was slimed with spittle. He started to wipe away the sticky foam with the bandage on his left wrist, but his hand was intercepted by Hergi, protecting her work. She gave him a disapproving headshake and wrung out a wet cloth instead. Ingrey swabbed and tried not to think about his father.

"The tongue *is* the Bastard's own sign and signifier upon our bodies," Hallana mused.

As forehead for the Daughter, navel for the Mother, genitals for the Father, and heart for the Brother. "The veins, tentacles, whatever they were, of the geas seemed to grow from all of my five theological points."

"That ought to *mean* something. I wonder what? I wonder if there are any manuscripts of Old Weald lore that would illuminate this puzzle? When I get back to Suttleaf, I will search our library, but I'm afraid we've mostly medical tracts. The Darthacan Quintarians who conquered us were more interested in destroying the old ways than in chronicling them. It was as if they wished to put the old forest powers out of reach of everyone, even themselves. I'm not sure they were wrong."

"When I was in the leopard—when I *was* the leopard," said Ijada, "I saw the phantasmal images, too. But then it was all shut away from me again." A faint regret tinged her tone.

"I, on the other hand"—the sorceress's fingers drummed on the closest level surface, which happened to be the top of her stomach—"saw nothing. Except for Lord Ingrey ripping his way out of iron chains that should have held a horse, that is. If that was typical of the strength their spirit animals lent the old warriors, it's no wonder they were prized."

If the old warriors had hurt like this afterward, Ingrey wasn't so sure their ghost animals would have been as prized as all that. If the forest kin had carried on as he just had . . . he wanted to ask about the noises he'd made, but was too mortified.

"If there was anything to see, *I* should have seen it," Hallana went on in increasing exasperation. She plunked down on a spare chair. "Dratsab, dratsab. Let us think." After a moment, she narrowed her eyes at Ingrey. "You say the thing is gone. If we cannot say what it was—can you at least now remember who put it on you?"

Ingrey leaned forward, rubbing his scratchy eyes. He suspected they were glaringly bloodshot. "I'd better have these boots off." At Hallana's gesture, Bernan knelt and assisted; Ingrey's ankles were indeed swelling and discolored. He stared down at them for a moment more.

"I did not feel the geas before I first saw Ijada," he said at last. "For all I know it could have been riding me for days, or months, or years. I thought it *was* years, at first—I thought it was my wolf, as much as I could think about it at all. If not for Lady Ijada's testimony, and . . . and what happened just now, I might still think that. If I had succeeded in slaying her, I would certainly have gone on believing so."

Hallana sucked on her lower lip. "Think harder. A compulsion to kill your prisoner was more likely laid on you between the time the news came of Boleso's death and the time you left Easthome for Boar's Head. Before then, there was no reason, and after, no time. Whom did you see in that time?"

Put like that, it was even more disturbing. "Not very many men. I was called to Lord Hetwar's chambers in the evening. The courier was still there. Hetwar, Hetwar's secretary of the chamber, Prince Rigild the king's seneschal, Earl Badgerbank, Wencel kin Horseriver, Lord Alca kin Otterbine, the kin Boarford brothers . . . We spoke but briefly, as Lord Hetwar gave me the news and my instructions."

"Which were?"

"Retrieve Boleso's body, transport his killer . . ." Ingrey hesitated. "Make his death discreet."

"What did that mean?" asked Ijada, sounding genuinely puzzled.

"Make all evidence of Boleso's indiscretions vanish." *Including his principal victim?*

"What? But aren't you an officer of the king's justice?" she said indignantly.

"Strictly speaking, I serve Sealmaster Hetwar." He added after a cautious moment, "It is Sealmaster Hetwar's steadfast purpose to serve the closest needs of the Weald and its royal house."

Ijada fell silent, dismayed, her brows drawing down.

The Temple sorceress tapped her lips with one finger. She, at least, did not look shocked. But when she spoke again, her swift thoughts had plainly darted down yet another road. "Nothing of spirit can exist in the world of matter without a being of matter to support it. Spells are sustained by sorcerers through their demons, which are necessary but not sufficient; the demon's sustenance must come from the sorcerer's body, ultimately. But *your* spell was being sustained by *you*. I suspect . . . hm. To use your word, Ijada, a parasite magic? The spell was somehow induced in you, and your life maintained it thereafter. If this strange sorcery has any resemblance to my own, it flows most readily, like water, downhill. It does not create, but steals its capabilities from its host."

This made a visceral sense to Ingrey, but it was not really something he wanted Lady Ijada to hear of him. All sorts of men had the capacity to kill for the convenience of their betters; though usually, the only spell required could be fitted in a clinking purse. He had ridden guard, ready to draw steel in his lord's defense, any number of times, and wasn't that much the same thing?

Wasn't it?

"But . . ." Ijada's lovely lips thinned with thought. "Sealmaster Hetwar must have a hundred swordsmen, soldiers, bravos. A half dozen of his guardsmen rode out with you. The . . . the person, whoever—might have laid the geas on any of them just as well. Why should the only man in Easthome who is known to bear an animal spirit be sent to *me*?"

A flash of expression—insight, satisfaction?—flew across Learned Hallana's face and vanished. But she did not speak, only sat back more intently, presumably because leaning forward more intently was not feasible. "Is it widely known, your spiritual affliction?" she asked.

Ingrey shrugged. "It is general gossip, yes. Variously garbled. My reputation is useful to Hetwar. I'm not someone most men want to cross." *Or have around them for very long, or invite to their tables, or, above all, introduce to their female kin. But I'm well accustomed to that, by now.*

Ijada's eyes widened. "You were chosen because your wolf could be blamed! Hetwar chose you. Therefore, he must be the source of the geas!"

Ingrey did not care for that thought. "Not necessarily. Lord Hetwar was in consultation for some time before I came. Any man in the room might have suggested me for the task." The wolf part, however, seemed all too plausible. Ingrey himself had been ready to blame his prisoner's death on his wolf-within. He'd have stood self-accused, incapable of his own defense. Presuming he'd even survived his attempt on Lady Ijada's life . . . he remembered yesterday's near-fatal swim. One way or another, victim and tool would both have been silenced.

Two extremely unpleasant realizations crept over Ingrey. One was that he was still bearing Lady Ijada toward her potential death. Her drowning in the river yesterday could have been no worse than some later poisoning or strangling in her cell, and a hundred times more merciful than the horrors of a dubious trial and subsequent hanging.

And the other was that an enemy of great and secret power was going to be seriously upset when they both arrived at Easthome alive.

6

INGREY WOKE FEVERISH FROM DIMLY REMEMBERED
nightmares. He blinked in the level light coming through the
dormer window in the tiny, but private, chamber high up in
the eaves of his inn. Dawn. Time to move.

Movement unleashed pain in every strained and sprained
muscle he possessed, which seemed to be most of them, and
he hastily abandoned his attempt to sit up. But lying back did
not bring relief. He gingerly turned his head, his neck on fire,
and eyed the trap of crockery he'd set on the floor by his
door. The teetering pile appeared undisturbed. Good sign.

The wraps on his wrists and right hand were holding, although stained with brown blood. He stretched and clenched
his fingers. So. Last evening had been no dream, for all its
hallucinatory terrors. His stomach tightened in anxiety—
painfully—as the memories mounted.

Groaning, he forced himself up again, lurched out of bed,
and staggered to his washstand. A left-handed splash of cold
water on his face helped nothing. He pulled on his trousers,
sat on the edge of his bed, and attempted his boots. They
would not slide over his swollen ankles. Defeated, he let
them fall to the floor. He lowered his body carefully into his

rumpled bed linens. Reason, in his head, seemed replaced by a kind of buzz. He lay for what was probably half the turning of a glass, judging by the creep of the sunlit squares across his wall, with no more useful thought than a surly resentment of his hopeless boots.

Hinges squeaked; a clatter of crockery was overridden by Rider Gesca's startled swearing. Ingrey squinted at the door. Gesca, grimacing in bewilderment, picked his way across the dislodged barrier of tumbling beakers and plates. The lieutenant was dressed for the road in boots and leathers and Hetwar's slate-blue tabard, and tidied for the solemnity of the duty: drab blond hair combed, amiable face new-shaved. He stared down at Ingrey in dismay. "My lord?"

"Ah. Gesca." When the noise of rolling saucers died away, Ingrey managed, "How is pig-boy this morning?"

Gesca shook his head, seeming caught between wariness and exasperation. "His delusions passed off about midnight. We put him to bed."

"See that he does not approach or annoy Learned Hallana again."

"I don't think that will be a problem." Gesca's worried eyes summed the bruises and bandages. "Lord Ingrey— what *happened* to you last night?"

Ingrey hesitated. "What do they say happened?"

"They say you were locked in with that sorceress for a couple of hours when suddenly a racket rose from the room—howling, and thumping to bring down the plaster from the ceiling below, and yelling. Sounded like someone being murdered."

Almost . . .

"The sorceress and her servants went out later as though nothing had happened, and you left limping, not talking to anyone."

Ingrey reviewed the excuses Hallana had called through the door, as well as he could remember them. "Yes. I was carrying a . . . ham, and a carving knife, and I tripped over a chair." No, she hadn't said a chair. "Upended the table. Cut my hand going down."

Gesca's face screwed up, as he no doubt tried to picture how this event could result in Ingrey's peculiar array of bandages and bruises. "We're almost ready to load up, out there. The Red Dike divine is waiting to bless Prince Boleso's coffin. Are you going to be able to ride? After your accident." He added after a reflective moment, "Accidents."

Do I look that bad? "Did you deliver my message for Lord Hetwar to the Temple courier?"

"Yes. She rode out at first light."

"Then . . . tell the men to stand down. I expect instructions. Better wait. We'll take a day to rest the horses."

Gesca gestured assent, but his stare plainly questioned why Ingrey had driven both men and animals to their limits for two long days only to spend the time so gained idling here. He picked up the crockery, set it on the washstand, gave Ingrey another bemused look, and made his way out.

Ingrey had scrawled his latest note to Lord Hetwar immediately upon their arrival last night, reporting the cortege in Red Dike and pressing for relief of his command, feigning inability to supply adequate ceremony. The note had contained, therefore, no word of the Temple sorceress or hint of the later events in that upstairs room. He hadn't mentioned the incident of the river, or, indeed, any remark upon his prisoner at all. Uneasy awareness of his duty to report the truth to the sealmaster warred now with fear, in his heart. Fear and rage. *Who placed that grotesque geas in me, and how? Why was I made a witless tool?*

And can it happen again?

His own anger frightened him even as his fear stoked his fury, tightening his throat and making his temples throb. He lay back, trying to remember the hard-won self-disciplines that had stilled him under the earnest holy tortures at Birchgrove. Slowly, he willed his screaming muscles to resistless quiet again.

His wolf had been released last night. *He* had unchained it. Was it leashed again this morning? And if not . . . what then? For all the aches in his body, his mind felt no different from any other morning of his adult life. So was his frozen hesitation here in Red Dike just old habit, or was it good sense? Simple prudence, to refuse to advance one step farther toward Easthome in his present lethal ignorance? His physical injuries made a plausible blind to hide behind. But were they a hunter's screen or just a coward's refuge? His caged thoughts circled.

Another tap at the door broke the tensing upward spiral of his disquiet, and a sharp female voice inquired, "Lord Ingrey? I need to see you."

"Mistress Hergi. Come in." Belatedly, Ingrey grew conscious of his shirtless state. But she was presumably an experienced dedicat of the Mother's order, and no blushing maiden. Still, it would be courteous to at least sit up. It would.

"Hm." Her lips thinned as she stepped to the bedside and regarded him, a coolly capable glint in her eye. "Rider Gesca did not exaggerate. Well, there is no help for it; you must get up. Learned Madam wishes to see your prisoner before she leaves, and I would have her on the road home at the earliest moment. We had enough trouble getting here; I dread the return trip. Come, now. Oh, dear. Let me see, better start with . . ."

She plunked her leather case down on the washstand and rummaged within, withdrawing a square blue glass bottle and pulling out the cork stopper. She poured a sinister syrup into a spoon, and as Ingrey creaked up on one elbow to ask, "What is it?" popped it into his mouth. The liquid tasted utterly vile. He swallowed, afraid to spit it out under her steely gaze.

"A decoction of willow bark and poppy, wine spirits, and a few other useful things." Her gaze traveled up and down his body; she pursed her lips, then bent and administered another spoonful. She nodded shortly and restoppered the bottle. "That should do it."

Ingrey swallowed medicine and a surge of bile. "It's revolting."

"Eh, you'll change your mind about it soon enough, I warrant. Here. Let's see how my work is holding up."

Efficiently, she unbound his wrappings, applied new ointment and fresh bandages, daubed the stitches in his hair with something that stung, combed out the tangles, washed his torso, and shaved him, batting his hands away as he tried to protest his own competence to dress himself. "Don't you be getting my new wraps wet, now, my lord. And stop fighting me. I'll have no delays out of *you*."

He hadn't been dressed like this by a woman since he was six, but his pain was fading most deliciously away, to be replaced by a floating lassitude. He stopped fighting her. The intensity of her concentration, he realized dimly, had nothing to do with him.

"Is Learned Hallana all right? After last night?" he asked cautiously.

"Baby's shifted position. Could be a day, could be a week, but there are twenty-five miles of bad roads between here and Suttleaf, and I wish I had her home safe *now*. Now, you mind me, Lord Ingrey; don't you dare do anything to detain her. Whatever she wants from you, give it to her without argument, if you please." She sniffed rather fiercely.

"Yes, Mistress," Ingrey answered humbly. He added after a blinking moment, "Your potion seems very effective. Can I keep the bottle?"

"No." She knelt by his feet. "Oh. Your boots won't do, will they? Do you have any other shoes with you . . . ?" She scavenged ruthlessly in his saddlebags, to emerge with a pair of worn leather buskins that she jammed onto his feet. "Up you come, now."

The agony, as she pulled on his arms, seemed pleasantly distant, like news from another country. She towed him relentlessly out the door.

❧

The sorceress-physician was already waiting in the taproom of Ijada's inn at the other end of Red Dike's main street. Learned Hallana eyed his bandages, and inquired politely, "I trust this morning finds you much recovered, Lord Ingrey?"

"Yes. Thank you. Your medicine helped. Though it made an odd breakfast." He smiled at her, a trifle hazily he feared.

"Oh. It would." She glanced at Hergi. "How much . . . ?" Hergi held up two fingers. Ingrey could not decide if the twitch of the divine's eyebrows was censure or approval, for Hergi merely shrugged in return.

Ingrey followed both women upstairs once more. They were admitted to the parlor, a little doubtfully, by the female warden. Ingrey looked around surreptitiously for signs of his late frenzy, finding none but for a few faint bloodstains and dents on the oak floorboards. Ijada stepped from the bed-chamber at the sound of their entry. She was dressed for travel in the same gray-blue riding costume as yesterday, but had put off her boots in favor of light leather shoes. Un-easily, Ingrey searched her pale face; her expression, return-ing his gaze, was sober and pensive.

More uneasily, he searched his own shifted perceptions. She seemed not so much *different* to him this morning as *more,* with an energetic density to her person that seized his focus. A heady warm scent, like sunlight in dry grass, arose from her. He found his lips parting to better taste that sun-smell—a futile effort, as it did not come through the air.

Hallana, too, had more than a taste of the uncanny about her, a dizzying busyness partly from her pregnancy but mostly from a subdued swirl, smelling like a whiff of wind after a lightning strike, that he took for her pacified demon. The two ordinary women, Hergi and the warden, seemed suddenly thin and flat and dry by comparison, as though drawn on paper.

Learned Hallana embraced Ijada and pressed a letter into her hands.

"I must leave very soon, or we won't be home before dark," the divine told her. "I wish I could go along with you, instead. This is all most disturbing, especially . . ." She jerked her head at Ingrey, indicating his late geas, and his lips twisted in agreement. "That alone would make this Temple business, even without . . . well, never mind. Five gods guard you on your journey. This is a note to the master of my order in Easthome, begging his interest in your case. With luck, he can take up with you where I am forced to leave off." She glanced Ingrey's way again, an untrusting tension around her mouth. "I charge you, my lord, to help see that this arrives at its destination. And no other."

He opened his hand in an ambiguous acknowledgment, and Hallana's lips thinned a little more. As Hetwar's agent, he had learned how to open and copy letters without leaving traces, and he was fairly certain she guessed he knew those tricks of a spy's trade. Yet the Bastard was the very god of spies; what tricks might His sorceress know? And to which of her two holy orders had she addressed her concerns? Still, if she had enspelled the missive in any way, it was not apparent to Ingrey's new perceptions.

"Learned . . ." Ijada's voice was suddenly thin and uncertain. *Learned,* not *dear Hallana,* Ingrey noted. Hergi stood alertly ready to usher her mistress out the door; she frowned in frustration as the divine turned back.

"Yes, child?"

"No . . . never mind. It's nothing. Foolishness."

"Suppose you let me be the judge of that." Hallana lowered herself into a chair and tilted her head encouragingly.

"I had a very odd dream last night." Ijada stepped nervously back and forth, then settled in the window seat. "A new one."

"How odd?"

"Unusually vivid. I remembered it in the morning right away, when I awoke, when my other dreams melted away out of my mind."

"Go on." Hallana's face seemed carved, so careful was her listening.

"It was brief, just a flash of a vision. It seemed to me I saw a sort of . . . I don't know. Death-haunt, in the shape of a stallion. Black as soot, black without gleam or reflection. Galloping, but very slowly. Its nostrils were red and glowing, and steamed; its mane and tail trailed fire. Sparks struck from its hooves, leaving prints of flame that burned all to ash in its wake. Clouds of ash and shadow. Its rider was as dark as it was."

"Hm. Was the rider male or female?"

Ijada frowned. "That seems like the wrong question to ask. The rider's legs curved down to become the horse's ribs, as if their bodies were grown together. In the left hand, it held a leash. At the end of the leash ran a great wolf."

Hallana's eyebrows went up, and she cast a glance at Ingrey. "Did you recognize this, ah, particular wolf?"

"I'm not sure. Maybe. Its pelt was pewter-black, just like . . ." Her voice trailed off, then firmed. "In my dream, anyway, I thought it felt familiar." Briefly, her hazel eyes bored into Ingrey's, her sober look returning, to his immense discomfort. "But it was altogether a wolf, this time. It wore a spiked collar, but turned inside out, with the sharp points digging inward. Blood splashed from its paws as it ran, turning the ash it trod to splotches of black mud. Then the shadow and the cinders choked my breath and my sight, and I saw no more."

Learned Hallana pursed her lips. "My word, child. Vivid, indeed. I'll have to think about that one."

"Do you think it might have been significant? Or was it just an aftershock from . . ." She gestured around the room, plainly recalling the bizarre events of last evening here, then looked at Ingrey sideways through her lashes.

"Significant dreams," said Hallana, a faint didactic tinge leaking into her tone, "may be prophecy, warning, or directive. Do you have any sense of which this might be?"

"No. It was very brief, as I said. Though intense."

"What did you feel? Not when you awoke, but then, within the dream? Were you frightened?"   ·

"Not frightened, exactly. Or at least, not for myself. I was more furious. Balked. As though I were trying to catch up, and could not."

A little silence fell. After a moment Ijada ventured, "Learned? What should I do?"

Hallana seemed to wrench her distant expression into an unfelt smile. "Well . . . prayer never hurts."

"That hardly seems like an answer."

"In your case, it might be. This is not a reassurance."

Ijada rubbed her forehead, as though it ached. "I'm not sure I want more such dreams."

Ingrey, too, wanted to beg, *Learned, what shall I do?* But what answer, after all, could she give him? To stay frozen here? Easthome would only come to him, with all due ceremony. Travel on, as was his plain duty? Surely a Temple divine could advise no other course. Flee, or set Ijada to flight? Would she even go? He'd offered escape to her once, in that tangled wood. She'd sensibly refused. But what if her flight were made more practical? An escape in the night, with no hint to Ingrey's masters, oh no, as to how or from whose hand she had acquired horse, pack, money . . . escort? *We must speak again of this.* Or could he give her over to the sorceress, her friend—send her in secret to Suttleaf? Surely, if such a sanctuary were possible, Learned Hallana would have offered it already. He strangled his beginning noise of inquiry in a cough, scorning to be dismissed with instructions to pray.

Hergi helped her mistress to rise again from her chair.

"Travel safely, Learned," said Ijada. She smiled crookedly at the pregnant woman. "I don't like to think that you might have put yourself in any danger because of me."

"Not for you, dear," said Hallana in an absent tone. "Or not for you alone, at least. This is all much more complex than I anticipated. I long for the advice of my dear Oswin. He has such a logical mind."

"Oswin?" said Ijada.

"My husband."

"Wait," said Ijada, her eyes growing round with astonishment. "Not—not *that* Oswin? Our Oswin, Learned Oswin, from the fen fort? That fussy stick? All arms and legs, with a neck like a heron swallowing a frog?"

"The very same." Oswin's spouse seemed unruffled by

this unflattering description of her mate; her firm lips softened. "He's improved with age, I promise you. He was very callow then. And I, well, I trust I may have improved a trifle, too."

"Of all the wonders—I can scarcely believe it! You two used to argue and fight all the time!"

"Only over theology," said Hallana mildly. "Because we both cared, you know. Well . . . mostly over theology." Her mouth twitched up at some unspoken memory. "One shared passion led to others, in due time. He followed me back to the Weald, when his cycle of duty was ended—I told him he just wanted to have the last word. He's still trying. He is a teacher, too, now. He still likes to argue—it's his greatest bliss. I should be cruel to deny it to him."

"Learned Sir has a way with words, he does," confirmed Hergi. "Which I do not look forward to hearing, if I don't get you home safe and soon as I promised him."

"Yes, yes, dear Hergi." Smiling, the sorceress at last turned to lumber out under the close attendance of her handmaiden. Hergi gave Ingrey a nod of judicious approval in passing, presumably for his cooperation, or at least, for his failure to interfere.

He glanced back at Lady Ijada, watching her friend depart. Regret darkened her expression. She caught his gaze and mustered a wan smile. Oddly warmed, he smiled back at her.

"*Oh,*" she said, one hand flying to her mouth.

"Oh what?" he inquired, puzzled.

"You can smile!" From her tone, this was a wonder tantamount to his sprouting wings and flapping up to the ceiling. He glanced upward, picturing himself doing so. The winged wolf. *What?* He shook his head to clear it of these odd thoughts, but it just made him dizzy. Perhaps it was as well that Hergi had taken the blue bottle away with her.

Ijada stepped to the window onto the street, and Ingrey followed. Together they watched Hergi load her mistress into the wagon, its wheel repaired, under Bernan's anxious eye. The groom, or smith, or whatever he was took up the reins, clucking at the stubby horses, and the wagon trundled up the street and turned out of sight. Behind them in the chamber, the warden made herself busy unpacking a case evidently bound up for the road, but like Boleso's coffin not loaded because of Ingrey's order of delay.

He was standing very close to Ijada, looking over her shoulder; he might readily reach up and rest his left hand on the nape of her neck, where her hair, lifted into its bundling net, revealed the pale skin. His breath stirred a stray strand there, yet she did not move away. She did turn her head, though, to meet his glance. No fear convulsed her features, no revulsion: just an intense scrutiny.

And yet she had seen not just that other vile thing, but his wolf; his defilement, his capacity for violence, was not rumor or gossip to her now, but a direct experience. Undeniable. *She denies nothing. Why does she not recoil?*

His perceptions spun. Turn it around: how did he feel about her cat? He had seen it, in that other reality, as clearly as she had seen his wolfishness. Logically, her defilement should seem twin to his own. Yet a god had passed her in the night, the mere brush of His cloak hem seeming a breath of exaltation. All the theological theories of all the Temple divines who'd dinned their lessons into Ingrey's unwilling ear seemed to melt away under the pitiless gaze of some great Fact, hovering just beyond the reach of his reason. *Her* secret beast had been gloriously beautiful. Terror, it seemed, had a new and entrancing dimension today, one Ingrey had never before suspected.

"Lord Ingrey," she said, and her low voice troubled his blood, "I would follow Learned Hallana's advice and go to the temple to pray." She cast a wary glance at her warden. "Privately."

His mind lurched back into motion. It would be perfectly unexceptionable to conduct his prisoner to the temple without her chaperone; at this hour, it would be nearly deserted, and they might converse in plain sight undisturbed. "No one would wonder if I escorted you to the altars of the gods to pray for mercy, lady."

Her lips twisted. "Say justice, rather, and it would do."

He backed a little from her and made a sign of assent. Turning, he dismissed the warden to whatever of her own affairs she cared to pursue for an hour, and saw Ijada out of the parlor. When they gained the street and turned up it, Ijada tucked her hand in his elbow and picked her way carefully over the damp cobbles, not looking at him. The temple loomed up at length, built of the gray stone of this district, its size and style and solidity typical of great Audar's grandson's reign, before the Darthacan conquerors demonstrated that they, too, were capable of racking themselves to ruin in bloody kin wars.

They walked past the iron gates into the high-walled, quiet precincts, and under the imposing portico. The inner chambers were dim and cool after the bright morning outside, with narrow shafts of sunlight streaming down from the round windows high above. Some three or four persons were on their knees, or prone, before the Mother's altar in Her chamber. Ijada stiffened briefly on Ingrey's arm; he followed her glance through the archway to the Father's altar to catch sight of Boleso's coffin, set up on trestles, blanketed with brocades, and guarded by soldiers of the Red Dike city militia. But both the Daughter's chamber and the Son's were empty at this hour; Ijada turned into the Son's.

She fell gracefully to her knees before the altar; less gracefully, Ingrey followed suit, sitting back on his heels. The pavement was cold and hard. A silence stretched between them as Ijada gazed upward. Ordering her prayers in her mind?

"What," Ingrey began quietly, "did you think would happen to you once you reached Easthome? What had you planned to do?"

Her glance shifted to him, though she did not turn her head. In a like undertone, she replied, "I expect I shall be examined, by the King's justiciars or the Temple inquirers, or both. I should certainly expect the Temple inquirers will take an interest now, given what has lately happened and Learned Hallana's letter. I plan to tell the exact truth, for the truth is my surest defense." A wry smile twitched her lips. "Besides, it's easier to remember, they say."

Ingrey let out a long sigh. "What do you imagine East-home is like, now?"

"Why—I've never been there, but I've always supposed it is a splendid place. The king's court must be its crown, of course, but Princess Fara told me tales of the river docks and the glassworks, the great Temple schools—the Royal College as well. Gardens and palaces. Fine dressmakers. Scriptoriums and goldsmiths and artisans of every sort. There are plays put on, and not just for holy days, but for the great lords in their high houses."

Ingrey tried again. "Have you ever seen a flock of vultures circling the carcass of some great and dangerous beast, bull or bear, that is not quite dead enough yet? Most hold back, waiting, but some dart in to peck and tear, then duck away. All hover closer as the day wears on, and the sight of the wheeling death watch draws in more distant kin, hot with fear of missing the best tidbits when all close in at last for the disembowelment."

Her lips thinned in distaste, and she turned her face toward him in question: *What now?*

"At present"—Ingrey dropped his voice to a growl—"Easthome is more like that. Tell me, Lady Ijada, who do you think will be elected the next hallow king?"

She blinked. "Why, I assume—Prince-marshal Biast." Boleso's elder and saner brother, now earning his rank under the tutelage of his father's military advisors on the northwest border.

"So many others had assumed, till the hallow king was struck down with that wasting disease, then this palsy-stroke. If the blow had held off for five more years, Hetwar believes the king might have secured Biast's election in his own lifetime. Or if the old man had died quickly—Biast might have been rammed through on the momentum of grief, before the opposition could muster. Few could have foreseen or planned for this living half death, lasting months, giving time and motive for the worst, as well as the best and all between, to maneuver. To think. To whisper to each other. To be tempted." Kin Stagthorne had held the hallow kingship for five generations; more than one other kin believed it might now be their turn to seize that high seat.

"Who, then?"

"If the hallow king were to die tonight, not even Hetwar knows who would be elected next week. And if Hetwar doesn't know, I doubt anyone else can guess, either. But by the pattern of bribes and rumors, Hetwar thought Boleso was to be a surprise candidate."

Her brows flew up. "A bad one, surely!"

"A stupid and exploitable one. From the point of view of certain men, ideal. *I* thought such men were underestimating just how dangerous his erratic nature had become, and would have lived to regret their success. And that was before I knew of any bleeding of the uncanny into the mix." Ingrey frowned. *Had* Hetwar known of Boleso's blasphemous dabblings? "The sealmaster was concerned enough to have me deliver a deposit of some one hundred thousand crowns to the archdivine-ordainer of Waterpeak, to secure his vote for Biast. His Grace thanked me in nicely ambiguous terms, I thought."

"The sealmaster bribed an *archdivine*?"

Ingrey winced at her tone, so innocently aghast. "The only thing unusual about the transaction was me. Hetwar normally uses me to deliver his threats. I'm good at it. I especially enjoy it when they try to bribe or threaten me back. One of my few pleasures, leading them into ambush and then, ah, into enlightenment. I think I was intended to be a double message, for the archdivine was nervous enough. A fact that Hetwar put . . . well, wherever he puts such things."

"Does the sealmaster confide in you?"

"Sometimes. Sometimes not." *Now, for example?* "He

knows I have a curious mind, and feeds me tidbits now and then. But I do not press. Or I should get none."

Ingrey took a deep breath. "So. Since you have not taken my hints to heart, let me lay it out for you more plainly. You did not just defend your virtue, there on the top of Boar's Head Castle. Nor did you merely offend the royal house of Stagthorne by making its scion's death a public scandal. You upset a political plot that has already cost someone hundreds of thousands of crowns and months of secret preparation. *And* involved illicit sorcery of the most dangerous sort. I deduce from my geas that somewhere in Easthome is a man—or men—of power who does not want you blurting the truth about Boleso to anyone at all. Their attempt to kill you subtly has miscarried. I am guessing that the next attempt will be less subtle. Or were you picturing some heroic stand before a justiciar or inquirer as brave and honest as yourself? There may be such men, I do not know. But I guarantee *you* will meet only the other sort."

Her jaw, he saw out of the corner of his eye, had set.

"I am . . . irritated," he finally chose. "I decline to be made a party to this. I can arrange your escape. Dry-shod, this time, with money and without hungry bears. Tonight, if you like." There: disloyalty of secret thought made public words. As the silence grew thicker, he stared at the floor between his knees.

Her voice was so low it vibrated. "How convenient for you. That way, you won't have to stand up to anybody. Nor speak dangerous truths to anyone for any honor's sake. All can go on for you just as it was."

His head snapped around. Her face had gone white.

"Scarcely," he said. "I have a target painted on my back now, too." His lips drew back in a sort of grin, the one that usually made men step away from him.

"Does that *amuse* you?"

Ingrey considered this. "It stirs my interest, anyway."

Ijada drummed her nails on the pavement. It sounded like

the clicking of distant claws. "So much for high politics. What about high theology?"

"What?"

"I felt a *god* brush past me, Ingrey! Why?"

He opened his mouth. Hesitated.

She continued in the same fierce whisper, "All my life I have prayed, and all my life I have been refused answer. I scarcely believed in the gods anymore, or if I did, it was only to curse them for their indifference. They betrayed my father, who had served Them loyally all his life. They betrayed my mother, or They were powerless to save her, which was as bad or worse. If a god has come to me, He certainly hasn't come *for* me! In all your calculating, how do you sum *that*?"

"High court politics," said Ingrey slowly, "are as godless as anything I know. If you press on to Easthome, you choose your death. Martyrdom may be a glory, but suicide is a sin."

"And just what do you press on to, Lord Ingrey?"

"I have Lord Hetwar himself as a patron." *I think.* "You will have no one."

"Not every Temple divine in Easthome can be venal. And I have my mother's kin!"

"Earl Badgerbank was *at* that conference that dispatched me. Are you so sure he was there in your interests? I'm not."

She hitched her skirts away from him. "I," she announced, "shall pray now for guidance. *You* may be quiet." She flounced forward into the pose of deepest supplication, prone on the floor, arms outflung, her face turned from him.

Ingrey lay on his back and stared at the domed ceiling, angry, dizzy, and a little ill. Hergi's potion was beginning to wear off, he feared. His frustrated thought circled, then drifted, but not into piety. He let his tired eyelids shut.

After a formless time, Ijada's tart voice inquired, "Are you praying or napping? And are you, in either case, done?"

He blinked his eyes open to find her standing over him. Napping, apparently, for he had not heard her rise. "I am at your disposal, lady." He started to sit up, stifled a yelp, and lay back more carefully.

"Yes, well, I'm not surprised, you know. Did you *look,* afterward, at what you did to those poor chains?" She held out an exasperated hand. Curious as to her strength, he grasped her hand and wrist with both hands. She leaned back like a sailor hauling on a rope, and he wallowed up.

As they made their way out under the portico into the autumn sun, Ingrey asked, "And what guidance did you receive for all your prayers, lady?"

She bit her lip. "None. Though my thoughts are less disordered, so a little quiet meditation did that much good at least." Her sideways glance at him was enigmatic. "Somewhat less disordered. It's just that . . . I can't help thinking about . . ."

He made an encouraging noise of inquiry.

She burst out, "I *still* can't believe that Hallana married *Oswin!*"

They found Ijada's warden in the taproom of her inn. She was sitting in the corner with Rider Gesca, their heads bent together, tankards and a platter with bread crumbs, cheese rinds, and apple cores on the table between them. The walk up the warm street had loosened Ingrey's stiff muscles a trifle, and he fancied he strolled rather than limped over to them. They looked up, and their talk ceased.

"Gesca." Ingrey nodded toward the platter, reminded that he had not eaten yet. "How is the food, down here?"

"The cheese is excellent. Stay away from the beer, though—it's gone sour."

Ijada's eyes widened, but she forbore comment.

"Ah. Thank you for the warning." He leaned over and nabbed the last bread crust. "And what have you two been finding to talk about?"

The warden looked frightened, but Gesca, with a hint of challenge, merely said, "I've been telling Ingrey stories."

"Ingrey stories?" Ijada said. "Are there many?"

Ingrey controlled a grimace.

Gesca, grinning at the encouragement, said, "I was just telling the tale of how Hetwar's train was attacked by those bandits in the forest of Aldenna, on the way home from Darthaca, and how you won your place in his household. It was my good word in the sealmaster's ear that did it, after all."

"Was it?" said Ingrey, trying to decide if Gesca was gabbling nervously or not. And if so, why.

"We were a large party," Gesca continued to the women, "and well armed, but this was a troop of outlaws who had fled to the forest and grown to over two hundred men, mostly by the addition of discharged soldiers and vagabonds and runaways. They were the plague of the country round about, and we likely looked rich enough that they dared to try us. I was right behind Ingrey in the van when they fell on us. They realized their mistake soon enough. Astonishing swordplay."

"I'm not that good," said Ingrey. "They were bad."

"I didn't say good, I said astonishing. I've seen swordmasters, and you're not, nor am I. But those bastard moves of yours—they should not have worked, but . . . When it became apparent that no one would best you if you had room to swing your steel, one bear of a fellow closed on you in a grapple. I was maybe fifteen feet away at the time, and I had my own troubles, but still—you tossed your sword in the air, grabbed the fellow's head, snapped his neck, caught the sword descending, and turned and beheaded the bandit coming up behind you. One continuous move."

Ingrey had no memory of the moment, though he recalled the attack, of course. The beginning and the end of it, anyway. "Gesca, you are making up tales to swagger with." Gesca was near a decade older than Ingrey; perhaps the staid middle-aged warden seemed a less unlikely object for dalliance to him.

"Ha. If I were making up grand lies for swagger, I'd tell them on *myself*. At that point, the rest turned and ran. You hewed down the slowest . . ." Gesca trailed off, not completing the story. Ingrey suddenly guessed why. He had come back to himself while methodically dispatching the wounded. Red to the elbows, the blood smell overpowering. Gesca, face appalled, gripping him by the shoulders and crying, *Ingrey! Father's tears, man, save some for hanging!* He had . . . not exactly forgotten that. He had merely refrained from revisiting the memory.

Gesca covered his hesitation by taking a swig of beer, evidently remembered its taste too late, and swallowed anyway. He made a face and wiped his lips. "It was at that point that I recommended to Hetwar that he make your place permanent. My thinking was purely selfish. I wanted to make sure that you never ended up on the opposite side to me in a fight." Gesca smiled up at him, but not with his eyes.

Ingrey's return smile was equally austere. *Subtlety, Gesca? How unlike you. What are you trying to say to me?*

The ache from his head blow day before yesterday was returning. Ingrey decided to repair to his own inn to find food. He bade the warden to her duty, instructing the women to lock their chamber door once more, and withdrew.

7

AFTER FORAGING A MEAL OF SORTS IN HIS INN'S COM-
mon room, Ingrey returned to his chamber to fall across his
bed once more. He was a day and a half late fulfilling the
Reedmere dedicat's prescription of rest for his aching head
blow, and he apologized humbly in his heart to her. But for
all his exhaustion, in the warming afternoon, sleep would
not come.

It was no good dashing about arranging all in secret for
Ijada's midnight escape if she refused to mount and ride
away. She *must* be persuaded. If her secret beast was discovered, would they burn her? He imagined the flames licking up around her taut body, evil orange caresses, igniting
the oil-soaked shift such prisoners were dressed in to speed
their agony. He visualized her swinging from a hemp rope
and oak beam, in vicious, senseless parody of an Old Weal-
ing sacrifice hanged from a sacred forest tree. Or would the
royal executioners allow her a silk rope, like her leopard, in
honor of her kin rank? Though the old tribes, lacking silk,
had used rope woven from shimmering nettle flax for their
highest born, he had heard. *Think of something else.* But his
thoughts circled in dreary morbidity.

They had begun as messengers to the gods, those willing human sacrifices of the Old Weald. Sacred couriers to carry prayers directly to heaven in unholy hours of great need, when all mere spoken words, or prayers of the heart or hands, seemed to fly up into the void and vanish into a vast silence. *Like mine, now.* But then, under the generations-long pressure from the eastern borders, the tribes' needs had grown, and so had their fears. Battles and ground were lost; woes waxed and judgment slipped; quality gave way to quantity, in the desperate days, and heroic holy volunteers grew harder to find.

Their ranks were filled by the less willing, then the un-willing; at the last, captured soldiers, hostages, kidnapped camp followers, worse. The sacred trees bore a bumper crop. Children, Ingrey had heard, in some of the Quintarian di-vines' favorite gruesome martyr tales. Enemy children. *And what benighted mind places the name of enemy on a bewil-dered child?* At the very least, the Old Wealding tribal mages might have reflected on what prayers that river of sacrifice had *really* borne to the gods, in their victims' weep-ing hearts.

Think of something useful, curse it. Ijada's tart words in the temple seemed to bore into his skin like biting insects. *You won't have to stand up to anybody, nor speak dangerous truths . . .* Five gods, what power did the fool girl imagine he had in Easthome? He himself lived on sufferance, under Het-war's shielding hand. Ingrey lent that hand a palpable force, yes, but so did the rest of Hetwar's household troops; lent, perhaps, a more unique and subtly useful air of uncanny threat, but in the sealmaster's web of authority he was surely a minor strand. Ingrey had never distributed favors, and so now had none to call in. If he had any chances at all to res-cue or redeem Ijada, they would end when the cortege en-tered the city gates.

His thoughts were growing worse, he was uncomfortably aware, but not wider. At length, he dozed. It wasn't a good doze, but it was better than the writhing that went before.

He woke as the autumn sun was going down, and took himself again to Ijada's inn to invite her to evening prayer.

She cocked an eyebrow at him, and murmured, "You are grown pious, of a sudden." But at his tight-lipped look of anguish, she relented and accompanied him to the temple once more.

When they were on their knees before the Brother's altar—both the Mother's and the Daughter's chambers were full of Red Dike supplicants again—he began under his breath, "Listen. I must decide tonight whether we ride or bide tomorrow. You cannot just drift into disaster with no plan, no attempt even to throw some rope to shore. Else it will become the rope that hangs you, and it drives me half-mad to picture you dangling as your leopard did. I should think you'd both have had enough of hanging."

"Ingrey, think," she returned in as low a voice. "Even assuming I could escape unseen, where would I go? My mother's kin could not take me in or hide me. My poor stepfather—he hasn't the strength to fight such high foes, and besides, his would be among the first places they'd look for such a fugitive. A woman, a stranger, alone—I would be utterly conspicuous, and a target for the vile." She had taken thought, too, it appeared.

He drew a breath. "How if I came with you?"

A long silence; he glanced aside to see her face gone still, staring straight ahead, wide-eyed. "You would do that? Desert your company and your duty?"

He set his teeth. "Perhaps."

"Then where would *we* go? Your kin could not take us in either, I think."

"I cannot imagine going back to Birchgrove for any reason. No. We would have to get out of the Weald altogether, cross the borders. To the Alvian League, perhaps—slip into the Cantons over the northern mountains. Or to Darthaca. I can speak and write Darthacan, at least."

"I cannot. I would be your mute . . . what? Burden, servant, pet, paramour?"

Ingrey reddened. "We could pretend you were my sister. I could swear to regard you with that respect. I wouldn't touch you."

"How very enticing." Her lips set in a flat line.

He paused, feeling like a man crossing river ice in winter and hearing a first faint cracking sound coming from under his feet. *What did she mean me to make of* that *remark?* "Ibran was your father's tongue, presumably. Do you speak it?"

"A little. Do you?"

"A little. We could make for the Peninsula, then. Chalion or Ibra or Brajar. You would not then be so mute." There was work for swordsmen there, too, Ingrey had heard, in the interminable border wars with the heretical Quadrene coastal princedoms—and few questions asked of foreign volunteers, so long as they signed the Five.

She vented a long sigh. "I've been thinking, this afternoon, about what Hallana said."

"Which? She talked a great deal. Clouds of chatter."

"Look to her silences, then."

That sounded so like one of Lord Hetwar's favorite aphorisms that Ingrey jerked. "Did she have any?"

"She said she sought me out—at a moment of great inconvenience, perhaps peril, for herself, mind you—for two reasons. Because she'd heard the news—and for the dreams, *of course*. Only Hallana could make that second reason sound like an afterthought. That *I* have had strange and dark dreams, nightmares almost as disturbing as my waking life, I take to be the result of fear, weariness, and . . . and Boleso's gift." She moistened her lips. "But why should *Hallana* dream of me or my troubles? She is a Temple woman to the bone, and no renegade, for all that she clears her own path. Did she speak to you of her dreams?"

"No. But I didn't think to ask."

"She asked many questions, learned I-know-not-what

from watching us, but she gave me no direction, one way or another. That, too, is a silence. All she gave me, in the end, was the letter." She touched her left breast, fingering the fine-embroidered fabric of her riding jacket. Ingrey fancied he heard a faint rustle of paper beneath the cloth, from some inner pocket. "She seemed to expect me to deliver it. As the only thing resembling guidance that she gave me, I am loath to give it up for some chancy flight into exile with . . . with a man I'd not met till four days ago." She was silent a moment. "*Especially* not as your little sister, five gods spare me!"

He did not understand her offense, but he certainly could not mistake her refusal. He said heavily, "We'll continue on toward Easthome tomorrow, then, with Boleso's coffin." Which would give him perhaps three more days to come up with some better argument or plan, less the time he spent sleeping. *If any.*

He escorted her back through the lowering twilight to her inn, and into the hands of her warden once more. The countrywoman's gaze upon him was now outright suspicious, though she made no comment at all. Starting back down the street, Ingrey began to wonder if he should be attending to *Ijada's* silences. There were certainly enough of them.

As he neared his inn, a dark shape thrust itself off the wall where it had been leaning. Ingrey's hand strayed to his sword hilt, but relaxed again as the figure moved into the yellow light of the lantern above the door, and he recognized Gesca. The lieutenant gave him a nod.

"Walk with me, Ingrey. I would have a word in private."

Ingrey's brows twitched up, but he fell in willingly enough. They matched steps on the cobblestones, took a turn about the next square up the street near the city gates, and settled on a wooden bench by the covered well in the square's center. A servant turned away and stumped off past them with a pair of dripping buckets hung from a yoke over his shoulders. Beyond, in the street, a couple hurried home, the woman holding a lantern, the man with a boy atop his shoulder, who curled his small hands in the man's hair; the man laughed protest at the grip. The man's eyes shifted to assay the two loitering swordsmen, took reassurance from their repose, and returned to his woman. Their footsteps faded.

Silence fell, and lengthened. Gesca's fingers drummed uneasily on his thigh. "Is there a problem in the troop?" Ingrey prompted at last. "Or with Boleso's men?"

"Huh." Gesca sat up and straightened his shoulders. "Maybe you'll tell me." He hesitated again, sucked on his lower lip, then said abruptly, "Are you falling in love with that accursed girl, Ingrey?"

Ingrey stiffened. "Why should you think that?"

Sarcasm edged Gesca's voice. "Well, let me see. What could possibly have suggested this thing? Could it be the way you speak to her apart at every chance? Or could it be the way you plunged like a madman into a raging torrent to save her? Could it have been how you were surprised, half-dressed, trying to sneak into her bedchamber at midnight? The pale and starveling look on your face, when you think no one is watching you, when you look at her? The way the lovesick circles darken daily under your eyes? I admit, only Ingrey kin Wolfcliff would ignite with lust for a woman who bludgeons her lovers to death, but for you, that's not a deterrent, it's a lure!" Gesca snorted.

"You have," said Ingrey coldly, "entirely the wrong impression of the matter." Dismay verging on horror gripped him at the blatant plausibility of Gesca's interpretation, succeeded by the arrested thought that it might not be so bad a public cloak for the stranger and more deadly reality of the geas, at that. Followed in turn by an even more frightening suspicion that Gesca might not be misled at all . . . *No. No.* "Anyway, it was only one lover."

"What?"

"That she bludgeoned." He added after a moment, "I admit, whatever her game bag lacks in numbers, it makes up in weight." And after another moment, "In any case, she isn't attracted to me, so your fears are moot."

"Not true. She thinks you a very comely man, though glum."

"How do you know *that*?" Ingrey rapidly reviewed the past days—when had Gesca ever spoken with the prisoner?

"She discussed you with her warden, or perhaps it was the other way around. Quite frank and outspoken, that one, when you get her going. The Mother's work does that to some women."

"The warden doesn't speak so to me."

"That's because you terrify her. I don't. At least by contrast. Very useful, from my point of view. But have you ever overheard two women discussing men? Men are crude liars, comparing their drabs, but women—I'd rather have a Mother's anatomist dissect me alive than to listen to the things the ladies say about us when they think they are alone." Gesca shuddered.

Ingrey managed not to blurt, *What else did Ijada say of me?* His prisoner, it occurred to him, would have had to fill the hours with something, when locked up with that countrywoman; and inconsequential chatter might conceal dire secrets better than silence itself. So. He ventured a blander, "Is there anything else I should know?"

"Oh, aye"—Gesca let his voice lilt upward into a feminine falsetto—"the lady thinks your smile is *devastating*."

Gesca's smile, Ingrey thought, was an altogether evil smirk. Evidently, however, the shadows were not deep enough yet to hide Ingrey's return glare, or possibly it burned through the darkness with its own heat, for Gesca sobered, raising a warding hand.

"Ingrey, look." Gesca's voice grew serious. "I don't want to see you do something stupid. You have a future in Hetwar's house, far beyond mine, and it's not just your kinship that gives you the leg up. For me, maybe I'll make guard captain someday. You're a lettered man in two tongues, Hetwar talks to you as an equal—not just in blood, but in wits— and you give him back as good as you get. Listening to the two of you makes my head spin round, sometimes. I don't even want to walk the paths you seem destined to tread.

Heights make me dizzy, and I like my head where it is. But most of all . . . I don't ever want to be the officer who's sent to arrest you."

Ingrey unset his teeth. "Fair enough."

"Right."

"We ride again tomorrow."

"Good."

"If I can get my boots on."

"I'll come help you."

And I will dismiss that prying, spying, gossiping warden back to Reedmere, and replace her with another. Or with none. Feminine chatter was annoying enough, but what if her gossip dared extend to the curious events she had witnessed swirling around Hallana's visits?

What if it already has?

They both rose and started back down the ill-lit street. Ingrey paused at the door of his inn; Gesca, with a half salute of farewell, walked onward. Ingrey studied his back.

So. Gesca watches me. But why? Idle—or carnal—curiosity? Self-interest, as he claimed? Worried comradeship? *Strange gossip?* It occurred to Ingrey that for all Gesca's modest claims to be an unlettered man, he was perfectly capable of penning a brief report. The sentences might be simple, the word choices infelicitous, the spelling erratic, but he could get his observations down in a logical enough order for all practical purposes.

And if Hetwar had both men's letters before him, which would be very like Hetwar . . . Ingrey's silences would shout.

Ingrey swallowed a curse and went indoors.

During the next day's ride, the autumn countryside passed in a blur of inattention for Ingrey. But he was all too keenly aware of Ijada, riding alongside the wagon near her new warden, a daunted young dedicat from the Daughter's Order in Red Dike, plucked by the local divine from her teaching duties for this unaccustomed task.

Once, when they first mounted up, Ijada smiled at him. Ingrey almost smiled back, till Gesca's mockery echoed in his mind, freezing his face in an uncomfortable distorted grimace that made her eyes widen, then slide away. He spurred ahead before his mouth muscles went into spasms.

He wondered what madness had seized his tongue last night in the temple. Of *course* Ijada must refuse to fly, even from the gallows, with a man who had tried to kill her, what, three times? Five? What sort of choice was *that* to lay before the girl? *Think, man.* Might he offer her another escort? Where could one be found, that he could trust? A vision of kidnapping her and riding off with her across his saddlebow led to even less useful imaginings. He knew the speed and ferocity his wolf could lend to him; what might her leopard do for her, woman though she most undoubtedly was? She had already slain Boleso, a bigger man than Ingrey, though admittedly, she had taken the prince by surprise. She'd even surprised herself, or so Ingrey read her. If she chose to resist him—if he then . . . and then she . . . The curiously absorbing reverie was shattered by his memory of Gesca's other jibe—*For you, it's a lure!*—and his scowl deepened.

And I am most certainly not falling in love with her, either, burn your eyes, Gesca.

Nor in lust.

Much.

Nothing that he could not fully control, anyway.

He spent the rest of the day not smiling at her, nor looking at her, nor riding near her, nor speaking to her, nor betraying any awareness of her existence in any way whatsoever. The effect seemed contagious; Gesca trotted near him to make some remark, took one look at his face, swallowed his words, and prudently retreated to the opposite end of the column. No one else approached him either, and Boleso's retainers shrank from his glower. At his few commands, men hastened to obey.

Their start had been late and their progress slow, seldom pushing the horses faster than a walk. As a result they arrived that afternoon at a smaller town than any prior stop, though still more miles nearer Easthome than Ingrey would have liked. Ingrey ruthlessly sent Boleso's men to bed down with their late master in Middletown's rustic temple, and seized the sole inn for himself, his prisoner and her duenna, and Hetwar's troop. He stalked the town's perimeter in the twilight, all too brief a task. There could be no excursion this night to that crowded temple for undervoiced argument. Tomorrow night, he must select a larger town for their halt, Ingrey determined. And the next night . . . there weren't enough next nights.

Since Gesca chose a bedroll in the taproom rather than to share Ingrey's chamber, Ingrey took his still-recovering hurts to bed early, and alone.

❧

With a short leg planned for their journey, Ingrey did not drive his men to an early start the next morning, either. He was still desultorily drinking bitter herb tea and nibbling bread in the little inn's taproom when Lady Ijada descended with her new warden. He managed to return her nod without undue distortion of his features.

"Was your chamber comfortable?" he inquired, neutrally polite, too aware of the two guardsmen in earshot still finishing their repast at the trestle table across the room.

"It sufficed." Her return frown was searching, but better than that hazardous smile.

He thought of asking after her dreams, but hesitated for the fear that this would prove not a neutral topic at all. Perhaps he might dare to ride by her side for a time later today; she seemed fully capable, once given the lead, of carrying on an oblique conversation before unfriendly ears that might convey more information than it appeared.

The sound of horses' hooves and a jingle of harness from

outside turned both their heads. "Halloo the house!" a hoarse voice shouted, and the tapster-and-owner scurried out through the hall to greet these new customers, pausing to send a servant to roust the stableboys to take the gentlemen's horses.

Ijada's nostrils flared; she drifted toward the door in the innkeeper's wake. Ingrey drained his clay beaker and followed, left hand reflexively checking his sword hilt. He came up behind her shoulder as she stepped onto the wooden porch.

Four armed men were dismounting. One was clearly a servant, two wore a familiar livery, and the last . . . Ingrey's breath stopped in surprise. And then blew out in shock.

Earl-ordainer Wencel kin Horseriver paused in his saddle, his reins gathered in his gloved hands. The young earl was a slender man, wearing a tunic from which gold threads winked under a leather coat dyed wine-red. The coat's wide collar was trimmed with marten fur, disguising his uneven build. His dark blond hair, lightened with a few streaks of premature gray, hung to his shoulders in ratty corkscrew strands, disheveled by his ride. His face was elongated, his forehead prominent, but his odd features were redeemed from potential ugliness by sharp blue eyes, fixed now on Ingrey. His presence here on this bright morning was unexpected enough. But the shock . . .

It seemed partly a scent, though borne on no breeze, partly a shadow, an intense density that made Wencel seem, somehow, vastly more *there* than any man around him. The scent was a little acrid, like urine, a little warm, like sweet hay, and deeply potent. And it appeared in Ingrey's mind without passing through his nostrils. *He bears a spirit animal.*

Too.

And I have never perceived it before.

Ingrey's head jerked toward Ijada; her face, also, had gone still with astonishment.

She senses it—smells it? Sees it? And it is a new thing to her as well. How new is it?

The perceptions, it appeared, ran three ways, for Wencel sat up with his head cocked, eyes widening, as his gaze first summed Ingrey, then turned to Ijada. Wencel's lips parted as his jaw dropped a fraction, then tightened again in a crooked smile.

Of the three of them, the earl recovered first. "Well, well, well," he murmured. A pair of gloved fingers waved past his forehead in salute to Ingrey, then went to his heart to convey a shadow-bow to Ijada. "How very strangely met we three are. I have not been so taken by surprise for . . . longer than you would believe."

The innkeeper began a gabble of welcome, intercepted, at a jerk of Wencel's chin, by one of his guardsmen, who took the man aside, presumably to explain what would be wanted of his humble house by his highborn guests. By trained civility, Ingrey went to Wencel's horse's head, though he did not really want to stand any nearer to the earl. The animal snorted and sidled at his hand on the bridle, and his grip tightened. The horse's shoulders were wet with sweat from the morning's gallop, the chestnut hairs curled and darkened, white lather showing between its legs. *Whatever brings him, Wencel wastes no time.*

Staring down at Ingrey, Wencel drew a long breath. "You are just the man I wanted to see, cousin. Lord Hetwar takes pity on your aversion to ceremony, so repeatedly expressed in your otherwise laconic letters. So I am sent to take over my late brother-in-law's cortege. A family duty, as I'm the only relative neither prostrate with grief, laid down with illness, or still stuck on bad roads halfway to the border. A royal show of equipment and mourners follows on to join us in Oxmeade. I had thought to meet you there last night, according to your ever-changing itineraries."

Ingrey licked dry lips. "That will be a relief."

"I thought it might be." His eyes went to Ijada, and the sardonic, rehearsed cadences ceased. He lowered his head. "Lady Ijada. I cannot tell you how sorry I am for what has happened—for what was done to you. I regret that I was not there at Boar's Head to prevent this."

Ijada inclined her head in acknowledgment, if not, precisely, in forgiveness. "I'm sorry you were not at Boar's Head, too. I did not desire this high blood on my hands, nor . . . the other consequences."

"Yes . . ." Wencel drawled the word out. "It seems we have much more to discuss than I'd thought." He shot Ingrey a tight-lipped smile and dismounted. At his adult height, Wencel was only half a hand shorter than his cousin; for reasons unclear to Ingrey, men regularly estimated his own height as greater than it was. In a much lower voice, Wencel added, "Strangely secret things, since you did not choose to discuss them even with the sealmaster. Some might chide you for that. Be assured, I am not one of them."

Wencel murmured a few orders to his guardsmen; Ingrey gave up the reins to Wencel's servant, and the inn's stableboys came pelting up to lead the retinue away around the building.

"Where might we go to talk?" said Wencel. "Privately."

"Taproom?" said Ingrey, nodding to the inn.

The earl shrugged. "Lead on."

Ingrey would have preferred to follow, but led off perforce. Out of the corner of his eye, he saw Wencel offer a polite arm to Lady Ijada, which she warily evaded by making play with lifting her riding skirts up the steps and passing ahead of him.

"Out," Ingrey said to Hetwar's two breakfasting men, who scrambled up in surprise at the sight of the earl. "You can take your bread and meat with you. Wait outside. See that no one disturbs us." He closed the taproom door behind them and the confused warden.

Wencel, after an indifferent glance around the old-fashioned rush-strewn chamber, tucked his gloves in his belt, seated himself at one of the trestle tables, and waved Ingrey and Ijada to the bench across from him. His hands clasped each other on the polished boards, motionless but not relaxed.

Ingrey was uncertain what creature Wencel bore within.

Of course, he'd had no clear perception of Ijada's, either, till his wolf had come unbound again. Even now, if he had not known from seeing both the leopard's corpse and its renewed spirit in their place of battle with the geas, he might not have been able to put a name to that disquieting wild presence within her.

Far more disturbing to Ingrey was the question, *When?* He had seen Wencel only twice since his own return from his Darthacan exile four years ago. The earl had been but lately married to Princess Fara, and had taken his bride back to his rich family lands along the lower Lure River, two hundred miles from Easthome. The first time the new-wed Horserivers had returned to the capital, for a midwinter celebration of the Father's Day three years back, Ingrey had been away on a mission for Hetwar to the Cantons. The next visit, he had seen his cousin only at a gathering at the king's hall when Prince Biast had received his marshal's spear and pennant from his father's hand. Wencel had been taken up with the ceremony, and Ingrey had been tied down in Hetwar's train.

They'd passed face-to-face but briefly. The earl had acknowledged his disreputable and disinherited cousin with a courteous nod, unsurprised recognition with no hint of aversion, but had not sought him out thereafter. Ingrey had thought Wencel vastly improved over the unprepossessing youth he remembered, and had assumed that the burden of his early inheritance and high marriage had matured him, gifted him with that peculiar gravity. Had there been something strange underlying that gravity, even then? The next time they had met was in Hetwar's chambers, a week ago. Wencel had been quiet, self-effacing, among that group of grim older men—mortified, or so Ingrey had guessed, for he would not meet Ingrey's eyes. Ingrey could barely remember his saying anything at all.

Wencel was speaking to Ijada, his eyes downcast in chagrin. "My lady wife has done you a great wrong, Ijada, and it is surely the gods' own justice that it has rebounded upon her head. She lied to me at first, claiming that it was your wish to stay with Boleso, until the courier from Boar's Head brought that dark enlightenment. I swear I gave her no just cause for her jealousy. I should be more furious with her than I am, if her betrayal had not so clearly contained its own punishment. She weeps incessantly, and I . . . I scarcely know how to unravel this tangle and reweave the honor of my house." He raised his head again.

The intensity of his gaze upon Ijada was not only, Ingrey thought, perturbation with her leopard. *I think Princess Fara was not so astray in her jealousy as Wencel feigns.* Four years married, and no heir to the great and ancient house of Horseriver; did that silence conceal barrenness, disaffection, some subtler impotence? Had it fueled a wife's fears, justly or no?

"I do not know how you may do so either," returned Ijada. Ingrey was uncertain if the edgy chill of this represented anger or fear, and stole a glance at her face. That pure profile was remarkably expressionless. He suddenly wanted to know *exactly* what she saw when she looked at Wencel.

Wencel tilted his head in no less frowning a regard. "What *is* that, anyway? Surely not a badger. I would guess a lynx."

Ijada's chin rose. "A leopard."

Wencel's mouth screwed up in surprise. "*That* is no . . . and where did that fool Boleso get a . . . and why . . . my lady, I think you had better tell me all that happened there at Boar's Head."

She glanced at Ingrey; he gave a slow nod. Wencel was as wound up in this as any of them, it seemed, on more than one level, and he appeared to have Hetwar's confidence. *So . . . does Hetwar know of Wencel's beast, or not?*

Ijada gave a short, blunt account of the night's deeds, factual as Ingrey understood the events, but with almost no hint of her own thoughts or emotions, devoid of interpretations or guesses. Her voice was flat. It was like watching a dumb show.

Wencel, who had listened with utmost attention, but without comment, turned his sharp gaze to Ingrey. "So where is the sorcerer?"

"What?"

He gestured at Ijada. "*That* did not happen spontaneously. There must have been a sorcerer. Illicit, to be sure, if he was both dabbler in the forbidden and tool to such a dolt as Boleso."

"Lady Ijada—my impression from Lady Ijada's testimony was that Boleso performed the rite himself."

"We were alone together in his bedchamber, certainly," said Ijada. "If I ever encountered any such person in Boleso's household, I never recognized him as a sorcerer."

Wencel absently scratched the back of his neck. "Hm. Perhaps. Yet . . . Boleso never *learned* such a rite by himself. He'd taken up many creatures, you say? Gods, what a fool. Indeed . . . No. If his mentor was not with him, he must certainly have been there recently. Or disguised. Hidden in the next room. Or fled?"

"I did wonder if Boleso might have had some accomplice," Ingrey admitted. "But Rider Ulkra asserted that no servant of the house had slipped away since the prince's death. And Lord Hetwar would surely not have sent even me to arrest such a perilous power without Temple assistance." Yes, Ingrey might have encountered something far less benign than salutary pig-delusions.

. . . *Such as a geas?* What if his murderous compulsion had *not* come with him from Easthome after all? He kept his eyes from widening at this new thought. "Hetwar could not have suspected the true events." But then why the sealmaster's insistence on Ingrey's discretion? Mere politics?

"The reports of the tragedy that Hetwar received that first night were garbled and inadequate, I grant you," said Wencel with a scowl. "Leopards were entirely missing from them, among other things. Still . . . I could wish you had secured the sorcerer, whoever he was." His gaze wandered back to Ijada. "At the least, confession from such a prisoner might have helped a lady of my household to whom I owe protection."

Ingrey flinched at the cogency of that. "I doubt I should be here, alive or sane, if I had surprised the man."

"An arguable point," Wencel conceded. "But you, of all men, should have known to look."

Had the geas been fogging Ingrey's thinking? Or just his own numb distaste for his task? He sat back a little, and, having no defense, countered on another flank: "What sorcerer did *you* encounter? And when?"

Wencel's sandy brows twitched up. "Can you not guess?"

"No. I did not sense your . . . difference, in Hetwar's chamber. Nor at Biast's installation, which was the last time I'd seen you before."

"Truly? I was not sure if I had managed to conceal my affliction from you, or you had merely chosen to be discreet. I was grateful, if so."

"I did not sense it." He almost added, *My wolf was bound,* but to do so would be to admit that it now was not. And he had no idea where he presently stood with Wencel.

"That's a comfort. Well. It came to me at much the same time as yours, if you must know. At the time of your father's death—or perhaps, I should say, of my mother's." At Ijada's look and half-voiced query, he added aside to her, "My mother was sister to Ingrey's father. Which would make me half a Wolfcliff, except for all the Horseriver brides that went to his clan in earlier generations. I should need a pen and paper to map out all the complications of our cousinship."

"I knew you had a tie, but I did not realize it was so close."

"Close and tangled. And I have long suspected that all those tragedies falling together like that were somehow bound up one in another."

Ingrey said slowly, "I knew my aunt had died sometime during my illness, but I had not realized it was so near to my father's death. No one spoke of it to me. I'd assumed it was grief, or one of those mysterious wastings that happen to women in middle age."

"No. It was an accident. Strangely timed."

Ingrey hesitated. "Ties . . . Did *you* meet the sorcerer who placed your beast in you? Was it Cumril for you, too?"

Wencel shook his head. "Whatever was done to me was done while I was sleeping. And if you think *that* wasn't the most confusing awakening of my life . . . !"

"Did it not sicken you, or drive you mad?"

"Not so much as yours, apparently. There was clearly something wrong with yours. I mean, over and above the horror that happened to your father."

"Why did you never say anything to me? My disaster was no secret. I wish I had known I was not alone!"

"Ingrey, I was thirteen, and terrified! Not least that if my defilement were discovered, they would do to me what they were doing to you! I didn't think I could survive it. I was never strong and athletic, like you. The thought of such torture as you endured sickened me. My only hope seemed concealment, at all costs. By the time I was sure of my own sanity again, and I began to regain my courage, you were gone, exiled, shuffled out of the Weald by your embarrassed uncle. And how could I have communicated? A letter? It would certainly have been intercepted and read, by your keepers or mine." He breathed deeply, and brought his rapid and shaky voice back under control. "How odd it is to find us roped together now. We could all burn jointly, you know. Back to back to back."

"Not me," Ingrey asserted, and cursed the nervous quaver in his voice. "I have a dispensation from the Temple."

"Powers that can grant such mercies can also rescind them," said Wencel darkly. "Ijada and I, then. Not the relation, front to front, that my wife feared, but a holy union of sorts."

Ijada did not flinch from this remark, but stared at Wencel with a tense new interest, her brows drawn in. Reassessing, perhaps, a man she'd thought she'd known, that she was discovering she had not known at all? *As I am?*

Wencel focused on Ingrey's grubby bandages. "What happened to your hands?"

"Tripped over a table. Cut myself with a carving knife," Ingrey answered, as indifferently as possible. He caught Ijada's curious look, out of the corner of his eye, and prayed she would not see fit to expand upon the tale. Not yet, anyway.

Instead, she asked the earl, "What is your beast? Do you know?"

He shrugged. "I had always thought it was a horse, for the Horserivers. That made sense to me, as much as anything in this could." He drew a long, thoughtful breath, and his chill blue eyes rose to meet theirs. "There have been no spirit warriors in the Weald for centuries, unless maybe some remnant survived hidden in remote refuges. Now there are three new-made, not just in the same generation, but in the same room. Ingrey and I, I have long suspected were of a piece. But you, Lady Ijada . . . I do not understand. You do not fit. I would urge you search for this missing sorcerer, Ingrey. At the very least, the hunt for such a vital witness might delay proceedings against Ijada."

"That would be a good thing," Ingrey conceded readily.

Wencel's hands spread flat on the table in unease. "We are all in each other's hands now. I had imagined my secret safe with you, Ingrey, but now it seems you were merely ignorant of it. I've been alone so long. It is hard for me to learn trust, so late."

Ingrey bent his head in wry agreement.

Wencel pulled his shoulders back, wincing as though they ached. "Well. I must refresh myself, and pay my respects to my late brother-in-law's remains. How are they preserved, by the way?"

"He's packed in salt," said Ingrey. "They had a plentiful supply at Boar's Head, for keeping game."

A bleak amusement flashed in Wencel's face. "How very direct of you."

"I didn't have him properly skinned and gutted, though, so I expect the effect will be imperfect."

"It's as well the weather is no warmer, then. But it seems we'd best not delay." Wencel let out a sigh, planted both palms on the tabletop, and pushed himself wearily to his feet. For an instant, the blackness of his spirit seemed to strike Ingrey like a blow, then he was just a tired young man again, burdened too soon in life with dangerous dilemmas. "We'll speak again."

The earl made his way out to the porch, where his retainers jumped alertly to their feet to escort him toward the town temple. In the door of the taproom, Ingrey touched Ijada's arm. She turned, her lips tight.

"What do you make of Wencel's beast?" he asked her, low-voiced.

She murmured back, "To quote Learned Hallana, if that's a stallion, I'm the queen of Darthaca." Her eyes rose to meet his, level and intent. "Your wolf is not much like a wolf. And his horse is not much like a horse. But I will say this, Ingrey; they are both a *lot* like each other."

8

INGREY RETURNED UPSTAIRS TO PACK HIS SADDLEBAGS, then sought Gesca. The lieutenant's gear was gone from the corner of the taproom. Ingrey walked down the muddy street of Middletown—better named Middlehamlet, in his view— to the small wooden temple, in hopes of finding him. He reviewed which of the half dozen village stables they had commandeered for their horses and equipment Gesca was likely to have gone to next, but the plan proved unnecessary; Gesca was standing in the shade of the temple's wide porch. Speaking, or being spoken to, by Earl Horseriver.

Gesca glanced up at Ingrey, twitched, and fell silent; Wencel merely gave him a nod.

"Ingrey," said Wencel. "Where is Rider Ulkra and the rest of Boleso's household now? Still at Boar's Head, or do they follow you?"

"They follow, or so I ordered. How swiftly, I do not know. Ulkra cannot expect much joy to await him in Easthome."

"No matter. By the time I have leisure to attend to them, they will have arrived there, no doubt." He sighed. "My horses could use a little rest. Arrange things, if you will, to depart at noon. We'll still reach Oxmeade before dark."

"Certainly, my lord," said Ingrey formally. He jerked his head at the unhappy-looking Gesca, and Wencel gave them a short wave of farewell and turned for the temple.

"And what did Earl Horseriver have to say to you?" Ingrey inquired of Gesca, low-voiced, as they trod down the street again.

"He's not a glad man. I cringe to think how black things would be if he'd actually *liked* his brother-in-law. But it's plain he does not love this mess."

"That, I had already gathered."

"Still, an impressive young fellow, in his way, despite his looks. I thought so back at Princess Fara's wedding."

"How so?"

"Eh. It wasn't that he did anything special. He just never . . ."

"Never what?"

Gesca's lips twisted. "I . . . it's hard to say. He never made a mistake, or looked nervous, never late or early . . . never drunk. It just crept up on you. Formidable, that's the word I want. In a way, he reminds me of you, if it was brains and not brawn that was wanted." Gesca hesitated, then, perhaps prudently, declined to pursue this comparison any farther down the slope into the swamp.

"We are cousins," Ingrey observed blandly.

"Indeed, m'lord." Gesca gave him a sideways glance. "He was very interested in Learned Hallana."

Ingrey grimaced. *Well, that was inevitable.* He would hear more from Wencel on that subject before the day was done, he was sure.

The Middletown Temple divine was a mere young acolyte, and had been thrown into panic by the descent upon him, on only a half day's notice, of the prince's cortege. But however much ceremony Earl Horseriver was sent to provide, it was clear it was not starting yet. The cavalcade left town promptly at noon with a grimmer efficiency than Ingrey in his vilest mood would have dared deploy. He applauded in his heart, and left the pallid acolyte a suitable purse to console him for his terrors.

Middletown was not yet out of sight on the road behind them when Wencel wheeled his chestnut horse around beside Ingrey's, and murmured, "Ride ahead with me. I need to speak with you."

"Certainly." Ingrey kneed his horse into a trot; he gave what he hoped was a reassuring nod to Ijada as they passed around her riding beside the wagon. Wencel favored her with a somewhat ambiguous salute.

Wencel turned in his saddle, as the distance between them and the cortege stretched out of any possible earshot, but only remarked, "Wherever did you find the beer wagon?"

"Reedmere."

"Ha. At least one thing about his funeral will match poor Boleso's taste. They're hauling that silver-plated royal hearse from Easthome to meet us in Oxmeade. I trust it will not collapse any bridges on the way."

"Indeed." Ingrey tried to keep his lips from twitching.

"My household awaits me in Oxmeade to attend to my comfort tonight. And yours, if you will join me. I recommend you do so. There will be no lodgings to be found for love nor money once the court arrives there for this procession."

"Thank you," said Ingrey sincerely. There had been duels fought by desperate retainers over the possession of haylofts, in certain unwieldy royal excursions of Ingrey's experience. Wencel would certainly have secured the best chambers available.

"Tell me of this Learned Hallana, Ingrey," said Wencel abruptly.

At least he did not tax Ingrey for his failure to mention her before. Ingrey wondered whether to feel relieved. "I judged her to be exactly what she claimed to be. A friend of Lady Ijada's who had known her as a child. She'd been a physician at some fort of the Son's Order out west in the fen marches—Ijada's father was a lord dedicat, and its captain, at the time."

"I knew something of Lord dy Castos, yes. Ijada has spoken of him. But my mind picks at the coincidence. A sorcerer with some connection with Lady Ijada—and her new affliction—disappears from Boar's Head. Days later, a sorcerer—or sorceress—with a connection with Ijada comes to her in Red Dike. Is this two sorcerers, or one?"

Ingrey shook his head. "I cannot imagine Learned Hallana passing without note at Boar's Head. Inconspicuous, she was not. And she was very pregnant, which I gather lays great constraint upon her use of her demon for the duration. She stays in a hermitage at Suttleaf, for safety. I admit my evidence is indirect, but I'm certain that Boleso was already deep into his disastrous experiments when he murdered his manservant so grotesquely, six months ago. Which must put his pet sorcerer at Easthome then, or near then, as well."

Wencel frowned in doubt.

"It is as much an error to take truth for lies, as lies for truth," Ingrey pointed out. "The dual-divine was a most unusual lady, but that she might also be Boleso's puppet is one too many things to believe about her. It doesn't fit. For one thing, she was no fool."

Wencel tilted his head, conceding the point. "Suppose she were his puppet master, then?"

"Less unlikely," Ingrey granted reluctantly. "But . . . no."

Wencel sighed. "I shall give up my simplifying conjecture, then. We have two separate sorcerers. But—how separate? Might Boleso's tool have fled to her, after the debacle? The two in league?"

An uncomfortable idea. It occurred to Ingrey suddenly that the suggestion—misdirection?—that his geas had been laid on him at Easthome had come from Hallana. "The timing . . . would not be impossible."

Wencel grunted disconsolately, staring between his

horse's ears for a moment. "I understand the learned divine wrote a letter. Have you read it yet?"

Curse you, Gesca. And curse that gossiping warden. How much else did Wencel already know? "It was not entrusted to me. She handed it directly to Lady Ijada. Sealed."

Wencel waved a hand in dismissal of this. "I'm sure you've been taught how to do the thing."

"For ordinary correspondence, certainly. This is one from a Temple sorcerer. I hesitate to think what might happen to the letter—or to me—if I attempted to tamper with it. Burst into flame, maybe." He left it to Wencel to decide if he meant the paper, or Ingrey himself. "Passing it on to Hetwar also has problems. At the least, he would need another Temple sorcerer to open it. I should think even the royal seal-master would find it a challenge to suborn one to pry into letters addressed to the head of his own order."

"An illicit sorcerer, then." At Ingrey's sour look, he protested, "Well, you must grant Hetwar could find one if anyone could—if he chose."

"If this multiplication of hypothetical sorcerers goes on, we shall have to hang them from the rafters like hams to make room." Although, Ingrey was uncomfortably reminded, there was still his strange geas to account for.

Wencel gave a short, unhappy nod, then fell silent for a little. "Yes, speaking of hams," he finally said. His voice grew conversational. "It is not, you know, that you lie well, cousin. It's merely that no one is foolhardy enough to call you on it. This may have given you an inflated idea of your skill at dissimulation." The voice hardened. "What really happened in that upstairs room?"

"If I had anything more to report, it would be my duty to report it first to Lord Hetwar."

Wencel's brows climbed. "Oh, really? First, and yet somehow . . . not yet? I saw your letters to Hetwar, such as they were. The number of items missing from them turns out to be quite notable. Leopards. Sorceresses. Strange brawls. Near drownings. Your romantic lieutenant Gesca would even have it that you have fallen in love—also, if more understandably, without hint in your scribblings."

Ingrey flushed. "Letters can go astray. Or be read by unfriendly eyes." He glowered, pointedly, at the earl.

Wencel's lips parted, closed. He attended for a moment to his horse, as he and Ingrey separated to ride around a patch of mire. When they were stirrup to stirrup again, Wencel said, "Your pardon if I seem anxious. I have a great deal to lose."

With false cheeriness, Ingrey replied, "While I, on the other hand, have already lost it all. Earl-ordainer."

Wencel touched a fist to his heart, in acknowledgment of the hit. But he added quietly, "There is also a wife."

It was Ingrey's turn to fall silent, abashed. Because Wencel's marriage was arranged—and, up till now, barren—did not necessarily entail that it was also loveless. On either side. Indeed, Princess Fara's betrayal of her handmaiden spoke of a hot unhappy jealousy, which could not be a product of bored indifference. And the hallow king's daughter must have seemed a great prize to so homely a young man, despite his own high rank.

"Besides," Wencel's voice lightened again, "burning alive is a most painful death. I do not recommend it. I think this missing sorcerer could be a threat to us both, in that regard alone. He knows many things that he should not. *We* should find him first. If he proves to contain nothing, ah, personally dangerous, I'd be glad enough to pass him along to Hetwar thereafter."

And if the sorcerer *was* dangerous to him, what did Wencel propose to do then? And, five gods, *how*? "Leaving aside all questions of duty—this is not an arrest I am equipped to handle, privately or otherwise."

"How if you were? Does having first knowledge not attract you?"

"To what end?"

"Survival."

"I am surviving."

"You were. But your dispensation from the Temple depends, in part, upon a bond of surety now broken."

Ingrey's eyes flicked to him, wary. "How so?"

Wencel's lips tightened in a small smile. "I could deduce it by the change in your perception of me alone, but I don't have to; I can see it. Your beast lies quietly within you, by long habit if nothing else, but nothing constrains it except that you do not call it up. Sooner or later, some Temple sensitive is bound to notice, or else you will make some revealing blunder." His voice grew low and intense. "There are alternatives to cutting off your hand for fear of your fist, Ingrey."

"How would you know?"

Wencel's hesitation was longer, this time. "The library at Castle Horseriver is a remarkable thing," he began obliquely. "Several of my Horseriver forefathers were collectors of lore, and at least one was a scholar of note. Documents lie there that I am certain exist nowhere else, some of them hundreds of years old. Things old Audar's Temple-men would not have hesitated to burn. The most amazing eyewitness accounts—I should tell you some of the anecdotes, sometime. Enough to lure a not very bookish boy to read on. And then, later—to read as though his life depended on it." His gaze found Ingrey's. "You dealt with your so-called defilement by running away from all knowledge, and acknowledgment. I dealt with mine by running toward. Which of us do you think has the best grip by now?"

Ingrey blew out his breath. "You give me a lot to think about, Wencel."

"Do so, then. But do not turn away from understanding, this time, I beg you." He added more softly, "Do not turn your back on me."

Indeed not. I should not dare. He gave Wencel an equivocal salute.

The cortege came then to a rocky ford, fortunately not in so great a spate as the near-disastrous crossing on the first day, and Ingrey turned his attention to getting all across in safety. A mile farther on, the wagon nearly bogged in a stretch of mud, then a guardsman's mount went lame from a lost shoe. Then, at a stop to water the horses, a fight broke out between two of Boleso's retainers, some smoldering private quarrel that burst into flame. Ingrey's customary menace almost did not contain it, and he turned away from the separated pair pale with worry, which they fortunately took for rage, about what might happen the next time if mere threat was not enough, and he was forced to follow with action.

He remounted his horse more blank-faced than ever. Wencel, he had to admit, had thrown his mind into chaos. The earl's twisting conversation gave Ingrey a sharp sense that the pair of them were fencing in the dark, blades stabbing at hidden targets. Both concealing and confiding dangerous secrets to each other, feint and parry . . . equally? *I think Wencel conceals more*. To be fair, Wencel had also seemed to reveal more.

Ingrey had thought his anxiety over the strange geas to be his most pressing problem. The notion that Wencel's *lore* might contain clues to the matter was doubly exciting. It suggested Ingrey might have an ally to hand. It equally suggested that Ingrey might have found his unknown enemy. Or, how was it that Wencel seemed to regard illicit sorcerers as minor inconveniences, to be so readily handled? He glanced toward the head of the cortege where Wencel now rode, beyond earshot once more, interrogating one of Boleso's men. The guardsman was a big fellow, yet his shoulders were bowed as though trying to make himself smaller.

Wencel had dragged a number of lures across Ingrey's trail, yet it was not the new mystery but the old one that most arrested him, caught and held him suspended between fascination and fear. *What does Wencel know about my father and his mother that I do not?*

❧

Oxmeade was larger than Red Dike, but Boleso's cortege was received at its big stone temple that afternoon with only moderate ceremony, mostly, it seemed, because the town was a madhouse of preparation for greater events tomorrow. Ingrey was hugely relieved finally to hand off responsibility for the corpse and its outriders to Wencel, who handed them in turn to his sober seneschal, a gaggle of Easthome Temple divines, and a formidable array of retainers and clerks. Princess Fara and her own household, Ingrey was glad to learn, had not followed on, but awaited them all in the capital. It was not yet twilight when Ingrey and his guard mounted up again with their prisoner and followed Wencel through the winding streets.

Passing along the edge of a crowded square, Wencel pulled up his horse, and Ingrey stopped beside him. A street market was open late, presumably to serve the needs of the courtiers and their households already starting to arrive for the last leg of Boleso's funeral procession. Ingrey was not sure at first what had caught Wencel's attention, but he followed the earl's gaze past the busy booths to a corner where a fiddler played, his hat invitingly laid upside down at his feet. The musician was better than the usual sort, certainly, and his mellow instrument cast a strange, plaintive song into the golden evening air.

After a moment Wencel remarked, "That is a very old tune. I wonder if he knows how old? He plays it . . . almost rightly."

Wencel kept his face averted until the song ended. When he looked forward his profile was strange. Tense, but not with anger or fear; more like a man about to weep for some inconsolable, incalculable loss. Wencel grimaced the tension away and clucked his horse onward without looking back, nor sending anyone to throw a coin in the hat, though the fiddler looked after the rich party with thwarted hope.

They came at length to the large house Wencel had rented, or commandeered, one of several in a row in this wealthy merchants' quarter. Bright brass bosses in sunburst patterns studded the heavy planks of its front door. Ingrey handed off his horse to Gesca, shouldered his saddlebags, and oversaw Lady Ijada and her young warden taken upstairs by a maid. By their strained greetings, this was a servant who had known Ijada before. The Horseriver household, it seemed, found the justice of Ijada's case as disturbingly ambiguous as did their master.

Before Wencel went off to deal with the sheaf of messages that had arrived in his absence, he murmured to Ingrey, "We shall eat in an hour, you and Ijada and I. It may be our last chance for private speech for a while."

Ingrey nodded.

He was guided to a tiny chamber on the top floor, where a basin and a can of hot water were already waiting for him. It was clearly a servant's room, of whatever wealthy family the earl had dislodged, but its solitude was most welcome to him. Horseriver's own servants were likely crowded into some lesser dormitory or stable loft in this crisis, and Gesca and his men would fare little better. Ingrey trusted Horseriver's cook would console them.

Ingrey washed efficiently. His wardrobe was too limited to take much time over; he had brought clothing for hard riding, not for courtly dining. Done and dressed, he considered the temptations of the cot, but feared if once he lay down, he would be unable to force himself up again. He wended down the narrow staircase instead, planning to explore the house and the street around it, and perhaps check on Gesca, if the stable proved to be nearby. He paused on the next landing, hearing Wencel's voice in the hallway. He turned that way instead.

Wencel was speaking to Ijada's warden, who was listening with a wide-eyed, daunted expression. He wheeled at the sound of Ingrey's step, and grimaced. "You may go," he said to the warden, who bobbed a curtsey and withdrew into what was presumably Ijada's chamber. Wencel joined Ingrey at the staircase, motioning him ahead, but excused himself when they reached the ground floor to go off and confer with his clerk.

Ingrey stepped outside in the dusk and made his circuit of

the environs of the house. Arriving again at the front door, he was passed from the porter to another servant and into a chamber at the back of the second floor. It was not the grand dining room, almost suitable to an earl's estate, but a small breakfast parlor, overlooking a kitchen garden and the mews. Its single door was heavy, and would muffle sound well, Ingrey judged. A little round table was set for three.

Ijada arrived escorted by a maidservant, who curtseyed to Ingrey and left her. She wore an overdress of wheatstraw-colored wool upon clean linen high to her neck. The effect was modest and maidenly, though Ingrey supposed the lace collar was mostly to hide the greening bruises on her throat. Wencel came in almost on her heels, glittering in the abundant candlelight, having also changed into richer garb than what he'd ridden in. And cleaner. Ingrey briefly wished his own saddlebags had held a better choice than *least smelly*.

At Wencel's gesture Ingrey brushed off his court manners and helped Lady Ijada to her chair, and Wencel to his, before seating himself. All equally distant from each other, tripod-tense. Servants, obviously instructed, bustled in around them, leaving covered dishes and withdrawing discreetly. The food, at least, proved good, if countrified: dumplings, beans, baked apples, a brace of stuffed woodcocks, sauces and savories, carafes of three sorts of wines.

"Ah," murmured Wencel, lifting a silver cover and revealing a ham. "Dare I ask you to carve, Lord Ingrey?"

Ijada blinked warily. Ingrey returned Wencel an equally tight smile and haggled off slices. He slipped his hands below the table, after, to pull his cuffs down again over the bandages on his wrists. He waited to see how Wencel would bend the talk next, which resulted in a silence for a space, as all applied themselves to the meal.

At length Wencel remarked, "I had nothing but second-hand reports about the dire events at Birchgrove that left your father dead and you . . . well. They were quite jumbled and wild. And certainly incomplete. Would you tell me the full tale?"

Ingrey, braced for more questions about Hallana, hesitated in confusion, then mustered his memories once more. He had held them for years in silence, yet now recounted them aloud for the third time in a week. His story seemed to grow smoother with repetition, as though the account were slowly coming to replace the event, even in his own mind. Wencel chewed and listened, frowning.

"Your wolf was different than your father's," he said, as Ingrey wound down after describing, as best he could, the wolfish turmoil in his mind that had blended into his weeks of delirium.

"Well, yes. For one thing, it was not diseased. Or at least . . . not in the same way. It made me wonder if animals could get the falling sickness, or some like disease of the mind."

"How did your father's huntsman come by it?"

"I do not know. He was dead before I recovered enough to ask anything."

"Huh. For I had *heard*"—a slight emphasis on that last word, a significant pause—"that it was not the wolf originally intended for you. That the rabid wolf had killed its pack mate, a day before the rite was to be held. And that the new wolf was found that night, sitting outside the sick wolf's cage."

"Then you have heard more than I was told. It could be, I suppose."

Wencel tapped his spoon beside his plate in a faint, nervous tattoo, seemed to catch himself, and set it down.

Ingrey added, "Did your mother say anything to you about your stallion? That morning when you awoke changed."

"No. That was the morning she died."

"Not of rabies!"

"No. And yet I have wondered, since. She died in a fall from a horse."

Ingrey pursed his lips. Ijada's eyes widened.

"It died in the accident, too," Wencel added. "Broke its

leg. The groom cut its throat—it was said. By the time I came to wonder about it—some time afterward—she was long buried, and the horse butchered and gone. I have meditated by her grave, but there is no lingering aura to be sensed there. No ghosts, no answers. Her death was wrenching to me, so soon, just four months after my father's. I was not insensible to the parallels with your case, Ingrey, but if Wolfcliff brother and sister had some plan concocted, some intent, no one confided it to me."

"Or some conflict," Ijada suggested thoughtfully, looking back and forth between the pair of them. "Like two rival castles, one on each side of the Lure, building their battlements higher."

Wencel opened a hand in acknowledgment of the possible point, though his frown suggested that the idea did not sit easily with him.

"In all this time, you must have developed *theories,* Wencel," said Ingrey.

Wencel shrugged. "Guesses, conjectures, fantasies, more like. My nights grew full of them, till I was wearied beyond measure with the wondering."

Ingrey chased his last bite of dumpling across his plate, and said in a lower tone, "Why did you never approach me before, then?"

"You were gone to Darthaca. Permanent exile, for all I knew. Then your family lost all trace of you. You might have been dead, as far as anyone had heard to the contrary."

"Yes, but what about after? When I returned?"

"You seemed to have reached a place of safety, under Hetwar's protection. Safer with your dispensation than I was with my secrets, certainly. I envied you that. Would you have thanked me for throwing your life back into doubt and disarray?"

"Perhaps not," Ingrey conceded reluctantly.

A crisp double knock sounded at the room's thick door. Ijada started, but Wencel merely called, "Come!"

Wencel's clerk poked his head around the door and murmured apologetically, "The message you were awaiting has arrived, my lord."

"Ah, good. Thank you." Wencel pushed back from the table, and to his feet. "Excuse me. I shall return in a few moments. Pray continue." He gestured at the serving dishes.

As soon as Wencel exited, a pair of servants bustled in to clear used plates, lay new courses, renew the wine and water, and retreat again with equally wordless bows. Ingrey and Ijada were left looking at each other. Some tentative exploration under the dish covers revealed dainties, fruits, and sweets, and Ijada brightened. They helped one another to the most interesting tidbits.

Ingrey glanced at the closed door. "Do you think Princess Fara knows of Wencel's beast?" he asked her.

She studied a piece of honeyed marzipan and ate it before replying. Her frown was not, Ingrey thought, for the food. "It would fit some things that I didn't understand about them. Their relationship seemed strange to me, although I didn't necessarily expect such a high marriage to be like my mother's. Either of hers. For all that he is not handsome, I think Fara *wanted* Wencel to be in love with her. In some more courtly fashion than he displayed."

"Was he not courtly?"

"Oh, he was always polite, that I saw. Cool and courteous. I never saw why she seemed to have always a touch of fear around him, for he never raised his hand or even his voice to her. But if it was fear *for* him, and not—or not just—*of* him, perhaps that explains it."

"And was he in love with her?"

Her frown deepened. "It's hard to say. He was so often moody, so distant and silent, for days on end it seemed. Sometimes, if there were visitors to Castle Horseriver, he would rouse himself, and there would be a spate of conversation and wit—he's really extraordinarily learned. Yet he has spoken more in one evening to you, here, than I ever heard him speak at any meal with his wife. But then . . . you are arresting to him in ways that she is not." Her eyes slid toward and away from him, and he knew she tested her inner senses.

So are you, now, Ingrey realized. "He has only a little time to assure himself of his own safety in this new tangle. Perhaps that explains why he's pushing. He is pushing— don't you think?" Ingrey at least felt pressed.

"Oh, yes." She paused in thought. "Too, it may be an outpouring long suppressed. Who *could* he speak to of this, before us, now? He's worried, yes, but also . . . I don't know. Excited? No—subtler or stranger than that. Surely *joyful* cannot be the word." Her lips screwed up.

"I shouldn't think so," Ingrey said dryly.

The door clicked open, and Ingrey's gaze jerked up. It was Wencel, returning. He seated himself again with an apologetic gesture.

"Is your business settled?" Ijada inquired politely.

"Well enough. If I have not yet said so, Ingrey, let me congratulate you on the speed of your mission. It does not look as though I shall be able to emulate it, to my regret. I'll likely send you ahead with Lady Ijada tomorrow, as her presence in the cortege is like to be, hm, awkward, as it is turned into a parade. At half march all the way on to Easthome, five gods spare me."

"Where in Easthome am I to be sent?" Ijada asked, a little tensely.

"That is a matter still being settled. I should know by tomorrow morning. No place vile, if I have my way." He stared at her through lidded eyes.

Ingrey stared at them both, daring to extend his senses beyond sight. "You two are different from each other. Your beast is much darker, Wencel. Or something. Her cat makes me think of sun-dappled shade, but yours . . . goes all the way down." Past the limits of his perceptions.

"Indeed, I think that leopardess must have been at the peak of its condition," said Wencel. He cast Ijada a smile, as if to reassure her that the comment was well meant. "It has a fresh and pure power. A Weald warrior would have been proud to bear it, if there had been such a clan as kin Leopardtree back then."

"But I am a woman, not a warrior," said Ijada, watching him back.

"The women of the Old Weald used to take in sacred animals as well. Did you not know?"

"No!" Her eyes lit with interest. "Truly?"

"Oh, seldom as warriors, though there were always a few such called. Some tribes used theirs as their banner-carriers, and they were valued above all women. But there was a second sort . . . another sort of hallowed animal made, that women took more often. Well, more proportionally; they were much rarer to start with."

"Banner-carrier?" Ijada echoed in an odd tone.

"Made?" said Ingrey.

Wencel's lips curved up at the tautness in his voice, in an angler's smile. "Weald warriors were made by sending the soul of a sacrificed animal into a man. But something else was made when the soul of an animal was sacrificed into another animal."

Ijada shook off her arrested look, and began, "Do you think Boleso was attempting—wait, no."

"I have still not quite unraveled what Boleso thought he was about, but if it was in pursuit of some rumor of this old magic, he had it wrong. The animal was sacrificed, at the end of its life, into the body of a young animal, always of the same sort and sex. And all the wisdom and training it had learned went with it. And then, at the end of its life, that animal was sacrificed into another. And another. And another. Accumulating a great density of life. And—at some point along the chain, five or six or ten generations or more—it became something that was not an animal anymore."

"An . . . animal god?" ventured Ijada.

Wencel spread his hands. "In some shadowy sense, perhaps. It's what some say the gods are—all the life of the world flows into them, through the gates of death. They accumulate us all. And yet the gods are an iteration stranger still, for they absorb without destroying, becoming ever more *Themselves* with each perfectly retained addition. The great hallowed animals were a thing apart."

"How long did it take to make one?" asked Ingrey. His heart was starting to beat faster, and he knew his breath was quickening. And he knew Wencel marked it. *Why am I suddenly terrified at Wencel's bedtime tale?* His very blood seemed to growl in response to it.

"Decades—lifetimes—centuries, sometimes. They were vastly valued, for as animals, they were tame and trainable, uncannily intelligent; they came to understand the speech of men. Yet this great continuity suffered continuous attrition, and not just through ordinary mischance. For when a Weald man or woman took one of the great beasts into their soul, they became something far more than a warrior. Greater and more dangerous. Few of the oldest and best of the creatures survived unharvested under the pressure of Audar's invasion. Many were sacrificed prematurely just to save them from the Darthacan troops. Audar's Temple-men were specially disposed to slay them whenever they were found, in fear of what they could become. Of what they could make us into."

"Sorcerers?" said Ijada breathlessly. "Wealding sorcerers? Is that what Boleso was attempting to become?"

Wencel bent his hand back and forth. "Let us not become confused in our language. A sorcerer, proper—or improper, if illicit and not bound by Temple disciplines—is possessed of an elemental of disorder and chaos, sacred to the Bastard, and the magic the creature endows is constrained into channels of destruction thereby. Such demons are bound up in the balance of the world of matter and the world of spirit. And the old tribes had such sorcerers, too, with their own traditions of discipline under the white god.

"The great hallowed animals were of *this* world, and had not ever been in the hands of the gods. Not part of their powers. Not constrained to destruction, either. A purely Wealding thing. Although their magic was wholly of the mind and spirit, they also could affect the body that the mind and spirit rule. The animal shamans had a quite separate tradition from the tribal sorcerers, and not always in alliance with them even in the same clan. One of the many divisions that weakened us in the face of the Darthacan onslaught." Wencel's eyes grew distant, considering this ancient lapse.

Ijada was looking back and forth between Wencel and Ingrey. *"Oh,"* she breathed.

Ingrey's face felt drained. It was as if his fortress walls were crumbling, inside his mind, in the face of Wencel's sapping. *No. No. This is rubbish, nonsense, old tales for children, some sort of vile joke Wencel is having on me, to see how much I can be persuaded to swallow.* What he whispered instead was, *"How?"*

"How came this wise wolf to you, you mean?" Wencel shrugged. "I, too, would like to know. When Great Audar"—his mouth gave the name a venomous twist—"tore out the heart of the Weald at Bloodfield—which was the great shrine of Holytree, before his utter desecration of it—even he did not manage to massacre all. Some spirit warriors and shamans were not present at the rite, by delay or chance. A few escaped the ambush."

Ijada sat up with an even sharper stare. A flick of Wencel's eyes acknowledged his audience, and he continued: "Even a century and a half of persecution afterward did not erase all knowledge, though not for lack of trying. Pockets endured, though very few in writing like the library at Castle Horseriver—specially collected by certain of my ancestors, to be sure, but collected *from* somewhere. But in remote regions, fens and mountains, poor hamlets—the Cantons broke from the Darthacan yoke early—traditions, if not their wisdom, continued for long. Passed down from generation to generation as secret family or village rites, always dimming in ignorance. What even Audar could not accomplish, Time the destroyer did. I had not imagined any to be left, after the relentless erosion of centuries. But it seems there were at least . . . two." His blue gaze pierced Ingrey.

Ingrey's thoughts felt like frantic claws scrambling and scraping on the floor of a cage. He managed only an inarticulate noise.

"For your consolation," Wencel continued, "it explains your long delirium. Your wolf was a far more powerful intrusion upon your soul than your father's or Ijada's simple creatures. Four hundred years old seems impossible—how many wolf generations must that be?—and yet . . ." His gaze on Ingrey grew uneasy. "*All the way down,* indeed. An apt description. The spirit warriors mastered their beasts with little effort, for the ordinary animals were readily subordinated to the more powerful human mind. In the Old Weald, if you'd been destined to be gifted with a great beast, you would have had much preparation and study, and the support of others of your kind. Not abandoned to find your own way, stumbling in fear and doubt and near madness. No wonder you responded by crippling yourself."

"Am I crippled?" Ingrey whispered. *And what fearsome thing would I be if I were not?*

"Oh, aye."

Ijada, her tone shrewd, said to Wencel, "And are you?"

He held a palm out. "Less so. I have my own burdens."

How much less so, Wencel? Yet Ingrey was less moved by the suspicion that he might have found the source of his geas, as by the notion that he might have found his mirror.

Wencel turned again to Ingrey. "In the event, yours was a happy ignorance. If the Temple had suspected what manner of beast you *really* bore, you would not have found that dispensation so easy to come by."

"It wasn't easy," muttered Ingrey.

Wencel hesitated, as if considering a new thought. "Indeed. To bind a *great* beast could have been no small task." A respectful, even wary, smile turned one corner of his mouth. He glanced at the candles burning down in their holders on the center of the table. "It grows late. Tomorrow's duties crowd the dawn. We must part company for a while, but Ingrey, I beg you—do nothing to draw fresh attention to yourself till we can talk again."

Ingrey scarcely dared breathe. "I thought my wolf was just a well of violence. Rage, destruction, killing. What else can it—*could* I do?"

"That is the next lesson. Come to me for it when we are both back in Easthome. Meantime, if you value your life, keep your secrets—and mine." Wencel pushed himself up, wearily. He ushered them out the door before him, plain signal that both the dinner and the revelations were done for the night. Ingrey, nearly sick to his stomach, could only be thankful.

9

THE SERVANT'S COT CREAKED IN THE NIGHT SILENCE OF the house as Ingrey sat down and clenched his hands upon his knees. Introspection was a habit he'd long avoided, for aversion to what it must confront. Tonight, at last, he forced his perceptions inward.

He pushed past the generalized dull terror, as through a too-familiar fog. Brushed aside clinging tendrils of self-deception, a veil on his inner sight. He had no time or patience for them anymore. Once, he had conceived of his bound wolf as a sort of knot under his belly, encysted, like an extra organ, but one without function. The knot, the wolf, was not there now. Nor in his heart, nor in his mind, exactly, though trying to see into his own mind felt like trying to see the back of his own head. The beast was truly unbound. So . . . where . . . ?

It is in my blood, he realized. Not a part, but every part of him. It wasn't just in him, now; it *was* him. Not to be ripped out as readily as cutting off his fist, or tearing out his eyes, no, no such trivial surgery would answer.

It came to him then, a possible reason why the fen folk practiced their peculiar blood sacrifices, a meaning lost in the depths of time even to themselves. The marsh people were old enemies of the Old Wealdings. They had faced the forest tribes' spirit warriors and animal shamans in battle and raid along their marches for centuries out of mind—taken captives, perhaps including prisoners far too dangerous to hold. Had those sanguinary drainings once had a more grim and practical purpose?

Could a mere physical separation, of blood from body, also create a spiritual one, of sin from soul?

Denial, it seemed, ran at the end of its long road down into a bog of blood. More in a sort of chill curiosity than any other emotion, Ingrey rummaged in his saddlebags and drew out his coil of rope. He laid it and his belt knife out on the quilt beside him and glanced upward in the light of his single candle at the shadowy ceiling beams. Yes, it could be done, the supreme self-sacrifice. Bind his own ankles, hoist himself up, loop a knot. Hang upside down. Lift the finely honed blade to his own throat. He could let his wolf out in a hot scarlet stream, end its haunting of him, right here and now. Free himself of all defilement in the ultimate *no*.

I can refuse the dark power. By stepping into a darkness more absolute.

So would his soul, rejected by the gods, just fade quietly into oblivion as the sundered and damned ghosts were said to do? It seemed no fearful fate. Or—if he had misjudged the rite—would his lost spirit, augmented by this unknown force, turn into something . . . else? Something presently unimaginable?

Did Wencel know what?

All those lures the young earl had thrown out, all that bait, were plain enough indicators of how Wencel thought of Ingrey, and about him. *I am prey, in his eyes. Watch me run.* He could deny Wencel his quarry.

Ingrey stood up, reached, felt along the beam, tucked the rope through a slight warped gap between the timber and the attic floor above, sat again and studied the cord's dangling length in the shadows. He touched the gray twist; his brain felt cool and distant, in this contemplation, and yet his hand shook. That much blood would make a mighty mess on the floor for some horrified servant to clean up in the morning. Or would it flow between the floorboards, seep through the ceiling of the room below? Announce the event overhead by a dripping in the dark, spattering wetly upon a pillow or a sleeping face? *Was that thunder, does the roof leak?* Until a light was struck, and its bright flare revealed the drizzle as a redder rain. Would there be screams?

Was Lady Ijada's room below his? He calculated the placement of corridors, and of the chamber door into which the warden had retreated. Perhaps. It hardly mattered.

He paused for a long time, barely breathing, balanced on the cusp of the night.

No.

His blood cried out for Ijada, but not like *this*. He considered the small miracle of her smile. Not the usual nervous polite grimace most women favored him with, never reaching their eyes; indeed, it seemed Ijada could smile at him with her eyes alone, fearlessly. Without concealed revulsion. Even delicately enjoying, it seemed, a sight she found inexplicably comely. His wolf was no less dangerous in its capacities to her than to any other woman he had not dared to touch or look upon, she was not *safe* from him, no . . . she was something unexpectedly else. She was dangerous right back at him.

The thought did very odd things to his heart. He rejected the poets' phrases as drivel; his heart did not turn over, nor inside out, nor, most *certainly* not *ever,* dance. It went on beating right side up in his chest as usual, if a little faster and tighter-seeming. Was he odd, to relish the peculiar perilous sensation so? It wasn't exactly pleasant. Exactly. But what he relished in the darkness of his dreams wasn't what most men he'd known spoke of, in the crude braggings of their lusts, as pleasant; he'd been aware of that for some time.

His hand drew back, clenched closed.

So if I choose not to wake you so redly, Ijada, what then?

He had come to the end of the road of *No;* he could go no further down it without drowning in his own blood. *I have three choices, I think.* To wade into the red swamp and never come up again. To linger in numbness and immobility as before—yet it was certain that neither the tide of events nor the relentless Wencel would permit the continuation of his paralysis very much longer. Or . . . he might turn around and walk the other way.

So what does that mean, or has my thinking turned altogether to a poet's twaddle? His bedchamber was so quiet he could hear the susurrus of the blood in his ears like an animal's panting.

Could he stop denying himself, and deny others instead? He tested the phrases on his tongue. *No, you are wrong, all of you, Temple and Court and folk in the streets. You always were wrong. I am not . . . am not . . .* what? *And are these the only terms I can think in, these shouted nos?* Ah, habit.

But if I turn and walk the other way, I do not know where the road goes. Or where it ends.

Or Who I may meet along it, and that thought disturbed him more than knife and cord and haunted blood together.

Though if I can find a darker dark along it than this one, I shall be surprised.

He rose, sheathed his knife, packed the rope away. Stripped for sleep and lay down under the servant's sheets. Old and thin and mended, they were, but clean; it was a rich household that afforded even its servants such refinements.

I do not know where I am going. But I am quite weary enough of where I've been.

❧

After the briefest dawn meeting with Wencel, all practicalities, Ingrey took his prisoner on the road. Hetwar's troop still escorted them, glad enough to be lighter by one dead prince and a dozen surly retainers and all their baggage. Ingrey had even sent the latest warden-dedicat home, her place taken by a middle-aged maidservant of Horseriver's household who rode pillion behind Gesca. The small cavalcade climbed out of the valley of Oxmeade into the breaking day, and began to wind through the settled country of the rich lowlands belonging to the earldom of Stagthorne.

Taking a lead from Horseriver, Ingrey edged his mount forward and without apology motioned Ijada to ride ahead with him. He was nonetheless conscious of Gesca's narrow gaze, following them. Just so they outdistanced the curious lieutenant's ears.

Ijada was unusually pale and withdrawn this morning, with gray smudges under her eyes. Her smile, returning his curt nod, was brief and muted. Was she finally coming to realize that she rode into a trap? Too late?

"We cannot continue to flounder along with no attempt at a plan," he began firmly. "You've rejected mine. Have you a better?"

"*Run away* was not my idea of a *plan*." She cocked an eye at him. "And when did *I* become *we*?"

His mouth, tightening, paused. *The first hour I saw you at Boar's Head, five gods help me.* "In the upstairs room of that inn at Red Dike," he answered instead.

She tilted her head in a conciliating nod.

"We share a certain problem apart from your legal morass," he continued. "Cat maiden."

"Oh, it's not apart. Dog lord."

Despite himself, his lips twisted up in return. Did he truly smile so little, that his mouth should feel so odd doing this? "Earl Horseriver has promised this much to shield you. He told me this morning that you are to be lodged in a house in the capital that he owns, with his servants about you. Better than some dank cell down by the river, and a sign, I think, that your destruction is not yet set in train. There may be a little time."

"He means to keep me close," she said thoughtfully.

"At Wencel's request, Lord Hetwar has appointed me your house warden for this arrest." No need to mention how his breath had skipped at this unexpected stroke of good fortune. "Judging by the note his courier brought me, Hetwar is glad enough to have you kept out of sight for a time."

Her eyes flew up. "Wencel means to keep us both close, then. Why?"

"I judge . . ." his voice slowed, uncertain. "I judge he is a little off-balance, just now. So much is happening at once, with the funeral and his distraught wife, atop the roil already with the hallow king's illness and—the Mother avert, but it seems most probable—the impending election. Biast and his retinue will be arriving in Easthome, and the prince will certainly draw his brother-in-law into the concerns of his party. Beneath that lie Wencel's other uncanny secrets, old and new. If Wencel can make one piece of his puzzle hold still till he has time to attend to it, well, so much the better. For him. As for me, I don't intend to hold still."

"What do you intend?"

"I've had one idea, so far. If, as I suspect, more than one power in Easthome would like to see your trial suppressed, this scandal swept quietly aside, it might even be accepted. Your kin might call on the old kin-law, and offer a blood-price for Prince Boleso."

She inhaled, brows climbing in surprise. "Will the Temple care to have its justiciars excluded from so high a case?"

"If the highest lords of kin Stagthorne and kin Badgerbank agree, the divines of the Father's Order will have no choice. There lies my first doubt, for the king is unfit to accept any proposal; at the time I left Easthome, Hetwar was uncertain that the old man had even been made to understand that Boleso had, um, met his death. Biast, once he arrives, will be half-prepared and wholly distracted. Clear decisions from the Court at Easthome have been hard to come by, these past weeks, and it will likely get worse before it gets better. But Earl-ordainer Badgerbank is no small power in his own right. If he could be convinced, for the honor of his house, to sponsor you, and Wencel urged to help persuade him, the scheme might have a chance."

"A prince's blood-price could be no small sum. Far beyond my poor stepfather's means."

"It would have to come from Badgerbank's purse. With Wencel, perhaps, helping fill it on the left hand."

"Have you met Earl Badgerbank? I did not think he had the reputation as a generous man."

"Um . . ." Ingrey hesitated, then answered honestly, "no, he doesn't." He glanced across at her, riding in the warming morning light. "But if the money—"

"Bribe?" she muttered.

"—were raised elsewhere, I think there would be less trouble coaxing him to lend his name. Your dower lands— how large are they?"

Her voice grew oddly reluctant. "They run for some thirty miles east and west along the roots of the Raven Range, and twenty miles north up to the rim of the watershed with the Cantons."

Ingrey blinked, taken aback. "That is rather larger than you led me to picture. A forested tract is no small resource; it may yield up game, timber, charcoal, mast for pigs, perhaps a great prize of minerals beneath . . . you have nearly the price of a prince right there, I think! How many villages or hamlets are to be found there, how many hearths in the tax census?"

"None. Not in those lands. No one hunts there. No one goes in."

The sudden tension in her tone arrested him. "Why not?"

She shrugged, unconvincingly. "They are accursed. Haunted woods, whispering woods. The Wounded Woods, they are called, and indeed, the trees seem sick. All who enter are plagued by nightmares of blood and death, they say."

"Tales," Ingrey scoffed.

"I went in," Ijada replied steadily. "After my mother died, and it was at last made clear that the tract had indeed come to me. I went to see for myself, for I believed I had the right. And duty. The forester was reluctant to escort me, but I made him. My stepfather's grooms and my maid were terrified. For a full day we rode in, then made a camp. Most of the land is raw and steep, all ravines and abrupt cliffs, briars and stones poking through, and gloomy hollows. At the center is one broad, flat valley, filled with great oak trees, centuries old. That is the darkest part, said to be the most haunted, a cursed shrine of the Old Weald. Local legend says it is lost Bloodfield itself, for all that two other earldoms along the Ravens claim that doubtful honor."

"Many old shrine sites have become farmers' fields, in time."

"Not this one. We slept there that night, much against the will of my escort. And indeed, we dreamed. The grooms dreamed of being torn apart by animals, and woke screaming. My maid dreamed that she drowned in blood. Come morning, they were all wild to get away."

Ingrey considered her words. And then he considered her silences. "But you were not?"

She hesitated so long this time he almost asked again, but held his tongue. His patience was rewarded at length when she murmured, "We all dreamed. It took me some time to realize that my dream was different."

Silences, he reminded himself, had a power all their own. He waited some more. She regarded him under her lashes, as if gauging his tolerance for further tales of the uncanny.

She began, he thought, obliquely. "Have you ever witnessed an almsgiver mobbed by famished beggars? How they gather in a vast swirl, each one weak, but in their numbers strong and frightening, frantic? *Give to us, give, for we starve* . . . Yet however much you gave, all that you had, it would not be enough; they might tear you apart and devour you without being satisfied."

He granted her a wary nod, uncertain where this was tending.

"In my dream . . . men came to me out of the trees. Bloody-handed men, many headless, in the rusted armor of the Old Weald. Some bore animal standards, the skulls all decorated about with colored stones, or wore capes of skins; stag and bear, horse and wolf, badger and otter, boar and lynx and ox and I know not what else. Faceless, blurred, horribly hacked. They raved around me in a great begging crowd, as though I were their queen, or liege-lady, come to spread some strange largesse among them. I could not understand their language, and their signs bewildered me. I was not afraid of them, for all they pawed my garments with rotting hands until my dress was soaked in cold black blood. They wanted something of me. I could not make out what it was. But I knew they were *owed* it."

"A terrifying dream," he said, in the most detached voice he could muster.

"I did not fear them. But they split my heart."

"Were they so pitiful?"

"No—I mean—really. Or not really, but in my dream—I parted my ribs, and reached into my chest, and brought out my beating heart and presented it to the revenant I took to be their captain. He was one of the headless ones—his head, in its helm, was fastened to his broad gold belt, and he bore a standard with its banner tight-furled. He bowed low, and placed my heart upon a stone slab, and cut it in two with the hilt-shard of his broken sword. Half he handed back to me again, with a sign of great respect. The other half, they raised high upon the standard's point, and they cried out again. I did not understand if it was pledge, or sacrifice, or ransom, or what, until . . ." She stopped, swallowed.

Began again. "Until Wencel said those words last night. *Banner-carrier.* I had half forgotten the dream, in the press of more recent woes, but at those words the memory of it slammed back, so vivid it was like a blow—I don't think you know how close I came to fainting."

"I . . . no. To me, you just looked interested."

She gave a relieved nod. "Good."

"And so what new thing do you make of your dream as a result?"

"I thought . . . I think . . . I think now the dead warriors made me their banner-carrier, that night." Her right hand rose from her rein to her left breast, and spread there in the sacred gesture; he thought the fingers clutched in a tiny spasm. "And I was suddenly reminded that the heart is the sign and signifier of the Son of Autumn. The heart for courage. And loyalty. And love."

Ingrey had tried to wrench their thoughts to shrewd politics, to good, solid, reasonable, practical plans. How had he stepped hip deep into the eerie once again? "It was but a dream. How long ago?'"

"Some months. The others could not wait to break camp and gallop home, next morning, but I rode slowly, looking back."

"What did you see?"

"Nothing." Her brows drew in, as if in remembered pain. "Nothing but trees. The others feared that country, but it drew my heart. I wanted to return to the woods, alone if no escort would come, and try again to understand. But before I could slip away, I was sent to Earl Horseriver's household, and, well." Her glance at him intensified. "But the Wounded Woods cannot be sold."

"Surely someone might be found who does not know their local reputation."

She shook her head. "You don't understand."

"What, are the lands entailed to you?"

"No."

"Already pledged for debt?"

"No! Nor shall they be. How would I ever redeem them?" She laughed mirthlessly. "No great marriage, or likely, any marriage, looms in my future now; and I have no other prospects of inheritance."

"But if it might save your life, Ijada—"

"You don't understand. Five gods help me, *I* don't understand. But . . . they laid the woods into my charge, the dead men. I cannot lay that charge down until my men are . . . paid."

"Paid? What coin can ghosts desire? Or hallucinations, as the case may be," he added testily.

She grimaced in frustration, and with a little slice of her hand batted down his doubting shot. "I don't know. But they wanted *something*."

"Then I shall just have to find another way," Ingrey muttered. *Or return to this argument later.*

Now it was her turn to stare thoughtfully at him. "And what plans have you made to seek out the source of your geas?"

"None, yet," he admitted. "Though after, um, Red Dike, I think no such thing could be laid upon me again without my seeing it. Resisting it." Stung by the doubtful quirk of her eyebrows, he added more sternly, "I plan to be on my guard, and look about me."

"I did wonder . . . are you so certain I was its true target? Perhaps, instead of you being a means to destroy me, I was just a means to destroy you. Whom have you offended?"

Ingrey's frown deepened at this unwelcome thought. "Many men. It's my calling. But I always figured an enemy would just send paid bravos."

"Do you think the average bravo would be inclined to take you on?"

His lips lifted a little at this. "They might have to raise the price."

Her lips curved, too. "Perhaps your unknown enemy is a pinch-purse, then. The bounty for a wild wolf warrior might be too steep for him."

Ingrey chuckled. "My reputation is more lurid than my sword arm can sustain, I'm afraid. An adversary has merely to send enough men, or shoot from behind in the dark. Easily enough done. Men alone are not hard to kill, despite our swagger."

"Indeed," she murmured bleakly, and Ingrey cursed his careless tongue. After a moment, she added, "It's still a good question, though. What would have happened to you if the geas had worked as planned?"

Ingrey shrugged. "Disgraced. Dismissed from Hetwar's service. Maybe hanged. Our drowning would have passed as an accident, true. Some several men might have been happy that I'd relieved them of a dilemma, but I should not have looked to them for gratitude."

"But it would be safe to say you'd have been removed as a force in the capital."

"I'm no force in the capital. I'm just one of Hetwar's more dubious servants."

"Such a charitable man Hetwar is to sponsor you, then."

Ingrey's lips opened, closed. "Mm."

"When I first saw Wencel's beast, my mind leapt to him as the possible source of your geas. Still more so, when he revealed its mystery. He as much as said he fancied himself a shaman."

You thought it, too? Ijada, Ingrey reminded himself, had never known Wencel as a small, slow child. But did that leave her to overestimate, or Ingrey to underestimate, his cousin?

Ijada continued, "But in that case, I do not understand why we were both allowed to leave his house alive today."

"That would have been too crude," said Ingrey. "A hired assassin is always his own witness, but the geas would have left none. The spell-caster, Wencel or not, desired greater subtlety. Presumably." He frowned in renewed doubt.

"He was never a comfortable man, but this new Wencel scares me to death."

"Well, he does not me." Ingrey's mouth and mind froze as he was suddenly reminded of how close he'd come to death at his own hand, not twelve hours past. A subtle enough death to pass unquestioned even under Wencel's roof? *It was no geas that time, though. I did it to myself. After Wencel cried wolf at me . . .*

"Now what makes you grow grim?" Ijada demanded.

"Nothing."

Her lips twisted in exasperation. "To be sure."

After a few more minutes of riding in silence, she added, "*I* want to know what else Wencel knows of Bloodfield—or Holytree, as he called it—if he's such a scholar of the Old

Weald as he claims. Tax him on it, if—when—you speak again. But do not tell him of my dream."

Ingrey nodded agreement. "Had you ever discussed your legacy with him?"

"Never."

"With Princess Fara?"

Ijada hesitated. "Only in terms of its value, or lack of it, as a bride-piece."

Ingrey drummed his fingers on the thigh of his riding leathers. "It must·have been but a dream. Most souls would have been taken up by the gods at the hour of their deaths, whether your woods were Bloodfield or some lesser Wealding defeat. Any sundered who refused the gods would have blurred to oblivion centuries ago, or so the divines taught me. Four hundred years is far too long for ghosts to survive so entire."

"I saw what I saw." Her tone neither offered nor requested rationalizations.

"Maybe that's what the addition of animal spirits does to men's souls," Ingrey continued in a spurt of inspiration. "Instead of dissolution, damnation becomes an eternal, cold, and silent torment. Trapped between matter and spirit. All the pain of death lingering, all the joy of life stripped away . . ." He swallowed in sudden fear.

Ijada's gaze grew distant, looking down the winding road. "I trust not. The warriors were worn and tormented, but not joyless, for they took joy in me, I thought." Her eyes, turning toward him, crinkled a little at the edges. "A moment ago, you said it must be a dream, but now you take it for truth, and your doom foreshadowed. You can't have it both ways, however delightfully glum piling up the prospects makes you."

Ingrey was surprised into a snort; his lips curled up at the sides, just a little bit. He yanked them back straight. "So which do you think it is?"

"I think . . ." she said slowly, "that if I could go back *now,* I would know." Her lids lowered briefly, and the next look she gave him seemed to weigh him. "I think you might, too."

They were interrupted then by a crowd on the road, some kin-lord's entourage from Easthome traveling to the funereal duty at Oxmeade. Ingrey motioned his men aside, scanning the mob of outriders for faces he recognized. He saw a few, and exchanged brief, sober salutes. Boarford's men, and therefore the two brother-earls and their wives sheltered in the tapestry-covered wagon that jounced along the ruts. Almost immediately thereafter, Ingrey's troop had to make way again for a procession of Temple-men, lord dedicats and high divines, richly dressed and well mounted.

When they had all sorted themselves out once more, Ingrey found Gesca's horse pressed up to his side, and the lieutenant favoring him with a mistrustful scowl. Ingrey spurred forward, and led on at a more rapid pace.

IO

THEY CRESTED THE RANGE OF LOW HILLS NORTHEAST OF the capital in the late afternoon. The town and the broad southern plains beyond spread out before their gaze. The river Stork curled away from the town's foot in a bright silver line, growing more crooked until lost in the autumn haze. A few boats, merchant craft, sculled laboriously up or drifted down its length, making their way from or to the cold sea some eighty miles distant. As Ingrey reined back beside her, Ijada rose in her stirrups and stared.

He studied her expression, which was part fascinated, part wary. Easthome might well be the largest city she'd seen in her life, for all that perhaps a dozen Darthacan provincial seats eclipsed it, and the Darthacan royal capital could have held it six times over.

"The town is divided into two halves, Templetown and Kingstown," Ingrey told her. "The upper town, on those high bluffs, holds the temple, the archdivine's palace, and all the offices of the holy orders. The lower town has the warehouses and the merchants' quarters. You can see the wharves beyond the wall, where the drainage runs out to join the Stork. The hallow king's hall and most of the kin-lords' houses are on the opposite end from the docks." His hand swept out the sections. "Easthome used to be two villages, back in the old days, belonging to two different tribes. They feuded and fought across the creek that divided them till it ran with blood, they say, practically up to the time Audar's grandson seized the place for his western capital, and stamped out all division with his new stonework. You can scarcely see the creek now, it is so built across. And no one now chooses to die for the sake of a sewer. Hetwar told me this tale; he takes it for a parable, but I'm not sure what he thinks the moral is."

The cavalcade descended the road to the easternmost gate on the Kingstown side. The stonework was good, it was true, the winding streets lined by high houses of tan blocks or whitewashed stucco, with glints of glass windows peering out from deep-browed embrasures. Red-tile roofs replaced wattle and flammable thatch; ordinary fires had probably destroyed more of the old twin towns than war. The defending walls were even more improved, although crowded with new building lapping too near and spilling beyond, compromising their purpose.

They came at length to a narrow curving street in the merchants' quarter, and dismounted before a slim stone house in a row of several such built abutting one another, though obviously at different times by different masons. Ingrey wondered if Horseriver owned not just this house but the row, and if such lucrative property had come to him with Princess Fara. The house was neither so rich nor so large as last night's lodging, but it appeared decent enough, quiet and close.

Ingrey dismounted and passed his and Ijada's horses to Gesca's care.

"Tell my lord Hetwar I will report to him as soon as I see the prisoner secured. Send me my manservant Tesko, if you find him sober, with what things I am likely to need for the next few days. Clean clothes, for one." Ingrey grimaced, stretching his aching back; his leathers reeked of horse and the grime of the road, and the stitches in his scalp were itching again, maddeningly. Ijada, stripping off her riding gloves and craning her neck, managed somehow to appear nearly as trim and cool as she had that morning.

The house's porter saw them inside; the woman warden-servant, guided by a housemaid, marshaled Ijada at once up the stairs, her leather-strapped case hoisted after by the porter's boy. Ingrey set down his saddlebags and stared around the narrow hall.

The porter ducked his head nervously. "The boy will be back in a moment to take you to your room, my lord."

Ingrey grunted, and said, "No hurry. If this place is to be my charge, I had best look it over." He prowled off through the nearest doorway.

The house seemed simple enough. The cellar and the ground floor were devoted to storage, a kitchen with antechamber and pallets for cook and scullion, an eating hall, a parlor, and a cubby under the stairs where the porter lurked. Ingrey poked his head out the only other outer door, which led to a back court with a covered well. The second floor included what might have been meant for a study, as well as two bedrooms. Passing the door of similar chambers on the next floor up, Ingrey heard the murmur of women's voices, Ijada and her warden. The top floor was divided up into smaller rooms for the servants.

He descended again to find the porter's boy lugging his saddlebags into one of the bedrooms on the second floor. The furnishings were sparse—narrow bed, washstand, a single chair, a battered wardrobe—and Ingrey wondered if the place had been tenanted or not before Horseriver's couriers had arrived last night demanding its possession. Light, distinctive footsteps and the creaking of, perhaps, a bed overhead marked Ijada's location. The proximity was both reassuring and unsettling. When he heard her steps on the stairs, he turned for the hall.

She had her hand raised to knock on his door as he opened it. In the other, she held Learned Hallana's letter, a little crumpled now. Her warden—or was that, Wencel's warden?—hovered behind her, peering suspiciously.

"Lord Ingrey," she said, reverting to formality. "Learned Hallana charged you to deliver this. Will you do so?" Her level eyes seemed to bore into his, silently reminding him of the rest of the sorceress's words: *to its destination, and no other.*

He took it, glancing at the scrawled direction. "Do you know who this"—he peered more closely—"Learned Lewko may be?"

"No. But if Hallana trusts him, he must be worthy of it, and no fool."

What does that prove? Hallana trusted me. And a Temple-man neither foolish nor untrue might yet be no friend to the defiled.

Still, Ingrey remained deathly curious as to what Hallana had reported of him, and of the strange events at Red Dike. The only way he might find out short of opening the letter himself was to be there when it was opened. And if he delivered it on his way to Hetwar's palace, he would be relieved of any possible need to conceal it or lie about it to his master. Hetwar could not demand it of him then. If chided, Ingrey could feign its faithful delivery was just the sort of virtuous act Hetwar might properly expect of his henchman.

"Yes. I will undertake the charge."

Ijada nodded intently, and he wondered if she read his corkscrew thoughts in his eyes, or not: or if she judged him as blithely as Hallana had.

He added, "Stay in; stay safe. Lock your inner doors as well. I presume whatever comforts this house may offer are yours for the asking." He let his eye fall on the servant-warden, and she made a circumspect curtsey of acknowledgment. "I don't know what else Lord Hetwar may want of me tonight, so eat when you will. I'll be back as soon as I can."

He tucked the letter in his jerkin, bowed her a polite farewell, and made his way down the stairs. He wanted a bath, clean clothes, and a meal, in that order, but all such niceties would have to wait.

Leaving instructions with the porter for his servant,

should Tesko arrive before he returned, Ingrey walked out into the town.

Familiar smells and sights subtly reassured him. He wound his way through the cobbled streets of Kingstown and across the half-buried creek, then climbed the steep steps up the near cliff of the temple side. Two switchbacks and a breathless ten minutes brought him to the stair-gate, winding crookedly under a tower and two houses, into the upper town. In the dark corner where the passage turned, a little shrine for the safety of the city stood, a few candles flickering in the dim drafts flanked by wilted garlands; reflexively, Ingrey made the fivefold sign in passing. He came out again into the early-evening light and turned right.

A few more minutes' walk brought him to the main square before the temple. He strode under the pillared front portico and into the sacred precincts.

The central court was open to the air, and in its middle the holy fire burned quietly on its plinth. Through an archway into one of the five great stone domes surrounding it, Ingrey could see a ceremony beginning—a funeral, he realized, for he could glimpse a bier, surrounded by shuffling mourners, being set down before the Father's altar. In a few days, Prince Boleso's body, too, would pass through these rites here.

On the other side of the court, the acolyte-grooms were marshaling their sacred animals for the little miracle of the choosing. Each creature, led by its handler dressed in the color of his or her order, would be presented before the bier, and the divine would interpret by its actions which god had taken up the soul of the recent dead. This not only guided the prayers of the mourners, but also their more material offerings, to the altar and the order of the proper god. Ingrey would be more cynical about this, but that he had more than once seen results clearly unexpected to all parties involved.

A woman in Mother's greens had a large green bird, which cawed nervously, perched upon her shoulder. A maiden in Daughter's blue held a young hen with purple-blue feathers tightly under her arm. An immensely fluffy gray dog cowered close to the gray robes of an elderly groom of the Father's Order. A young man in the reds and browns of the Son led a skittish chestnut colt, its coat brushed to a shimmering copper and its eyes rolling whitely. The animal snorted and sidled, yanking its groom almost off his feet, and in a moment, Ingrey saw why.

Pacing slowly after the others loomed the most enormous white ice bear Ingrey had ever seen. The thing was as tall as a pony, and as wide as two. Its narrow eyes were the color of frozen urine, and about as expressive. At the far end of a long, thick silver chain, its handler followed, dressed in the white robes of the Bastard's Order. The young man bore an expression of suppressed terror, and his head swiveled a little frantically between his charge and a towering man who followed after, murmuring encouragement.

The man was nearly as arresting as the bear. He was broad-shouldered to match his height, with hair in a dense red horsetail down his back. Thick silver clamps held it in place, and thick silver bracelets clanked on his arms. Bright blue eyes held an expression of amiable bemusement which Ingrey was not sure whether to take as acuity or vacuity. His clothes—tunic, trousers, a swinging coat—were simple enough in cut, but colorfully dyed and decorated with elaborate embroidery. Big boots were stamped with silver designs, and the hilt of his long sword glittered with crudely cut gems. In the belt sheath at his back rested not a knife, but an ax, also elaborately inlaid, its blade gleaming razor-honed.

A brown-haired man in similar but less gaudy dress, a good head shorter than his fellow yet still tall, leaned against a pillar with his arms folded, watching the proceedings with a most dubious expression. Some of the grooms shot him looks of supplication, which he steadfastly ignored.

Ingrey tore his attention from this peculiar drama as he saw an older woman in the white-and-cream robes of the Bastard, the loops of a divine's braid bouncing on her shoulder and her arms laden with folded cloth, scurry through the court, evidently intent upon some shortcut. Ingrey barely caught her sleeve as she sped past. She jerked to a halt and eyed him unfavorably.

"Excuse me, Learned. I carry a letter for one Learned Lewko, which I am charged to deliver into his hand."

Her expression altered at once into something, if not more friendly, much more interested. She looked him up and down; indeed, he imagined he looked the part of a road-weary courier, just now.

"Come with me, then," she said, and abruptly reversed direction. Though Ingrey's legs were longer than hers, he had to stretch his stride to keep up.

She led him through a discreet side entry, down and up some steps, back outside behind the temple, and past the archdivine's palace into the next street. Down one more narrow alley they came to a long stone building some two stories high, passed through a side door, and wended up more stairs. Ingrey began to be grateful he hadn't just asked for directions. They passed a succession of well-lit rooms devoted to scriptoria, judging by the heads bent over tables and scratching of quills.

Coming to a closed door in the same row, she knocked, and a man's calm voice bade, "Enter."

The door swung open on a narrower room, or perhaps that was an illusion created by the contents. Crammed shelves lined the chamber, and a pair of tables overflowed with books, papers, scrolls, and a great deal of more miscellaneous litter. A saddle sat propped on its pommel in one corner.

The man, sitting in a chair beyond one table near the window, looked up from the sheaf of papers he was reading and raised his brows. He, too, was dressed in Bastard's whites, but the robes were slightly shabby and without any mark of rank upon them. He was middle-aged, spare, perhaps a little taller than Ingrey, clean-shaven, with sandy-gray hair trimmed short. Ingrey would have taken him for some important man's clerk or secretary, except that the woman divine pressed her hand to her lips and bowed her head in a gesture of utmost respect before she spoke again.

"Learned, here is a man with a letter for you." She glanced up at Ingrey. "Your name, sir?"

"Ingrey kin Wolfcliff."

No special reaction or recognition showed in her face, but the spare man's brows notched a trifle higher. "Thank you, Marda," he said, polite dismissal clear in his tone. She touched her lips again and withdrew, shutting the door behind Ingrey.

"The Learned Hallana instructed me to deliver this letter to you," said Ingrey, stepping to the table and handing it over.

Learned Lewko set down his sheaf of papers rather abruptly and sat up to take it. "Hallana! Not ill news, I trust?"

"Not . . . that is, she was well when I last saw her."

Lewko eyed the missive more warily. "Is it complicated?"

Ingrey considered his answer. "She did not show me the contents. But I expect so."

Lewko sighed. "As long as it's not another ice bear. I don't think she would gift me with an ice bear. I hope."

Ingrey was briefly diverted. "I saw an ice bear in the temple court, as I came in. It was, um, most impressive."

"It is utterly horrifying, *I* think. The grooms were weeping. Bastard forfend, are they actually trying to use it in a funeral?"

"So it appeared."

"We should have just told the prince *thank you*, and put it in a menagerie. Somewhere out in the country."

"How did it come here?"

"By surprise. Also by boat."

"How big was the *boat*?"

Lewko grinned at Ingrey's tone, and looked suddenly younger thereby. "I saw it yesterday, tied up at the wharf below Kingstown. Not *nearly* as big as one would think." He ran a hand through his hair. "The beast was a gift, or perhaps a bribe. Brought by this giant red hairy fellow from some island on the frozen side of the south sea, who is either a prince, or a pirate—it is hard to be sure. Prince Jokol, fondly nicknamed by his loyal crew Jokol Skullsplitter, I am informed. I didn't think those white bears could be tamed, but he seems to have made a pet of this one since it was a cub, which makes the gift even more dear, I suppose. I cannot imagine what the voyage was like; they say they met storms. I suspect he is quite mad. In any case, he also brought several large ingots of high-grade silver for the bear's upkeep, which apparently robbed the temple menagerie-master of the wits to refuse the gift. Or bribe."

"Bribe for what?"

"The Skullsplitter wants a divine, to carry off to his glacier-ridden island in place of his bear. This is a fine work of missionary duty that any divine should be proud to undertake. Volunteers have been called for. Twice. If none steps forth by the time the prince is ready to cast off again, one will simply have to be found. Dragged from under a bed, perhaps." His grin flickered again. "I can afford to laugh; they can't send *me*. Ah, well." He sighed once more and set the letter before him on the table, with the wax seal uppermost. He bent his head over it.

The amusement drained from Ingrey, and he came alert. His blood—*that* blood—seemed to spin up like a vortex. Lewko did not bear the braid of a sorcerer, he did not *smell* of a demon, and yet Temple sorcerers answered to him . . . ? Threw their most complicated dilemmas in his lap?

Lewko laid his hand across the wax seal, and his eyes closed briefly. Something flared about him. It was nothing Ingrey saw with his eyes or smelled with his nose, but it made the hair stir at the nape of his neck. He'd felt a trace of this stomach-wrenching awe once before, from a stronger source, but with inner senses at the time much weaker. At the end of his futile pilgrimage to Darthaca, in the presence of a small, stout, harried fellow, to all appearances ordinary, who sat down quietly and let a god reach through him into the world of matter.

Lewko's not a sorcerer. He's a saint, or petty saint. And he knew who Ingrey was, and he had seemingly been here at the temple for years, judging by the state of his study, but Ingrey had never seen—or was that, noticed?—him before. Certainly not in the company of any of the high Temple divines who waited upon the sealmaster or the king's court, all of whom Ingrey had dutifully memorized.

Lewko glanced up; there was not much humor in his eyes now. "You are Sealmaster Hetwar's man, are you not?" he inquired mildly.

Ingrey nodded.

"This letter has been opened."

"Not by me, Learned."

"Who, then?"

Ingrey's mind sped back. From Hallana to Ijada to him . . . Ijada? Surely not. Had it ever been out of her possession, parted from her bosom? It had rested in that inner pocket of the riding habit, which she had worn . . . all but at the dinner at Earl Horseriver's. And Wencel had left the table to receive an urgent message . . . *indeed.* Easy enough for the earl to overawe and suborn that warden to rifle Ijada's luggage, but had Wencel thought to use some shaman trick to fool a sorcerer about his prying? *But Lewko is not a sorcerer, now, is he. Not exactly.* Ingrey temporized: "Without proof, any guess of mine would be but slander, Learned."

Lewko's look grew uncomfortably penetrating, but to Ingrey's relief he dropped his eyes to the letter again. "Well, let us see," he muttered, and stripped it open, scattering wax.

He read intently for a few minutes, then shook his head and stood to lean nearer to the window. Twice, he turned the closely written paper sideways. Once, he glanced across at Ingrey and inquired rather plaintively, "Does the phrase *broke his chants* mean anything to you?"

"Um, could that be, *chains*?" Ingrey ventured.

Lewko brightened. "Ah! Yes, it could! That makes much more sense." He read on. "Or perhaps it doesn't . . ."

Lewko came to the end, frowned, and started over. He waved vaguely toward a wall. "I believe there is a camp stool under that pile. Help yourself, Lord Ingrey."

By the time Ingrey had extracted it, snapped it open, and perched himself upon its leather seat, Lewko looked up again.

"I pity the spy who had to decipher this," he said, without heat.

"Is it in code?"

"No: Hallana's handwriting. Written in haste, I deem. It takes practice—which I grant I have—to unravel. Well, I've suffered worse for less reward. Not from Hallana, she always touches the essential. One of her several uncomfortable talents. That demure smile masks a holy recklessness. And ruthlessness. The Father be thanked for Oswin's moderating influence. Such as it is."

"You know her well?" Ingrey inquired. *Or, why does this paragon write to you, alone of all the Temple functionaries in Easthome?*

Lewko rolled the letter and tapped it gently on the edge of the table. "I was assigned to be her mentor, many years ago, when she so unexpectedly became a sorceress."

Surely it took one sorcerer to teach another. Therefore and therefore . . . Like a stone across the water, Ingrey's mind skipped two begged questions to arrive at a third. "How does a man become a former sorcerer? Undamaged?" It was the task of that Darthacan saint to destroy illicit sorcerers, who were reported to fight like madmen against the amputation of their powers, but Learned Lewko had surely not been such a renegade.

"It is possible to lay down the gift." Lewko's mouth hovered between faint amusement and faint regret. "If one chooses to in time."

"Is it not a wrench?"

"I didn't say it was easy. In fact"—his voice softened still further—"it takes a miracle."

What *was* this man? "I have served four years here in Easthome. I'm surprised our paths have not crossed before."

"But they have. In a sense. I am very familiar with your case, Lord Ingrey."

Ingrey stiffened, especially at Lewko's choice of words: *case*. "Were you the Temple sorcerer sent to Birchgrove with the inquiry to examine me?" He frowned. "My memories of that time are confused and dark, but I do not remember you."

"No, that was another man. My involvement at the time was less direct. The inquirer brought me a bag of ashes from the castle, to turn back into a letter of confession."

Ingrey's brow wrinkled. "Isn't that what I believe Learned Hallana would call a bit uphill for Temple magic? Chaos forced back to order?"

"Indeed and alas, it was. It cost me a month's work and probably a year of my calling. And all for very little, as it turned out, to my fury. What do you remember of Learned Cumril? The young Temple sorcerer whom your father suborned?"

Ingrey stiffened still further. "From an acquaintance lasting the space of an hour's meal and a quarter of an hour's rite, not much. All his attention was on my father. I was an afterthought." He added truculently, "And how do you know who suborned whom, after all?"

"That much was clear. Less clear was how. Not for money. I think not for threats. There was a reason—Cumril imagined himself doing something good, or at least heroic, that went horribly awry."

"How can you guess his heart when you don't even know what his mind was about?"

"Oh, that part I don't have to guess. It was in his letter. Once I'd reassembled it. A three-page screed descanting upon his woe, guilt, and remorse. And scarcely one useful fact that we didn't already know." Lewko grimaced.

"If Cumril wrote the confession, who burned it?" asked Ingrey.

"Now, that *is* a guess of mine." Lewko leaned back in his chair, eyeing Ingrey shrewdly. "And yet I am surer of it than many an assertion for which I had more material proof. Do you understand the difference between a sorcerer who rides his demon, and one who is ridden?"

"Hallana spoke of it. It seemed subtle."

"Not from the inside. The difference is very clear. The gulf between a man who uses a power for his purposes, and a power that uses a man for its purposes, is . . . sometimes less than an ant's stride across. I know. I rode dangerously close to that line myself, once. It is my belief, after the debacle that left your father dead and you . . . well, as you are, Cumril was taken by his demon. Whether despair made him weak, whether he was overmatched from the first, I can't now guess, but I believe in my heart that the writing of that confession was Cumril's last act. And the burning of it, the demon's first."

Ingrey opened his mouth, then closed it. In his mind, he had always cast Cumril in the part of betrayer; it was uncomfortable to consider that the young sorcerer, too, might have been in some strange sense betrayed.

"So you see," said Lewko softly, "Cumril's fate concerns me. More, it *nags* me. I fear I cannot encounter you without being reminded of it."

"Did the Temple ever find out if he was alive or dead?"

"No. There was a report of an illicit sorcerer in the Cantons some five years ago that might have been him, but all trace was lost thereafter."

Ingrey's lips started to shape the word *Who* . . . but he changed it: "What *are* you?"

Lewko's hand opened. "Just a simple Temple overseer, now."

Of what? Of all the Temple sorcerers of the Weald, perhaps? *Just* seemed scarcely the word for it, nor did *simple. This man could be very dangerous to me,* Ingrey reminded himself. *He knows too much already.*

And he was about to learn more, unfortunately, for he glanced down at the paper and asked Ingrey to describe the events at Red Dike. No great surprise; Ingrey had certainly guessed those at least would be in the letter.

Ingrey did so, honestly and completely, but in as few words as he could coherently muster. Disaster was in the details, every spare sentence skirting a morass of more questions. But his stiff little speech seemed to satisfy the divine, or at least, questions about the restraint of Ingrey's wolf did not immediately arise.

"Who do you think placed this murderous compulsion, this strange scarlet geas, upon you, Lord Ingrey?"

"I very much wish to know."

"Well, that makes two of us."

"I am glad of that," said Ingrey, and was surprised to realize it was true.

Then Lewko asked, "What do *you* think of this Lady Ijada?"

Ingrey swallowed, his mind seeming to spiral down like a bird shot out of the air. *He asked me what I think about her, not what I feel about her,* he reminded himself firmly. "She undoubtedly bashed Boleso's head in. He undoubtedly deserved it."

A silence seemed to stretch from this succinct obituary. Did Lewko, too, understand the uses of silences? "My lord Hetwar did not desire all these posthumous scandals," Ingrey added. "I think he has even less than your relish for complications."

More silence. "She sustains the leopard spirit. It is . . . lovely in her." *Five gods, I must say something to protect her.* "I think she is more god-touched than she knows."

That won a response. Lewko sat up, his eyes suddenly cooler and more intent. "How do you know?"

Ingrey's chin rose at the hint of challenge. "The same way I know that you are, Blessed One. I feel it in my blood."

The jolt between them then made Ingrey certain he'd overstepped. But Lewko eased back in his chair, deliberately tenting his hands. "Truly?"

"I am not a complete fool, Learned."

"I do not think you are a fool at all, Lord Ingrey." Lewko tapped his fingers on the letter, looked away for a moment, then looked back. "Yes. I shall obey my Hallana's marching orders and examine this young woman, I think. Where is she being held?"

"More housed than held, so far." Ingrey gave directions to the slim house in the merchants' quarter.

"When is she to be bound over to stand her indictment?"

"I would guess not till after Boleso's funeral, since it is so near. I'll know more once I speak with Sealmaster Hetwar. Where I am obliged by my duty to go next," Ingrey added by way of a broad hint. Yes—he needed to escape this room before Lewko's questions grew even more probing. He stood up.

"I shall try to come tomorrow," said Lewko, yielding to this move.

Ingrey managed a polite, "Thank you. I shall look for you then," a bow, and his removal from the room without, he trusted, looking as though he were running like a rabbit.

He closed the door behind himself and blew out his breath in unease. Was this Lewko potential help or potential harm? He remembered Wencel's parting words to him: *If you value your life, keep your secrets and mine.* Had that been a threat, or a warning?

He had at least managed to keep all mention of Horseriver from this first interview. There could be no hint of Wencel in the letter; his cousin had not impinged on Ingrey's life until after Hallana had been left behind, thankfully. But what about tomorrow? What about half an hour from now, when he stood in his road dirt before Hetwar to report his journey and its incidents?

Horseriver. Hallana. Gesca. Now Lewko. Hetwar. Ingrey was starting to lose track of what all he had not said to whom.

He found the correct direction and began to retrace his steps back to the shortcut through the temple, keeping the cadence of his footfalls deliberate.

It struck him only then that in delivering Hallana's letter to Lewko, he had also, without any need for spell or geas, delivered up himself.

II

AS INGREY MADE HIS WAY UP THE CORRIDOR TOWARD THE side entrance of the temple court, a cry of dismay echoed along the walls. His steps quickened in curiosity, then alarm, as the cry was succeeded by a scream. Frightened shouts erupted. His hand gripped the hilt of his sword as he burst into the central area, his head swiveling in search of the source of the uproar.

A bizarre melee was pouring out of the archway to the Father's court. Foremost was the great ice bear. Clamped in its jaws was the foot of the deceased man, an aged fellow dressed in clothes befitting a wealthy merchant, the stiff corpse bouncing along like some huge doll as the bear growled and shook its head. At the end of the silver chain hooked to the bear's collar, the groom-acolyte swung in a wide and stumbling arc. Some of the braver or more distraught mourners pelted after, shouting advice and demands.

His voice nearly squeaking, the panicked groom advanced on the bear, yanking the chain, then grabbing for the corpse's arm and pulling. The bear half rose, and one heavy paw lashed out; the groom staggered back, screaming in earnest now, clutching his side from which red drops spattered.

Ingrey drew his blade and ran forward, skidding to a stop before the maddened beast. From the corner of his eye he could see Prince Jokol, grasped in a restraining hug from behind by his companion, struggling toward him. "No, no, no!" cried the red-haired man in a voice of anguish. "Fafa only thought they were offering him a *meal*! Don't, don't hurt him!"

By *him*, Ingrey realized, blinking, Jokol meant the *bear* . . .

The bear dropped its prize and rose up. And up. And up . . . Ingrey's head tilted back, his eyes widening at the snarling jaws, the massive shoulders, the huge, outspreading paws with their wicked ivory-tipped claws, looming high over his head . . .

Everything around him slowed, and Ingrey's perceptions came alight, in the black exultation of his wolf ascending, seemingly pumped from his heart up into his reeling brain. The noise in the court became a distant rumble. His sword in his hand felt weightless; the tip rose, then began to curve away in a glittering backswing. His mind sketched the plunge of the steel, into the bear's heart and out again before it could even begin to react, caught as it was in that other, more sluggish stream of time.

It was then that he felt, more than saw, the faint god light sputtering from the bear like sparks off a cat petted in the winter dark. The light's beauty confounded him, burning into his eyes. His heightened perceptions reached for it in a desperate grasping after the fading god, and suddenly, his mind was *in* the bear's.

He saw himself, foreshortened: a doubled image of leather-clad man and moving blade, and a vast, dark, dense wolf with glowing silver-tipped fur spewing light in an aureole all around him. As his heart reached after the god light, so the bear's astounded senses reached toward him, and for an instant, a three-way circle completed itself.

A laughing Voice murmured in his mind, but not in his

ear: "I see my Brother's pup is in better pelt, now. Good. Pray continue . . ." Ingrey's mind seemed to explode with the weight and pressure of that utterance.

For a moment, the bear's dazed and wordless memories became his. The recent procession into the Father's court, with the other animals all about. The distraction of the groom, the stink of his fear, but the reassurance of the familiar one, his smell and his voice, providing a link to calm in this disordered stone world. Voices droning, on and on. A dim comprehension of movement, positioning, yes, there had been food not long ago, when he did this, and let them lead him over there . . . And then his bear-heart swelled and burst with the overwhelming arrival of the god, followed by the happy certainty of a rocking amble toward the bier. Then confusion and pain; the small man hooked on the end of his chain was pulling back, yanking, punishing him for doing this thing, frustrating his happiness. He lunged forward in an attempt to complete his god-given task. More of these puny creatures ran about getting in his way. A red rage rose in his brain like a tide, and he grabbed that cold odd-smelling lump of meat and lumbered off with it toward the laughing light Who called him, Who was, confusingly, everywhere and yet nowhere . . .

The monstrous creature gave a snarl of pain and wrath, towering like a fur avalanche above Ingrey's head.

Ingrey seemed to reach deep into his chest, his belly, his bowels, and brought out one word: *"Down!"* The command flew through the air with the weight of a stone from a catapult.

His sword tip circled once, then fell in a silver arc to the pavement before his feet. The bear's snout tracked it, following it down, and down, until the great beast was crouched before Ingrey's boots, pressing its jaw to the tiles, its paws drawn in close to its head, its massive haunches bunching up behind. The yellow eyes looked up at him in bear-bewilderment, and awe.

Ingrey glowered around to find the groom-acolyte scrabbling away on hands and knees nearby, white robes bloodied, eyes now more huge on Ingrey than they'd been on the ice bear. The claws had merely grazed his ribs, else he might have been disemboweled. The bear's rage still boiled up in Ingrey's brain. Letting his sword fall with a clang, he advanced upon the man. He scooped him up by the front of his robes, jamming him against the plinth of the holy fire. The man was as tall as Ingrey, and broader in the beam, but he seemed to float in Ingrey's grasp. Ingrey bent him backward over the licking heat. The groom's flailing feet sought the floor, without success, and his squeaking strained up beyond sound into silence.

"What did they pay you, to thwart the god's blessing? Who dared this execration?" Ingrey snarled into the groom's contorted face. His voice, pitched low and vibrating, snaked all around the stone walls like a rustle of velvet, and back into his own ears like a purr.

"I—I—I—I'm *sorry*!" squealed the groom. "Arpan said, Arpan said, it would do no harm . . ."

"He lies!" yelped the groom in the Father's livery, dragging his frightened gray dog on its lead, circling wide around the still-crouching bear.

The white-clad groom's eyes focused on Ingrey's, inches from his face, and he inhaled deeply and screamed, "I confess! Don't, don't, don't . . ."

Don't what? With difficulty, Ingrey straightened, opened his hands, and let the man fall back to his feet. He kept on going down, however, knees crumpling, till he was curled up in a bleeding ball at the base of the plinth, sniveling.

"Nij, you *fool*!" screamed the Father's groom. "Shut up!"

"I couldn't help it!" cried the Bastard's groom, cowering from Ingrey. "His eyes shone silver, and his voice had a terrible weirding on it!"

"Then you'd best listen, hadn't you," said an unsympathetic voice at Ingrey's elbow.

Ingrey jerked away to find Learned Lewko, out of breath, exasperation manifest in the set of his teeth, standing looking over the chaotic scene.

Ingrey inhaled deeply, desperately trying to slow his heart, will time to its normal flow, calm his exacerbated senses. Light, shade, color, sound, all seemed to strike at him like ax blades, and the people all around him burned like fires. It was gradually borne in upon him how *many* people were staring at him now, mouths agape: some thirty or so mourners, the divine conducting the ceremony, all five groom-acolytes, Prince Jokol and his dumbfounded friend, and now, Learned Lewko. Who was not looking at all dumbfounded.

I have let my wolf ascend, Ingrey reflected in a dizzied delirium. *In front of forty witnesses. In the middle of the main temple court of Easthome.*

At least I seem to have amused the white god . . .

"Learned, Learned, help me, mercy . . ." mumbled the injured groom, crawling to Lewko's feet and grabbing the hem of his robe. Lewko's look of exasperation deepened.

A dozen people now seemed to be arguing at once, accusations and counteraccusations of both bribes and threats, as the mourners fell apart into two camps. An inheritance seemed to be at stake, from the fragments of speech that reached Ingrey's ears, although the thread of this instantly tangled with other old grudges, slights, and resentments. The hapless divine who had been conducting the funeral ceremony made a few feeble attempts to restore order among his flock while simultaneously threatening discipline upon his grooms, then, thwarted in both tasks, turned instead to an easier target.

He whirled to Prince Jokol, and pointed a shaking hand at the bear. "Take that thing *back*," he snarled. "Get it *out* of this temple at once! Never return!"

The towering red-haired man seemed nearly in tears. "But I was promised a divine! I must have one! If I do not bring one back to my island, my beautiful Breiga will not marry me!"

Ingrey stepped forward, chin up, and put all the authority of Sealmaster Hetwar's most dangerous sword hand into his voice. And perhaps . . . something extra. "The Temple of Easthome will give you a missioner in exchange for your silver ingots, Prince. Or perhaps I missed the offer to return *them*?" He let his eye fall stonily on the harassed divine.

Learned Lewko, in a tone seeming singularly calm compared to everyone else's, soothed, "The Temple will make all right, Prince, once we have ironed out this regrettable internal fault. It seems that your fine bear was the victim of an impious machination. For now, will you please take Fafa back to your boat for safekeeping?"

He added out of the corner of his mouth to Ingrey, "And you, my lord, would oblige me vastly if you would go with them, and see that they both get there without eating any small children on the way."

Ingrey melted with relief at the thought of escape. "Certainly, Learned."

Lewko's eyelids flicked down; he added, "And take care of that."

Ingrey followed his glance. New blood was leaking in a dark trickle down his fingers from beneath the soiled bandage on his right hand. Something half-healed had burst during his manhandling of the guilty groom, presumably. He'd felt nothing.

He looked up to find himself fixed with a fierce blue stare. Jokol's eyes narrowed; he bent his head for a low-voiced, rapid exchange with his brown-haired comrade. Then he looked up and favored Lewko with an abrupt nod, which he extended to Ingrey. "Yes. We like this one, eh, Ottovin?" He gave his companion a nudge in the ribs that might have knocked over a lesser man, and marched over to his bear. He picked up the silver chain. "Come, Fafa."

The bear whined and shuffled a little, but kept its crouching pose.

Lewko's hand griped Ingrey's shoulder; a nearly soundless breath in his ear said, "Let it up again, Lord Ingrey. I think it is calmer now."

"I . . ." Ingrey stepped nearer to the bear, and scooped up

and resheathed his sword. The bear shuffled about some more, pressed its black nose to Ingrey's boots, and stared up at him piteously. Ingrey swallowed, and tried in a cracked voice: "Up."

Nothing happened. The bear whimpered.

He reached down into a deep, deep well within himself, and brought up the word again; but a word given weight, a growling song that made his own bones vibrate. *"Up."*

The great animal seemed to unfold. It lumbered to its master then, and Jokol dropped to his knees and petted the huge beast, big hands ruffling the thick fur of its neck, murmuring soothing endearments in a tongue Ingrey's ear could not translate. The ice bear rubbed its head on the prince's embroidered tunic, smearing it with bear spit and white hairs.

"Come, my good friend, Fafa's friend!" said Jokol, standing up and giving Ingrey an expansive wave of his hand. "Come share a bowl with me." He gave the silver chain a shake. His glance swept over the mob arguing in the court, and he gave a sniff of disdain and turned toward the outer doors. Ottovin, his face screwed up, followed loyally after. Ingrey hurried to catch up, keeping Jokol between himself and the bear.

The short, strange parade exited the temple, leaving Learned Lewko to manage the babble and wailing left in their wake. Ingrey heard his crisp voice, addressed to the still-yammering groom and anyone else within earshot, ". . . then it must have *been* a trick of the light." At Ingrey's last glance over his shoulder, Lewko's eyes met his, and his lips formed the word *Tomorrow*. Ingrey found it an unreassuring but credible promise.

His eyes shone silver, and his voice had a terrible weirding on it . . . Familiar pain crept over Ingrey, and he realized he had done some most unpleasant things to his still-healing back, as well as to his hand. But the ringing in his ears was new, as was the thick tightening in his raw throat.

His memory returned unbidden to his old torments at

Birchgrove. Of his head shoved under the Birchbeck, his lungs pulsing with red pain. Not even screams had been possible in that breathless cold. Of all his trials, that had proved the most effective, and his excited handlers had repeated it often, until his lucidity locked in. The strength of his silence, appallingly grim in a barely-boy, had been forged and quenched in that icy stream: stronger than his tormentors by far, stronger than fear of death.

He shook off the disquieting recollection and attended to guiding the island men back to the docks below Kingstown through the least crowded streets he could find. Lewko's concerns seemed less a joke when they picked up a tail of excited children, all pointing and chirping at the bear. Jokol grinned at them. Ingrey scowled and waved them off. His intensified senses seemed to be quieting, his heart slowing at last. Jokol and Ottovin spoke to each other in their own dialect, with frequent glances in Ingrey's direction.

Jokol dropped back beside Ingrey. "I thank you for helping poor Fafa, Lord, Lord Ingriry. Ingorry?"

"Ingrey."

Jokol grimaced apologetically. "I fear I am a very stupid man in your talk. Well, my mouth will get better."

"You speak Wealdean well," said Ingrey diplomatically. "My Darthacan is hardly more fluent, and I do not speak your tongue at all."

"Ah, Darthacan." Jokol shrugged. "That is a hard talk." His blue gaze narrowed. "Do you write?"

"Yes."

"That is good. I cannot." The big man sighed mournfully. "All feathers break in these." He held out one thick hand for Ingrey's inspection; Ingrey nodded in an attempt at sympathy. He did not doubt Jokol's assertion in the least.

At the ice bear's ambling pace, they came at length to the gate in the Kingstown walls that led out to the cut-stone embankment and wooden wharves. A grove of masts and spars made a black tangle against the luminous evening sky. The working riverboats were flat and crude, for the most part, but scattered among them were a few seagoing vessels of light draft, up from the mouth of the Stork. Above Easthome no such ships went, for the rising hills created impassable rapids, although timber and other goods, on rafts or in barrels, were routinely floated down them whenever the water rose high enough.

Jokol's ship, tied up alongside one outthrusting jetty, proved altogether a different breed. It was easily forty feet long, curved out in the middle as gracefully as a woman's hips, narrowing on each end to where matching prows curled up, artfully carved with entwined rows of sea birds. It had a single mast, and a single deck; its passengers must presumably suffer the elements when it sailed, although at the moment, a large tent was arranged along the back half.

The ship looked big enough on the river, but to Ingrey's mind it seemed insanely small for the open seas. It looked even smaller when the bear slouched aboard, snuffling, and flopped down amidships in what was evidently its accustomed place with a great, exhausted sigh. The boat rocked, then settled again, as Jokol snapped the chain to a hook on the mast. Ottovin, with an anxious smile, gestured Ingrey up the wobbly board that served as a gangplank and thumped down to the deck after him. In the twilight, the glow from the lamps set within the tent seemed welcoming, and Ingrey was reminded of the little wooden boats bearing candles that he and his father had released into the Birchbeck for the Son's Day ceremonies, in happier times, before wolves had eaten their world.

A crew of perhaps two dozen welcomed their prince back gladly, and the bear, if less gladly, at least familiarly. They were all strong-looking men, though none so tall as their leader: most as young, but a few grizzled. Some kept their hair in similar horsetails, some braided, and one had a shaved head, though judging from his pale and mottled scalp, that might have been in some desperate recent attempt to combat an infestation of vermin. None was ill clothed, and, taking a swift count of the weapons neatly stored along the vessel's sides with the shipped oars, none ill armed. Retainers, warriors, sailors, rowers? All men here did all work, Ingrey suspected; there could be no room for purposeless distinctions on this boat when the seas rose high.

The bear delivered, Ingrey considered escape, but as Hetwar's man he supposed he'd better accept Prince Jokol's *bowl* first, lest he give some offense that might reflect on the sealmaster. He trusted the ritual would be brief. Jokol waved Ingrey into his tent, which made a spacious enough hall. The fabric was wool, made waterproof with fat; Ingrey decided his nose would grow used to its odor soon. Two trestle tables with benches were set up within, and another bench at the side to which his host led Ingrey. Jokol and Ottovin plunked down on either side of him; the other men bustled about, efficiently setting out utensils and food.

A blond young man with a quite valiant reddish ring-beard standing out like a halo around his chin bowed before the three of them and distributed, indeed, wooden bowls. Another man followed with a jug, from which he poured an opaque liquid, first to the guest, then to the prince, then to Ottovin. Wavering vapors arose from the sloshing brew. Ottovin, whose Wealdean was more broken than Jokol's, gave Ingrey to understand, with various baffling gestures, that it was brewed from mare's milk, or possibly blood. *Or possibly urine,* Ingrey reflected after his first taste. If that noise had been meant as a whinny, horses had something to do with it, anyway. He would choke down this one drink for courtesy, then take his leave, Ingrey decided. He could plead his duty to Hetwar and extract himself tactfully.

Beyond the far end of the tent, through an open flap, a brazier and temporary kitchen were set up, and a smell of grilling meat made Ingrey's mouth abruptly water. "We will eat much soon," Jokol assured him, with the smile of a host anxious to please.

Ingrey would have to eat sometime, to be sure; and drinking this pungent brew on an empty stomach seemed a dangerous indulgence just before an interview with the sealmaster. He nodded. Jokol slapped him on the back and grinned.

Jokol's grin faded as his eye fell on Ingrey's gory right hand. The prince caught a comrade by the sleeve, and gave a low-voiced order. In a few minutes, one of the older men appeared, laden with a basin, cloths, and a bundle. He evicted Ottovin from the bench and signed Ingrey to give over his wounded hand. As the grubby bandage came off, the man winced at the new rupture and the aging, dark purple bruises. Ottovin, leaning over to watch, gave a short whistle, and said something that made Jokol bark a laugh. Jokol kindly held the drinking bowl to Ingrey's lips again before the grizzled fellow stabbed and sewed the flesh once more. When the fellow had finished, wrapped the hand, gathered his gear, ducked his head, and gone off again, Ingrey resisted the strong desire to put his head down between his knees for sheer dizziness. It was plain he was not going anywhere just yet.

As promised, the food was both soon and much. It happily included no dried fish, stony journey-bread, or other repellent sea rations, but rather appeared to have been gathered fresh from the town markets. Cooks in the noble houses of Easthome might prepare more delicate feasts, but it was all good, far beyond the camp fare Ingrey had been expecting. Ingrey, giving it the attention it deserved, failed to fend off the fellow intent on refilling his bowl whenever the fluid level dropped below half.

Full night had fallen before the men began actively to resist their cheerful kitchen comrades' attempts to reload their platters. Ingrey's plan to let time and the meal sober him enough to rise and go seek the sealmaster's palace seemed to need more time. Or less meal . . . The lamps blazed brightly on flushed and shining faces all around.

A babble of talk resolved in one man making some petition to their prince, who smiled and shook his head, but then made some compromise involving offering up Ottovin.

"They want tales," Jokol whispered to Ingrey, as Ottovin

rose and put one booted foot on the bench, and cleared his throat. "We shall have many, this night."

Now, a new drink was offered around. Ingrey sipped cautiously. This one tasted like pine needles and lamp oil, and even Jokol's men took it in small glasses.

Ottovin launched into the sonorous speech of the islands, which seemed to bounce around the tent in rich rhythms. The dialect lay, maddeningly, just on the other side of Ingrey's understanding, though recognizable words seemed to spring out of the stream here and there. Whether they were Wealdean cognates or just accidents of similar sound, Ingrey was not sure.

"He is telling the tale of Yetta and the three cows," Jokol whispered to Ingrey. "It is a favorite."

"Can you translate it?" Ingrey whispered back.

"Alas, no."

"Too difficult?"

Jokol's blue eyes danced, and he blushed. "Too filthy."

"What, don't you know all those short words?"

Jokol sniggered happily, leaned back, and crossed his legs, his hand tapping his knee keeping time to Ottovin's voice. Ingrey realized that he'd just managed to make a joke. Across a language barrier. And had not even given offense. He smiled muzzily and took another sip of his liquid pine needles. The men crowding the benches and ranged along the walls laughed uproariously, and Ottovin bowed and sat, collecting his due drink; the custom seemed to involve tipping it back in one gulp. The islanders applauded, then began shouting at their prince, who acquiesced and rose in turn to his feet. After a rustling and murmur, the tent fell so silent Ingrey could hear the river waves lapping gently on the hull.

Jokol drew a deep breath and began. After the first few sentences, Ingrey realized he was listening to verse, rhythmic and alliterative. After the first few minutes, he realized that this was to be no short or simple offering.

"This is an adventure tale, good," Ottovin confided to Ingrey in the usual behind-the-hand whisper. "These days, it is hard to get anything but love stories out of him."

The sound of Jokol's voice washed over Ingrey like the rocking of a boat, a cradle, a horse's stride. The beat never wavered; he never seemed to pause at a loss for a word or phrase. His listeners sometimes giggled, sometimes gasped, but most often sat as though enspelled, lips parted, the lamplight caressing their faces and gleaming from their eyes.

"He's *memorized* all that?" Ingrey whispered in astonishment to Ottovin. And at the man's slightly blank look, repeated, tapping his forehead, "The words are all in his head?"

Ottovin smiled proudly. "That and a hundred hundred more. Why do you think we call him Skullsplitter? He makes our heads burst with his tales. My sister Breiga will be the happiest of women, aye."

Ingrey eased back on the bench, swallowed some more pine needles, and reflected on the nature of words. And presuppositions.

At astounding length, Jokol finished, to the enthusiastic applause of his men; they cheered as he knocked back his drink. He grinned sheepishly and waved away an immediate demand for more, with some vociferous debate over the selection. "Soon, soon! It will be ready for you soon," he promised, tapping his lips, and sat for a time, smiling absently.

One of the other men took a turn then, though not in verse this time; judging from the raucous laughter, it was another that Prince Jokol might be too shy to translate.

"Ah," said Jokol, leaning close to Ingrey to refill his glass. "You grow less glum. Good! Now I shall honor you with Ingorry's Tale."

He rose again, and seemed to settle into himself, his face growing solemn. He launched again into verse, serious and, at moments, even sinister, judging from the riveted looks of his listeners. In very short order, Ingrey realized Jokol was retelling the tale of the corrupted funeral, and of Ingrey's rescue of the bear and the situation, for Ingrey's own name, in Jokol's rolling pronunciation, and that of Fafa, appeared often. The titles of the gods were quite distinct. And, to Ingrey's dismay, so was the term *weirding*. Which, judging by the way the men's eyes shifted to look warily at Ingrey, meant much the same thing in the island dialect as it did in the Weald.

Ingrey studied Jokol once more, considering the nature of a mind that could take his disaster of sunset and transmute it into heroic poetry by midnight. Extemporaneously. Or perhaps that was, into a campfire tale—the sort designed to send one's spooked listeners off to bed, but not to sleep . . . If the sense was represented by the sound, Jokol's observations had been more acute and detailed than Ingrey would have believed possible, not that his own had been exactly coherent. There seemed not to be any references to wolves, though.

The response when Jokol finished this time was not raucous applause but something more like a sigh of awe. It became a murmur of commentary and, Ingrey suspected from certain voices rising from the back row, interested critique. Jokol's smile was more sly, this time, as he tipped back his glass.

The feast fragmented then, with more food and more drink forcibly circulating. Some men broke out bedrolls and seized corners, and rolled over to snore untrammeled by the noise; Ingrey wondered if they also slept through sea storms. Ottovin, a good lieutenant, averted potential disaster by forbidding the drunken ax-throwing contest to have live targets. Jokol stretched his shoulders, eased his strained voice with another drink, and smiled at Ingrey in a curiosity that Ingrey returned full fold.

"Tomorrow night," said Jokol, "I will make them listen to a love story, in honor of my beautiful Breiga, or they shall get none. You are a young fellow like me, I think, Lord Ingorry. Do you love a one?"

Ingrey blinked, a bit owlishly. Hesitated. Claimed. "Yes. Yes, I do." Sat shocked to hear those words coming from his mouth, in this place. *Curse that horse urine.*

"Ah! That is a good thing. Happy man! But you do not smile. Does she not love you back?"

"I . . . don't know. But we have other troubles."

Jokol's brows rose. "Unwilling parents?" he inquired sympathetically.

"No. It's not like . . . It's . . . She may be under a death sentence."

Jokol sat back, stunned serious. "No! For why?"

It was the inebriated haze he was seeing everything through, Ingrey decided, that made this southern madman seem such a cheerful confidant, a brotherly repository of the most intimate fears of his heart. Maybe . . . maybe no one would remember these words in the morning. "Have you heard of the death of Prince Boleso, the hallow king's son?"

"Oh, aye."

"She beat in his brains with his own war hammer." This seemed too bald. He added by way of clarification, "He was trying to rape her at the time." The uncanny complications seemed beyond explanation, at the moment.

Jokol gave a little whistle, and clucked in sympathy. "That is a hard tale." He offered after a moment, "Still, she sounds a good, strong girl. My beautiful Breiga and Ottovin once killed two horse thieves that came to their father's farm. Ottovin was littler, then."

Brother indeed! "What came of it?"

"Well, *I* asked her to marry me." Jokol's grin flashed. "They were my horses. The thieves' blood-price was made low, because of the dishonor of their crime. I added it to her bride gift, aye, to please her father." He glanced benignly over at Ottovin—his future brother-in-law?—who had slid off the bench a short while ago and now sat draped half over it with his head pillowed on his arm, snoring gently.

"Justice is not so simple, in the Weald." Ingrey sighed. "And the blood-price of a prince is far beyond my purse."

Jokol cocked an interested eye. "You are not a landed man, Lord Ingorry?"

"No. I have only my sword arm. Such as it is." Ingrey flexed his bandaged right hand ruefully. "No other power."

"I think you have one more thing than that, Ingorry." Jokol tapped the side of his head. "I have a good ear. I know what I heard, when my Fafa bowed to you."

Ingrey froze. His first panicked impulse, to deny everything, died on his lips under Jokol's shrewd gaze. Yet he must discourage further dangerous gossip on this topic, however poetic. "This"—he pressed his hand to his lips, then spread it on his heart, to indicate what he dared not name aloud—"must stay bound in silence, or the Temple will make me outlaw."

Jokol pursed his lips, sat up a little, and frowned as he digested this.

Ingrey's somewhat liquefied thoughts sloshed in his head and tossed up a new fear on the shores of his wits. Jokol's face bore no look of dismay or revulsion, though his interest was plainly deeply stirred. Yet even a good ear could not recognize something it had never before heard. "This, earlier"—he touched his throat, swept his hand down his torso—"have you ever heard the like?"

"Oh, aye." Jokol nodded.

"How? Where?"

Jokol shrugged. "When I asked the singing woman at the forest's edge to bless my voyage, she gave me words in such a weirding voice as that."

The phrase seemed to slide through Ingrey's head as sharply as the scent of pine needles. *The singing woman at the forest's edge. The singing woman at . . .* Yet Jokol seemed untouched by the uncanny; no demon-smell hung about him, certainly, no animal spirit hid within him, no geas clung to him like some acrid parasite. He gazed back at Ingrey with a blank affability that one might easily—fatally—mistake for oxlike stupidity.

A thump sounded upon the deck from outside the tent, then a silvery rattling, a bass growl, and a strangled cry.

"Fafa at least does not sleep through his watch," murmured Jokol in satisfaction, and rose to his feet. He prodded Ottovin with a booted toe, but his kinsman-to-be merely stirred and mumbled. Jokol slipped a big hand under Ingrey's elbow and heaved up.

"I don't," Ingrey began. *"Whups . . ."* The ship's deck heaved and swayed under his feet, though the tent's sides hung slack in the windless and waveless night. The lamps were burning low. Jokol's smile twitched, and he kindly kept Ingrey's arm, guiding him toward the tent flap. They stepped out into the gilded shadows to find Fafa sniffing and straining at the end of the taut chain toward an immobilized figure with his back pressed to the vessel's thwart.

Jokol murmured some soothing words in his own tongue to his pet, and the bear lost interest in its quarry and returned to flop down again by the mast. Ingrey staggered as the boat really rocked, this time, and Jokol's grip on his arm tightened.

"Lord Ingrey," Gesca's voice choked from the shadows. He cleared his throat, stood upright again, and stepped forward into the lapping orange light of the cresset in its clamp beside the gangplank. His eyes shone a trifle whitely about the rims as he glanced again at Fafa.

"Oh," said Ingrey. "Gesca. 'Ware the bear." Ingrey smiled at his rhyme. The big islander shouldn't own all the good poetry. "Yes. I was just coming to see m'lord Hewwar. *Het*-war."

"My lord Hetwar," said Gesca, recovering his dignity and a frosty tone, "has gone to bed. He instructed me to— after I found you—inform you that you may wait upon him first thing tomorrow morning."

"Ah," mumbled Ingrey wisely. *Ouch.* "Then I'd best get some sleep. Hadn't I."

"While you can," muttered Gesca.

"A friend?" Jokol inquired, with a nod at Gesca.

"More or less," said Ingrey. He wondered which. But Jokol seemed to take him at his word, and he handed off Ingrey to his lieutenant. "I don't need . . ."

"Lord Ingorry, I thank you for your company. And other things, you bet. Any man who can drink my Ottovin off his bench is welcome on my ship anytime. I hope I see you again, in Easthome."

"You . . . you, too. Give my bes' to dear Fafa." He groped with his numb tongue for further suitably princely farewells, but Gesca was steering him toward the gangplank.

The gangplank proved a challenge, as it was seized with the same wavering motions as the ship, and was much narrower, after all. Ingrey, after a short pause for consideration, solved the problem by tackling it on all fours. After crawling across without falling into the Stork, he rolled over and sat up triumphantly upon the dock. "See?" he told Gesca. "Not so drunk. Jokol is a prince, you know. S'all good diplomacy."

With a growl, Gesca hauled Ingrey to his feet and draped his arm across his shoulders. "Grand. Explain all this to the sealmaster, tomorrow. I want my bed. Now, walk."

Ingrey, a little sobered in mind, though his body still lagged, made an effort to put his boots one in front of the other for a time, as they made their way up through the gates and began to wind through the dark streets of Kingstown.

Gesca said in a voice of aggravation, "I've been hunting all over the city for you. At the house, they said you'd gone to the temple. At the temple, they said you were carried off by a pirate."

"No; worse." Ingrey cackled. "A poet."

Gesca's face turned; even in the shadows, Ingrey could see the lieutenant was looking at him as though he'd just put his head on backward.

"Three people up there said they'd seen you enspell a giant ice bear. One said it was a miracle of the Bastard. Two others said it was no such thing."

Ingrey remembered the Voice in his head, and shivered. "You know what nonsense frantic folks in crowds come up with." He was starting to feel steadier on his feet. He withdrew his arm from Gesca's shoulder. Anyway, in the absence of a menacing bear in the midst of a funeral miracle, it hardly seemed something likely to happen again. No god-voice jarred him now, and animals were a quite different proposition from men. "Don't be gullible, Gesca. It's not as though I could say"—he reached down within himself for that hot velvet rumble—"*halt,* and have you suddenly—"

Ingrey became aware that he was walking on alone.

He wheeled around. Gesca was standing frozen in the dim light from a wall lantern.

Ingrey's belly twisted up in a cold knot. "Gesca! *That's not amusing!*" He strode back, angry. "Stop that." He gave Gesca a short shove in the chest. The man rocked a little, but did not move. He reached up with his bandaged hand—it trembled—and took Gesca by the jaw. "Are you mocking me?"

Only Gesca's eyes, wide with horror, moved, and that only to blink.

Ingrey licked his lips, stepped back. His throat seemed almost too tight to speak at all. He had to take two breaths before he could reach down again, and that barely. *"Move."*

The paralysis broke. Gesca gasped, scrambled back to the nearest wall, and drew steel. Both wheezing, they stared at each other. Ingrey was suddenly feeling far too sober. He opened his hands at his sides, placating, praying Gesca would not lunge.

Slowly, Gesca resheathed his sword. After a moment, he said in a thick voice, "The prison house is just around the corner. Tesko is there waiting to put you to bed. Can you make it?"

Ingrey swallowed. He had to force his voice above a whisper. "I think so."

"Good. Good." Gesca backed along the wall, then turned and walked rapidly away into the shadows, glancing often over his shoulder.

Jaws clamped shut, hardly daring to breathe, Ingrey paced the other way, turning at the corner. A lantern hanging on a bracket beside the door of the narrow house burned steadily, guiding him in.

12

INGREY DIDN'T HAVE TO POUND ON THE DOOR TO WAKE the house, for the porter, though wearing a nightshirt and with a blanket wrapped around his shoulders, came at his first quiet knock. The firm way the man locked up again behind Ingrey did convey a strong hint that this should be the last expedition of the night. He readied a candle in a glass holder to assist Ingrey's way up the stairs.

Ingrey took it with muttered thanks and scuffed up the steps. Light glimmered above on his landing, which proved to be from both a lamp burning low on a table and another candlestick sitting on the steps up to the next floor. Beside it, Lady Ijada crouched, wrapped in a robe of some dark material. She raised her head from her knees as Ingrey swung out of the constricted staircase with a slight clatter of his sword sheath against the wood.

"You are safe!" she said huskily, rubbing her eyes.

Ingrey blinked around into the shadows, startled. The last time any woman had waited up in concern for him was . . . beyond the reach of his memory. There was no sign of her warden, nor of his servant Tesko. "Should I not be?"

"Gesca came, three hours ago or more, and said you'd never come to Lord Hetwar's!"

"Oh. Yes. I was diverted."

"I was imagining the most bizarre things befalling you."

"Did they include a six-hundred-pound ice bear and a pirate poet?"

"No . . ."

"Then they weren't the most bizarre after all."

Her brows drew down; she rose and stepped off the stairs, recoiling as his no-doubt vaporous breath reached her flaring nostrils. She waved a hand to disperse the reek and made a face. "Are you drunk?"

"By my standards, yes. Although I can still walk and talk and dread tomorrow morning. I spent the evening trapped with twenty-five mad southern islanders and the ice bear on their boat. They did feed me. Have you seen Tesko?"

She nodded toward his closed door. "He came with your things. I think he fell asleep awaiting you."

"Unsurprising."

"What of my letter? I worried it had gone astray."

Oh. It was her *letter* she'd feared for, why she had waited up in the dark. "Safely delivered." Ingrey considered this. "Delivered, anyway. How safe a man Learned Lewko is, I would hesitate to guess. He dresses like a Temple clerk, but he's not one."

"You once said what sort of Temple-men you thought would take up my case. Which did you judge him to be? Straight or crooked?"

"I . . . doubt he's a bribable man. It does not follow that he will be on your side." Ingrey hesitated. "He is god-touched."

She cocked her head. "You look a little god-touched yourself, just now."

Ingrey jerked. "How can you tell?"

Her pale fingers extended, in the flickering shadows, as if to feel his face. "I once saw one of my father's men dragged by his horse. He was not badly hurt, but he rose very shaken. Your face is more set, and not covered with blood and dirt, but your eyes look like his did. A bit wild."

He almost leaned into her hand, but it fell back too soon. "I've had a very strange night. Something happened at the temple. Lewko is coming to see you tomorrow, by the way. And me. I think I'm in trouble."

"Come, then, and tell me." She drew him down to sit beside her on the steps, her eyes wide and dark with renewed disquiet.

Ingrey stumbled through a description of his encounter with the bear and its god in the temple court, which twice made her gasp and once made her giggle. He was a little taken aback at the giggle. She listened with fascination to his description of Jokol, his boat, and his verse. "I thought," said Ingrey, "what happened with Fafa was the white god's doing, in His wrath at the dishonest grooms. But just now, coming back here with Gesca, it happened again. The weirding voice. I did not know if it was my wolf, or me. Five gods, I am no longer sure where I leave off and it begins! It has never spoken like this before. It has never spoken at all."

Ijada said thoughtfully, "The fen folk claimed that wisdom songs were magical, once. Long ago."

"Or far away." *The singing woman at the forest's edge . . .* "This is here, and now, and in deadly earnest. What I wonder is, does Wencel know of such powers? Does he possess them? Why did he not use them on us? I think he stole and read your letter while we were at dinner with him, by the way. Learned Lewko says it was opened."

Ijada sat up and caught her breath. "Oh! What did the letter say?"

"I did not read it, but I gather it described the events at Red Dike in some detail. So, at least from the time he came back in to join us at the table, Wencel knew of the geas, and he knew that I concealed it from him. Did you sense a change in his conversation, then?"

Ijada frowned. "If anything, he seemed more forthcoming. In hope of coaxing a like frankness?"

Ingrey shrugged. "Perhaps."

"Ingrey . . ."

"Hm?"

"What do *you* know of banner-carriers?"

"Scarcely more than I know of shamans. I have read some Darthacan accounts of battles with the Old Wealdings. The Darthacans did not love our bannermen. The spirit warriors, and indeed, all the kin warriors, fought fiercely to defend their standards. If the banner-carrier refused to retreat, then the warriors would fight to the last around him—or her, I suppose, if Wencel speaks true. Audar's soldiers always tried to bring the banners down as quickly as possible, for that reason. It was said one of the banner-carrier's tasks was to cut the throats of our own who were too wounded to carry away. It was considered an honorable ending. The wounded warrior, if he still could speak, was expected to bless the bannerman and thank the blade."

Ijada shivered. "I did not know that part."

Her expression grew inward for a moment, on what thoughts Ingrey could scarcely guess. Her dream at the Wounded Woods? But warriors already dead could scarcely require such a gruesome service from their bannerwoman.

Ijada added, "See what Wencel knows, when you ask him about Holytree."

"Mm, and there's another meeting I'm not looking forward to. I don't think Wencel is going to be best pleased with me over this spectacle tonight. Farcical as it was, I drew the Temple's attention in the most serious way. I am afraid of Lewko."

"Why? If he is a friend and mentor of Hallana's, he cannot be dishonorable."

"Oh, I'm sure he would be a good friend. And an implacable enemy. It is merely worrisome to imagine him on the other side." Or was this just habit? He remembered the earnest divines at Birchgrove, torturing him back to silent sanity. It had left pain as an unreliable guide to Ingrey of the line between his friends and his enemies.

Ijada said impatiently, "What side do you imagine you are on?"

Ingrey's thoughts came to a full stop. "I don't know. Every wall seems to curve away from me. I spin in circles." He glanced up, finding her eyes, close to his, turned amber in the shadows. The pupils were wide in the dimness, as if to drink him in. He might fall into them as deep wells, and drink deep in turn. She possessed physical beauty, yes, and beneath that the edgy thrilling wildness of her leopard spirit. But beyond that . . . something more. He wanted to reach through her to that something, something terribly important . . . "You are my side. And you are not alone."

"Then," she breathed, "neither are you."

Oh. Neither time nor his heart stopped, surely, and yet he floated for the space of a breath as though he'd stepped from some great height, but not begun to fall. Weightless. "Sweet logician."

Closing the handbreadth between their lips was the work of a second. Her eyes flared open.

Her lips were as soft as he'd ever imagined, as warm as sunlight. The first touch was chaste, hesitant, but a great shock seemed to roll through his body, his belly, and echo back up his limbs, which left his hands trembling. He stilled them by gripping her around the waist, around the back of her head, fingers clenching in her loose dark hair. A warm arm wound around his shoulder, flattened to his back, pressed him inward. Fingers gripped his upper arm in turn, spasming. Her lips parted.

A wave of lust ran in the track of that first shock, firing his loins, kindling an awareness of just how long it had been since he'd held a woman like this. . . . No, he'd *never* held a woman like *this*. The kiss grew abruptly passionate, and not chaste at all. He explored her mouth in desperate haste, and the white hands wrapping him fairly wrenched him toward her, crushing the softness of her body against his. Their breath synchronized; their heartbeats began hammering in time.

And then they were reaching *through* each other . . .

A magical kiss was suddenly not a romantic turn of phrase. It was not, in fact, romantic at all. It was terrifying beyond breath. She choked, he gasped, they drew apart, though their hands still gripped; not lustful now, but more like two people drowning.

Her eyes, wide before, were huge, the pupils stretched black with only a narrow ring of gold iris shimmering around them. "What are you . . . ?" she began, as he panted, "What have you done?"

One hand released him to clutch at her heart, beneath the dark robe. "What *was* that?"

"I don't know. I've never . . . felt . . ."

A creak of floorboards, a clank, a scrape; Ingrey sprang back as his chamber door opened. Ijada folded her arms together like a woman freezing, and spat an unexpected short word under her breath. He had just time to cock a wry eyebrow at her, and she to grimace back at him, before he twisted to see Tesko poke his yawning face through the door into the dim hallway.

"M'lord?" he inquired. "I heard voices . . ." He blinked in mild surprise at the pair sitting on the steps.

Ijada rose, snatched up her candlestick, gave Ingrey a mute look of scorching intensity, and fled up the stairs.

For a brief, self-indulgent moment, Ingrey pictured himself drawing his steel and beheading his servant. Alas, the hall was too narrow for such a swing to be executed properly. He gave over the vision with a long sigh and levered himself to his feet.

Tesko, perhaps sensing Ingrey's displeasure at the ill-timed interruption, bowed him warily into his chamber. The clubfooted youth had been issued half-trained to Ingrey when he had first taken up his place as Hetwar's more-than-courier. Used to caring for his own needs, Ingrey had treated the menial with an indifference that had overcome Tesko's initial terror of his violent reputation a little too completely. The day he had caught Tesko pilfering his sparse property, however, he had replaced repute with a vivid demonstration. After that Hetwar's other servants did more to whip their junior into shape than Ingrey ever had, for if Tesko were dismissed, he would have to be replaced with one of *them*.

Ingrey let Tesko remove his boots, gave curt orders for the predawn, and fell into bed. But not to sleep.

He was too spun up to sleep, too drunk to think straight, too exhausted to sit up. His blood seemed to hiss through his veins, growl in his ears. He was intensely conscious of every faint creak from overhead. Did Ijada's breathing still rise and fall in time with his? He was still aroused, and more than half-afraid to do anything about it, because if she felt his every heartbeat and movement the way he seemed to feel hers . . .

They had surely been falling toward that moment of meeting for days. He felt coupled to her now as though they were two hunting dogs, leashed to each other for their training. *So who is the huntsman? What is the quarry?* The heavy click of that binding reverberated in his bones: chains thinner than gossamer, stronger than iron, less readily parted.

He didn't have to hear the creaks, as she turned in her bed. He knew where she was as certainly as he knew the position of his own body in the dark. He held out a hand in the dimness. *This is an illusion. I am simply going mad with unrequited lust.* Except that it hadn't seemed as unrequited as all that, now, had it? A perfectly demented grin stretched his mouth, briefly.

❧

He must have slept eventually, for Tesko nearly had to pull him from the covers and onto the floor to wake him again. Tesko's jerky motions betrayed a fear balanced between the dangers of dealing with an Ingrey half-awake and the dangers of disobeying; Ingrey swallowed the glue from his mouth and assured his servant that disobeying would have been worse. Sitting up proved painful but not impossible.

He let Tesko help wash, shave, and dress him, in the interest of protecting his new bandage; Ingrey frowned to see it nearly soaked through again with browning blood, but there was not time to change it now. The filthy covering on his left wrist he at last abandoned, as that wound was now better than half-healed, all black scabs and new pink scars and greening bruises. The sleeves of his town garb—gray and dark gray—covered it well enough. With sword, knife, and clean boots, he was made presentable, if one ignored the bloodshot eyes and pale face.

He rejected bread with loathing, gulped tea, and took the stairs down with a faint clatter. He glanced up through two opaque floors. *Ijada still sleeps. Good.*

The chill, moist air outside was tinged with just enough light for Ingrey to make his way through the streets. He arrived at the opposite end of Kingstown with his head, though still aching, a little clearer for the walk.

Color was leaking back into the world with the dawn. The stolid cut stone of the wide front of Hetwar's palace took on a buttery hue. The night porter recognized Ingrey at once through the hatch in the heavy carved front doors, and swung one leaf just wide enough to admit him into the hushed, rich dimness. Ingrey turned down the offer of a page to announce him and made his way up the stairs toward the sealmaster's study. A few servants moved quietly about, drawing back curtains, stirring fires, carrying water.

Ingrey blinked and hesitated when he rounded the corner to find Prince-marshal Biast's own bannerman, Lord Symark kin Stagthorne, leaning against the wall outside Hetwar's chamber. Symark exchanged a familiar nod with Ingrey.

"Is the prince here?" Ingrey murmured to him.

"Aye."

"When did you arrive?"

"We reached the Kingstown gate about two hours ago. The prince left his baggage train in the mire near Newtemple. We rode all night." Symark hitched his shoulders, dislodging a few small lumps of drying mud from his coat.

"Is that you, Ingrey?" Hetwar's voice called from within. "Enter."

Symark raised a brow at him; Ingrey slipped inside. Hetwar, seated at his desk, motioned him to close the door behind him.

Ingrey made his bow to the prince-marshal, seated with his booted legs stretched out before him in a chair opposite Hetwar, then to the sealmaster. Both men returned acknowledging nods, and Ingrey stood with his hands clasped behind his back to await his next cue.

Biast looked as mud-flecked and road-weary as his bannerman. Prince Biast was a little shorter than his younger brother Boleso, and not quite as broadly built, but still shared the Stagthorne athleticism, brown hair, and long jaw, resolutely shaved. His eyes were a touch shrewder, and if he shared Boleso's sensuality and temper, they were rather better controlled. Biast had become heir presumptive only three years ago, on the untimely death through illness of the eldest Stagthorne brother, Byza. Prior to those expectations falling so heavily upon him, the middle prince had been guided toward a military career, the rigors of which had left him little time to match either Byza's reputation for courtly diplomacy or Boleso's notoriety for self-indulgence.

Hetwar was already dressed for the day not in his usual sober simplicity, but in full court mourning, his chains of office lying heavy on his fur-trimmed tunic. Presumably, he meant to depart soon to join Boleso's funeral procession on its last leg into Easthome this afternoon. The sealmaster was of middle height, middle age, middle build; indulgences of the flesh were not among Hetwar's temptations, surrounded by opportunities though he might be here at the high court. It struck Ingrey that Learned Lewko shared something of the same deceptive mild manner Hetwar routinely bore, concealing complex mastery, which was a curious and unsettling thought.

What neither sealmaster nor prince-marshal bore was any smell of the uncanny, to Ingrey's newly awakened inner senses. The perception did not ease him much. Magical powers worked sometimes; material powers worked all the time, and this chamber, these two men, fairly resonated with the latter.

Hetwar ran a hand through his thinning hair and favored Ingrey with a glower. "About time you showed up."

"Sir," said Ingrey neutrally.

Hetwar's brows rose at his tone, and his attention sharpened. "Where were you last night?"

"What have you heard so far, sir?"

Hetwar's lips curved a little at the cautious riposte. "An extraordinarily garbled tale from my manservant this morning. I trust that you did not actually enspell a giant rampaging ice bear in the temple court yesterday evening. What really happened?"

"I had gone up there for a brief errand on my way here, sir. Indeed, an acolyte had lost his hold on a new sacred animal, which had injured him. I, um, helped them regain control of the beast. When the Temple returned it to its donor, Learned Lewko requested me to accompany it back through town, for safety's sake, which I did."

Hetwar's eyes flashed up at Lewko's name. So, *Hetwar* knew who Lewko was, even if Ingrey had not.

Ingrey continued, "The owner, Jokol, proclaimed himself as a prince from the southern islands, and it seemed to me undiplomatic to refuse the hospitality of his ship, which he pressed upon me. The islanders' drinks proved deadly and their poetry, very lengthy. When Gesca rescued me, it was too late to attend upon you."

A small snort from Biast, with a renewed look at Ingrey's pallor, testified to the prince-marshal's amusement. Good. Better to be the butt of a tale of drunken foolishness than the nexus of out-of-control illegal magic, shattering miracle, and worse.

Ingrey added, "Learned Lewko was witness to the whole

of the incident with the bear, and the only one I would suggest that you regard as reliable."

"He is peculiarly qualified."

"So I understood, sir."

A passing stillness of Hetwar's hands was all that revealed his reaction to this. He frowned and went on. "Enough of last night. I am told your journey with Prince Boleso's coffin was more eventful than your letters to me revealed."

Ingrey ducked his head. "What did your letters from Gesca say?"

"Letters from Gesca?"

"He was not reporting to you?"

"He reported to me yesterday evening."

"Not before?"

"No. Why?"

"I suspected he was penning reports. I assumed it was to you."

"Did you see this?"

"No," Ingrey admitted.

The eyebrows climbed again.

Ingrey took a breath. "There are some things that happened on the journey even Gesca does not know."

"For example . . . ?"

"Were you aware, sir, that Prince Boleso was experimenting with spirit magic? Animal sacrifice?"

Biast jerked in surprise at this; Hetwar grimaced, and said, "Rider Ulkra apprised me of some dabblings. Leaving a young man with that much energy too idle may have been a mistake. I trust you removed any unfortunate traces, as I requested; there is no point in besmirching the dead."

"They were not idle dabblings. They were serious and successful attempts, if ill controlled and ill-advised, that led directly to a state of mind I can only name violent madness. Which also leads me to wonder, for obvious reasons, how long they had been going on. Wen—it is suspected the prince had the aid of an illicit sorcerer at one point or another. Lady Ijada testifies Boleso had some garbled theory that the rites were going to give him an uncanny power over the kin of the Weald. He strangled a leopard the night he tried to rape her, and she killed him trying to defend herself."

Hetwar glanced worriedly at Biast, who was now sitting up listening with a darkening frown. Hetwar said, "Lady Ijada testifies? I trust you see the problem with that."

"I saw the leopard, the strangling cord, the paint traces on Boleso's body, and the chamber. Ulkra and several others among the prince's household can confirm this. I believe her without reservation. I believed her from the first, but later, another incident confirmed my conviction."

Hetwar opened a hand, inviting Ingrey to go on. His expression was anything but happy.

"It became apparent to me . . . it was revealed that . . ." This was harder than Ingrey had expected. "Someone, in Easthome or elsewhere, had undertaken a plot to murder my prisoner. It is not clear to me who, or why." He kept half an eye on Biast as he said this; the prince looked startled. "It became clear how."

"So who was this assassin?"

"Me."

Hetwar blinked. "Ingrey . . ." he began warningly.

"It was revealed to me, through four failed attempts on my prisoner's life and the help of a Temple sorcerer we met in Red Dike, one Learned Hallana—who was once a pupil of Learned Lewko's, by the by—that a compulsion or geas had been placed upon me by magical means. Hallana says it was not common demon magic, not something related to the white god's powers."

Hetwar stared his swordsman up and down. "Understand, Ingrey, I do not—yet—accuse you of raving, but I fail to see how anyone, let alone an ordinary young woman, could survive any sort of single combat with you."

Ingrey grimaced. "It turned out she could swim. Among other talents. The sorceress broke the geas in Red Dike, fortunately for us all." Close enough to the truth, for his current purposes. "The event was extremely peculiar, from my point of view."

"Gesca's, too, it seems," muttered Hetwar.

In a perfectly calm, level voice, Ingrey said, "I am infuriated beyond bearing to have been so used."

He had meant his tone to convey restrained displeasure; by the heat in his belly and tremble of his hands, he realized just how much truer his words were than he'd intended. Biast snorted at the odd juxtaposition of tone and content, but Hetwar, who was watching his body, went still.

"I wondered if it had been by you, sir," Ingrey continued in the same deadly cadences.

"No, Ingrey!" said Hetwar. His eyes had gone a little wide; his hands, flat on the desk top, did not reach for the hilt of his court sword. Ingrey could see the strain of that withheld motion.

Ingrey had spent four years watching Hetwar spin out truth or lies as the occasion demanded. Which was it now? His head was pounding, and his blood seemed to simmer. Was Hetwar conspirator, tool, blameless? It came to him that he did not have to guess.

"Speak truth."

"I didn't!"

Silence fell, with the force of an ax blade. Biast was suddenly plastered back in his chair.

Or perhaps I should have bitten my tongue in half.

"That is very good to know, sir," Ingrey said, in a spuriously tranquil tone, deliberately easing his stance. *Scramble out of this, now.* "How does the hallow king fare?"

The silence stretched too long, as Hetwar stared at him. Without taking his eyes from Ingrey's mouth, he made a little commanding gesture at the dismayed Biast.

Biast, after a questioning look at the sealmaster, licked his lips. "I visited my father's bedside before I came here. He is worse than I had imagined. He recognized me, but his speech was very slurred, and he is very yellow and weak. He fell back to sleep almost at once." The prince paused, and his voice fell further. "His skin is like paper. He was always . . . he was never . . ." The voice stopped before it broke, Ingrey thought.

"You must," said Ingrey carefully, "both be giving thought to the risk of an election very soon."

Hetwar nodded; Biast nodded more reluctantly. The prince-marshal's lidded eyes only half concealed a lingering alarm, and his glance at Hetwar plainly questioned whether Ingrey's eerie revolt was usual behavior for the sealmaster's infamous wolf-swordsman, or not. Hetwar's expression was grimly uninformative.

Ingrey said, "I am more than half-convinced that Boleso's forbidden experiments were aimed at a grasp for the hallow kingship."

"But he is the younger!" objected Biast, then added, "Was."

"That was potentially correctable. Given magical means, your assassination might have been effected undetectably. As I discovered."

Hetwar suddenly looked furiously thoughtful. "It is true," he murmured, "that more votes have been bought and sold than actually exist. I'd wondered where the sink could be . . ."

"How much doubt is there of the prince-marshal's succession?" Ingrey asked Hetwar, with a diplomatic nod at Biast. "Should the king chance to die when so many are gathered in Easthome for Boleso's funeral, it seems to me the election could come to a head very quickly."

Hetwar shrugged. "The Hawkmoors, and their whole eastern faction, have long been preparing for such a moment, as we all know. It has been four generations since their kin lost the kingship, but they still hunger for a return to their old ascendancy. They had not, I judged, secured enough certain votes, but given the uncertain ones . . . If Boleso had been secretly gathering those, they are now scattered again."

"Do you see such scatterings returning to his brother's

faction?" Ingrey glanced at Biast, who looked as though he was still digesting the intimation of fratricide, without pleasure.

"Perhaps not," muttered Hetwar, brows drawn deeply down. "The Foxbriar kin, though they know their lord cannot win, surely know they hold a deciding edge if things run too close. If the ordainers were to fail repeatedly to effect a clear outcome, the argument could go to swords."

Biast's frown was no happier, but his hand drifted resolutely to his hilt at these last words, a gesture Hetwar did not miss; he held up a restraining palm.

"Were Prince Biast removed," said Ingrey carefully, "indeed, whether he were removed or not, it seems to me that a spell that could compel a murder could as secretly compel a vote."

Ingrey had thought he'd held all of Hetwar's attention before. He'd been mistaken.

"Really," breathed Hetwar. He could hardly grow more still, but the stillness turned much colder. "And—Ingrey—can you perceive such spells?"

"I can now."

"Hm." His stare on Ingrey grew freshly appraising.

And so I am saved, in Hetwar's eyes. Maybe.

Hetwar vented a noise between a groan and a sigh, running his hands through his hair once more. "And here I thought bribery, coercion, threats, and double-dealing were enough to contend with." His eyes rose to Ingrey again, narrowing in new thought. "And whom do you suspect of this illicit magic? If not me," he added dryly.

Ingrey gave him a polite, apologetic shrug. Apologetic, but unabashed. *If you value your life, keep your secrets and mine . . .* "I possess no proof yet sturdy enough to stand on. It's a serious accusation."

Hetwar grimaced. "Your gift for understatement has not deserted you, I see. This is going to be Temple business, you know."

Ingrey nodded, briefly and unhappily. He wanted the

mage—even in his mind, he yet withheld the too-specific terms *sorcerer* or *shaman*—who had laid that evil geas upon him to be brought low. He was not at all sure he wished to be brought down with him. But to know that Hetwar, at least, was one wall that stood squarely at his back was an enormous relief. Ingrey prayed he had not damaged that wall in the testing of it.

And if Hetwar was not in league with Ijada's would-be murderer, then perhaps a plea for justice would have a chance, here? When else, indeed, was Ingrey likely to come face-to-face with Biast in the next few days? He took a breath.

"There remains the matter of Lady Ijada. If you desire to draw a veil over Boleso's late madness and blasphemy, a trial is the last thing you want. Let the inquest return a verdict of self-defense, or better still, accident, and let her go."

"She killed my *brother,*" said Biast, a little indignantly.

"Then let her pay a suitable blood-price, perhaps, in the manner of the Old Weald—nothing too impossibly high," Ingrey added cautiously. "Honor served, discretion preserved."

"The precedent is scarcely a good one for the royal house," said Hetwar. "As well declare hunting season on Stagthornes, or all high lords. There are sound reasons the Father's Order spent so much effort eliminating that old custom. The rich might without fear purchase the lives of the poor."

"And they don't now?" said Ingrey.

Hetwar gave him a little warning growl. "It is certainly to be preferred that her execution be swift and as painless as possible. Perhaps she might be granted a sword, instead of a rope or the pyre, or some like mercy."

And I a swordsman. "There is more going on here than is yet . . . clear." He had not wanted to play this card, but their closed expressions terrified him. He had planted his ideas in their heads; perhaps he should give them time to germinate. *Should her life be forfeit, then, because I am afraid to speak?* "I think she is god-touched. You pursue her at your peril."

Biast snorted. "A murderess? I doubt it. If so, let the gods send her a champion."

Ingrey held his breath lest it huff from his mouth like that of a man punched in the gut.

It seems They have. He's just not a very good one. You would think the gods could do better . . .

His pent breath found other words. "How long, my lords, has it been since the hallow kingship grew so hollow? This was once a sacred thing. How did we dare to come to treat it as merchandise to be bought and sold at the best market price? When did god-sworn warriors become peddlers?"

The words stung Hetwar, at least, for he sat up in open exasperation. "I use the gifts the gods have given me, including judgment and reason. My task, my tools. I have served the Weald since before you were born, Ingrey. There never was a golden age. It was always only iron."

"The gods have no hands in this world but ours. If we fail Them, where then can They turn?"

"Ingrey, peace!"

Biast was rubbing his brow, as though it ached. "Enough of this! If I am to attend the procession, I must go wash and dress." He stood and stretched, wincing.

Hetwar rose at once. "Indeed, Prince-marshal. I, too, must ride out." He frowned in frustration at Ingrey. "We will continue this when you have regained a more considered temper, Lord Ingrey. In the meantime, do not speak of these matters."

"Learned Lewko desires to interview me."

Hetwar blew out his breath. "Lewko, I know. A most unhelpful man, in my experience."

"I defy the Temple at my gravest risk."

"Oh? That's a new twist. I thought you defied anyone you damned well pleased."

How long they would have locked each other's gazes, Ingrey was not sure, but Biast reached the door first. Hetwar perforce followed, waving Ingrey out. "You had better not lie to Lewko. I'll speak with him later. And with you later." His gaze flicked down. "Don't drip on my carpets."

Ingrey flinched, and clasped his right hand with his left. The bandage was wet through, and leaking.

"What happened to your—no, tell me later. Attend on me at the funeral rite. Dress properly," Hetwar ordered.

"Sir." Ingrey bowed to his retreating back. Symark, who had wandered away down the hall to examine Hetwar's tapestries, hurried to join the prince.

So. Hetwar was going to think before reacting. Ingrey did not find this wholly reassuring.

It was full morning in Easthome, lively with bustling crowds, when Ingrey regained the street and turned toward the river. Ijada was awake now, he felt in his heart. Awake, and not, at the moment, unduly distressed. The reassurance eased him. Without what he now realized was an endemic state of covert panic driving his strides, his feet found their own pace, and it was a slow one. Did this strange new perception run two ways? He would have to ask her. He trudged wearily back toward the narrow house.

13

THE PORTER ADMITTED INGREY AGAIN TO THE HALL. Ingrey's gaze flicked up. Ijada was above, locked in with her
warden as instructed, presumably. It crossed Ingrey's mind
that while Horseriver's servants and one somewhat-
damaged swordsman might be enough to keep a docile naïve
girl from escaping this imprisonment, it was a woefully inadequate force to ward off attack. Ingrey might foil one as-
sailant—well, a few—several—but a sufficiently determined
enemy had merely to send enough men, and the conclusion
would be grimly certain.

For some subtler, uncanny attack . . . the outcome was not
so obvious. Could the weirding voice prove a defense? The
hum of questionable power in his blood unnerved him still.
Earl Horseriver apparently knew, even if Ingrey did not, of
the full range of Ingrey's new capacities. Wencel's oblique
promise of some sort of training troubled Ingrey's thoughts.

The porter produced a slightly crumpled piece of paper.
"Temple messenger brought this for you, my lord."

Ingrey broke the seal to find a short note from Learned
Lewko, the penmanship blocky and neat. *It appears my time*

will be taken today with that matter of internal Temple discipline you helped to uncover yesterday, for which I thank you, it read. *I will wait upon you and Lady Ijada as soon as I may following the prince's funeral rites tomorrow.*

Ingrey could imagine that the Temple would urgently wish to correct the dereliction of its acolytes before the state occasion. It was perhaps not entirely his imagination that he sensed a tart aggravation between the brief lines. Relief warred with disappointment in his heart. Lewko unsettled him, but he could think of no one better to ask about the laughing Voice that he had heard in his head during yesterday's scuffle in the temple court. Although his greatest secret hope, that Lewko would assure him it must have been a hallucination, seemed increasingly forlorn.

He climbed to his rooms to have Tesko help change his soaked bandage and take away his town garb to clean the bloodstains. The new stitches proved intact, and the spaces between them had scabbed over again. The unhealing wound was beginning to disturb him. His episodes of bleeding had perfectly reasonable explanations, most having to do with his own carelessness; it was only in his nervous fancy that they were beginning to seem like unholy libations. *And if small magics draw a small blood sacrifice, what would a great one do?*

His bed beckoned, and he sank down on it. The notion of food was still repulsive, but perhaps sleep would help him heal. He no sooner lay down than his thoughts began spinning again. He had been assuming from the beginning that the motivation of Ijada's mysterious assassin must be political, or revenge for her killing of Boleso. Perhaps such theorizing was an effect of his being so long in Hetwar's train. Yet trying to widen his thinking only made it feel more diffuse and foolish. *I know less and less each day.* What was the end of this progression, a glum future as a village idiot? The absurd images trailed off at last in muzzy exhaustion.

❧

He woke later than he had intended, thirsty, but feeling as if he had paid off some accumulated debts to his body. Inspired, he sent down orders via Tesko that dinner should be served to him and his prisoner in the ground-floor parlor. He donned town garb again, combed his hair, wondered why he owned no lavender water, considered sending Tesko out to buy some tomorrow, scrubbed his teeth, and shaved for the second time that day as the shadows deepened outside. He took a breath and descended the stairs.

He turned into the parlor to find Ijada already standing there in the illumination of the sconces, in the wheat-colored dress looking like candlelight herself. She turned at the sound of his step, and a smile flared on her face that made his lips part.

He could not very well fall upon her like a ravening wolf, not least because the accursed warden stood at her side, hands and lips tightly folded. The table, he saw to his dismay, seemed to have been reflexively set for three. Horseriver's servant was surely Horseriver's spy. Simply to dismiss the duenna bore unknown dangers.

Regardless of his own strangely shifting internal allegiances, he supposed he must guard his own reputation as well as Ijada's, or risk being relieved of his post. But he might hazard a smile, and did. He might chance a touch of her hand, brought formally to his lips. The scent of her skin, so close, seemed to bring all of his senses to heightened sharpness. The sheer intensity of her, at this range, almost overwhelmed him.

One desperate return squeeze, her nails biting fiercely into his skin, was all her opportunity to say, *I feel it, too*. She muted her smile to something social, the trained courtesy of a high household, as he helped her to her seat and a manservant brought their meal.

"I believe this is the first time I have seen you out of your riding leathers, Lord Ingrey." Her tone seemed to be quite approving.

He touched the fine black cloth of his jerkin. "Lady Hetwar makes sure that her husband's men do not disgrace her house."

"She has a good eye, then."

"Oh? Good." Ingrey swallowed wine without choking. "Good." His thoughts tangled on too many levels at once: the arousal of his body, the political and mortal fear of their situation, the remembered shock of that mystical kiss. He dropped a bite of food off his fork, and tried surreptitiously to retrieve it from his lap.

"Learned Lewko did not come."

"Oh. Yes. He sent a note; he means to come tomorrow, after the funeral."

"Did anything further come of your ice bear? Or your pirate?"

"Not yet. Though the rumors had already reached my lord Hetwar."

"How did your conference with the sealmaster go?"

He tilted his head. "How would you guess?" *Do you sense where I am, how I feel, as I do you?*

She gave a small nod in return, and essayed slowly, "Tense. Uncertain. There was . . . an incident." Her gaze now seemed to dig under his skin. She glanced at the warden, who was chewing and listening.

"Truly." He drew breath. "I believe Sealmaster Hetwar is to be trusted. His concerns, however, are wholly political ones. I am less and less of the opinion that your concerns are wholly political ones. Prince-marshal Biast was there, which I did not expect. He did not warm at once to the idea of a blood-price, but at least I had a chance to set the idea in his mind."

She pushed some noodles across her plate with her fork. "I think the gods have little interest in politics. Only in souls. Look to souls, Lord Ingrey, if you seek to guess Their minds." She looked up, frowning.

Conscious of the glowering warden, Ingrey asked more lightly after Ijada's day; she returned in kind a description of an amusing old book of household hints, apparently the only reading matter the house had offered up. After that the conversation fell flatly silent for a space. Not what he had hoped, but at least they were both in the same room, alive and breathing. *I must raise my standards for dalliance.*

A sharp rap on the front door, the shuffle of the porter, voices; Ingrey tensed, aware he'd left his sword upstairs and bore only his belt knife, then relaxed a trifle as he recognized the new voice as Wencel's. He rose to his feet as the earl-ordainer entered the parlor, and the warden scrambled up and curtseyed apprehensively.

"Ingrey. Lady Ijada." Wencel nodded to them. He was dressed in full court mourning, a little grimed, and looked weary to the point of exhaustion. The darkness within him was quiescent, as if benumbed or suppressed. His eye summed the chairs. "You may be excused," he said to the warden. "Take your plate."

The woman curtseyed again and removed herself promptly. She did not need to be told, by Wencel at least, to close the door behind her.

"Have you eaten?" Lady Ijada inquired civilly.

"This and that." He waved. "Just some wine, please."

She poured from the carafe, and he took the beaker and sat back in his chair, his legs stretched out, his head tilted back. "You are well, lady? My people are seeing to your needs?"

"Yes, thank you. My material needs, anyway. It is news that I lack."

Wencel's chin came down. "There is no news, at least of your plight. Boleso has arrived in Templetown, where his body will rest tonight. By this time tomorrow, that carnival, at least, will be over." He grimaced.

And Ijada's legal one will begin? "I have been thinking, Wencel . . ." Succinctly, Ingrey explained his blood-price ploy once more. "If you really seek to redeem the honor of your house, cousin, this could be one way. If the Stagthornes and the Badgerbanks could both be persuaded. Which you are also in a position to do, I would point out."

Wencel gave him a shrewd look. "I see you are not an impartial jailer."

"If such a jailer was what you really wanted, I'm sure you could have found one," Ingrey returned dryly.

Wencel lifted his beaker in an only half-mocking salute, and drank. After a moment he added, "Speaking of indirect evidence, I presume by the fact that I am not yet arrested for defilement that you have kept our secrets."

"I have managed to keep you out of my conversations so far, yes. I don't know how much longer I can succeed. I've drawn some unfortunate attention from the Temple. Did you hear about the ice bear yet?"

Wencel's lips twisted. "This funeral procession today being short on piety and long on gossip, yes. The tales I heard were lurid, conflicting, and ambiguous. I was possibly the only confidant to whom the events were crystal clear. Congratulations upon your discovery. I didn't imagine you would learn of that power for quite some time yet."

"My wolf never spoke like this before."

"The great beasts have no speech. That shaping must come from the man. The whole is a different essence from either part; they alter each other as they merge."

Ingrey contemplated this remark for a moment, finding it plangent but maddeningly vague. He decided to leave out mention of that other Voice.

"And," Wencel added, "your wolf was truly bound before. Separated from you even while trapped within. Neither the Temple nor I was mistaken on that, I promise you. It is its unbinding that remains a mystery to me." Wencel raised his brows invitingly.

Ingrey ignored the hint. "What else might it—might I—we—do?"

"The weirding voice is actually a great and subtle power, nearer the heart of the matter than you know."

"Since I know practically nothing, that is no great observation, Wencel."

Wencel shrugged. "Indeed, the shamans of the forest

tribes bore other powers. Visions that did not deceive. Healings, of wounds of the body or mind, of fevers, of sicknesses of the blood. Sometimes, they could follow men who had fallen into great darkness of mind and bring them back out again. Sometimes their powers were reversed; they could plunge victims into those darknesses, or thwart healing, even unto death. Darker necromancies still, consuming mortal sacrifices."

Casting geases? Ingrey wondered silently.

"Great powers," Wencel continued more lowly, "and yet—even in the days of the Old Weald's greatest glory and heartbreak, not great enough. Outnumbered, the shamans and spirit warriors were borne down under the weight of their most implacable enemies. Let that be a lesson to you, Ingrey. We are far too alone in this. Secrecy is our only source of safety."

Ijada took a breath and ventured, "I have heard that great Audar overcame Wealding sorceries with swords alone, in his last push. Swords and courage."

Wencel snorted. "Darthacan lies. He had gathered all the Temple saints and sorcerers that Darthaca could muster in his train. It took the gods' own betrayals to bring us down at Holytree."

Ingrey guessed at Ijada's direction, and followed her lead. "Yes, what does your library at Castle Horseriver have to say about Bloodfield that the Darthacan chronicles do not?"

Wencel's lips curled up in a weird little smile. "Enough to know that whatever they've taught you of it in these degenerate days is fabrication."

Ingrey said, "Whatever evil rites the Wealdings were attempting, Audar won. No lie there."

Wencel's shoulders jerked in aggravation. "Not evil, but a great, if desperate, deed. The Weald was sorely pressed. We had lost half our lands to the Darthacans in the past generation. The bravest of our young men were dying in droves beneath the Darthacan lances."

"The military accounts I have read all assert that Audar's

army was better organized, trained, and led, and its baggage train a wonder, by the standards of the day," Ingrey observed. "They built their own roads through the forests almost as fast as they could march."

"Hardly that fast, but indeed, their descent on any tribal district fell as a destructive plague. With all of their own resources and half of ours in Darthacan hands, courage alone was no longer enough to stem their advance. The hallow king in that day—the last true consecrated servant of our people, and by the way one of my Horseriver ancestors—met with all the shamans of all the kin he could gather, and together they devised a great rite to make their spirit warriors invincible. Men of might, who could not be wounded or slain, to meet the Darthacans in battle and throw them back across the river Lure forever. Men whose bodies and spirits would be bound to the sacred Weald itself, renewed by its life until the victory was gained. The wisdom songs they composed to effect the bindings were to last for three days, all the voices blended together in a chant of overwhelming majesty, greater and more unified than anything attempted before. They sang up strength out of the very forest."

Ijada, listening with breathless attention, murmured, "So what went wrong?"

Wencel shook his head, his lips tightening to paleness. "It would have worked, had not Audar, with the aid of his sorcerers and the gods, come upon us too soon. A forced march at unprecedented speed through the forests and hills, then, instead of waiting till dawn for the light and to rest his men, an immediate attack in the darkness. It was the night of the second day of the great rite, and we were unprepared and vulnerable, the kin shamans exhausted and drained with their labors, the king already bound but the men still partly not."

"You—we did fight, though?" she pressed.

"Oh, fiercely. But Audar had concentrated three times our numbers. I—no one thought he could gather that many, that fast, and move them so far."

"Still, magically healing warriors must have been hard to overcome. How?"

"When bodies are buried in one pit, and all their heads buried in a pit half a mile away, even such uncanny men die. Eventually. They slew the hallow king, the hub of the spell, first, though I grant not by beheading. They broke his limbs and cast him into the first pit, and piled the decapitated bodies of his comrades in upon him. He took hours to die. Suffocated—drowned in their beloved blood—at the last." Wencel's eyes glittered in the candlelight.

"Audar's men worked all night and all day," he continued, "red to their waists and half-mad with the task. Some broke from the horror of their own deeds, sat and rocked and wept. They slew all they found within the bounds of Holytree, whether surrendered or resisting: shamans, spirit warriors, innocent camp followers, males, females, children. They were taking no more chances. They leveled every structure, killed every animal, cut down and burned the Tree of Sacrifice. The hallow king's eldest son and holy heir they beheaded last, at the end of the next day, after he had witnessed it all. When no living thing was left within the sacred bounds except the trees, they withdrew, and forbade entry. As if to bury their own sins along with us. And the rains came, and the snows of many winters, and men died, and forgot Holytree, and all the glory that had passed there."

Ingrey found his breath had nearly stopped, so caught up was he in Wencel's impassioned delivery of this old tale. What else might Wencel be prodded into revealing? "They say Audar was made furious with tribal treaty betrayals, and was sorry afterward for the massacre. He made great gifts to the Temple for the forgiveness of his soul."

"*His* Temple!" Wencel scoffed. "He received with his left hand what he gave with his right. And a forced treaty is no treaty at all, but a robbery. The Darthacan encroachment was never-ending, and their treaties, self-serving lies."

"I don't know," said Ingrey judiciously. "It's clear enough from the chronicles that the Darthacans did not start out intending to conquer the Weald. They slid into it over two generations. Every time they set up a boundary, they found themselves with a new frontier to defend, and the unruly kin tribes picking piecemeal at their defenses, until they moved the outposts farther to defend those lines, and it started all over again."

"You are half a Darthacan yourself, Ingrey." Wencel's tone fell from impassioned back to dry once more.

"Most of us are, these days."

"Yes. I know."

"But some kin warriors escaped to the borders," said Ijada, watching Wencel closely. Her hands were tight in her lap. "They fought on, our ancestors. We fought back. In time, we won. The Weald was renewed."

Wencel snorted. "Audar's empire fell to the squabbles and stupidities of his great-grandsons, not for any virtue remaining in the Weald. What came back, a century and a half later, was a shadow and a mockery of the Old Weald, emptied of its essences and its beauties, stamped in the mold of Darthacan Quintarian orthodoxy. The men who re-created that parody of the hallow kingship thought they were restoring something, but they were too ignorant even to know what had been lost. The great free days, the forest days, were gone, netted under the roads and mills, cut down with the trees turned to towns, weighted beneath the groaning stones of Audar's temples. A hundred and fifty years of tears and strain and blood had been spent for *nothing*. They congratulated themselves most smugly, the new kin lords, the grand rich earl-ordainers—and archdivine-ordainers, what a travesty!—but their vaunted throne was empty of anything but men's buttocks. They should have been weeping in the ashes, on that day of final betrayal."

Wencel at last seemed to grow conscious of the wide-eyed stares of both his listeners. "Faugh! So ends the lesson, children." He exhaled. "I grow morbid. It has been an ugly day, and too long. I should go home." His lips compressed. "To my wife."

Ijada said in a constricted voice, "How is she taking it all?"

"Not well," Wencel conceded.

Ingrey worried suddenly how much of a push against Ijada might come from that quarter. Princess Fara was one Stagthorne who might well want blood, not money, in order to wash her own hands of a grievous guilt. And Fara surely had not only Wencel's ear, but her brother Biast's.

Wencel pushed back his chair, pinched the bridge of his nose, and rose to his feet. His eyes were dark-circled, Ingrey noticed. And too old for his face.

Ingrey saw him out the front, then nipped back into the parlor and closed the door once more before the warden could reappear. Ijada was frowning, as he seated himself beside her.

"I wonder," she said slowly, "what dreams Wencel has been having?"

"Hm?"

She tapped two fingers on the table edge. "He did not speak of Bloodfield as one who has read or heard. He spoke as one who'd seen."

"As you have—do you think? Yet at a different time."

"My dream was in the present, I thought. Why should he dream of the past? Why should *he* dream of my men at all?"

Ingrey noted her unthinking possessive. "He seems to feel they are—were—*his* men." He hesitated. "His father had a reputation for a historical mania. So did his grandfather, I think, from some things my father and aunt said. He was not drawn in to his sires' passions as a child, that I know, but perhaps some crept upon him as he studied their writings later. He must have been frantic for explanations of what had happened to him." He added after a moment, "Have you dreamed again of the Wounded Woods since you were there?"

She shook her head. "There was no . . . no need. The task, whatever it was, was done. It didn't need to be done twice. Nothing of it has faded or changed since then." Her eyes sought his face. "Until you came along, that is."

Alone as they briefly were, Ingrey was torn between desire and fear of another kiss. What else might such a caress reveal? His bandaged hand crept toward hers and closed over it, and a small grateful smile flashed at him from those dizzying lips.

Her eyes narrowed. "Kin shaman. Spirit warrior. Banner-carrier. Holytree. Why should all these symbols of the Old Weald be resurrected here, now? We three are linked and linked again—you and Wencel by blood and old tragedy, he and I by . . . recent events, you and I by . . ." She took a breath. "We should be trying to figure it out."

"We should be trying to stay alive, Ijada!"

"I am not at all sure," she said rather quietly, "that staying alive is what this is all about."

His hand clutched hers on the tabletop despite the twinge of pain. "Don't you become fey!"

"Why not? Do you imagine feyness is only your task?" Her brows twitched up in sudden amusement. "It is most becoming upon you, I admit. Unfairly so." She leaned toward him, and he froze between terror and joy as her lips brushed his. Only flesh on flesh this time, only a touch of warmth.

Before he could lunge at her in a quest for holy fire, the door clicked open. The warden entered and eyed them both, unsmiling. Unwillingly, he released Ijada's hand and eased back. He was conscious that his breath was coming too fast.

The warden sketched a curtsey. "Begging your pardon, my lord. The earl instructed me to keep close to my lady."

"I am obliged for his consideration," said Ijada, in a voice so expressionless even Ingrey could not decide if it was sincere or dry. She tipped up and drained her beaker and set it down. "Should we retire again to that dull chamber?"

"If it please you, my lady, it was what the earl said."

Beneath the woman's stodgy stubbornness Ingrey perceived a real unease. The earl-ordainer's secular powers alone were enough to overawe his servants, Ingrey supposed, but did they sense—or had they experienced—more?

"Perhaps it is as well to turn in early," Ingrey conceded

reluctantly. "I must attend Lord Hetwar at the funeral rites tomorrow morning."

Ijada nodded and rose. "I should be grateful if you would wait upon me after, and tell me of them."

"Certainly, Lady Ijada."

He watched her pass out of the parlor. It was only in his overwrought fancy that the room seemed to grow darker for her going from it.

14

THE TEMPLE SQUARE WAS ALREADY CROWDED WITH courtly and would-be-courtly mourners when Ingrey arrived there in the midmorning. His eye picked out a few of Gesca's men at the outer edges of the mob, indicating that Lord Hetwar was already within. Ingrey lengthened his stride and shouldered through the press. Those who recognized him gave way at once.

The sky was a bright autumn blue, and he shrugged in relief as he stepped out of the sun into the shade of the portico. His best court dress was heavy and a trifle hot, the somber sleeveless coat swirling about his ankles and tending to tangle with his sword. The sunbeams shone down also into the open central court, where the holy fire burned high on its plinth, and he blinked at the adjustment from light to dark to light. He spotted Lady Hetwar, attended by Gesca and Hetwar's oldest son, made his way to her side, and bowed. She gave him an acknowledging nod, her glance approving his garb, and shifted a little to make him space to loom in proper retainer's style beside Gesca at her back. Gesca gave him a nervy sideways stare, but by no other sign revealed any aftereffects of their last tense encounter, and Ingrey began to hope Gesca had kept the eerie incident to himself.

Beyond the plinth, Ingrey also noted Rider Ulkra and some of Prince Boleso's higher servants; good, the exiled household had arrived in Easthome as instructed. Ulkra cast him a polite nod of greeting, though most of the retainers who had ridden escort to Boleso's wagon with him avoided his eyes—whether conscious of his contempt or simply unnerved by him, Ingrey could not tell.

From a stone passage, the sound of a temple choir started up, the echoing effect making the fine, blended voices sound appropriately distant and doleful. At a slow pace, the singing acolytes entered the court: five times five, a quintet for each god, robed in blue, green, red, gray, and white. The archdivine of Easthome followed solemnly. Behind him, six great lords carried the prince's bier. Hetwar was among them, both kin Boarford brothers, and three more earl-ordainers.

Boleso's body was tightly wrapped in layers of herbs beneath his perfumed princely robes, Ingrey guessed, though his swollen face was exposed. The delay in his burial pushed the limits of a decomposition that would necessitate a closed coffin. But the death of one so highborn demanded witnesses, the more the better, to prevent later imposters and pretenders from troubling the realm.

The principal mourners followed next. Prince-marshal Biast, resplendent of dress and weary of face, was attended by Symark, holding the prince-marshal's standard with its pennant wrapped and bound to its staff as a sign of grief. Behind them, Earl Horseriver supported his wife, Princess Fara. Her dark garb was plain to severity, her brown hair drawn back and without jewels or ribbons, and her face deathly white by contrast. She had not her brothers' height, and the long Stagthorne jaw was softened in her; she was not a beauty, but she was a princess, and her proud carriage and presence normally made up for any shortfall. Today she just looked haggard and ill.

Horseriver's spirit horse seemed stopped down so tight as

to be mistakable for a mere blackness of mood. *I must find out from Wencel how he does that.* Ingrey began to see how Wencel might long evade the lesser among the Sighted, but he wondered at the cost.

Ingrey was relieved to see that the hallow king had not been dragged from his sickbed and propped in some sedan chair or litter to attend his son's funeral. It would have been too much like one bier following another.

Ingrey trailed Lady Hetwar as she took her place in the procession entering the high-vaulted Son of Autumn's court. The wide, paved space filled; lesser hangers-on crowded up and peeked through the archway from the central court. The high lords set down the bier before the Son's altar, the choir chanted another hymn, and Archdivine Fritine stepped forth to conduct the ceremonies of Boleso's send-off. Ingrey widened his stance, clasped his hands behind his back, and prepared to endure the obsequies. On the whole, and fortunately in his view, the speakers kept their words brief and formal, with no references to the embarrassing manner of the prince's death. Even Hetwar restricted himself to a few platitudes about young lives cut tragically short.

A rustling sounded from the central court as the crowd parted to allow the procession of the sacred animals to pass. Three of the stiff-looking groom-acolytes who led them were not the ones Ingrey had seen the other day. Fafa the impressive ice bear had been replaced by a notably small long-haired white cat curled tamely in the arms of a new woman groom in the Bastard's whites. The boy who led the copper colt was the same as before, though; while he kept his attention on his animal and the archdivine, his glance did cross Ingrey's once, above Lady Hetwar's head, and his eyes widened in alarmed recognition.

With extreme circumspection, each animal was led to the bier to sign the acceptance, if any, of Boleso's soul by its god. No one much expected a blessing from the Daughter of Spring's blue hen nor the Mother of Summer's green bird, but nerves stretched as the copper colt was led forth. The horse's response was ambiguous to nonexistent, as were those of the gray dog and the white cat. The grooms looked worried. Biast appeared grim indeed, and Fara seemed ready to faint.

Was Boleso's soul sundered and damned, then, rejected by the Son of Autumn Who was his best hope, unclaimed even by the Bastard, doomed to drift as a fading ghost? Or defiled by the spirits of the animals he had sacrificed and consumed, caught between the world of matter and the world of spirit in chill and perpetual torment, as Ingrey had once envisioned to Ijada?

The archdivine motioned Biast, Hetwar, and Learned Lewko—who had been lurking in the background so unobtrusively even Ingrey had not seen him before—to his side for a low-voiced conference, and the grooms began to lead up the animals one by one and present them again to the bier.

The heat and the tension were suddenly too much for Ingrey. The chamber wavered and lurched before his eyes. His right hand throbbed. As quietly as he could, he stepped back to the wall to brace his shoulders against the cool stone. It wasn't enough. As the copper colt clopped forth once more, his eyes rolled back and he crumpled to the pavement in a boneless heap, the only sound a faint clank from his scabbard.

❧

And then, abruptly, he was standing in that other *place,* that unbounded space he had entered once before to do battle. Only it seemed not to be a battle to which he was called now. He still wore his court garb, his jaw was still human . . .

Out of an avenue of autumn-scented trees a red-haired young man appeared. He was tall, clothed as for a hunt in leggings and leathers, his bow and quiver strapped across his back. His eyes were bright, sparkling like a woodland stream; freckles dusted across his nose, and his generous mouth laughed. His head was crowned with autumn leaves, brown oak, red maple, yellow birch, and his stride was wide.

He pursed his lips and whistled, and the sharp sweet sound pierced Ingrey's spirit like an arrow.

Bounding out of the mists, a great dark wolf with silver-tipped fur ran to the youth's side, jaws agape, tongue lolling foolishly; the huge beast crouched at his feet, licked his leg, rolled to one side and let the red-haired youth crouch and thump and rub its belly. A collar of autumn leaves much like the youth's crown circled the thick fur of its neck. The wolf seemed to laugh, too, as the youth stood once more, legs braced.

Pacing in a more dignified manner, but still eagerly, the spotted leopard appeared. Ijada, looking bewildered, walked beside it. The leopard's neck was bound with a garland of autumn flowers, all purple and deep yellow, and a plaited chain of them ran up to circle Ijada's wrist like a leash, but which was leader and which was led was not clear. Ijada wore the spotted yellow dress in which Ingrey had first seen her, the one she'd been wearing during the nightmare of Boleso's death, but the bloodstains were fresh and red, shimmering like rubies embroidered across her breast. Her expression, as she saw the youth's bright face, changed from bewildered to wide-eyed, exalted, and terrified. The leopard rubbed against the youth's legs on the other side from the wolf, nearly knocking him over, and its rumbling purr sawed through the air like some serrated song.

The youth gestured; Ingrey's and Ijada's heads turned.

Prince Boleso stood before them in an agonized paralysis. He, too, wore what he'd been found in the night he'd died: a short coat and daubs of paint and powder across his waxy skin. The muted colors made Ingrey's head ache; they clashed, not rightly composed. They reminded Ingrey of an ignorant man, hearing another language, responding with mouthed gibberish, or of a child, not yet able to write, scribbling eager senseless scrawls across a page in imitation of an older brother's hand.

Boleso's skin seemed translucent to Ingrey's eyes. Beneath his ribs, a swirling darkness barked and yammered, grunted and whined. Boar there was, and dog, wolf, stag, badger, fox, hawk, even a terrified housecat. *An early experiment?* Power there was, yes; but chaos even greater, an unholy din. He remembered Ijada's description: *His very mind seemed a menagerie, howling.*

The god said softly, "He cannot enter My gates bearing these."

Ijada stepped forward, her hands held out in tentative supplication. "What would You have of us, my lord?"

The god's eye took in them both. "Free him, if it be your will, that he may enter in."

"You would have us choose the fate of another?" she asked breathlessly. "Not just his life, but his eternity?"

The Son of Autumn tilted his wreathed head a trifle. "You chose for him once, did you not?"

Her lips parted, closed, set a little, in fear or awe.

He ought to feel that awe, too, Ingrey supposed. Ought to be falling to his knees. Instead he was dizzy and angry. With a piercing regret, he envied Ijada her exaltation even as he resented it. As though Ingrey saw the sun through a pinhole in a piece of canvas, while Ijada saw the orb entire. *But if my eyes were wider, would this Light blind me?*

"You would—you would take *him* into Your heaven, my lord?" asked Ingrey in astonishment and outrage. "He slew, not in defense of his own life, but in malice and madness. He tried to steal powers not rightly given to him. If I guess right, he plotted the death of his own brother. He would have raped Ijada, if he could, and killed again for his sport!"

The Son held up his hands. Luminescent, they seemed, as if dappled by autumn sun reflecting off a stream into shade. "My grace flows from these as a river, wolf-lord. Would you have me dole it out in the exact measure that men earn, as from an apothecary's dropper? Would you stand in pure water to your waist, and administer it by the scant spoon to men dying of thirst on a parched shore?"

Ingrey stood silent, abashed, but Ijada lifted her face, and said steadily, "No, my lord, for my part. Give him to the river. Tumble him down in the thunder of Your cataract. His loss is no gain of mine, nor his dark deserving any joy to me."

The god smiled brilliantly at her. Tears slid down her face like silver threads: like benedictions.

"It is unjust," whispered Ingrey. "Unfair to all who—who *would* try to do rightly. . . ."

"Ah, but I am not the god for justice," murmured the Son. "Would you both stand before My Father instead?"

Ingrey swallowed nervously, not at all sure the question was rhetorical, or what might happen if he said *yes*. "Let Ijada's be the choosing, then. I will abide."

"Alas, more shall be required of you than to stand aside and act not, wolf-lord." The god gestured to Boleso. "He cannot enter in my gates so burdened with these mutilated spirits. This is not their proper door. Hunt them from him, Ingrey."

Ingrey stared through the bars of Boleso's ribs. "Clean this cage?"

"If you prefer that metaphor, yes." The god's copper eyebrows twitched, but his eyes, beneath them, glinted with a certain dark humor. Wolf and leopard now sat on their haunches on either side of those slim booted legs, staring silently at Ingrey with deep, unblinking eyes.

Ingrey swallowed. "How?"

"Call them forth."

"I . . . do not understand."

"Do as your ancestors did for each other, in the purifying last rites of the Old Weald. Did you not know? Even as they washed and wrapped each body for burial, the kin shamans looked after the souls of their own. Each helped his comrade, whether simple spirit warrior or great mage, through Our gates, at the end of their lives, and looked to be helped so in turn. A chain of hand to hand, of voice to voice, cleansed souls flowing in an unending stream." The god's voice softened. "Call my unhappy creatures out, Ingrey kin Wolfcliff. Sing them to their rest."

Ingrey stood facing Boleso. The prince's eyes were wide

and pleading. *I imagine Ijada's eyes were wide and pleading that night, too. What mercy did she get from you, my graceless prince?*

Besides, I cannot sing worth a damn.

Ijada's eyes were on *him,* now, Ingrey realized. Confident with hope.

I have no mercy in me, lady. So I shall borrow some from you.

He took a breath, and reached down into himself farther than he'd yet done before. *Keep it simple.* Picked out one swirl by eye, held out his hand, and commanded, *"Come."*

The first beast's spirit spun out through his fingers, wild and distraught, and fled away. He glanced at the god. "Where—?"

A wave of those radiant fingers reassured him. "It is well. Go on."

"Come . . ."

One by one, the dark streams flowed out of Boleso and melted into the night. Morning. Whatever this was. They all floated in a *now* somewhere outside of time, Ingrey thought. At last Boleso stood before him, still silent, but freed of the dark smears.

The red-haired god appeared riding the copper colt, and extended a hand to the prince. Boleso flinched, staring up in doubt and fear, and Ijada's breath caught. But then he climbed quietly up behind. His face held much wonder, if little joy.

"I think he is still soul-wounded, my lord," said Ingrey, watching in bare comprehension.

"Ah, but I know an excellent Physician for him, where we are going." The god laughed, dazzlingly.

"My lord—" Ingrey began, as the god made to turn the unbridled horse.

"Yes?"

"If each kin shaman delivered the next, and him the next . . ." He swallowed harder. "What happens to the last shaman left?"

The Lord of Autumn stared enigmatically down at him. He extended one lucent finger, stopping just short of brushing Ingrey's forehead. For a moment, Ingrey thought he was not going to answer at all, but then he murmured, "We shall have to find out."

He clapped his heels to the copper colt's sides, and was gone.

❧

Ingrey blinked.

He was lying on hard pavement, his body half-straightened, staring up at the curve of the dome of the Son's court. Staring up at a ring of startled faces staring down at him: Gesca, a concerned Lady Hetwar, a couple of men he did not know.

"What happened?" whispered Ingrey.

"You fainted," said Gesca, frowning.

"No—what happened at the bier? Just now?"

"The Lord of Autumn took Prince Boleso," said Lady Hetwar, glancing over her shoulder. "That pretty red colt nuzzled him all over—it was very clear. To everyone's relief."

"Yes. Half the men I know were betting he'd go to the Bastard." A twisted grin flitted over Gesca's face.

Lady Hetwar cast him a quelling frown. "That is *not* a fit subject for wagering, Gesca."

"No, my lady," Gesca agreed, dutifully erasing his smirk.

Ingrey hitched up to sit leaning against the wall. The motion made the chamber spin in slow jerks, and he squeezed his eyes shut, then opened them again. He had felt numb and bodiless during his vision, but now he was shuddering in waves radiating out from the pit of his belly, though he did not feel cold. As though his body had experienced some shock that his mind was denied.

Lady Hetwar leaned forward and pressed a stern maternal hand to his damp brow. "Are you ill, Lord Ingrey? You do feel rather warm."

"I . . ." He was about to firmly deny any such weakness, then thought better of it. He wanted nothing more passionately than to remove himself from this fraught scene at once. ". . . fear so, my lady. Pray excuse me, and excuse me to your lord husband." *I must find Ijada.* He clambered to his feet and began to feel his way along the wall. "I would rather not pitch up my breakfast on the temple floor in the middle of all this."

"Indeed not," she agreed fervently. "Go on, quickly. Gesca, help him." She waited just long enough to see Gesca grasp his arm, then turned back to her son.

Over by the altar, the choir was again singing, forming up to lead the procession out, and people were beginning to shuffle themselves back into their positions. Ingrey was grateful for the covering noise. Across the crowd, he thought he saw Learned Lewko crane his neck toward his disruption, but he did not meet the divine's eyes. Keeping to the walls, half for support and half to skim around the throng, he made his escape. By the time they exited the portico, he was towing Gesca.

"Leave me," he gasped, shaking off Gesca's hand.

"But Ingrey, Lady Hetwar said—"

He didn't even need the weirding voice; Gesca recoiled at his glower alone. He stood staring in bewilderment as Ingrey weaved away through the crowded square.

By the time Ingrey reached the stairway down to Kingstown, he was nearly running. He bolted down the endless steps two and three at a time, at risk of tumbling head over tail. By the time he passed over the covered creek, he was running, his long coat flapping around his boot heels. By the time he pounded on the door of the narrow house, and stood a moment with his hands on his knees, wheezing for breath, he had nearly made his lie to Lady Hetwar true; his stomach was heaving almost as much as his lungs. He fell through the door as the astonished porter opened it.

"Lady Ijada—where is she?"

Before the porter could speak, a thumping on the stairs

answered his question. Ijada flew down them, the warden in her train crying, "Lady, you should not, come back and lie down again—"

Ingrey straightened, grasping her hands as she grasped his. "Did you—"

"I saw—"

"Come!" He yanked her into the parlor. *"Leave us!"* he shouted back over his shoulder. Porter, porter's boy, warden, and housemaid all blew back like leaves in a storm gust. Ingrey slammed the door upon them.

The handgrip turned into a shaken embrace, having in it very little romance but a great deal of terror. Ingrey was not sure which of them was trembling more. "What did you see?"

"I saw Him, Ingrey, I heard *Him*. Not a dream this time, not a fragrance in the dark—a daylight vision, clear." She pushed him back to stare into his face. "And I saw you." Her look turned to disbelief, though not, apparently, of her vision. "You stood face-to-face with a god, and you could find nothing better to do than to *argue* with Him!" She gripped and shook his shoulders. "Ingrey!"

"He took Boleso—"

"I saw! Oh, grace of the Son, my transgression was lifted from me." Tears were running down her real face, as they had her dream face. "By your grace, too, oh, Ingrey, such a deed . . ." She was kissing his face, cool lips slipping across hot sweat on his brow, his eyelids, his cheeks.

He fell back a little, and said through gritted teeth, "I don't do this sort of thing. These things do not *happen* to me."

She stared. "They happen to you rather a lot, *I'd* say."

"No! Yes . . . Gods! I feel as though I've become some unholy lightning rod in the middle of a thunderstorm. Miracles, I have to stay away from funeral miracles, they dodge aside from their targets and come at me. I don't, I can't . . ."

Her left hand squeezed his right. She looked down. "Oh!"

The wretched bandage was soaked again. Wordlessly, she turned to the sideboard, rooted briefly in a drawer, and found a length of linen. "Here, sit." She drew him to the table, stripped off the red rag, and wrapped his hand more tightly. Their mutual wheezing was dying down at last. *She* had not run across half of Easthome, but he did not question her breathlessness.

"A physician should look at that," she said, knotting the cloth. "It's not right."

"I won't say you're mistaken."

She leaned forward and pushed a lock of sweat-dampened hair off his forehead. Her gaze searched his face, for what he did not know. Her expression softened. "I may have murdered Boleso—"

"No, only killed."

"But thanks to you I did not encompass his sundering from the gods. It's something. No small thing."

"Aye. If you say so." For her, then. If his actions had pleased Ijada, perhaps they were worthwhile. Ijada and the Son. "That was it, then. That was what we were chivvied here for. Boleso's undeserved redemption. We have accomplished the god's will, and now it's over, and we are discarded to our fates."

Her lips curved up. "That's very Ingrey of you, Ingrey. Always look on the dark side."

"*Someone* has to be realistic, in the midst of this madness!"

Now her brows rose, too. She was *laughing* at him. "Utterly bleak and black is not the sum of realism. All the other colors are real, too. It was *my* undeserved redemption as well."

He ought to feel offended. Not buoyed up by her laughter as if floating in some bubbling hot spring.

She took a breath. "Ingrey! If one soul trapped in the world by an anchor of animals is such an agony to the gods that they make miracles out of, of such unlikely helpers as us, what must four thousand such souls be?"

"You think of your Wounded Woods? Your dream?"

"I don't think we're done. I don't think we're even *started* yet!"

Ingrey moistened his lips. He followed her jump of inspiration, yes. He wished it wasn't so easy to do. If freeing one such soul had been an experience of muted terror to him . . . "Nor shall we be, if I am burned and you are hanged. I do not say you are wrong, but first things first."

She shook her head in passionate denial. "I still do not understand what is wanted of me. But I *saw* what is wanted of you. If your great-wolf has made you a true shaman of the Weald, the very last—and the god's own Voice said it was so—then you are their last hope indeed. A purification—the men who fell at Bloodfield were never purified, never released. We need to go there." She jerked in her seat as if ready to leap up and run out the door at once and down the morning road on foot.

His hands tightened on hers, as much to hold her in place as anything. "I would point out, we have a few hindrances here. You are arrested and bound for trial, and I am your arresting officer."

"You offered to smuggle me away once before. Now I know where! Don't you see?" Her eyes were afire.

"And then what? We would be pursued and dragged back, perhaps even before we could do anything, and your case would be worse than before, and I would be wrenched from you. Let us solve this problem in Easthome first, *then* go. That is the logical order of things. If your men have waited four hundred years for you, they can surely wait a little longer."

"Can they?" Her brows drew down in a deep frown. "Do you know this? How?"

"We must concentrate on one problem at a time, the most urgent first."

Her right hand touched her heart. "This feels most urgent to me."

Ingrey's jaw set. Just because she was passionate and loving and beautiful and god-touched didn't mean she was right in all things.

More than god-touched. Personally redeemed by miracu-

lous intervention. No wonder she seemed a conflagration just now. He might melt in her radiance.

But only redeemed in her soul and sin. Her body and crime were still hostage to the world of matter and Easthome politics. Whatever he was called to, it was not to follow her into plain folly.

He drew breath. "I did not dream your dream of the Woods. I have only your—admittedly vivid—description to go on. Ghosts fade, starved of nourishment from their former bodies. Why have not these? Do you imagine they've been stuck in the blasted trees for four centuries?"

He'd meant it for half a joke, but she took it wholly seriously. "I think so. Or something of a sort. *Something* alive must be sustaining them in the world of matter. Remember what Wencel said, about the great rite that Audar interrupted?"

"I don't trust anything Wencel says."

She regarded him doubtfully. "He's your cousin."

Ingrey couldn't decide if she meant that as an argument for or against the earl.

"I do not understand Wencel," Ijada continued, "but that rang true to me, it rang in my bones. A great rite that bound the spirit warriors to the Weald itself for their sustenance, until their victory was achieved." A most unsettled, and unsettling, look stole over her face. "But they never achieved victory, did they? And the Weald that came back, in the end, was not what they'd lost, but something new. Wencel says it was a betrayal, though I do not see it. It was not their world to choose, anymore."

A knock sounded on the street door of the narrow house, making Ingrey flinch in surprise. The porter's shuffle and low voice sounded through the walls, the words blurred but the tone protesting. Ingrey's teeth clamped in irritation at the untimely interruption. *Now what?*

15

A PERFUNCTORY RAP SHIVERED THE PARLOR DOOR, AND it swung inward. The porter's voice carried from the hall, "... no, Learned, you daren't go in there! The wolf-lord ordered us not—"

Learned Lewko stepped around the frame and closed the door firmly on the porter's panicked babble. He was dressed as Ingrey had glimpsed him earlier that morning, in the white robes of his order, cleaner and newer than what he'd worn in his dusty office but still unmarked with any rank. Unobtrusive: against the busy background of Templetown, surely nearly invisible. He was not exactly wheezing, but his face was flushed, as if he'd been walking quickly in the noon sun. He paused to reorder his robes and his breathing, his gaze on Ingrey and Ijada penetrating and disturbed.

"I am only a *petty* saint," he said at last, signing himself, his touch lingering on his heart, "but *that* was unmistakable."

Ingrey moistened his lips. "How many others there saw, do you know?"

"As far as I know, I was the only Sighted one present." He tilted his head. "Do you know any differently?"

Wencel. If there had been signs apparent to Lewko, Ingrey rather thought Wencel could not have been unaware. "I'm not sure."

Lewko wrinkled his nose in suspicion.

Ijada said tentatively, "Ingrey . . . ?"

"Ah." Ingrey jumped to his feet to perform introductions, grateful to take refuge for a moment in formality. "Lady Ijada, this is Learned Lewko. I have, um . . . told you each something of the other. Learned, will you sit . . . ?" He offered the third chair. "We expected you."

"I fear I cannot say the same of you." Lewko sighed and sank down, flapping one hand briefly to cool his face. "In fact, you become more unexpected by the hour."

Ingrey's lips quirked up in brief appreciation as he sat again by Ijada. "To myself as well. I did not know . . . I did not intend . . . What *did* you see? From your side?" He did not mean, from Lewko's side of the chamber, but from the look on the divine's face Ingrey had no need to explain that.

Lewko drew breath. "When the animals were first presented at the prince's bier, I feared an ambiguous outcome. We do try to avoid those; they are most distressing to the relatives. Disastrous, in this case. The groom-acolytes are normally under instruction to, ah, amplify their creature's signs, for clarity. Amplify, mind you, not substitute or alter. I fear that this habit became misleading to some, and led to that attempt at fraud the day before yesterday. Or so our later inquiries revealed. None of the orders was pleased to learn that this was not the first time recently that some of our people let themselves be tempted by worldly bribes or threats. Such corruption feeds on its own success when it meets no correction."

"Did they not fear their gods' wrath?" asked Ijada.

"Even the wrath of the gods requires some human opportunity by which to manifest itself." Lewko's eye gauged Ingrey. "As the wrath of the gods goes, your performance the other day was remarkably effective, Lord Ingrey. Never have I seen a conspiracy unravel itself and scramble to confession with such alacrity."

"So happy to be of service," Ingrey growled. He hesitated. "This morning was the second time. The second god I've . . . crossed, in three days. The ice bear now seems a prelude—*your* god was there, within the accursed creature."

"So He should be, for a funeral miracle, if it be a true one."

"I heard a voice in my mind when I faced the bear."

Lewko stiffened. "What did it say? Can you remember exactly?"

"I can scarcely forget. *I see my Brother's pup is in better pelt, now. Good. Pray continue.* And then the voice laughed." Ingrey added irritably, "It did not seem very helpful." And more quietly, "It frightened me. I now think I was not frightened enough."

Lewko sat back, breathing out through pursed lips.

"*Was* it your god, in the bear? Do you think?" Ingrey prodded.

"Oh"—Lewko waved his hands—"to be sure. Signs of the Bastard's holy presence tend to be unmistakable, to those who know Him. The screaming, the altercations, the people running in circles—all that was lacking was something bursting into flame, and I was not entirely sure for a moment you weren't going to provide *that,* as well." He added consolingly, "The acolyte's scorches should heal in a few days, though. He does not dare complain of his punishment."

Ijada raised her brows.

Ingrey cleared his throat. "It was not your god this morning, though."

"No. Perhaps fortunately. Was it the Son of Autumn? I saw only a little stir by the wall when you collapsed, a felt *Presence,* and a flare like orange fire as the colt signed the body at last. Not," he added, "seen with my eyes, you know."

"I know now," sighed Ingrey. "Ijada was there. In my vision."

Lewko's head whipped around.

"Let her tell of it," Ingrey continued. "It was her . . . it was her miracle, I think." *Not mine.*

"You two shared this vision?" said Lewko in astonishment. "Tell me!"

She nodded, stared a moment at Lewko as if determining to trust him, glanced again at Ingrey, and began: "It came upon me by surprise. I was in my room upstairs, here. I felt odd and hot, and I felt myself sink to the floor. My warden thought I had fainted, and lifted me to my bed. The other time, at Red Dike, I was more aware of my body's true surroundings, but this time . . . I was wholly in the vision. The first thing I saw was Ingrey, in his court dress—what he wears now, but I had never seen it before." She paused, eyeing his garb as if about to add some other comment, but then shook her head and went on. "His wolf ran at his heels. Great and dark, but so handsome! I was leashed by a chain of flowers to my leopard, and it pulled me forward. And then the god came from the trees . . ."

Her level voice recounted the events much as Ingrey had experienced them, if from another angle of view. Her voice shook a little as she quoted the god's words. Verbatim, as nearly as Ingrey could recall—it seemed she shared the effect he'd felt, of speech that wrote itself across the mind in letters of everlasting fire. He looked away when many of his own graceless comments were quoted back at him as well, and set his teeth.

Tears glistened at the corners of her eyes as she finished, ". . . and Ingrey asked him what happens to the last shaman left, if there are none to deliver *him*, but the god did not say. It almost seemed as if He did not *know*." She swallowed.

Lewko leaned his elbows on the table and rubbed his eyes with the heels of his hands. "Complications," he muttered, not approvingly. "Now I remember why I fear to open letters from Hallana."

Ingrey asked, "Could this affect Ijada's case, do you think? If it should be brought to testimony? How goes the preparation for her case? I think—I am guessing—you hear all such news early." If Lewko's subtle resemblances to Hetwar extended beyond age and style, that is.

"Oh, aye. Temple gossip is worse than court gossip, I swear." Lewko sucked on his lower lip. "I believe the Father's Order has empaneled five judges for the pretrial inquiry."

That in itself was news of significance; minor cases, or cases that were to be treated as minor, would only get three such judges, or one, or if the accused was especially unlucky, a junior acolyte just learning his trade. "Do you know anything of their characters?" *Or against them?*

Lewko raised a brow at that question. "Highborn men, experienced in capital cases. Serious-minded. They will probably begin to question witnesses as early as tomorrow."

"Huh," said Ingrey. "I saw that Rider Ulkra had arrived. All of Prince Boleso's household will have come from Boar's Head with him. Nothing to delay the inquiry, then. Will they call me to testify?"

"As you were not there at the time of the prince's death, perhaps not. Do you wish to speak?"

"Perhaps . . . not. I'm not sure. How experienced are these serious men in matters of the uncanny?"

Lewko grunted and sat back. "Now, that's always a problem."

Ijada was following this with a frown. "Why?"

He cast her a measuring glance. "So much of the uncanny—or the holy, for that matter—is inward experience. As such, testimony about it tends to be tainted. People lie. People delude themselves, or others. People are swayed or frightened or convinced they have seen things they have not. People are, frankly, sometimes simply mad. Every young judge of the Father's Order soon learns that if he were to dismiss all such testimony at the first, he would not only save endless time and aggravation, he would be right nine times out of ten, or better. So the conditions for acceptance of such claims in law have become strict. As a rule, three Temple sensitives of good reputation must vouch for each other and the testimony."

"You are a Temple sensitive, are you not?" she said.

"I am only one such."

"There are three in this room!"

"Mm, sensitive perhaps, but somewhat lacking the further qualifications of *Temple* and *good reputation,* I fear." His dry glance fell as much on Ingrey as Ijada.

Hallana, it occurred to Ingrey, might be another valid witness. But difficult at present to call upon. Although if he wanted a delaying tactic, sending all the way to Suttleaf for her would be one, to be sure. He filed the thought away.

Ijada rubbed her forehead, and asked plaintively, "Do you not believe us, Learned?"

Lewko's lips compressed. "Yes. Yes, I do, Bastard help me. But belief enough for private action, and evidence sufficient for a court of law, are two separate things."

"Private action?" said Ingrey. "Do you not speak for the Temple, Learned?"

He made an equivocal gesture. "I both stand within and administer Temple disciplines. I am also barely god-touched, though enough to know better than to wish for more. I am never sure if my erratic abilities are my failure to receive, or His failure to give." He sighed. "Your master Hetwar has always resisted understanding this. He plagues me for aid with unsuitable tasks and dislikes my telling him no. My order's sorcerers are at his disposal; the gods are not."

"*Do* you tell him no?" asked Ingrey, impressed.

"Frequently." Lewko grimaced. "As for great saints—no one commands them. The wise Temple-man just follows them around and waits to see what will happen."

Lewko looked briefly introspective: Ingrey wondered what experiences he might have had in this regard. Something both rare and searing, at a guess. Ingrey said, "I am no saint of any kind."

"Nor I," said Ijada fervently. "And yet . . ."

Lewko glanced up at them both. "You say true. And yet. You have both been more god-touched than anyone in the strength of such wills ought to be. It is the abnegation of self-will that gives room for the gods to enter the world through saints. The rumors of their spirit animals making the Old Weald warriors more open to their gods, mediating grace as the sacred funeral beasts do for us, have suddenly grown more convincing to me."

So is my dispensation as much in danger as Wencel asserts? Ingrey decided to probe the question more obliquely. "Ijada is no more responsible for receiving the spirit of her leopard than I was my wolf's. Others imposed it upon her. Cannot she be granted a dispensation like mine? It makes no sense to save her from one capital charge only to lose her to another."

"An interesting question," said Lewko. "What does Sealmaster Hetwar say of it?"

"I have not mentioned the leopard to Lord Hetwar yet."

Lewko's brows went up.

"He does not like complications," Ingrey said weakly.

"What *are* you playing at, Lord Ingrey?"

"I would not have mentioned it to you, except Hallana's letter forced my hand."

"You might have undertaken to lose that missive on the way," Lewko pointed out mildly. Wistfully?

"I thought of that," Ingrey confessed. "It seemed but a temporary expedient." He added, "I could ask the same question of you. Pardon, Learned, but it seems to me your allegiance to the rules flexes oddly."

Lewko held up his outspread hand and wriggled it. "It is murmured that the thumb is sacred to the Bastard because it is the part He puts upon the scales of justice to tip them His way. There is more truth than humor in this joke. Yet almost every rule is invented out of some prior disaster. My order has an arsenal of rules accumulated so, Lord Ingrey. We arm ourselves as needed."

Making Lewko equally unpredictable as ally *or* enemy, Ingrey realized unhappily.

Ijada looked up as another knock sounded at the street door. Ingrey's breath stopped at the sudden fear it might be Wencel, following up this morning's events as swiftly as

Lewko, but judging from the muffled arguing in the porter's voice, it could not be the earl. At length, the door swung inward, and the porter warily announced, "Messenger for Learned Lewko, m'lord."

"Very well," said Ingrey, and the porter retreated in relief.

A man dressed in the tabard of Prince Boleso's household shouldered past him; a servant, judging by the rest of his clothes, his lack of a sword, and his irresolute air. Middle-aged, a little stooped, with a scraggly beard framing his face. "Your pardon, Learned, it is urgent that I speak—" His eye fell on Ingrey, and widened with apparent recognition; his voice ran down abruptly. *"Oh."*

Ingrey's return stare was blank, at first. His blood seemed to boil up in his head, and he realized that he smelled a demon, that distinctive rain-and-lightning odor, spinning tightly within this man. One of Lewko's sorcerers in disguise, reporting Temple business to his master? No, for Lewko's expression was as devoid of recognition as Ingrey's, though his body had stiffened. *He smells the demon, too, or senses it somehow.*

It was the voice more than the appearance that did it. Ingrey's mind's eye scraped away the beard and eleven years from the servant's face. "You!"

The servant choked.

Ingrey stood up so fast his chair fell over and banged on the floor. The servant, already backing up, shrieked, whirled, and fled back out the door, slamming it behind him.

"Ingrey, what—?" Ijada began.

"It's *Cumril*!" Ingrey flung over his shoulder at her, and gave chase.

By the time Ingrey wrenched open both doors and stood in the street, the man had disappeared around the curve, but the echo of running footsteps and a passerby's astonished stare told Ingrey the direction. He flung back his coat, put his hand on his sword, and dashed after, rounding the houses just in time to see Cumril cast a frightened look back and duck into a side street. Ingrey swung after him, his stride lengthening. Could youth and fury outrun middle age and terror?

The man is a sorcerer. What in five gods' names am I going to do if I catch him? Ingrey gritted his teeth and set the question aside as he bore down on Cumril, his hand stretching for the man's collar. He made his grab, yanked back, whipped the man around, and flung him against the nearest wall with a loud thump, following up to pin him there with the weight of his body and glare.

Cumril was gasping and whimpering: "No, no, help . . . !"

"So enspell me, why don't you?" Ingrey snarled. Sorcerers and shamans, Wencel had said, were old rivals for power. With the dizzied remains of his reason, Ingrey wondered which was the stronger, and if he was about to test the question.

"I dare not! It will ascend, and enslave me again!"

This response was peculiar enough to give Ingrey pause; he let his hand, now clenched on Cumril's throat, ease somewhat. "What?"

"The demon will t-take me again, if I try to call on it," Cumril stammered. "You need, need, need have no fear of me, Lord Ingrey."

"By my father's agony, the reverse is not true."

Cumril swallowed, looking away. "I know."

Ingrey's grip eased yet more. "Why are you here?"

"I followed the divine. From the temple. I saw him in the crowd. I want to, I was going to try to, I meant to surrender myself to him. I wasn't expecting *you*."

Ingrey stood back, his brows climbing toward his hairline. "Well, I have no objection to that. Come along, then."

Keeping a grip on Cumril's arm just in case, Ingrey led him back to the narrow house. Cumril was pale and trembling, but as he recovered his breath, his initial shock seemed to pass off. By the time Ingrey pushed him through the door of the parlor and closed it again behind them, Cumril had revived enough to shoot him a look of resentment before he straightened his tabard and stood before Lewko.

"Learned. Blessed One. I, I, I . . ."

Lewko's eyes were intent. He motioned to Ingrey's abandoned chair, which Ijada set upright. "Sit. Cumril, is it?"

"Yes, Learned." Cumril sank down. Ijada returned to her own seat; Ingrey folded his arms and leaned against the nearby wall.

Lewko pressed his palm to Cumril's forehead. Ingrey was not at all sure what passed between the two, but Cumril eased back yet more, and the demon-scent grew weaker. His panting slackened, and his gaze, wandering to some middle distance, bespoke the lifting of an invisible burden.

"Are you truly of Prince Boleso's household?" Ingrey asked, nodding to the tabard.

Cumril's eyes refocused on Ingrey. "Yes. Or I was. He, he, he passed me off as his body servant."

"So, *you* were the illicit sorcerer who aided him in his forbidden rites. I . . . it was guessed one must exist. But I never saw you at Boar's Head."

"No, I made very sure you, you, you did not." Cumril gulped. "Rider Ulkra and the household arrived here late last night. I had no other way to get back to Easthome except with them. I, I could not come sooner." This last seemed to be addressed to Lewko.

"Did anyone else of Boleso's household know what you really were?" Ingrey pressed.

"No, only the prince. I—my demon—insisted upon secrecy. One of the few times its will overrode Boleso's."

"Perhaps," Lewko interrupted gently, "you should begin at the beginning, Cumril."

Cumril hunched. "Which beginning?"

"The burning of a certain confession might do."

Cumril's gaze shot up. "How did you know about that?"

"I reassembled it for the inquiry. With great difficulty."

"I should think so!" Cumril's obvious fear of Lewko gave way to something like professional awe.

Lewko held up a restraining finger. "It was my guess that the destruction of that document marked the loss of your control over your power."

Cumril ducked his head in a nod. "It was so, Blessed One. And the beginning of my, my, my slavery."

"Ah." A brief smile of satisfaction tugged Lewko's lips at this confirmation of his theory.

"I will not say the beginning of my nightmare," Cumril continued, "for it was blackest nightmare before. But in my despair after the disasters at Birchgrove, my demon ascended and took control of my body and mind. I, we, it fled with my body, which it was overjoyed to possess, and we began a strange existence. Exile. Always, its first concern was to keep out of sight of the Temple, and then, on to whatever erratic pleasures in matter the thing desired. Which were not always what I would call pleasures. The months it decided to experiment with pain were the worst"—Cumril shuddered in memory—"but that pass, pass, passed off like every other passion. Fortunately. I swear it had the mindfulness of a mayfly. When Boleso found . . . us . . . and pressed us into his service, it became quite rebellious in its boredom, but it dared not thwart him. He had ways of asserting his will."

Lewko moistened his lips and leaned forward. "How did you regain control? For that is a very rare thing to happen, after a sorcerer's demon has turned upon him."

Cumril nodded, and glanced somewhat fearfully at Ijada. "It was her."

Ijada looked astonished. "What?"

"The night Boleso died, I was in the next chamber. To assist him in enspelling the leopard. There was a knothole in the wall, from which we could remove the knot and look and listen through."

Ijada's expression congealed. Cumril flinched under it. Was he, however demonized, to have been a wet-lipped spectator to her rape? Ingrey's hand, which had been idly caressing his sword hilt, tightened upon it.

Cumril bore up under their speculative glowers, and continued, "Boleso believed that the animal spirits he took in would allow him to bind each kin to himself. He had a, a, theory that the leopard was *your* kin animal, Lady Ijada, by reason of your father's Chalionese bloodlines. He meant to use it to bind your mind and will to his, to make you his perfect paramour. Partly, partly for lust, partly to test his powers before he took them into the arena of politics, partly because he was half-mad with suspicion of everyone by this time and only by such iron control dared to have any woman so close to his person."

"No wonder," said Ijada, her voice shaking a little, "he took no trouble to court me."

Lewko said quietly, "That was grave sin and blasphemy indeed, to attempt to seize another's will. Free will is sacred even to the gods."

"Was the leopard spirit meant to go into Ijada, then?" asked Ingrey, puzzled. "Did you put it there?" *As you once gave me my wolf?*

"No!" Cumril fell silent a moment, then gathered himself again. "Boleso took it, had just taken it, when the lady fought free from under him. And then . . . something happened that no one controlled. I know not by what courage she seized the war hammer and struck him, but death, death opens the world to the gods. It all happened at once, in a moment. I was still working upon the leopard as Boleso's soul was torn from his body, and the god . . . the shock . . . my demon . . . Boleso's soul struggled wildly, but could not get free of its defilements either to advance or retreat from the Presence.

"The leopard, so barely anchored, was torn from him, and fell into . . . no, was *called* into the lady. I heard a music like hunting horns in a distant dawn, and my heart seemed to burst with the sound. And my demon fell screaming in terror from it, and released its hold upon my mind, and fled in the only direction it could, inward and inward into a tight knot. It cowers there still"—he touched his chest—"but I do not know for how long." He added after a moment, "Then I ran away and hid in my room. I wept so hard I could not breathe, for a time." He was weeping again now, a quiet sniveling, rocking in his chair.

Lewko blew out his breath and rubbed the back of his neck.

From his place by the wall, Ingrey growled, "I would know of an earlier beginning, Cumril."

Cumril looked, if possible, more fearful, but he ducked his head in acquiescence.

Ingrey breathed exhilaration and dread. Finally, some truths. He contemplated the miserable sorcerer. *Maybe some truths.* "How came you to my father? Or did he come to you?"

"Lord Ingalef came to me, my lord."

Ingrey frowned; Lewko nodded.

"His sister Lady Horseriver had fled to him in great fear, begging his aid. She had a frantic tale of her son Wencel having become possessed by an evil spirit of the Old Weald."

Lewko's head came up. "Wencel!"

Ingrey choked back a curse. In one sentence, a whole handful of new cards was laid upon the table, and in front of Lewko, too. "Wait . . . this possession occurred before Wencel's mother's death? Not after?"

"Indeed, before. She thought it had happened at the time of his father's death, some four or so months earlier. The boy had changed so strangely then."

So already Wencel was caught in a lie. Or Cumril was. Or both could be lying, Ingrey reminded himself; but both could not be telling the truth. "Go on."

"The two concocted a plan for the rescue of her son, they thought. Lady Horseriver feared to go to the Temple openly, in part for terror that they might burn her boy if they could not release him from the possession." Cumril swallowed. "She meant to fight Old Weald magic with Old Weald magic."

Indeed, the Temple sorcerers had not been able to evict Ingrey's wolf from him; Wencel's mother had not been wrong to attempt some other way to spare her son. Ingrey scowled. "I know how badly awry that plan went! The rabid wolf that slew my father—was that chance or design?"

"I, I, to this day I do not know. The huntsman spoke to me on his deathbed, half-raving by then; he, he, he was not bribed to the deed, of that I am sure. He did not guess his animals were diseased, or I think he would have handled them more carefully himself!"

Ijada asked curiously, "Where was young Wencel when all this was going on at Birchgrove?"

"His mother had left him at Castle Horseriver, I understood. She meant to keep her actions secret from him until she could bring help."

And the implications of this were . . . "She feared him? As well as for him?" asked Ingrey.

Cumril hesitated, then ducked his head again. "Aye."

So . . . if a geas could be set in a man to make him kill at another's will, as the parasite spell had been set in Ingrey, how much easier would it be to set one in a wolf—or in a horse? Was the death of Lady Horseriver, trampled by her mount, no accident either? *What, now you suspect that Wencel killed his own mother?* Ingrey's blood was thudding in his head now, but mostly in a sick headache.

But the *why* of his wolf was answered at last. A lethal mix of family loyalty, good intentions, bad judgment . . . and secret uncanny malice? Or was that last some lesser intent, gone wrong? Had the unseen foe meant to kill Lord Ingalef, or just his animals? "My wolf—what of *my* wolf, which arrived so mysteriously?"

Cumril shrugged helplessly. "When its effect on you proved so disastrous, I thought it must have been sent like the rabid ones."

Had Wencel sent it, then? *Does he have some unseen leash upon me? Going all the way back to Birchgrove?* Ingrey unset his teeth and hitched his shoulders against the wall to fight their painful tightness. Ijada caught the gesture and frowned at him in worry.

Lewko was pinching the bridge of his nose, his eyes squeezed shut. "Lord Ingrey. Lady Ijada. You have both seen

Earl Horseriver lately, and not just with mortal eyes. What do you say of this accusation?"

"You have seen him, too," said Ingrey cautiously. "What did you sense?"

Lewko glanced up in irritation; Ingrey thought him about to snap, *I asked first!*, but instead he took a controlling breath, and said, "His spirit seems dark to me, though no more so than many a man who courts death as though to embrace it. It crossed my mind to fear for him, and for those near him, but not like this!"

"Ingrey . . . ?" said Ijada. Her question was clear in her rising tone: *Should we not speak?*

Wencel had been right: once the Temple started looking, they must find. And silence was the only sure safety. And it would, indeed, have been prudent to find and question Cumril before the Temple authorities did. Ingrey wondered grimly what else he would discover Wencel to have been right about. "Wencel bears a spirit animal, yes. Its evil or good I cannot judge. I had guessed Cumril must have laid it in him, too, as part of the same dire plot that gave me mine, but now it seems not."

"No, no," muttered Cumril, rocking again. "Not me."

"You did not mention this earlier," said Lewko to Ingrey, his tone suddenly very flat.

"No. I did not." He returned the tone precisely.

"Wild accusations," murmured Lewko, "a questionable source, not a shred of material proof, and the third highest lord in the land. What more joys can this day bring me? No, don't answer that. Please."

"Gods," said Ijada. "Remember?"

Lewko glowered at her.

Cumril's confessions didn't make sense, in Ingrey's head. Why sacrifice one child to save another? What gain could there be in both heirs being defiled? His thrill at the seeming chance of uncovering old truths faded. "*How* was making my father and me into spirit warriors supposed to rescue Wencel?"

"Lady Horseriver did not tell me."

"What, and you did not ask? It seems a blithe disregard for your famous Temple disciplines, oh sorcerer, to kick them all aside at a woman's word."

Cumril stared at the floor, and muttered with extreme reluctance, "She was god-touched. Most . . . most grievously."

A new thought chilled Ingrey. If bearing an animal spirit sundered one from the gods, like Boleso, what had happened to Lord Ingalef's soul? That funeral had long been over before Ingrey had recovered enough to ask about it. None had told him that his father was sundered. *None told me otherwise, either.* Lord Ingalef had been as well buried in tacit silences as in earth.

He must have been sundered. There was no shaman at Birchgrove to cleanse him.

Oh. Wait. There had been one, hadn't there. Potentially. Ingrey's heart seemed to halt. *Might I have saved . . . ?*

He gulped back the unbearable realizations and stared at Cumril in a frustrated, hostile silence. Lewko's silence was far less revealing. Their gazes crossed and clashed. Ingrey began to suspect he was not the only man here who preferred to collect the information first and dole it out at his discretion later. The divine rose abruptly to his feet.

"You had best come up with me to the temple now, Cumril, till I can make better arrangements for your safety. We will speak further on these matters." *In private* hung unspoken.

Cumril nodded as if in understanding and clambered up as well. Ingrey gritted his teeth. Safety from what? Cumril's demon reascending? Wencel? Nosy Temple inquirers? Ingrey? *Aye, Lewko had damned well better protect Cumril from me.*

He saw shepherd and lost sheep out the front door; Lewko bade him and Ijada farewell with a promise, or threat, to meet again soon. Now that they seemed to have emerged officially from the private conclave, the warden fell upon her charge and hustled her upstairs once more. Ijada, her face set with dark thought, did not resist.

Ingrey took the stairs two at a time to his room, there to shed his court finery for clothing he could better move in, which would not catch his blades. He had a visit to make, and without delay.

16

IN THE WANING AFTERNOON LIGHT, INGREY MADE HIS way through the crooked streets of Kingstown. He wended past the old Rivermen's Temple that served the folk of the dock quarter, then around the town hall and the street market in the square behind it. The market was closing down for the day, with only a few peddlers left under awnings or with their goods spread out on mats, sad leftover vegetables or fruits, wilting flowers, rejected leatherwork, picked-over piles of clothing new or used. He threaded his way upslope into the district of great houses nearest the King's Hall, deliberately dodging over one street to avoid Hetwar's mansion and the heightened chance of encountering men he knew.

Earl-ordainer Horseriver's Easthome manse was a bride gift from Princess Fara, the cut-stone facade decorated with a frieze of bounding stags for the Stagthornes. Only the banner over the door displayed the running stallion above the rippling waters of the Lure, the badge of the old high kin that marked the earl as in residence.

In residence, but not yet at home, Ingrey shortly discovered from the liveried door guards. The earl and princess's party had not yet returned from the interment and whatever funeral feast had followed in the hallow king's hall. Ingrey encouraged the porter's assumption that he bore some important message from Sealmaster Hetwar, letting himself be escorted to Wencel's study, provided with a polite glass of wine, and left to wait.

He set the wine aside untasted and circled the room restlessly. Afternoon sun crept across thick carpets. The bookcases were but half-filled, mostly with dusty tomes that would seem to have been inherited with the house. The heavy, carved writing table was tidied and free of work in progress or correspondence; a promising drawer proved locked. Ingrey decided it was just as well, when only the barest sound of footsteps in the hall heralded the door opening on Wencel. This interview was likely to be difficult enough without his being caught reading the earl's mail. Though he doubted Wencel would have been surprised.

The earl still wore the somber court garb Ingrey had seen him in at the funeral. He was shrugging out of his long coat as he shouldered through the door and shut it behind him. He folded the cloth over his arm and circled around Ingrey, who circled around him, each keeping a wary distance as though they were on two ends of a rope. The earl tossed the coat over a chair and half sat, half leaned against the writing table, motionless but not relaxed, not yielding any advantage of height or tension. His stare at Ingrey was speculative; his only greeting a murmured, "Well, well, well."

Ingrey took up a careful position against the nearest bookcase, arms crossed. "So what did you see?"

"My senses were tightly furled, as they always must be when I risk contact with the Temple's Sighted. But I hardly needed more; I could infer it all well enough. The Lord of Autumn could not have taken Boleso uncleansed, yet take him He did. There were but two men present who might have turned the task, and I knew it wasn't me. Therefore. Your masteries proceed apace, shaman." His slight bow might or might not have been mockery. "Had Fara known and been capable of understanding, I'm sure she would have thanked you, wolf-lord."

Ingrey returned a nod equally balanced on the edge of irony. "It seems you are not my sole source of instruction after all. Horse-lord."

"Oh, fine new friends you have—until They betray you. If the gods toy with you, cousin, it is for Their ends, not yours."

"Still, it seems I might be gifted with the salvation of more than Boleso. I could rescue you from your secret burden, save you from your fear of Temple pyres. How if I attempt to relieve you of your spirit horse?" A safe offer; Ingrey suspected Wencel would rather be stripped of his skin.

Wencel's lips curled up. "Alas, there is an impediment. I am not dead. Souls yet anchored to matter do not yield their loyal companions, any more than you could sing my life itself out of my body." Ingrey wasn't exactly sure what his expression revealed, but Wencel added, "Don't believe me? Try it, then."

Ingrey moistened his lips, half closed his eyes, and reached down. He lacked the floating glory of the god's inspiration, but as it was the second trial, he might make up for it in confidence, he thought. He felt for that furled shadow within Wencel, extended his hand, and rumbled, *"Come."*

It was like tugging on a mountain.

The shadow unfurled a little, but did not follow. Wencel's brows rose in brief surprise, and he caught a breath. "Strong," he allowed.

"But not strong enough," Ingrey conceded in return.

"No."

"Then you cannot cleanse me, either," Ingrey followed this out.

"Not while you live, no."

Ingrey felt his careful course between opposed sides, Wencel and the Temple, to be narrowing dangerously. And if he did not choose before he lost all turning room, he risked betraying both powers. It was surely better to have one powerful enemy and one powerful ally than two offended enemies. But which should be which? He drew a long breath. "I met an unexpected old acquaintance this afternoon. We had a long talk."

Wencel lifted his chin in inquiry.

"Cumril. Remember him?"

A flare of nostrils and a sharp intake of breath. "Ah."

"Coincidentally, he proved to be just the man you were looking for as well. Remember your insistence that Boleso must have suborned an illicit sorcerer? Cumril was the one. I'd missed encountering him at Boar's Head, for he recognized and avoided me."

Wencel's eyes glittered with interest. "Not so coincidental as all that. Illicit sorcerers are few, and the Temple expends much effort toward making them even fewer. He, at least, was one Boleso might have heard about, and secretly sought." He hesitated. "It must have been an interesting chat. Did Cumril survive it?"

"Temporarily."

"Where is he now?"

"I can't say." *Precisely.*

"At some point very soon, I am going to grow tired enough to stop humoring you. It has been a long and most unpleasant day."

"Very well, I shall come to the point. A question for you, Wencel. Why did you try to make me kill Ijada?" A shot not quite in the dark, but Ingrey held his breath to see what target it found.

Wencel grew perilously still, but for a slight flare of his eyes. "Where do you come by this conviction? Cumril? Not the most reliable of accusers."

"No." Ingrey quoted back to him: "There were but two men present who might have turned to the task, and I knew it wasn't me. Therefore." He added after a moment, "I must find out how you make a geas. I suspect necromancy."

Wencel paused for a long time, as though sorting through

a wide variety of responses. "In a sense." He sighed, by the squaring of his shoulders seeming to come to some unwelcome decision. "I would not call it a mistake, for if it had succeeded, it would have simplified my present life immeasurably. I would call it a false move, because of its peculiar consequences. I note merely, I am not playing against *you*."

"Whom do you play against, then?" Ingrey pushed off the wall and began to pace in a half circle around the earl. "At first I thought this was all about Easthome politics."

"Only indirectly."

Ingrey resolutely ignored the shivering in his belly, the thudding in his ears. The whirling confusion in his mind. "What is really going on here, Wencel?"

"What do you think is going on?"

"I think you will do anything to protect your secrets."

Wencel tilted his head. "Once, that was true." He added more softly, "Though not for much longer, I . . . well, do not pray."

Ingrey's body felt like a coiled spring. His hand caressed his knife haft. Wencel's glance did not miss the gesture.

"How if I release your soul the old hard way?" Ingrey returned as softly. "Whatever your powers, I doubt they would survive if I sawed off your head and tossed it in the Stork."

At least Wencel did Ingrey's menace the compliment of holding very, very still. "You cannot imagine how very much you would regret such an act. If you seek to rid yourself of me, that is exactly the wrong method. My heir."

Ingrey blinked in bafflement. "I am no heir to kin Horseriver."

"At law and in property, no. By the laws of the Old Weald, however, a nephew is next to a son in kinship. And as it seems this ill-made body of mine will not engender a son on Fara, you are the heir of my blood, should you be living when I next die. This is no particular joy or choice of mine, understand. The spell adopts you."

The conversation had tilted too suddenly and violently for it to be all Ingrey's doing; Wencel had met his daring push with a mighty yank, which was doubtless why Ingrey felt as though he were hanging upside down just now. Over a dire drop. Into a most uncertain darkness. The pressure of his hand on his hilt sagged. "*Next* die?"

"Remember how I told you the shamans' spirit animals were made, by the accumulation of life upon life, death upon death? Something akin was made to work for men's souls, too. Once."

"Oh, gods, Wencel, is this another of your bedtime tales?"

"This one shall keep you awake, I promise you." He drew breath. "For sixteen generations of Horserivers, my soul has passed from father to son in an unbroken chain, save when it passed between brothers. It has proved an evil heritage. The death of this clay will not release me from the world of matter, but only into the next male body in my line. Which is yours, at the moment. My blood coils in you through your mother's and your father's sides both, for all that the unruly Wolfcliff camp lends so much to your singular surliness." Wencel grimaced.

Ingrey envisioned it: not a great beast, but a great man? And if the piled-up spirits of animals blended and transmuted into something more powerfully uncanny, what strange thing might the piled-up souls of men become? "You have told me many lies, Wencel. Why should I believe this one?"

Ingrey had spiraled toward the table as he paced, as though drawn on a cord. Wencel bent his head toward the threat looming at his shoulder, and his eyes glimmered steel-colored with a crush of emotions too strange for Ingrey to unravel: anger and scorn, pain and cruelty, curiosity and animosity. "Shall I show you? It would be a just punishment for your presumption, I think."

"Aye, Wencel," Ingrey breathed. "Tell me true. For once."

"Since you ask so pressingly . . ." Wencel rotated until they were face-to-face, inches apart, and placed his stubby hands on either side of Ingrey's head. "I am the last high holy king of the Weald. Or Old Weald, so-called to distinguish it from modern mockeries."

The writing table stopped Ingrey's backward jerk. "You said the last real holy king died at Bloodfield."

"Not at all. Or twice, depending on how you look at it." The earl's fingers found Ingrey's temples, caressing them in small sweaty circles, and he continued, "I was a young man, heir to my high house, hunting in the meadows along the Lure before ever Audar was born to soil his swaddling clothes. The Darthacans pressed my kin tribe, squatted on our lands, cut down our forests, sent missionaries to defile our shrines, then soldiers to drag the missionaries' bodies home. My people fought and fell. I saw my father die, and my hallow king."

Pictures bloomed in Ingrey's head as Wencel spoke, too vivid to be his own imagination. *This is a weirding voice indeed, to make me remember what I never saw.* Dark forests, green valleys, palisades of timber embracing village houses built of wattle and daub, smoke rising sharp-scented from vents in their thatched roofs. Horsemen armored in boiled leather passing out the gates to battle, or back in, bloodied and drooping, their scant metal chinking in the chill air. Exhausted voices carried by the winter fog in a tongue that just eluded Ingrey's mind, but recalled Jokol's rolling poetry.

"The next election cast the kingship upon me, for I was grown leader of a grim people by then, with sons to follow at my back. They made me their torch, and I burned for them in the gathering shadows. Our hearts were hot. But the gods denied our sacrifices and turned Their faces from us."

A tawny young man, anxious and resolute, nude but for signs painted upon his body, stood high on an oak branch in flickering torchlight. A halter of silky nettle flax circled his neck, and blood ran down his limbs from a careful series of cuts. He raised his outstretched hands high, and spoke, vibrant voice marred by a quaver; then fell forward as a man might dive off a high rock into a pool. Nearly to the ground the fall was jerked to a neck-cracking stop . . . Wencel's dilated eyes shivered. *Was that one of the princely sons, sent to the gods as courier from his hallow king . . . ?* This was truth by the riverful; Ingrey felt as if he were being held head down in it till his brain might burst. The visions flowed on, engendered by the whispered words, in an overwhelming stream.

"We wove Holytree itself into the spell for invincibility and, as hallow king, I was its hub."

Voices sang, beating upward against the night like wings. The trees shivered as if caressed by the breath of them. The deep blended tones made Ingrey's every hair rise.

"But we could not risk the continuity of the kingship in battle, for if I were to fall, the spell would shatter, and all who were bound into it would be lost in the instant. So my eldest son . . ."

Bearded blond youth, faithful face etched by strain to untoward age. Some kinship in both those features and that strain, yes, to the tawny youth in the oak—brother or cousin?

". . . and I together undertook the great binding, so that kingship, soul, horse, hub, and all together might be handed down without a break, regardless of where or when or how our bodies met their ends. Until the victory was ours."

Wencel paused. "You do begin to see where this is going . . . ?"

Ingrey made a faint noise through parted lips, not quite a squeak, not quite a sigh. Wencel shifted to place himself more square to Ingrey. He did not draw back; his breath ghosted against Ingrey's face as he spoke.

"Audar's troops took me in the first hours of the fight. Broke my body, wrapped me in my royal banner, threw me in the first ditch they dug. They began the butchery even before the fighting was done. I died with my mouth full of black blood and dirt . . ."

The stench of it made Ingrey gag, a soup of filth and blood and urine.

". . . and awoke in the body of my child, man-child by

then. Prisoner, by then. Our eyes were spared no horror. The ax fell upon our neck like a lover's welcome kiss, at the end. I thought it ended. Defeat was ashes in my mouth . . ."

Cold splinters of a tree stump, already soaked with gore, pressed into Ingrey's stretched throat. Out of the corner of his eye, a weary voice grunted with effort, a steely arc fell, and a crunch shattered his keening woe as his vertebrae split.

". . . then I awoke in the body of my second son, miles away upon the border. I had escaped the massacre at Blood-field in the hardest way, upon the wings of our weirding. His mind was unprepared for me. I had to wrestle him for speech, motion, the light of his eyes. We were all mad for a little while, we three, trapped in his skull. But first I won his body, then began my war to win back the Weald."

Ingrey gulped for control of his own voice, if only to be reassured by the sound of it that he was still inside his own head. "I have heard of that Horseriver prince, I think. He was a famous battle lord. Campaigned for twenty years along the fens, till his defeat and death."

"Defeat, yes. Death—ah. My son's son was but twenty when I took his body from him. Holytree was an abandoned waste by then . . ."

A sodden woods, leafless in an icy mist, struggled up from black mire. The trees were twisted, knotted with cysts from which cold sap smeared down in frozen grains like phlegm from rheumy eyes.

". . . every kin warrior who had been spell-bound there was dead, by battle or accident or age, even the few who had escaped the massacre. Save one."

Wencel's own eyes, boring into Ingrey's, now seemed something from a dream. The visions circled in those pupils, sucked away as by a drain. *Visions that did not deceive,* Wencel had once said. Perhaps; but Ingrey, too, knew how to lie with truth, truth and selected silences. *I believe what I see. What do I not see?*

"The resistance went ill. There were many deaths in quick succession, among the exiled Horseriver kin of the old royal line. I found myself trapped in the body of a useless child, and in my impatience ate him; they treated us as mad. It was thirty years and another death before I won my way to leadership again. But no kin would fight for us anymore. I turned to politics, to the attempt to win back the Weald from within. I amassed wealth, and what power I could, and learned to bend men when I could not break them. I watched for fissures in the Darthacan royal house and applied myself to widening them."

The visions were fading, as if fading passion aged them to pale ghosts, impotent. "That was the Earl Horseriver they called the kingmaker, was it not?" said Ingrey faintly. "That was you, too?"

"Aye, and his son, and his son's son. I cascaded from body to body, amassing a great density of life. But my sons were not voluntary sacrifices to me, anymore. The gods, they say, accumulate souls without destroying them, which is proof, if any were needed, that I was no god on earth. If the invaded minds were not to explode in madness, only one could dominate. There was by then no choice of whose.

"For a hundred and fifty years I fought, and schemed, and bled, and died, and defiled my soul by fatal error and the cannibal consumption of my children's children's children. And for one glorious moment I thought myself done, the Weald renewed. But the new kingship had no weirding in it, no song of the land, none of the old forest powers. It was adulterated by the gods. I was not released from my cycle of torment. My war was over but not won.

"Thus began that line of strange and famously reclusive Earls Horseriver . . ."

"Can you not be released from your spell?" Ingrey whispered. "Somehow?"

Wencel's voice and face both cracked. "Do you think I have not *tried*?"

Ingrey flinched at the shout. "You need a miracle, I think."

"Oh, the gods have long hunted me." Wencel's grin grew

unholy. "They harry me hard, now. They want me; but I do not want them, Ingrey."

Ingrey had to force his voice to an audible volume. "What do you want, then?"

Wencel's expression grew distant, as of grief withheld so long as to turn stone. "What do I *want*? I have wanted many things, over the course of centuries. But now my wants are grown simple indeed, as befits such an addled senility. Such simple things. I want my first wife back, and my sons in the mornings of their lives. . . ."

The vision returned in breathtaking light, drenched in color. A man, a laughing woman, and a gaggle of youths reined in their horses on the reedy margins of the Lure, and watched in awe as a family of gray herons flew up into the bursting gold of dawn.

And for an instant, Horseriver's eyes cried, *Damn you for making me remember that!* The hour of drowning in blood and despair had borne with it a less piercing pain. His trembling grip tightened on Ingrey's face, fingers pressing hard enough to bruise. *"I want my world back."*

Ah. That was not an image doled out by design. It escaped. Ingrey moistened his lips. "But you can't have it. No one could."

The brief flare faded back into dry dark, darkness absolute, and Ingrey knew the visions were over.

"I know. Not all the gods together, by any miracle they might devise, can give me my desire."

"Do you fear the gods will destroy you?"

That disturbing smile again. "That is not a fear. That is a prayer."

"Or . . . do you fear their punishment? That they would plunge your soul into some eternal torment?"

Wencel leaned forward, up on his toes. "That," he breathed in Ingrey's ear, "would be redundant." To Ingrey's intense relief he finally released his grip, stepping back once more. He cocked his head as if studying Ingrey's face. "But you'll learn all about that, if your luck holds ill."

Ingrey should have thought he'd faced a raving lunatic, but for the stream of searing sights Wencel had sent spinning through his head. Whatever truth he had sought to shake from Wencel, it had not been *this*. Staggered he was, and Wencel could doubtless tell it from the winded way he sagged against the table, for all that he clutched the edge to conceal any betraying shudder in his body. Disbelieving . . . he merely wished he could be.

Ingrey felt for the gaps in the tale. There were many, both old and recent, but Ijada's army of ghosts at the Wounded Woods seemed the vastest. How could Horseriver bewail Bloodfield, yet make no mention of his abandoned and accursed comrades? That Wencel had laid the murderous geas against Ijada, he had admitted when he could no longer evade doing so, but the *why* of it he'd evaded naming still. Were the two silences connected?

A knock sounded on the chamber door, and both men jerked. "What?" the earl called, his sharp tone not inviting entry.

"My lord." The dutiful voice of some senior servant. "My lady is ready to depart and begs your company."

Wencel's lips thinned in annoyance, but he called back, "Tell her I come anon." Footsteps faded outside, and Wencel sighed and turned back briefly to Ingrey. "We are to attend upon her father. It is going to be an unpleasant evening. You and I shall have to continue this later."

"I, too, would wish to go on," Ingrey conceded, considered his words, and decided to let the dual meaning—speaking or just breathing—stand unaided.

Wencel measured him, still wary. "You understand, our family curse is asymmetrical. While my death would be your disaster, the reverse does not hold."

"Why do you not slay me as I stand, then?" For all of Ingrey's fighting edge, he did not doubt Wencel could do so. Somehow.

"It would stir up troubles I am still contemplating. At present, the spell would merely replace you with another, perhaps more inconvenient. Your Birchgrove cousin, likely. Unless you have some Darthacan by-blow I know nothing of."

"I . . . none that I know of. Do you not *know* who is your next heir after me?"

"The matter shifts, over time, in ways I do not control. You might have died in Darthaca. Fara might have conceived a son." Wencel's mouth twisted. "Others might be born or die. I learned long ago not to exhaust myself grappling problems that time will carry away on its tide." He walked back and forth once across the chamber, as if to shake the tension out of his body. Ingrey wished he might dare do the same.

At the end of his circuit, Wencel turned again. "It seems we are to be saddled with each other for a little, will or nil. How if you enter my service?"

Ingrey rocked back. He had a thousand questions, to which Wencel, and possibly Wencel alone, held the answers. Close attendance upon the earl must reveal *something* more. *And if I say no, how long do I get to live?* He temporized. "I owe Lord Hetwar much. I would not lightly leave his house, nor would he lightly release me, I think."

Wencel shrugged. "How if I begged you of him? He would not lightly refuse Princess Fara's husband such a favor."

No, but I might beseech Hetwar to evade or delay. "If Hetwar gives his leave, then."

"A nice loyalty. I cannot fault it, who would have a like one from you."

"I admit, your offer interests me strangely."

Wencel's dry smile acknowledged all the possible meanings of those ambiguous words. "I have no doubt of it." He sighed and walked to the chamber door, indicating this interview was drawing to its end. Obediently, Ingrey followed him.

"Tell me one thing more tonight, though," Ingrey said as he reached the portal.

Earl Horseriver raised his brows in curious permission.

"What happened to Wencel? The boy I knew?"

Horseriver touched his forehead. "His memories still exist, lost in a sea of such."

"But Wencel does not? He is destroyed?"

The earl shrugged. "Where is the fourteen-year-old Ingrey, then, if not there"—he gestured to Ingrey's head in turn—"in like disarray? They are both victims of a common enemy. If there is one thing that I have come to hate more than the gods, it is time." He gestured Ingrey out. "Farewell. Find me tomorrow, if you will."

There seemed something terribly wrong with Wencel's argument, but in his present dizzied state Ingrey could not finger what. In a few moments he found himself in the street again, blinking in the sunset light. It somehow surprised him that Easthome was still standing. It felt as though the city ought to have been churned to rubble during the small eternity he'd spent within, not one stone left upon another.

As I have been?

Gaps. Silences. Things not mentioned. For a man so sick with a surfeit of time, why was Wencel so anxious now? What drove him out of his reclusive routine, and into, apparently, such unaccustomed action? For Ingrey read him as a man pressed, and silently furious to be so.

He shook his aching head and turned for the sealmaster's palace.

17

HE WAS HALFWAY TO HETWAR'S WHEN THE REACTION SET in, turning his knees to tallow. A low abutment along a house wall flanking the street made a good enough bench, and he sank down upon it, bracing his hands on his thighs and his back against the day-warmed stone. He blinked and breathed deeply against his dizziness. It felt peculiarly like the aftermath of one of his wolf-fits, tumbling back into a stream of time he had temporarily exited; like falling back to earth after a dream of flight. Except that it was his mind, and not his body this time, that had ascended into that state where response flowed without thinking in some desperate dance for survival.

A passing matron paused and stared at him as he wrapped his arms around himself and rocked but, perhaps taking in his sex, age, and cutlery, passed on without daring to inquire into his well-being. In time, the trembling in his body ran its course, and his mind began to move again.

That was real, Wencel's tale. Five gods.

Horseriver's tale, he amended this thought. How much of Wencel lived on in that slight and crooked body was hard to say.

His second thought was a flash of envy. To live forever! How could a man not achieve happiness, with so many chances to flee old errors, to make it right? To build up wealth and power and knowledge? The envy faded upon reflection. Horseriver had paid for his many lives with many deaths, it seemed, and the spell gave him no respite from any horror entailed. *Burning is a painful death. I do not recommend it,* Wencel had once remarked, and Ingrey had thought him joking. In retrospect, the tone seemed more the judgment of a connoisseur.

Would surety of his own survival make a man more brave in battle? It was true that many of Wencel's ancestors . . . *rephrase,* that Earl Horseriver had many times died not-peacefully. Or would the knowing of how much pain a death could inflict make one more afraid? Two of the most grotesque endings, Ingrey had just relived body and mind along with Horseriver, and the mere memories shook him near to vomiting. More ghostly suggestions of other such fates spun outward in repetition like a man's image caught between two mirrors, and the thought of them going on past counting made his stomach clench again.

Realization of the other cost came to him then, not one Horseriver had held up before his mind's eye, but still leaking in around all of the searing visions. Ingrey had no child, had scarcely considered the possibility, but the dream of a son inspired in him a fierce vague sense of protectiveness nonetheless. Rooted, perhaps, in his own child-mind's hunger for a father's regard, bolstered by his happier memories of Lord Ingalef, Ingrey at least had some notion of what a father *ought* to be.

What must it have been like for Horseriver, watching son after son grow, knowing their fates? *Making* them, knowing? Did he warn them of what was to befall them, as he had just warned Ingrey? Or did he take them by ambush? Some of each? At what ages? What differences to Horseriver, to his heirs, between taking a bewildered child, a frightened youth, or an outraged mind come to full maturity, with a life, choices, perhaps a bride and children of his own? Whatever the differences, Horseriver had had time to cycle through them all.

And not just bodies and wives. Where did the souls go of all those spell-seized sons? Bound into the whole, digested but not wholly destroyed . . . it seemed the spell stole not only lives, but eternities. Carrying them along in broken pieces to the next generation, the next century, a jumbled, melting accumulation. Had Horseriver—the thought gave Ingrey more pause than all that had gone before—had Horseriver himself ever slain an especially beloved child before his own foreseen death, to spare that soul before it could be bound into this horror?

I think that may have happened a time or two, as well. In four centuries of lives frequently shortened by violence, there had surely been opportunity for every variation on the theme.

Dangerous, powerful, magical, immortal . . . and mad. Or nearly so. Wencel's brittle glibness took on a new tone, in retrospect. His baffling actions, wrenching back and forth between spurts of energy and withdrawal, still bewildered Ingrey, but Ingrey no longer reached for the reasons of ordinary men to explain them. He still did not understand Wencel, but the depth of his own misapprehension was at least revealed to him. *Look to souls, Ingrey,* Ijada had said. Indeed.

How many more iterations before Wencel lost even his present fragile function, and became so deranged as no longer to pass as lucid at all? As the spell spun on, it might look to the outside eye perhaps like some family disease, one blood relative after another struck down by dementia in youth, or middle age.

One more iteration, I think. The next transfer was going to be different, if Ingrey lived to receive it. His wolf would make it so. Different, but not, necessarily, *good*.

No. Not good.

Save for when he had received his wolf, this day was shaping up to be the most devastating Ingrey had ever experienced, beginning with looking a god in the eye and ending with Wencel's terrifying visions. He wanted nothing more now than to stagger home to clutch Ijada and howl the news into her ear. *Home?* The narrow house was surely no home to him. *But wheresoever she is, there is my place.* In the chaos and confusion of a battlefield, the standard held up above the swirl was the meeting point for the battered and lost, the place to regroup, find a trusted comrade against whom to place one's own bleeding back, and face outward again.

And she must be warned of this threatened transformation. It was disturbing beyond measure to realize that Wencel's fearsome heritage had been hanging over his head for years, and he had never known it. The timing of his body's capture was wholly in Wencel's power. The earl could have taken a knife to his own throat at any time and effected his preternatural transfer at will. Although . . . upon reflection, Ijada was perhaps the only person in the Weald who might be able to perceive his soul's adulteration upon sight. Perceive, but not necessarily understand; and Wencel's lies, coming out of Ingrey's mouth in Ingrey's voice, would surely be artful and practiced.

He forced himself back to his feet and started down the street again, trying not to weave like a drunken man. The motion helped settle his stomach and mind a little. He found himself passing the yellow stone front of Hetwar's palace, home of sorts for the past four years, and hesitated, reminded of his first panicked impulse to run to his patron. He was suddenly entirely unsure of what he wanted to tell Hetwar about Horseriver now, but the sealmaster had instructed Ingrey to see him earlier; at least he should discover if new orders awaited. He turned in.

The porter warned him, "My lord is in council."

Ingrey nearly decamped, but said instead prudently, "Tell him I wait, and ask his pleasure of me."

The porter dispatched a page, who returned shortly. "My lord bids you attend upon him in his study, Lord Ingrey."

Ingrey nodded, made his way up the wide stairs, and turned down the familiar corridor. He weaved around a servant lighting wall sconces against the gathering twilight. A rap on the study door elicited Hetwar's voice: "Enter."

He turned the latch and slipped within, then controlled a recoil against the closing door. Grouped around Hetwar's writing table were Prince-marshal Biast, Learned Lewko, and the archdivine-ordainer of Easthome himself, Fritine kin Boarford. Gesca stood against a wall in a strained posture that hinted of a man making difficult reports to his superiors. The whole array of eyes turned upon Ingrey.

"Good," said Hetwar. "We were just discussing you, Ingrey. Are you recovered from your morning's indisposition?"

His expression was decidedly ironic. Concluding, after a short mental review of the options, that the question was unanswerable, Ingrey returned a mere nod and studied his unwelcome audience.

Archdivine Fritine was an uncle of the present twin earls, a scion of the prior generation of Boarfords, dedicated to Temple service when too many older brothers made his chance of achieving high place in his kin lands unlikely. A long and typical career of a noble Temple-man lay behind him, by no means unhonorable; if he favored his kin, he equally ensured that they disgorged a steady return of favors to the Temple. His appointment to Easthome, with its important ordainer's vote, had occurred some seven years ago, the culmination of that career. And those favors.

In Ingrey's observation, Fritine and Hetwar tolerated each other fairly well, both men being equally practical. Through them, Kingstown and Templetown worked more often in tandem than opposed—often, but not invariably. A certain tension lay between them at present over the impending election, as Hetwar counted Fritine's vote among the uncertain; the archdivine had connections on his mother's side to both the Hawkmoors and the Foxbriars. And Fritine had used the excuse of his mediating Temple position to avoid promising his vote to anyone, yet. No doubt he found that uncertainty useful.

Of the archdivine's tolerance of his wolf, Ingrey had never been sure. It was his predecessor who had signed Ingrey's dispensation, a document Ingrey had preserved for the past decade when every other possession had been lost, now locked away in his room upstairs in this very palace. Ingrey didn't know if Fritine's distaste for the uncanny was theological or personal, for he seemed as oblivious to the allure of the mystical as Hetwar. *So what does he make of Lewko, I wonder?*

Who was presently chewing on his knuckles and staring at Ingrey in a most unsettling fashion, Ingrey realized. Ingrey favored him with a polite nod and waited for someone else to begin. *Anyone but me. Five gods, my wits are unfit for this perilous company just now.*

The archdivine plunged in at once. "Learned Lewko tells us you claim to have experienced a miracle in the Temple court this morning."

Ingrey wondered how Fritine would react if he said, *No, I granted one. I was disinclined, but the god begged me so prettily.* Instead, he replied, "Nothing I could prove in a court of law, sir. Or so I am informed."

Lewko shifted uncomfortably under his level look.

"I was there," said the archdivine coolly.

"So you were."

"I saw nothing." To Fritine's credit, in his expression of mixed worry and suspicion, worry seemed uppermost.

Ingrey inclined his head in a suitably infuriating gesture of utter neutrality. *Yes, let them reveal their thoughts first.*

Prince-marshal Biast said, rather hopefully, "One could assert that the Son of Autumn taking Boleso's soul was good evidence against the accusation of his tampering with animal spirits."

"One could assert anything one pleased," Ingrey agreed cordially. "And as long as one's eyewitness Cumril was found floating facedown in the Stork by tomorrow morning, there would be none to gainsay it. Certainly not me."

The archdivine jerked, looking angry at what might be construed as veiled slander. Or possibly suggestion. Or perhaps threat. Or counterthreat. Ingrey trusted it was hard to be sure. Lewko's shrewd eyes glinted in renewed curiosity, regarding Ingrey.

"That will not happen," said the archdivine. "Cumril is in strict custody. Justice will be served."

"Good. Then howsoever Boleso's soul be rescued, at least his character will get what it deserves."

Biast winced.

Hetwar said firmly, "So tell me, Lord Ingrey. At what point did you discover that Lady Ijada had also been infected with an animal spirit?"

Ah, they had indeed been comparing Ingrey stories. No help for it now. "The first day out from Boar's Head."

With his usual deceptive calm, Hetwar inquired, "And you did not think this worthy of mention to me?"

Gesca, standing by the opposite wall and doing his best to appear invisible, shrank at that tone. *And who were you penning your letters to, Gesca, if not Hetwar?* Horseriver, judging by the neat way he'd turned up on the road. And if so, was Gesca a conduit to him still?

Ingrey replied, "At first opportunity, I placed the problem before Temple authority in the person of Learned Hallana. Who sent me to Learned Lewko." *In a sense.* "I awaited his guidance, it being clearly a Temple concern, but alas it was delayed by the crisis of the ice bear. By the time we had another chance to speak, this afternoon, it was rather overridden by other matters." Other matters? Or the same matter, from another angle of view? Who but the gods saw around all corners simultaneously? It was a disturbing new thought. Well, shift the blame to the saint—who was watching Ingrey's shuffle with a certain dry appreciation—and see who in this room dared to chide *him*.

Not Hetwar, for he frowned and veered off. "So it seems.

The girl will be dealt with in due course. A more urgent accusation has come to our ears. What do you say of Cumril's charge that Wencel kin Horseriver also now bears a spirit animal?"

Ingrey drew a long breath. "That such a grave charge is surely a matter for a proper Temple inquiry."

"And what would that inquiry find?"

How great were Wencel's powers of concealment? Better than Ingrey's own, that was certain. "I imagine that would depend upon their competence, sir."

"Ingrey." Hetwar's warning tone, the special one pushed through his teeth, made both Gesca and Biast flinch, this time. Ingrey stood fast. "The man is an earl-ordainer, and we are on the verge of an election. I *thought* he was a staunch advocate of the rightful heir."

He nodded to Biast, who nodded back gratefully. Fritine blinked, and said nothing.

Hetwar continued, "If this is not the case, I need to know! I cannot afford to lose his support in some untimely arrest."

"Well," said Ingrey blandly, "then your solution is simple. Wait until after you have extracted his vote to turn and attack him."

Biast looked as though he'd bitten into a worm. Hetwar seemed, for a moment, as if he was actually considering this. Fritine looked blank indeed, and Ingrey wondered anew where his ordaining vote was promised.

Had Cumril's chances of kissing the Stork just gone up? *Do I care?* Ingrey sighed. *Probably.* Ingrey came to the glum realization that there was not a man in this room that he would fully trust with his newest revelations about Horseriver. *I want Ijada.*

Ingrey clenched his hands behind his back. *My turn.* "Archdivine. You are both theologian and ordainer. You must know if anyone does. Can you tell me—what is the precise *theological* difference between the hallow kingship of the Old Weald and its renewed form under Quintarian orthodoxy?"

Hetwar stared at him, a look of *Where in five gods' names*

did that question come from, Ingrey? writ plain on his face. But he eased back in his seat and gestured Fritine to answer, clearly just as curious to see where the answer would take them.

Fritine drummed his fingers on the arm of his chair. "The old hallow king was elected by the heads of the thirteen strongest kin tribes. The new, by eight great kin houses and five Temple ordainers. The rights of blood and primogeniture are given greater precedence"—he glanced at Biast—"after the Darthacan manner. Since the election of the hallow king more often than not used to be a pretext for tribal warfare, this more peaceful transfer of powers between generations itself seems the mark of godly blessings." His further nod to Biast gave impulsion to the hint, *And let us keep it that way.*

"A political answer was not what I asked for," said Ingrey. "Was the old hallow king always a spirit warrior, or . . . or a shaman?" And how unsafe was it going to prove, to release that particular term into the conversation?

Lewko sat up with a look of growing interest. "I have heard something of the sort. The old hallow king was supposed to be the hub of many intertribal rites; perhaps more mage than holy, in truth."

Ingrey tried to imagine any hallow king in the recent past as magical, and failed. *Nor holy either, in truth.* "So that—uncanny power—is all gone from the kingship?"

"Yes?" said Lewko.

Ingrey wasn't sure if that rising inflection was meant as assent or encouragement. "So—what's left? What makes the hallow kingship hallowed now?"

The archdivine's eyebrows went up. "The blessings of the five gods."

"Your pardon, Learned, but I get blessed by the five gods every Quarterday Service. It does not make me holy."

"Truly," muttered Hetwar, almost inaudibly.

Ingrey ignored him and forged on. "Is there any more to this kingly blessing than pious good wishes?"

The archdivine said sonorously, "There is prayer. The five archdivine-ordainers pray for guidance in their vote; all invite their gods for a sign."

Ingrey rather thought he had delivered a couple of those *signs* himself, in clinking bags. It had not made him feel like a messenger of the gods. "What else? What other changes? There *must* be something more." The slight strain in his voice betrayed too much urgency, and he swallowed to bring it back under close control. Five old kin groups were now missing from the mix, true, three of them extinct, two diminished. Five Temple-men replaced them smoothly enough, and who could say they were any less true representatives of their people? Yet the election had *created* Horseriver a mage-king once, created him something extraordinary. *Aye, and he never stopped being it, did he?* Was the present kingship empty in part because Horseriver held on to something in his deathlessness that he should have yielded back?

Biast, who had been jittering in his chair during this, interrupted. "If the accusation against Wencel is true, I am deeply concerned for the safety of my sister."

Ingrey bore no love for Fara, after what she had done to Ijada, but considering his suspicions of the fate of Horseriver's *last* wife-mother, he had to allow the point. "Your concern seems valid to me, my lord."

Hetwar sat up at that admission.

Ingrey added, "I am reminded, Sealmaster. Earl Horseriver has lately hinted to me that he desires my service. I beg you, if he asks, to say you will not release me. I fear to refuse him to his face. I don't wish to invoke his enmity."

Hetwar's brows drew down in furious thought. The archdivine stared, and said, "*Two* spirit-defiled men to be in the same house? Why does he desire this?"

"You assume your conclusion, Archdivine," Ingrey pointed out. "The earl is accused, not yet convicted."

Fritine turned in his seat. "Lewko . . . ?"

Lewko spread his hands. "I would need a closer look at him. And the aid of the god, which I cannot force."

Fritine turned back to Ingrey, frowning. "I would have you speak more plainly, Lord Ingrey."

Ingrey shrugged. "Consider what you demand, Archdivine. If you wish my testimony of the unseen and the uncanny, you cannot pick and choose. You must take all, or none. And I doubt you are ready to accept me as some sort of courier from the gods, bearing orders for you."

While Fritine was digesting the implications of *that* remark, Ingrey continued, "As for Wencel, he claims to be reminded of our cousinship. Belatedly enough." Well, that too was true in a sense.

Biast said indignantly, "You would leave my sister unprotected in a house where you fear to go yourself?" His brow wrinkled, and he added more slowly, "You are loyal to my lord Hetwar, are you not?"

He has never betrayed me. Yet. Ingrey gave a little ambiguous bow.

Biast continued, "But if the accusation is true . . . who better to protect the princess from, from any uncanny act her husband might take, or to rescue her from that place if the need arises? And you might observe, inform, report . . ."

"Spy?" said Fritine, in an interested tone. "Could he do that, do you think, Hetwar?"

Ingrey raised a brow. "Now you would have me take a lying oath of service, my lords?" he inquired sweetly.

"Ingrey, *stop that,*" snapped Hetwar. "Your graveyard notions of humor have no place in this council."

"That was humor?" muttered Biast.

"As close as he ever comes to it."

"I wonder that you endure it."

"His trying style has proved to have its uses. From time to time. He wanders his own twisted path, and brings back prizes no logical man would have even suspected were there. I've never been sure if it was a talent or a curse." Hetwar sat back and regarded Ingrey acutely. "*Could* you do this?"

Ingrey hesitated. It would make official what he had been doing half-awarely all along; playing both ends against the middle while desperately collecting fragments that he hoped would fall into some pattern. And keeping his own counsel betimes.

He could say no. He could.

"I admit," he said instead, slowly, "I, too, desire to understand more of Wencel." He added to Biast, "And why do you suddenly think your sister in danger now, and not anytime these past four years?"

Biast looked a trifle embarrassed. "These past four years, I was scarcely paying attention. We met but once after her wedding, and wrote seldom. I assumed, assumed she was well disposed of by my father, and content withal. I had my own duties. It was not till she spoke with me—well, I taxed her—this past day that she revealed how unhappy she had grown."

"What did she say to you?" asked Hetwar.

"She'd intended no such harm to fall out of the, um, events at Boar's Head. She thought Boleso had grown too wild, yes, but hoped that perhaps he and, um, Lady Ijada might grow content with one another, in time. That the girl might calm him. Fara feels her lack of children keenly, though I must say, it is not clear to me that the fault in that is *hers*. She thought her husband's eye had fallen on her new handmaiden, for it was he who brought her into Fara's household."

That last is new, thought Ingrey. Ijada had thought the offer the work of her Badgerbank aunt, but who had stirred up the aunt to remember her? *Could* Wencel have been thinking of a new heir, to place between himself and Ingrey? Or were his motives in securing Ijada something altogether else? *Altogether else, I now think. He would not so bestir himself without reason, but his reasons are not those of other men.*

"Lady Ijada claims the earl offered her no insult," Ingrey put in. "I grant you she may be naïve enough not to have recognized one unless it were gross, and Wencel is not given to grossness. I hold Fara much at fault in this whole chain of events. Though I admit, Boleso was well along on his own dark path, and it was better he was stopped sooner than later." Reminded by Hetwar's quick glare of a need for civility, he added to Boleso's bereaved brother, "I'm sorry it had to be so cruelly."

The prince-marshal vented an unhappy *Mm.* It was not a noise of disagreement.

The archdivine cleared his throat. "I would observe, Lord Ingrey, that by your testimony to Learned Lewko—and certain other evidences—it seems your spirit wolf is now unbound. You stand in violation of your dispensation."

His bland tone concealed not so much menace, or acute fear, as pressure, Ingrey decided. So. He knew how to deal with simple pressure.

"It was not by my will, sir." A safely uncheckable assertion. "It was an accident that occurred when Learned Hallana took the geas off me. And so, in a sense, the Temple's own doing." *Yes, blame the absent.* "While I can't say it was the gods' will, two gods have been quick enough to make use of it." Was that the barest nervous flinch on Fritine's part? Ingrey took a breath. "Now you desire to make use of it, too, setting me to guard Princess Fara. This seems to me a grave mandate, for a man you do not trust. Or do you mean to extract the use of me first, then turn on me? I warn you, I can swim."

Fritine considered this bait for a long moment and shrewdly declined to bite. "Then it behooves you to continue to make yourself useful, don't you think?"

"I see." Ingrey favored him with a slightly too-sweeping bow. "It seems I am at your service, Archdivine."

Hetwar shifted a little uncomfortably at this blatant exchange. It was not that he was above threats, but he had always managed to find smoother ways to move Ingrey to his will, a courtesy Ingrey appreciated aesthetically if nothing else.

"Since you put it so compellingly," said Ingrey—Hetwar grimaced, he saw out of the corner of his eye—"I will undertake to be your spy. And the princess's bodyguard." He gave Biast a polite nod, which Biast, at least, had the mother wit to return.

"This brings up the disposition of the prisoner," said Hetwar. "If Wencel is suspect, so is his courtesy of housing Lady Ijada. It may be time to move her to more secure quarters."

Ingrey froze. Was Ijada to be torn from his wardenship? He said carefully, "Would that not prematurely reveal your suspicions to Wencel?"

"By no means," said the archdivine. "Such a change was inevitable, after the funeral."

"It seems to me her present lodging is adequate," protested Ingrey. "She makes no attempt to run, trusting to Temple justice. I did mention she was naïve," he added, by way of a jab at Fritine.

"Yes, but you cannot guard two places at once," Biast pointed out logically.

Hetwar, finally growing alive to the sudden tension in Ingrey's stance, held up a restraining hand. "We can discuss this later. I thank you for volunteering in this difficult matter, Lord Ingrey. How soon do you think you might slip into Horseriver's household?"

"Tonight?" said Biast.

No! I must see Ijada! "It would look odd, I fear, if I were to arrive before he begged me of you, Lord Hetwar. Nor should you let yourself be persuaded too readily. And I am in need of food and sleep." That last was unblunted truth, at least.

"I would have my sister guarded now," said Biast.

"Perhaps you might arrange to visit her yourself, then."

"*I* have no uncanny powers to set against Wencel!"

You begin to believe you need me unburned, then, do you? Good. "Is there no Temple sorcerer to set in guard, meanwhile?"

"The ones I deem suitable are out on tasks," said Lewko. "I shall dispatch an urgent recall as soon as I may." Fritine nodded to this.

"Peace, prince," said Hetwar to Biast, who was opening his mouth again. "I think we can take no further sensible action tonight." He pushed up from his writing table with a tired grunt. "Ingrey, step out with me."

Ingrey excused himself to the seated powers, making sure to direct a special little farewell bow to Gesca just to worry him. If Gesca was Horseriver's spy, how would Wencel react when *this* report reached him? Although the earl must have anticipated Cumril's accusation. At least Gesca might testify that the suspicion hadn't come from Ingrey. *Yes. Let Gesca run, for now. Follow his scent, see if it goes where I think.*

Ingrey followed Hetwar down the dim, carpeted corridor, well out of earshot of the closed study door. "My lord?"

Hetwar turned to him and stood close under a sconce. The candlelight edged his troubled features. "It had been my belief before now that Wencel's keen interest in the upcoming election was on his brother-in-law's behalf. He has been deep in my councils therefore. Now I've cause to wonder if, like Boleso, it is some much closer desire."

"Has he made new actions aside from his odd interest in Ijada?"

"Say rather, old actions seen in a new light." Hetwar rubbed his forehead, and squeezed his eyes shut, briefly. "While you are guarding Fara, keep your eyes open for evidences of any, shall I say, unhealthily personal interest on Wencel's part in the next hallow kingship."

"I am very sure Wencel is not interested in mere political power," Ingrey said.

"This statement does not reassure me, Ingrey. Not when a certain wolf-lord has uttered the words *kingship* and *magery* in the same breath. I know very well you left things unsaid in there."

"Wild speculation bears its own hazards."

"Indeed. I want *facts*. I do not wish to lose a valuable ally through offensive false accusations, nor conversely to fail to guard against a dangerous enemy."

"My curiosity in this matter is as great as yours, my lord."

"Good." Hetwar clapped him on the shoulder. "Go, then, and see about that food and sleep you mentioned. You look like death on a platter, you know. Are you sure you weren't really ill, this morning?"

"I should have much preferred it. Did Lewko report my confession?"

"Of your so-called vision? Oh, aye, and a lurid tale it was." He hesitated. "Though Biast seemed to take some comfort in it."

"Did you believe it?"

Hetwar cocked his head. "Did you?"

"Oh," breathed Ingrey, "yes."

Hetwar stood very still, first seeking Ingrey's eyes, then, after a moment, dropping his gaze uncomfortably. "I regret missing that entertainment. So what did you and the god really say to each other?"

"We . . . argued."

Hetwar's lips curled up in a genuine, if dry, smile. "Why does this not surprise me? I wish the gods well of you. May They have better luck getting straight answers from you than I ever did." He began to turn away.

"My lord," said Ingrey suddenly.

Hetwar turned back. "Aye?"

"If, ah . . ." Ingrey swallowed to moisten his throat. "A favor. If, for any reason, my cousin Wencel should suddenly die in the next few days, I beg you will see that I am brought at once before a Temple inquiry. With the best sorcerers Lewko can muster doing the examination."

Hetwar frowned, staring at him. The frown deepened. He started to speak, but closed his lips again. "I suppose," he said at last, "you imagine you can just hand me a thing like that and walk off, eh?"

"So you swear, yes."

"You are confusing *swear* and *curse,* I think."

"Swear."

"Yes, then."

"Good."

Ingrey bowed and retreated. Hetwar did not call him back. Though a low and breathy cursing did, indeed, drift to Ingrey's ears as he turned for the stairs.

18

Ijada was sitting at the bottom of the staircase as the porter admitted Ingrey to the prison-house's entry hall, hunched over with her arms wrapped even more tightly about herself than the last time. Her warden sat a few steps above her, looking on in disquiet. Ijada sprang to her feet, her eyes searching Ingrey's face for he knew not what, but she seemed to find it, for she pounced upon him. Grasping his arm, she dragged him into the side room, slamming the door on the disapproving but cowed face of the warden.

"What *was* that, a while ago?" Ijada demanded. "What happened to you?"

"What did you—did you see something, too?"

"Visions, Ingrey, terrible visions. *Not* from the god, I swear. Some little while after you went out, I was overcome again. My knees gave way. The world around me did not fade altogether this time, but the pictures were stronger than memory, less than hallucination. Ingrey, I saw Bloodfield, I saw my men! Not tattered and worn as they were in my dream in the Wounded Woods, but from before, when they yet lived." She hesitated. "Died."

"Did you sense Wencel? Did you see him or hear his voice?"

"No, not . . . not as he is. These visions were in *your* mind, I think. Were they not?"

"Yes. Pictures from before-times, yes? The Old Weald. The massacre at Bloodfield."

She shuddered and touched her own neck, and the horrible crunch of the ax parting bone sounded again in Ingrey's memory. *She felt that, too.*

"*Why* do we share such things? What has happened between us?" she asked.

"The pictures, those visions—Wencel put them in me. He is not just spirit warrior like you, not just shaman like me. He's more. Lost out of time, terrible in his power and pain. He thinks he is—he claims to be—hallow king."

"But old Lord Stagthorne is king, has been since before I was born—how can there be two?"

"I think that is some problem, some mystery, that I have not yet come to the core of. I went to Wencel planning to beat the truth out of him if I had to. Instead, he beat it into me . . ."

He guided her into a chair and sat next to her, their hands still gripping each other across the tabletop. Haltingly, Ingrey described his terrifying interview with the earl. Ijada seemed to have shared only the mystic visions, not their context; Ingrey thought she must have spent the last hours wild with bewilderment, for even now her eyes were dilated and her body shivering.

"Wencel claims I am his soul's heir, my body to be seized by his spell whether he or I will it or not. How long this has been so, I do not know. There might once have been some other cousin between us, who died more lately, but . . . but it may even go back to the death of my father. Which raises yet more questions without answers about what my father intended with his wolf rite."

"My other dream," she breathed. "Of the burning horseman, the leashed wolf racing through the ash. It was you! It was *both* of you."

"Do you think? Perhaps . . ."

"Ingrey, I *recognized* Holytree, I recognized my men. I am bound to them as certainly as I am bound to you, though I do not know how. And if Wencel spoke true, he is bound to them as well, and they to him."

"Wencel's tale was full of gaps, but he did not lie about that," said Ingrey certainly. "That binding is at the very heart of all this."

"Then the circle is complete. You are bound to me, me to my ghosts, they to Wencel, and Wencel, it seems, to you. Is Wencel trying to work some great magic with all of us here?"

"I'm not sure. This is not all Wencel's doing, exactly. For one thing, the choice of his mystical heir is not his own, or he would surely have picked someone other than me. Which makes a sort of sense; the spell must have been made to work in the chaos and heat of battle, when both king and next heir might fall in the same hour—as happened at Bloodfield, more or less. The transfer must take place without attention or will on the part of the hallowed ones. So *that* part of the spell must be bound up with the dead spirit warriors in the Wounded Woods. It's as if the whole of the Old Weald, or what remains of its kin powers, chooses its heir *through* Wencel." There seemed to Ingrey to be an enigmatic, daunting validation in the notion.

Ijada's eyes narrowed. "Are we all three supposed to go to Bloodfield, then? And if so, what are we supposed to do when we get there?"

"And who—or Who—presses us to that end?" Ingrey muttered. He sat back, frowning. "The spell was locked tighter, heretofore. Just the Horserivers and the dead warriors, around and around for sixteen generations. You—you broke into it from the outside. The spell broke out to claim *me*. Its boundaries are not what they were. Boundaries between death and life, spirit and matter. Bloodline and bloodline. The Weald and an outer land. Changes—for the first time in centuries, changes are breaking in."

Ijada rubbed her wrinkled brow. "What am I, in this? Half-in, half-out—do I even belong? I am alive, they are dead; I am a woman, they are men—mostly—I think . . . My leopard is not even a proper Wealding beast! I did nothing for Boleso's soul this morning; I just stood there stupidly gaping. It's *you* that's wanted, Ingrey, you who might free the ghosts from their old creatures!" Her gaze upon him was devouring in its conviction.

"A door in a wall is at once both inside and outside," said Ingrey slowly. "Half and half, as you are in your very blood, by your father's grace. And you were wanted, too, though not, I think, by Wencel. Did your ghosts not choose you? Of all who slept and dreamed in the Woods that night?"

She hesitated, straightened a little. "Yes."

"So, then." *Then what?* Ingrey's exhausted brain did not supply an answer. "More matters arose, after the visions. Wencel wants very much to keep me closer, I think. He coaxed me with an offer of a post in his household. More than coaxed. Coerced."

She frowned in new worry.

"Hetwar," Ingrey continued, "instead of protecting me, wants me to take up the station so as to spy for him. Cumril raised the suspicion that Wencel bears a spirit animal, though the Temple and Hetwar do not yet know how much else he claims to be. I did not tell them. I'm not sure what consequences will spin from that, nor how quickly Wencel's darker secrets will unravel. Nor how I will be caught up in the tangle. Worse, Biast has taken a fear of his brother-in-law and wants to set me to guard Fara." Ingrey grimaced.

"Biast may not be not so far abroad as all that," said Ijada slowly. "I surely do not want my disasters to be the death of any more Stagthornes."

"You don't see. If I am drawn off to Horseriver, they will take you from my charge, give you over to some other jailer. Maybe shut you up in some other prison, less easy of access. Or of escape."

Tension tightened her face. "I must not be . . . must not be constrained, when it is finished. When it is time to go."

"When what is finished?"

Her hand grasped air in a gesture of frustration. "This. Whatever this is. When the god's hunt closes in upon what He seeks. Do you not feel it, Ingrey?"

"Feel, yes, I am feverish with the strain, but I do not see it. Not clear."

"What *is* Wencel about?"

Ingrey shook his head. "I am less certain all the time that he is *about* anything, besides defending his old secrets. His mind is so full, he actually seems to have trouble paying attention at moments. Not that this makes him less dangerous. What does he really fear? He cannot, after all, be slain, it would seem." Execution would not stop the earl. Imprisonment, were Wencel desperate enough, he might escape the same hard way, no matter how deep the dungeon or heavy the guard. It came to Ingrey that he really didn't want to risk Wencel being imprisoned.

Ijada's lips twisted in new puzzlement. "And how has the earl been getting through his funerals, all these centuries, if his soul never goes to the gods?"

Ingrey paused, considering the lack of rumor, then made a little gesture of negation. "Occupying the body of his own heir, he would usually be in close charge of his own rites. I'm sure he became expert in arranging them to display what he willed. And if he missed a few, well, some men *are* sundered."

The strangeness of it disturbed Ingrey's imagination anew. What must it have been like for Horseriver to watch his own body being buried, over and over? In a bereavement twisted back on itself, knowing that it was not the father but the son being lost in that hour?

Ijada nodded, some similar reflection sobering her face. She tapped the tabletop. "If the Temple were brought to attend upon his spell, what might they do?"

"I'm not sure. Nothing, I think, except by sorcery or miracle."

"The gods are already hip deep in this. With very little reference to the Temple."

"So it would seem." Ingrey sighed.

"So what are we to do?"

Ingrey rubbed the back of his neck, which ached. "Wait, I think. Still. I will go to Horseriver's household. And spy, but not only for Hetwar. Maybe I will find something there to make sense of this, some piece yet lacking."

"At what danger to yourself?" she fretted.

Ingrey shrugged.

She looked dissatisfied. "Something feels horribly unbalanced in this pause."

"What pause?" Ingrey snorted. "This unmerciful day has battered me half to bits."

Her hands waved in renewed exasperation. "While I have been mewed up in this house!"

He leaned forward, hesitated for a fraction of fear, and kissed her. She did not retreat. There was no sudden shock this time, no change in his sense of her, but that was only because her steady presence had never faded from their first kiss. He could feel it, a current like a millrace flowing between them. The arousal of his body was muted now in exhaustion, the pleasure of her lips drowned in a desperate uneasiness. She clutched him back not in lust or love, it seemed, but starveling trust: not in his dubious abilities, but in him whole. Wolf and all. His heart heated in wonder. He trembled.

She drew back and smoothed his hair from his brow, half-smiling, half-worried. "Have you eaten?" she asked practically.

"Not lately."

"You look so tired. Perhaps you should."

"Hetwar said the same."

"Then it is so." She rose. "I will order the kitchen to bestir itself for you."

He pressed the back of her hand to his throbbing forehead, before reluctantly releasing her.

Halfway to the door, she looked over her shoulder, and said, "Ingrey . . ."

"Hm?" He lifted his head from where it had sunk down upon his arms crossed on the table.

"If Wencel is truly some mystical hallow king, and you are truly his heir . . . what does that make you?"

Terrified, mostly. "Nothing good."

"Huh." She shook her head and went out.

Ingrey slept later than he'd intended the next morning, and his new orders arrived earlier than he'd expected, by the hand of Gesca.

Still adjusting the jerkin and knife belt he'd just donned, Ingrey descended the staircase to meet his erstwhile lieutenant in the entry hall. Gesca lowered his voice to Ingrey's ear as the porter shuffled out the door to the kitchen, calling for his boy.

"You are to report to Earl Horseriver."

"Already? That was fast. What of my prisoner?"

"I am to take your place as house warden."

Ingrey stiffened. "In whose name? Hetwar's or Horseriver's?"

"Hetwar's, and the archdivine's."

"Do they plan to move her elsewhere?"

"No one has told me yet."

Ingrey's eyes narrowed, studying the nervous lieutenant. "And whom did you report to after Hetwar's meeting, last night?"

"Why should I have reported to anyone?"

With a casual step that fooled no one, Ingrey backed the man to the wall, leaning on his braced arm and turning to trap Gesca's gaze. "You may as well admit you went to

Horseriver. If Wencel means me to serve him as I served Hetwar, I will be deep in his councils before long."

Gesca's lips parted, but he only shook his head.

"No good, Gesca. I knew of your letters to him." It was another shot in the almost-dark, but by the lieutenant's jerk, it hit the target.

"How did you—I thought there was no harm in it! He was Lord Hetwar's own ally! I just thought I was doing a favor for m'lord's friend."

"Suitably recompensed, one feels certain."

"Well . . . I am not a rich man. And the earl is not a nip-purse." Gesca's brows drew down in new wariness. "How did you know? I'd swear you never saw."

"By Wencel's so-timely arrival at Middletown. Among other things."

"Oh." Gesca's shoulders slumped, and he grimaced.

So was Gesca unhappy to have been lured into disloyalty to Hetwar, or merely unhappy to have been caught at it? "Slipping down the slope, are you? It makes a man as vulnerable to give favors as to take them. I seldom do either, therefore." Ingrey smiled his most wolfish, the better to uphold the illusion of his invulnerability in Gesca's mind.

Gesca's voice went small. "Are you going to turn me in?"

"Have I accused you yet?"

"That's not an answer. Not from you."

"True." Ingrey sighed. "If you were to confess yourself to Hetwar, instead of waiting for an accusation, you'd be more likely to earn a reprimand than a dismissal. Hetwar cares less for perfect honesty from his men, than that he understands precisely the limits of their guile. It's a comforting certainty of a kind, I suppose."

"And what of your limits, then? What comfort does he find in them?"

"We keep each other alert." Ingrey looked Gesca over. "Well, there could be worse wardens."

"Aye, and worse-looking wards."

Ingrey dropped his tone of edgy banter in favor of a much

purer menace. "You will treat Lady Ijada with the strictest courtesy while she is in your charge, Gesca. Or the wrath of Hetwar, the Temple, Horseriver, and the gods combined will be the least of your worries."

Gesca flinched under his glower. "Give over, Ingrey. I am no monster!"

"But I am," Ingrey breathed. "Clear?"

Gesca scarcely dared inhale. "Very."

"Good." Ingrey stepped away, and though he had in fact not touched him, Gesca slumped like a man released from a throttling grip, patting his throat as if to probe for bruises. Or tooth marks.

Ingrey scuffed back upstairs to roust Tesko to pack his meager belongings again for transfer to Horseriver's mansion. He reviewed his last night's meeting with Hetwar and its probable effect, as filtered through Gesca's memory and wits, on Horseriver. As long as Ingrey was not so stupid as to pretend to conceal it from the earl, he doubted Horseriver would be much disturbed by the assignment to spy on him. And the earl would surely have gleaned from Gesca the fact that Ingrey had kept the darkest of his secrets. On the whole, Gesca's little betrayal of trust might prove more useful than not, Ingrey decided.

As Tesko tottered off down the stairs under a load of his master's gear, Ingrey mounted the next flight and rapped on Ijada's door. He was pleased to hear the bolt scrape back before the door opened to reveal the woman warden's suspicious eye.

"Lady Ijada, if you please."

Ijada shouldered past the woman into the little upstairs hall, her expression grave and questioning.

Ingrey ducked his head at her. "I am called away to Earl Horseriver's already. Gesca will be taking my place as your keeper, for a time."

She brightened at the familiar name. "That's not so bad, then."

"Perhaps. I'll try to come back and speak with you if I find, um, better understandings of things."

She nodded. Her expression was more thoughtful than panicked, though what she was thinking, Ingrey could scarcely guess. She possessed no more answers than he did, but he admired her talent for finding very uncomfortable questions. He suspected he would be in want of it shortly.

He clasped her hands, in lieu of the good-bye kiss they could not make under watchful eyes. The strange current that seemed to flow between them still lingered, in that grip. "I will know if they move you."

She nodded again, releasing him. "I'll be listening for you, too."

He managed a ghost of a bow and tore himself away.

Ingrey repeated his uphill walk of yesterday through Kingstown, trailed this time by a puffing Tesko burdened with his belongings. Horseriver's porter was plainly expecting them, for they were shown at once to Ingrey's new room. It was no narrow servant's stall under the eaves, but a gracious chamber on the third floor appointed for highborn guests, with an alcove for Tesko. Leaving his servant to arrange his scant wardrobe, Ingrey left to explore the mansion. He wondered if Horseriver would expect him to clear the rest of his possessions from Hetwar's palace, and what the earl would construe if he did not.

Passing a sitting room on the second floor, its moldings gracefully carved in birch wood, Ingrey glanced in to see Fara and one of her ladies. The matronly lady sat bent over some sewing; Fara stood with her hand upon the drape, staring pensively out the window, strained features silvered by the morning light. Her rather rectangular face was pale, her body short and solid in her drab dress; she would be stout in old age, Ingrey thought. Her head turned at some creak or clink from Ingrey, and her dark eyes widened in recognition.

"Lord Ingrey—is it?"

"Princess." Ingrey essayed a sketchy salute, his hand to

his heart recalling, but not quite completing, a sign of the Five.

She looked him over, frowning. "Biast told me last night you were to enter my husband's service."

"And, ah . . . yours?"

"Yes. He told me that." She glanced at her attendant. "Leave us. Leave open the door." The woman rose, curtseyed, and slipped out past Ingrey; Fara beckoned him within.

She looked up at him in wary speculation as he came to the window. Her voice was low. "My brother said you would protect me."

Keeping his tone neutral and equally quiet, Ingrey said, "Do you feel in need of protection?"

She made an uncertain gesture. "Biast said a dire suspicion has fallen upon Wencel. What do you think of it?"

"Can you not tell if it is so, lady?"

She shook her head, not exactly in negation, and raised her long chin. "Can not you?"

"The presence of a blood-companion such as mine is not what defiles a man; it is what he does with it. Or so I must believe. My dispensation tacitly concedes the same. Have you suspected nothing uncanny of your husband, in all this time?"

Her thick black brows drew down in deeper unhappiness over this not-quite-answer. "No . . . yes. I don't know. He was strange from the start, but I thought him merely moody. I tried to lighten his spirit, and sometimes, sometimes it seemed to work, but always he fell back into his blackness again. I prayed to the Mother for guidance, and, and more— I *tried* to be a good wife, as the Temple teaches us." Her voice quavered, but did not break. Her frown darkened. "Then he brought that girl in."

"Lady Ijada? Did not you like her—at first?"

"Oh, at first—!" She gave an angry little shrug of her shoulders. "At first, I suppose. But Wencel . . . *attended* to her."

"And what was her response to this regard of his? Did you tax her about it?"

"She pretended to laugh. I didn't laugh. I watched him, watching her—I had never seen him so much as look twice at another woman since we wed, or before for that matter, but he looked at *her*."

Ingrey composed a question that would lead to Fara's version of the events at Boar's Head, though it scarcely seemed needful. No searing intellect here, no subtle guile, no eerie powers, just a hurt bewilderment. There seemed to be no uncanny tracks lingering *upon* her, either; Wencel did not choose to bespell his wife, it seemed. Why not?

But Fara's mind was circling in another direction. "Biast's accusation . . ." she murmured. Her gaze upon Ingrey sharpened. "It could be so, I suppose. I can tell nothing by looking at you, after all. If you really hide a wolf within, it is as invisible as any other man's sins. It would explain . . . much." She drew breath, and demanded abruptly, "How did you get your dispensation?"

His brows went up. "I suppose I had a particularly charitable Temple inquirer. He was sorry for a sick orphan. At length, I gave some proof of control of my affliction that seemed to satisfy my examiners. Not enough to give a castlemastership into my young hands, of course. Later—later, Hetwar supported me."

"If Wencel controls his beast so well that even I cannot tell he carries it, is that not proof enough to gain a like pardon?" she asked, a plaintive note leaking into her voice.

Ingrey moistened his lips. "You would have to ask the archdivine. It is no decision of mine." Was Fara thinking in terms of protecting and preserving her husband? *Could* Wencel slip through a Temple examination such as the one that had vacillated so long over Ingrey's case? Horseriver had so much more to conceal, but also, it seemed, more power to bring to bear on the task. If he desired. Perhaps he would be driven, through the destruction of his old concealments now in progress, to attempt some such ploy.

In fact, one would think the task would claim all his attention. *He pursues something else. Intently.* What?

For whatever private reasons, Fara clearly found the accusation that Wencel possessed a spirit beast to be alarmingly believable, once presented to her imagination. She had the look of a woman fitting together some long-worked puzzle, the last pieces falling into place faster and faster. Frightened, yes, both of and for her husband, and for herself.

"Why not ask Wencel these questions yourself?" said Ingrey.

"He did not come to me last night." She rubbed her face, and her eyes. The hard friction might be supposed to account for their reddening. "He doesn't, much, lately. Biast said to say nothing to him, but I do not know . . ."

"Wencel already knows he is privately accused. You would betray no one's secret by trying him."

She stared timidly at him. "Are you so much in his confidence already, then?"

"I am his closest living cousin." *Temporarily.* "Wencel's need for kinship has no nearer source of satisfaction, in this crisis." So to speak.

Her hands wrung each other. "I shall be glad of you, then."

That remains to be seen. Unfortunately, he could not very well express his low opinion of her betrayal of her handmaiden and simultaneously expect to cultivate her confidences. He stiffened, his senses attuned to an approaching presence even before the sound of a light step wafted from the corridor and a throat was cleared in the doorway.

"Lord Ingrey," said Wencel, in a cordial voice. "They told me you had arrived."

Ingrey made his little sketch bow. "My lord Horseriver."

"I trust you have found your new chambers to your liking?"

"Yes, thank you. Tesko thinks we rise in the world."

"So you might." Wencel's gesture of greeting to his wife was unexceptionably polite. "Attend on me, if you please, Ingrey. Lady, pray excuse us."

Fara's return nod was equally cool, only a slight rigidity of her body betraying her confusion of emotions.

Ingrey followed Wencel out and down two turnings of the halls to his study. Wencel pulled the door firmly shut behind them; Ingrey turned so as not to present his back to his host. Horseriver had certainly had time to prepare a magical attack, if he were so disposed. But the hairs on the back of Ingrey's neck stirred in vain, for Wencel merely waved him to a chair and hitched his hip over the edge of his writing table. He swung one leg and studied Ingrey through narrowed eyes.

"Hetwar released you most promptly," Wencel observed. "Did Gesca tell you why?"

"Oh, aye."

"Biast is most concerned for his sister. Fara dreams of saving you, I believe. How you came to deserve your wife's love, I cannot guess."

"Nor can I." Horseriver grimaced and spun one graying-blond ringlet, strayed to overhang his face, in his fingers in a gesture almost nervous. "I suspect her governesses allowed too much court poetry to rot her brain, before marriage. I have buried over a score of wives; I do not allow myself to become fond, these days. I can hardly explain what these women look like to me now. It is one of the subtler horrors of my present existence."

"Like kissing a corpse?"

"Like being the corpse so kissed."

"She seems not to know this."

The earl shrugged. "For some notion now discarded—habit—I began this union intending to engender one more son, and for that, the body must be aroused somehow. Fortunately, this one is still young, and simple Wencel would have been quite pleased with his princess, I think."

Did Horseriver allow that half-digested soul to surface, when feigning to make love to his bride? And how appallingly confusing for Fara, when the eager lost boy of the night gave way to the glacial stranger at breakfast . . . Could

Horseriver call other faces to the fore, when dealing with other tasks? The princess might well spin herself dizzy, trying to follow such a progression of moods in her spouse.

Wencel had fallen into one of his forthcoming humors again, for whatever purpose. Ingrey decided to pursue the opportunity. "Why did you bring Lady Ijada into your household? Considering the consequences, that would seem to have been a mistake."

Wencel grimaced. "Perhaps. In hindsight."

"Fara thought her intended for your new Horseriver broodmare."

The scowl deepened. "So it seems. I did say Fara was a romantic."

"If not that, then . . . for the Wounded Woods? And not merely Ijada's inheritance of the tract." It went against Ingrey's habits to give away information, but in this case, it might prime the pump. "She told me of her dream of it."

"Ah, yes," said Wencel grimly. "So you do know about that, now. I wondered."

"Did she tell you of it, too?"

"No. But I dreamed it with her, if from another angle of view. Since it was more than dream: it was event. Even acting as the gods' cat's-paw, she could not very well trouble my own waters without the ripples reaching me." Wencel sighed. "She created me a very great puzzle thereby. I brought her into my household to observe her, but I could discover nothing unusual. If the gods intended her for bait, I declined to bite. She had undoubtedly become bound into the spell during her night camping at Holytree, but she remained as sightless and powerless as any other ignorant girl."

"Until Boar's Head."

"Indeed."

"Did the gods *intend* all of this? Boleso's death as well?"

Wencel drew a long, thoughtful inhalation. "Resisting the gods somewhat resembles playing a game of castles and riders with an opponent who can always see several moves ahead of you. But even the gods cannot see infinitely far ahead. Our free wills cloud Their vision, even though Their eyes are more piercing than ours. The gods do not *plan,* so much as *take advantage.*"

"Why then did you send me to kill her? Mere prudence?" Ingrey kept his tone casual, as if the answer were of only scholarly interest to him.

"Hardly mere. Once she had slain Boleso, she was most assuredly bound for the gallows. If there is a more perfect symbolic representation of an Old Weald courier sacrifice than to hang an innocent virgin by a sacred cord from a tree, with divines singing blessings about her, I cannot think of it. Death opens a gate to the gods. *Her* death in that mode would have opened Holytree wide, barricaded against Them as it has been these four centuries."

"And her murder would not? What's the difference?"

Wencel merely shrugged, and made to slip off his perch and turn away.

"Unless"—Ingrey's mind leapt ahead—"there was more to that geas than murder."

Wencel turned back. His face bore that deeply ironic look that masked irritation, which Ingrey took as a sign that his digging was striking something worthwhile. "It would have bound her murdered soul to yours in a haunting, until it faded into nothingness. Keeping her, and her link to Holytree, beyond the reach of the gods. It was a variant of an old, old spell, and I spent far too much blood on it; but I was hurried."

"Charming." Ingrey failed to keep the snarl out of his voice now. "Murder and sundering both."

Wencel turned his palms out in a *What would you?* gesture. "Worse: a redundancy. For her leopard spirit would have done the same. If I had known of it. That move, I must concede to my Opponents. I still do not know if we were counterblocking each other to stalemate, or were all victims of Boleso's idiocy, or if more lies hidden beyond." He hesitated. "For the haunting to be effected without the murder first was not in my plans. But it happened. Didn't it." Wencel's eyes were cool upon Ingrey now, and it came to him that he was not the only man digging, here. Wait, was Horseriver saying that the current of awareness between Ingrey and Ijada was *his* doing?

At Ingrey's sudden silence, he added kindly, "Did you imagine you had fallen in love with her, cousin? Or she with you? Alas that I must shatter that idyllic illusion. Truly, I would have thought you—though perhaps not her—harder-headed."

Ingrey almost rose to this bait. *Aye, all the way out of the water, trailing foam.* But he remembered how Wencel's soft persuasions had almost had him cutting his own throat, not long back. *The man scarcely needs magic to wind me into knots.* The peculiar link between Ingrey and Ijada might indeed be a side effect of Wencel's defeated geas, but Wencel did not control it any longer. *And he does not like what he does not control, not when it lies so close to the heart of his matter.* Whatever that matter was. *And there is more between Ijada and me now than whatever you put there, Wencel.* Ingrey managed a gesture of dry dismissal. "Howsoever. Now I am in your service, what duties would you have of me, my lord?"

Wencel did not look entirely convinced of Ingrey's placidity, in the face of this, but he did not pursue the issue. "In truth, I have scarcely had time to consider the possibilities."

"Inventing as you go, are you?"

"Yes, I am quite godlike in that way, if no other. Perhaps I shall give you a horse."

"Hetwar spared me that expense. I rode his nags at need, and he fed them whether they were needed or not."

"Oh, the beast would be stabled at my expense. It would uphold the distinction of my house to mount you properly."

Ingrey was put instantly in mind of Horseriver's last wife-mother's death in her so-called riding accident, but he said merely, "Thank you, then, my lord."

"Be at your leisure this morning. Plan to attend on me when I go out, later."

"I am at your disposal, cousin."

Wencel's mouth quirked in mockery. "I trust so."

Ingrey took this for a sufficient dismissal and retreated from the study.

Whatever Wencel was about, he was not making *all* of it up as he went. He had some fixed goal in sight. And if it was the hallow kingship, as Hetwar feared, it was not for any reason that Hetwar could imagine.

Nor I. Yet. Ingrey shook his head. He had much to think upon, in the next hours.

19

By relentless prowling, Ingrey familiarized himself with every corner of the Horseriver mansion that day, to little effect. Wencel had arrived here bare weeks ago to attend on the hallow king in his worsening illness, and Fara had followed shortly despite her fatal diversion to Boar's Head. The city house was but lightly occupied, as though the couple were merely camping in it. There were no old secrets buried here, though five gods knew what Ingrey might find at Castle Horseriver. But the earl's haunt was two hundred miles away on the middle Lure, and Ingrey doubted anyone would be going back there till all this was long over.

As promised—or threatened—Earl Horseriver did conduct Ingrey later that afternoon to his stable mews, a stone building a few streets down the hill. Most of the great kins' livestock was kept outside the walls, in pastures along the Stork above the glassworks and the tanners. Horseriver's household was no exception, but a few beasts were kept nearby for the lord and lady, for grooms to use to collect other mounts at need, and for couriers. As befit the earl's state, the appointments within the mews were very fine: the central corridor paved with colored stone, the stall walls of rubbed oak, the metal bars decorated with twining bronze leaves. Ingrey was bemused to spy Ijada's showy chestnut mare, moving restlessly in a straight stall.

Ingrey refrained from patting its haunches, lest he be kicked. "I know this one—I'd guessed it might be one of yours."

"Aye," said Wencel absently. "She was too mettlesome for Fara. I was glad to find someone else to ride her."

Wencel stopped before a box stall on the opposite side and gestured. A dark gray gelding snuffled up to him, then snorted and shied away as Ingrey approached. "His name is Wolf," said Horseriver blandly. "For his color, formerly, but now one suspects a secret destiny. And who am I to argue with destiny? He is yours."

The gelding was undoubtedly a beautiful beast, well muscled, clean-limbed, its dappled coat polished to a shimmer by the earl's grooms. Ingrey suspected the animal concealed an explosive burst of speed. What else it might conceal—deadly geases sprang to mind—Ingrey could not tell. Did Wencel imagine it a bribe? So he might. Well, Ingrey could not look this gift in the mouth while the earl was watching. "Thank you, my lord," he said, in a tone to match Horseriver's.

"Would you care to try his paces?"

"Later, perhaps. I am not wearing my leathers." And ever since his be-wolfing at Birchgrove he'd always made new mounts peculiarly tense; he preferred to make their first acquaintance in private, in an enclosed space where the spooked horses might be more readily recaught and remounted till they had come to mutual understanding, or at least mutual exhaustion. This one looked as though it might take some time to wear down to tameness, under him.

"Ah. Pity."

Two stalls away, an unhorselike movement caught Ingrey's eye. Frowning, he walked down to peer into another loose box. His nostrils flared in surprise. An antlered stag abruptly raised its head from where it was lipping at a pile of hay, snorted, and sidled about. It banged its rack twice against the boards, causing a desultory wave of motion among the horses nearby.

"I think your presence disturbs him," murmured Wencel, in a tone of dry amusement.

After turning in a few more circles, the handsome beast stilled at the back of the stall, though it did not yet lower its head again to the hay. Its dark and liquid eye glowered at the men. Ingrey judged it captive for some time, for it no longer struggled; new-taken stags could kill themselves in their first frenzy to escape.

"What are you planning to do with it?" asked Ingrey, in a lighter tone than he felt. "Dinner? A gift for your in-laws?" And what sort of uncanny gift might Wencel make of it?

Wencel's lips twisted a little as he studied the nervous beast past Ingrey's shoulder. "When one plays against such far-sighted opponents as I do, it is as well to have more than one plan. But chances are it is fated for a spit. Come away, now."

Horseriver did not look back as they exited the mews. Ingrey inquired, "Do you ride much for sport, these days? As I recall you were excited by your father's horses." It had been one of the few topics his slow young cousin had actually chattered about, in fact.

"Was I?" said Horseriver absently. "I fear I feel about horses much as I feel about wives, these days. They last such a short time, and I am weary of butchering them."

Unable to think of a response to that, Ingrey followed him silently up the hill.

He considered the method in Wencel's madness, or perhaps it was the other way around. Wencel's rationale for his murderous attempt on Ijada and its equally swift abandonment was too peculiar to be a lie, but it did not follow that he was necessarily correct in it. Still, Wencel's erratic tactics against the gods must have worked before. In naming Ijada god-bait, he was surely not mistaken. That alarm alone must be enough to trigger his nervous malice. He'd eluded four hundred years of this hunt if his claims were true.

The gods would do better to wait at some choke point and let Wencel flail all he liked till he arrived there. But the strange intensity of Wencel's greetings when they'd all met on the road to Easthome was now explained; the man must have been thinking five ways at once. *Yes, but so must his Enemies.*

A disturbing notion came to Ingrey: perhaps Ijada had not been the bait at that fated meeting after all. *Perhaps I was.*

And Wencel has swallowed me down whole.

The next day, Princess Fara was called upon to testify before the board of judges at the inquest upon Prince Boleso's death.

Fara's first response was angered insult that a daughter of the hallow king would be ordered before the bench like a common subject—her secret fears taking shelter in injured pride, Ingrey judged. But some clever man—Hetwar, no doubt—had made Prince-marshal Biast the deliverer of the unwelcome summons. Since Biast had less interest in defending dubious actions, and more in finding the truth, his levelheaded persuasion overcame his sister's nervous protests.

Thus it was that Ingrey found himself pacing up the steep hill to Templetown as part of a procession consisting of the prince-marshal, his banner-carrier Symark leading the princess's palfrey, Fara's two ladies-in-waiting who had attended her at Boar's Head, and Fara's matched twin pages. In the main temple court, Symark was dispatched to find directions to where the judges sat, and Fara slipped her brother's leash, briefly, to lead her ladies to kneel and pray in the Mother's court. Whether Fara was trying to call upon the goddess who had so signally ignored her prayers in the past, or merely wanted an unassailable excuse to compose herself in semiprivacy for a few minutes, Ingrey could not guess.

In either case, Ingrey was standing with Biast when an unexpected figure exited the Daughter's court.

"Ingorry!"

Prince Jokol waved cheerfully and trod across the pavement past the holy fire's plinth to where Ingrey waited. The giant islander was shadowed as usual by his faithful Ottovin, and Ingrey wondered if the young man was under instructions from his formidable-sounding sister to make sure her betrothed was returned from his wanderings in good order, or else. Jokol was dressed as before in his somewhat gaudy island garb, but now he had a linen braid dyed bright blue tied around his thick left biceps, mark of a prayer of supplication to the Daughter of Spring.

"Jokol. What brings you here?"

"Eh!" The big man shrugged. "Still I try to get my divine I was promised, but they put me off. Today, I try to see the headman, the archdivine, instead of those stupid clerks who always tell me to go away and come back later."

"Do you pray for an appointment?" Ingrey nodded to Jokol's left sleeve.

Jokol clapped his right hand on the blue braid and laughed. "Perhaps I should! Go over his head, eh."

Ingrey would have thought the Son of Autumn to be Jokol's natural guardian, or perhaps, considering recent events, the Bastard, not that praying to the god of disasters was exactly the safest course. "The Lady of Spring is not your usual Patroness, surely?"

"Oh, aye! She blesses me much. Today, I pray for poetry."

"I thought the Bastard was the god of poetry."

"Oh, Him, too, aye, for drinking songs and such. And for those great songs of when the walls come crashing down and all is burning, aye, that make your hairs all stand up, those are fine!" Jokol waved his arms to mime horripilating tragedies suitable for epic verse. "But not today. Today, I mean to make a beautiful song to my beautiful Breiga, to tell her how much I miss her in this stone city."

Behind him, Ottovin rolled his eyes. Ingrey took it for silent comment on the sisterly object of the proposed song, not on the song itself. Ingrey was reminded that in addition to being the goddess of female virgins, the Daughter was also associated with youthful learning, civil order, and, yes, lyric poetry.

Biast was staring up at Jokol, looking impressed despite himself. "Is this by chance the owner of your ice bear, Ingrey?" he inquired.

Though longing to deny all association with the ice bear, now and forever, Ingrey was reminded of his social duties. "Pardon me, my lord. Allow me to present to you Prince Jokol of Arfrastpekka, and his kinsman Ottovin. Jokol, this is Prince-marshal Biast kin Stagthorne. Son of the hallow king," he added, in case Jokol needed a touch of native guidance among the perils of Easthome high politics.

But Jokol was neither ignorant nor overawed. He signed the Five and bowed his head, and Biast returned both greeting and blessing, as confident chieftains of two races neither vassal nor allied, but with some such possibilities hovering in the future, not to be scorned.

The promising mutual appraisal of the two princes was interrupted by the return of Symark, clutching the arm of a gray-robed acolyte. Having secured a guide to the proliferating hodgepodge of buildings that made up the Temple complex, Biast went to collect his sister from the Mother's court.

Jokol, taking the hint, made to bid Ingrey farewell. "I must try harder to see this archdivine fellow. It may take some time, so I should start, eh?"

"Wait," said Ingrey. "I'll tell you who you should see. In a building two streets back, second floor—no, better." He darted over to pluck a passing boy in Bastard's whites, a young dedicat of some sort, out of the thin stream of people passing through the central court bound on various errands. "Do you know the way to Learned Lewko's office?" he demanded of the boy.

The boy gave him an alarmed nod.

"Take this lord to him now." He handed off the dedicat to a bemused Jokol. "Tell him Lord Ingrey sends a complication for his collection."

"Will this Lewko help me to see the archdivine?" asked Jokol hopefully.

"Either that, or he'll go over Fritine's head. Threaten to give him Fafa; that will stimulate him on your behalf." Ingrey grinned; for the god of vile jokes, this practically constituted a prayer, he decided.

"He is a power in the Temple?"

Ingrey shrugged. "He is a power of a god who does not wait on clerks, at least."

Jokol pursed his lips, then nodded, brightening. "Very good! I thank you, Ingorry!" He trudged off after the boy, trailed by the dubious Ottovin.

Ingrey thought he heard someone laughing in his ear, but it wasn't Symark, who stood looking on somewhat blankly. A trick of the court's acoustics, perhaps. Ingrey shook his head to clear it, then pulled himself to an attitude of grave attention as Biast returned with the ladies.

Biast, after a glance around the court, gave Ingrey a peculiar stare, uncertain and searching. It occurred to Ingrey that the last time all of this party had been present in this place was two days ago, for Boleso's funeral. Was Biast wondering whether to believe in Ingrey's claimed shaman-miracle of cleansing his late brother's soul? Or—almost more disturbing—belief accepted, was he wondering what further consequences must flow from it?

In any case, the gray-robed acolyte led them around the temple into the maze of buildings housing clerks and works of the various holy orders. Some structures were new and purpose-built, but most were old and reassigned. They passed between two noisy and busy, if slightly dilapidated, former kin mansions, one now a foundling hospital run by the Bastard's Order, the other the Mother's infirmary, its colonnades echoing with the steps of physicians and green-clad acolytes, its tranquil gardens sheltering recovering patients and their attendants.

In the next street over they came to a large edifice, three stories high and built of the same yellow stone as Hetwar's palace, dedicated to the libraries and council rooms of the Father's Order. A winding staircase circled a spacious hall and brought them at length to a hushed, wood-paneled chamber.

The inquiries were already under way, it seemed, for a pair of retainers Ingrey thought he recognized from Boar's Head were just shouldering back out the door, looking daunted but relieved. They recognized the prince-marshal and princess and hastened to get out of their way, signing sketchy gestures of respect. Biast managed a return nod of polite acknowledgment, although Fara's neck stayed stiff, pride starched with mortification. Fara caught her breath in a little snort like a startled mare when the first person they encountered on the other side of the door was Boleso's housemaster, Rider Ulkra. Ulkra bowed, looking at least equally queasy.

A long table stretched across the head of the room, and five men sat along it with their backs to the draped windows. Two wore the gray-and-black robes and red shoulder braids of divines of the Father's Order, and the other three wore the chains of office marking judges of the King's Bench. At a small table to one side, a scribe sat with her quills and inks and papers. Other benches lined the walls. Near the scribe, on the bench on the far side of the room, another divine sat, a gangling fellow with untidy graying black hair that seemed to echo his robes. His red shoulder braid had a gold cord running through it, the mark of a senior scholar of jurisprudence. A counselor to the counselors?

The judges all rose and made obeisance to the prince-marshal and courtesies to the princess; a couple of dedicat-servants were sent scurrying to secure padded chairs for the Stagthorne haunches. While this was going on, Ingrey circled in on Ulkra, who swallowed nervously but returned his greeting.

"Have you been questioned yet?" Ingrey inquired politely.

"I was to be next."

Ingrey lowered his voice. "And do you plan to tell the truth, or lie?"

Ulkra licked his lips. "What would Lord Hetwar desire of me, do you suppose?"

Did he still think Ingrey was Hetwar's man? So was Ulkra exceptionally shrewd, or just behindhand on capital gossip? "If I were you, I should be more worried about what Hetwar's future master desires." He nodded toward Prince Biast, and Ulkra followed his glance, warily. "He is young now, but he won't stay that way for long."

"One would think," Ulkra angled, speaking almost under his breath, "he would desire to shield his sister from reproach and censure."

"Would one?" said Ingrey vaguely. "Let's find out." He beckoned to Biast, who trod over curiously.

"Yes, Ingrey?"

"My lord. Rider Ulkra here cannot decide if you would wish him to tell the exact truth, or shade it to spare your sister chagrin. What that says about your reputation, I must leave you to decide."

"Sh, Ingrey!" whispered Ulkra in furious embarrassment, with a fearful glance over his shoulder at the table down the room.

Biast looked taken aback. He said cautiously, "I promised Fara that none would shame her here, but certainly no man should violate his oath of truthsaying before the judges and the gods."

"You set the path for your future court starting even now, prince. If you discourage men from speaking unpalatable truths in front of you, I trust you will develop your skill for sifting through pretty lies, for you will spend the rest of your reign, however short, wading in them." Ingrey let his mild tone suggest that it was a matter of utter indifference to him which Biast chose; Ingrey would manage just the same.

Biast's lips twisted. "What was it Hetwar said of you? That you defy whom you choose?"

"Whom I please. I please Hetwar best so. But then, Hetwar is no man's fool."

"Verily." Biast's eyes narrowed; then he surprised and gratified Ingrey altogether by turning to Ulkra, and saying shortly, "Tell the exact truth." He inhaled, and added on a sigh, "I'll deal with Fara as I must."

Ulkra, eyes wide, bowed and backed away, presumably before Ingrey could wind him into further coils. The chairs arrived; Ingrey gave Biast a slight, sincere bow, rather ironically returned, and took his place on the rear bench where he could watch the whole room, and the door.

A futile speculation crossed his mind: if Boleso had possessed a friend with the backbone to stand up to him at critical junctures, would he still have turned onto the crooked roads that had led to his death? Boleso had always been the most difficult of the princely brood. Maybe nothing would have saved him, at the end.

After a short, whispered consultation among the judges, Ulkra was called up to take his oath and answer the inquirers. Ulkra stood before them with his hands clenched behind his stout back, feet apart, taking some refuge in the soldier-like pose. The questions were to the point; the panel had already, it appeared, acquired some grasp of the outline of events at Boar's Head.

As nearly as Ingrey could discern, Ulkra did tell the exact truth of the chain of deeds that had led to Boleso's death, insofar as he was eyewitness. He did not leave out the leopard, nor his suspicions about Boleso's earlier "dabblings," though he managed to cloak his own complicity of silence under protestations of the loyalty and discretion due from a senior servant. No, he had not suspected that Boleso's body servant was the illicit sorcerer Cumril. (So, the judges had heard of Cumril's existence—from Lewko?) At one point, the scholarly divine on the side bench silently passed a note across to one of the judges, who read it and followed up with a couple of especially penetrating and shrewd questions of the housemaster.

The unsubtle ugliness of Ijada's sacrifice at Boleso's bedroom door came through clearly enough to Ingrey's ear, despite Ulkra's self-serving phrasing of it. By the stiffening of Fara's features, this was the first fully objective account she had heard of the consequences at Boar's Head after she had abandoned her maiden-in-waiting there. She did not weep in whatever shame she swallowed, but her face might have been carved in wood. *Good.*

When Ulkra was dismissed, to flee from the chamber as swiftly as he decently could, Fara was called up. Ingrey, playing the courtier, made of helping her from her chair the chance to breathe in her ear, "I will know if you lie."

Her eyes shifted to him, coldly. "Should I care?" she murmured back.

"Would you really want to put such a weapon in my hand, lady?"

She hesitated. "No."

"Good. You begin to think like a princess."

Her gaze grew startled as he squeezed her arm in encouragement before letting her go. And then, for a moment, thoughtful, as though a new road had opened up before her not previously perceived.

The judges kept their questions to her brief and courteous, as befit equally law and prudence. The truth she spoke was, like Ulkra's, softened in her own excuse, and the motivation of her jealousy largely left out, which Ingrey thought all to the good. But the most critical elements in his view—that the demand had come from Boleso, been accepted without consultation by Fara, and that Ijada was no seductress nor cheerful volunteer—seemed plain enough, between the lines. Fara was released with diplomatic thanks by the panel; her eyes squeezed shut in bleak relief as she turned away.

With Fara leading the way, her two senior ladies-in-waiting told the truth as well, including a few side incidents not witnessed by Fara that were even more damaging to

Boleso. Biast looked decidedly unhappy, but made no move to interfere with the testimony; though there was no doubt the judges were very conscious of the prince-marshal's presence and expressions. The scholarly divine, Ingrey noticed, also sent sharp if covert glances Biast's way. If Biast had chosen to cast the right frowns, snort, or shift at the key moments, might he have shaped the questions? Distorted them in his late brother's favor? Perhaps; but instead he listened in guarded neutrality, as befit a man seeking truth before all other aims. Ingrey hoped that the idea of a blood-price might now be sounding better to him.

Shuffling echoed in the room as the party rose to leave. Ingrey directed the page to go in pursuit of his twin and bring around the princess's palfrey; the boy bobbed a bow, and replied, "Yes, Lord Ingrey!" in his high, clear voice before scampering out. The scholarly divine's head swiveled; he stared at Ingrey, frowning, then went to bend over the shoulder of one of the empaneled divines and murmur in his ear. Brows rising, the judge nodded, cast a glance Ingrey's way, and murmured back. He then raised his hand and his voice, and called, "Lord Ingrey! Would you stay a moment?"

Despite the polite tone, it was clearly a command, not query or invitation. Ingrey returned a nod and stood attentively. Biast, shepherding his sister out the door, frowned in frustration, apparently torn between assuaging Fara's anxiety to escape and his own desire to hear what was wanted of the wolf-lord now.

"I will catch you up, my lord," said Ingrey to him. Biast, with an expression that plainly said they would speak together later, nodded and followed his sister out.

Ingrey took up a stance before the judges' table reminiscent of Ulkra's, and waited, concealing extreme unease. He had not expected to be questioned today, or possibly at all.

The scholarly divine stood behind his colleague and folded his arms, shoulders hunched and face outthrust in his concentration upon Ingrey. With his beaklike nose and receding chin, he resembled a stork wading in the shallows, intent upon some fish or frog concealed below the water's surface. "I understand, Lord Ingrey, that you had an experience at Prince Boleso's funeral very pertinent to these proceedings."

This man had to have spoken with Lewko. How much had the Bastard's divine conveyed to the Father's scholar? The two orders were not usually noted for their mutual cooperation. "I fainted from the heat. Anything else is not such testimony as is admissible in a trial, I thought."

The man's lips pursed, and to Ingrey's surprise, he nodded in approval. But then said, "This is not a trial. It is an inquiry. You will observe I have not requested your oath."

Was that of some arcane legal significance? From the slight nods of a couple of the judges, apparently so. The scribe, for one thing, had set aside her quill and showed no sign of taking it up again, although she was staring at Ingrey in some fascination. It seemed they were speaking, at the moment, off the record. Given the company, Ingrey was not sure this was any aid to him.

"Have you ever fainted from heat before?" asked one of the King's Bench judges.

"Well . . . no."

"Please describe your vision," said the scholarly divine.

Ingrey blinked, once, slowly. If he refused to speak, how much pressure would they bring to bear? They would likely place him under oath; and then both speaking and silence would have potentially more dire consequences. Better this way. "I found myself, Lady Ijada, and Prince Boleso's sundered soul all together in a . . . place. A boundless place. I could see through Prince Boleso's torso. It was full of the spirits of dead animals, tumbling over each other in chaos and pain. The Lord of Autumn appeared." Ingrey moistened his lips and kept his voice dead level. "The god requested me to call the animal spirits out of Boleso. Lady Ijada endorsed the request. I did so. The god took up Boleso's soul and went away. I woke up on the temple floor." There, not too bad; as truthful as any madman and with quite a number of complications left out.

"How?" asked the divine curiously. "How did you call them out?"

"It was but a dream, Learned. One does not expect things to make sense in a dream."

"Nevertheless."

"I was . . . given a voice." No need to say how, or by whom, was there?

"The weirding voice? As the voice you used on the rampant ice bear two days before?"

A couple of heads along the panel came up at that.

Damn. "I have heard it called that."

"Could you use it again?"

It was all Ingrey could do not to use it right now; paralyze this roomful of men and escape. Or else squeeze his strangely diffuse wolf into a tight little invisible ball under his heart. *Fool, they cannot see it anyway.* "I do not know."

"More specifically," the divine went on crisply, "Lady Ijada is imputed to have been defiled with the spirit of a dead leopard. It is the teaching of Temple history, which your vision with the late prince would seem to support, that such a defilement sunders a soul from the gods."

"A dead soul," Ingrey corrected cautiously. For both he and Ijada bore animal spirits, and yet the god had spoken to both. Not to Boleso, though, Ingrey realized. He was moved to explain how the shamans of the Old Weald had cleansed their departed comrades' spirits, then thought better of it. He was not at all moved to explain how he'd learned all this.

"Quite so. My question, then, is: were Lady Ijada to be executed as a result of her future trial, could you, Lord Ingrey, remove the defiling animal spirit from her soul as you did for Prince Boleso's?"

Ingrey froze. The first memory that roared back into his mind was of Wencel's worried vision of Ijada as an Old Weald courier sacrifice, opening Holytree to the gods. Wencel had thought that path safely blocked by Ijada's defilement. Not so safe, and not so blocked, if Ingrey could un-block it again. *And I could.* Five gods, and curse Them one and five, was *this* the unholy holy plan for the pair of them? *Is this why You have chased us here?* Thoughts tumbling, In-grey temporized, "Why do you ask, Learned?"

"It is a theological fine point that I greatly desire clari-fied. Execution, properly speaking, is a punishment of the body for crimes in the world of matter. The question of the salvation or sundering of a soul and its god is not more af-fected than by any other death, nor should it be; for the im-proper sundering of a soul would be a heinous sin and burden upon the officers charged with such a duty. An exe-cution that entails such an unjust sundering must be resisted. An execution that does not may proceed." A silence fol-lowed this pronouncement; the divine added solicitously, "Do you follow the argument, my lord?"

Ingrey followed it. Claws scrabbling, dragged as by a leash. *If I say I can cleanse her soul, it frees them to hang her body with a blithe good will.* If he said he could not . . . he would be lying, but what else? He whispered, "It was only . . ." Stopped, cleared his throat, forced his voice to a normal volume. "It was only a dream, Learned. You refine too much upon it."

A warm autumnal voice murmured, somewhere between his ear and his mind, *If you deny Me and yourself before this little company, brother wolf, how shall you manage before a greater?*

Ingrey did not know if his face drained white, though sev-eral of the judges stared at him in alarm. With an effort, he kept himself from swaying on his feet. Or, five gods forbid, falling down in a faint. Wouldn't *that* be a dramatic devel-opment, coming pat upon his words of disavowal.

"Hm," said the scholarly divine, his gaze narrowing. "The point is an important one, however."

"How, then, if I simplify it for you? If I have not this abil-ity, the point is moot. If I have . . . I refuse to use it so." *Eat that.*

"Could you be forced?" The divine's tone conveyed no hint of threat; it seemed the purest curiosity.

Ingrey's lips drew back in a grin that had nothing to do with humor, at all, at all; several of the men pushed back in their seats in an instinctive recoil. "You could *try*," he breathed. Under the circumstances—under *those* circumstances, with Ijada's dead body cut down from a gallows and laid at his feet—he might just find out everything his wolf could *really* do. Until they cut him down as well.

"Hm." The scholarly divine tapped his lips; his expression, strangely, seemed more satisfied than alarmed. "Most interesting." He glanced down the panel. "Have you any more questions?"

The senior judge, looking vastly disturbed, said, "Not . . . not at this time. Thank you, Most Learned, for your . . . um . . . always thought-provoking commentary."

"Yes," muttered another under his breath, "trust *you* to come up with a horrible complication no one else ever thought of."

A slight tilt of the scholarly divine's head and a glint in his eye took this as more compliment than complaint, despite the tone. "Then I thank you, Lord Ingrey."

It was clearly a dismissal, and not a moment too soon; Ingrey managed a civil nod and turned away, quelling an urge to run. He turned onto the gallery outside the chamber and drew a long breath, but before he could entirely compose himself again, heard footsteps behind him. He glanced back to see the strange divine following him out.

The lanky man signed the Five by way of greeting; a swift gesture, but very precise, neither perfunctory nor sketched. Ingrey nodded again, started to rest his hand on his sword hilt, decided the gesture might be interpreted as too threatening, and let his hands drift to clench each other behind his back. "May I help you, Learned?" *Over the gallery rail, headfirst, perhaps?*

"My apologies, Lord Ingrey, but I just realized that I was

introduced before your party came in, but not again after. I am Learned Oswin of Suttleaf."

Ingrey blinked; his mind, briefly frozen, bolted off again in a wholly unexpected new direction. "*Hallana's* Oswin?"

The divine smiled, looking oddly abashed. "Of all my titles, the truest, I fear. Yes, I'm Hallana's Oswin, for my sins. She told me much of your meeting with her at Red Dike."

"Is she well?"

"Well, and delivered of a fine little girl, I am pleased to say. Who I pray to the Lady of Spring shall grow up to look like her mother and not like me, else she will have much to complain of when she is older."

"I'm glad she is safe. Both safe. Learned Hallana worried me." *In more ways than one.* He touched his still-bandaged right hand, reminded of how close he had come to retrieving his sword, in his scarlet madness in that upstairs room.

"Had you time to know her better, she would not have worried you."

"Ah?"

"She would have terrified you, just like the rest of us. Yet somehow, we all survived her, again. She sent me here, you see. Quite drove me from her bedside. Which many women tend to do to their poor husbands after a childbirth, but not for such reasons."

"Have you spoken with Learned Lewko?"

"Yes, at length, when I arrived last night."

Ingrey groped for careful wording. "And on whose behalf did Hallana send you?" It occurred to him belatedly that the divine's alarming theological argument back in the chamber might well have been intended to impede Ijada's execution, not speed it.

"Well . . . well, now, that's a little hard to say."

Ingrey considered this. "Why?"

For the first time, Oswin hesitated before he answered. He took Ingrey by the arm and led him away, around the corner of the gallery, well out of earshot of the door where a couple of what looked like more servants from Boar's Head were just being led inside by a gray-robed dedicat. Oswin leaned on the rail, looking down thoughtfully into the well of the hall; Ingrey matched his pose and waited.

When Oswin resumed, his voice was oddly diffident. "You are a man with much experience in the uncanny and the holy, I understand. The gods speak to you in waking visions, face-to-face."

"No!" Ingrey began, and stopped. Denial again? "Well . . . in a way. I have had many bizarre experiences lately. They crowd upon me now. It does not make me *deft*."

Oswin sighed. "I cannot imagine growing deft in the face of this. You have to understand. I had never had a direct experience of the holy in my life, for all that I tried to serve my god as seemed best to me, according to my gifts as we are taught. Except for Hallana. She was the only miracle that ever happened to me. The woman seems vastly oversupplied with gods. At one point, I accused her of having stolen my share, and she accused me of marrying her solely to sustain a proper average. The gods walk through her dreams as though strolling in a garden. *I* just have dreams of running lost through my old seminary, with no clothes, late for an examination of a class I did not know I had, and the like."

"Taking the examination, or giving it?" Ingrey couldn't help asking.

"Either, variously." Oswin's brow furrowed. "And then there are the ones where I am wandering through a house that is falling apart, and I have no tools to repair . . . well, anyway." He took a long breath, and settled into himself. "The night after our new daughter was born, I slept once again with Hallana. We both shared a significant dream. I woke crying out in fear. *She* was utterly cheery about it. She said it meant we must go at once to Easthome. I asked her if she had run mad, she could not rise and go about yet! She said she could put a pallet in the back of the wagon and rest the whole way. We argued about it all day. The dream came again the next night. She said that cinched the matter. I said she had a duty to the babe, to the children, that she could neither abandon them nor drag them along into danger. She gave way; I gloated. I took to my horse that afternoon. I was ten miles down the road before I realized that I had been neatly foxed."

"How so?"

"Separated, there was no way for me to continue the argument. Or to stop her. I have no doubt she's upon the road right now, not more than a day behind me. I wonder if she will have brought the children? I shudder to picture it. If you see her, or her faithful servants, in this town before I do, tell her I have taken rooms for all of us at the Inn of Irises across from the Mother's Infirmary."

"Would, um, she be traveling with the same ones I met in Red Dike?"

"Oh, yes, Bernan and Hergi. They would not be separated from her. Bernan was one of her early triumphs in sorcerous healing, you see. Hergi brought him to her in agony from the stones, clawing himself and shrieking of suicide, close to heart failure from the pain, his life and sanity despaired of. Hallana exploded the stones within his body, and he passed them at once—she had him on his feet and smiling in a day. They would follow her into any folly she chose." Oswin snorted. "I construct the most excellent arguments in the Father's name that my intellect and deep training can devise, yet with all my reason I cannot move people as she does just by—by standing there *breathing*. It is entirely unjust." His tone tried to be incensed, but only managed wistful.

"The dream," Ingrey reminded him.

"My apologies. I do not normally rattle on like this. Perhaps that explains something about my Hallana . . . I have laid it before Learned Lewko, now you. There were five people in it: Hallana, me, Lewko, and two young men I had never seen before. Until today. Prince Biast was one of them. I nearly fell off my bench when he walked into the chamber and was named. The other was a stranger fellow still; a giant man with long red hair, who spoke in tongues."

"Ah," said Ingrey. "That would be Prince Jokol, no doubt. Tell him to give Fafa a fish for me, when you meet him. In fact, you might catch him now; I just sent him to Lewko. He could still be there."

Oswin's eyes widened, and he straightened as though to dash off at once, but then shook his head and continued. "In the dream . . . I am a man of words, but I scarcely know how to describe it. All the five were god-touched. More, worse: the gods put us on and wore us like gauntlets. We shattered . . ."

They harry me hard, now, Horseriver had said. So it seemed. "Well, should you determine what it all meant, let me know. Were any others in the dream?" *Me or Ijada, for example?*

Oswin shook his head. "Just the five. So far. The dream did not seem finished, which upset me yet Hallana took in stride. I both long and fear to sleep, to find out more, but now I have insomnia. Hallana may be willing to run off into the dark, but *I* want to know where the stepping-stones will be."

Ingrey smiled grimly at this. "It was lately suggested to me, by a man with longer experience of the gods than I can rightly imagine, that the reason the gods do not show our paths more plainly is that They do not know either. I haven't decided if I find this reassuring or the reverse. It does hint they do not torment us solely for Their amusement, at least."

Oswin tapped a hand on the railing. "Hallana and I have argued this point—the foresight of the gods. They are the *gods*. They *must* know if anyone does."

"Perhaps no one does," said Ingrey easily.

The expression on Oswin's face was that of a man forced to swallow a vile-tasting medicine of dubious value. "I shall try Lewko, then. Perhaps this Jokol will know something more."

"I doubt it, but good luck."

"I trust we will meet again soon."

"Nothing would startle me, these days."

"Where might I reach you? Lewko said you were set as a spy upon Earl Horseriver, who also seems somewhat involved in this tangle."

Ingrey hissed through his teeth. "I suppose it's fortunate Horseriver already knows that I spy on him, with that sort of loose gossip circulating."

Oswin shook his head vehemently. "Neither loose nor gossip, and the circle is a tight one. Lewko had something like the dream, too, from what he says."

Somewhat involved, indeed. "Stay away from Horseriver for the time being. He is dangerous. If you wish to see me, send a message there, but put no matter of import in the writing—assume it will be intercepted and read by hostile eyes before I see it."

Oswin nodded, frowning. They walked together down the circling stairs and out to the street. Ingrey bade the divine farewell and turned his quickening steps down the hill toward Kingstown.

20

INGREY COULD NOT MUSTER MUCH SURPRISE WHEN, AFTER crossing the buried creek into the lower city, he rounded a corner and found Hallana's wagon blocking his path.

The two stubby horses, dusty and sweaty from the road, were standing hip-shot and bored, and Bernan sat on the driver's box with reins slack and his elbows on his knees. A riding horse, unsaddled, was tied on behind the wagon by a rope to its halter. Hergi crouched behind Bernan's shoulder. Hallana was hanging off the front brace of the canopy with one hand, shielding her gaze with the other, and peering dubiously up an alley too narrow for the wagon to enter.

Hergi pounded on Bernan's shoulder, pointed at Ingrey, and cried, "Look! Look!"

Hallana swung around, and her face brightened. "Ah! Lord Ingrey! Excellent." She gave Bernan a pat on the other shoulder. "See, did I not say?" The smith gave a weary sort of head bob, halfway between agreement and exasperation, and Hallana stepped over him to hop down to the street and stand before Ingrey.

She had abandoned her loose and tattered robes for a natty traveling costume, a dark green coat upon a dress of pale linen, notably cinched in around the waist. Her shoulder braids were absent—traveling incognito? She remained short and plump, but trimmer, with her hair neatly braided in wreaths around her head. There were no visible signs of children or other trailing chaos.

Ingrey gave her a polite half bow; she returned a blessing, although her sign of the Five more resembled a vague check mark over her torso. "So glad to see you," she told him. "I'm seeking Ijada."

"How?" he couldn't help asking. Presumably, she was once more in command of her powers.

"I usually just drive around until something happens."

"That seems . . . oddly inefficient."

"You sound like Oswin. He would have wanted to draw a grid over a chart of the city, and mark off sections in strict rotation. Finding you was *much* faster."

Ingrey started to consider the logic of this, then thought better of it. "Speaking of Learned Oswin. He told me to tell you he has taken rooms for you all at the Inn of the Irises, across from the Mother's Infirmary on Temple Hill."

A slight groan from Bernan greeted this news.

"Oh!" Hallana brightened still further. "You have met, how nice!"

"You are not surprised to be expected?"

"Oswin can be terribly stodgy at times, but he's not *stupid*. Of course he would realize we'd be coming. Eventually."

"Learned Sir will not be pleased with us," Hergi predicted uneasily. "He wasn't before."

"Pish posh," said Oswin's spouse. "You survived." She turned back to Ingrey, and her voice dropped to seriousness. "Did he tell you about our dream?"

"Just a little."

"Where *is* Ijada, anyway?"

The passersby all seemed ordinary folk, so far, but Ingrey declined to take chances. "I should not be seen talking to you, nor overheard."

Hallana jerked her head toward the canopied wagon, and Ingrey nodded. He swung up after her into the shadowed interior, clambering over bundles and seating himself on a trunk, awkwardly adjusting his sword. Hallana sat down cross-legged on a pallet padded thickly with blankets and looked at him expectantly.

"Ijada is being kept in a private house not far from the quayside." Ingrey kept his voice low. "Her house warden is Rider Gesca, for the moment, who is Hetwar's man, but the house belongs to Earl Horseriver. The servants there are the earl's spies, and Gesca's discretion is not to be trusted at all. You must not go there as yourself. Have Learned Lewko take you, perhaps in the guise of an examining physician for the inquest or some such. That would give you an excuse to exclude the servants and speak privately with Ijada."

Hallana's eyes narrowed. "Interesting. Is Fara's husband no friend to Ijada after all—or too much the reverse? Or is it that wretched princess who is the problem?"

"Fara is a tangle of problems, but Wencel's interest in her handmaiden was not the simple lechery she had imagined. Wencel has secret powers and unknown purposes. Hetwar has just set me in his household to spy upon him in an effort to determine those purposes. I don't want the waters there muddied worse than they are already."

"You think him dangerous?"

"Yes."

"To *you*?" Her brows went up.

Ingrey bit his lip. "It has become suspected that he bears a spirit animal. Like mine. This is . . . true but incomplete." He hesitated. "The geas we broke in Red Dike—he was the source of it."

She huffed out her breath. "Why is he not arrested?"

"No!" said Ingrey sharply. And at her stare, more quietly, "No. In the first place, I have not determined how to prove the charge, and in the second, a premature arrest could trigger a disaster." *For me, at least.*

She blinked up at him in a friendly way. "Oh, come, Lord Ingrey. You can tell *me* more."

He was sorely tempted. "I think . . . not yet. I am at the stage of things . . . I don't yet . . . I am still driving around in circles waiting for something to happen."

"Oh." A look of sympathetic enlightenment crossed her features. "*That* stage. I know it well." After a moment she added, "My condolences."

He ran a hand through his hair. It was growing again around the stitches, which were surely ready to come out. "I cannot linger. I must catch up with Prince Biast and Princess Fara. Your husband was at Ijada's inquest this morning, and can likely tell you more of it than I can. Lewko knows something as well. I wonder"—Ingrey faltered—"if I can trust you."

Her head came up, cocking a little to one side. She said dryly, "I assume that was not meant as an insult."

Ingrey shook his head. "I stumble through a murk of lies and half lies and stranger tales right now. The legal thing, the obvious thing—like arresting Wencel—may not be the right thing, though I cannot explain it. All feels fluid. As though the gods themselves hold Their breaths. Something is about to happen."

"What?"

"If I knew, if I *knew*—" Ingrey heard the rising tension in his own voice, and yanked it to a stop.

"Shh, hush," Hallana soothed him, as though calming a nervy mount. "Can you trust me, at least, to move cautiously, speak little, listen, and wait?"

"Can you?"

"Unless my gods compel me otherwise."

"Your gods. Not your Temple superiors."

"I said what I said."

Ingrey nodded and took a breath. "Ask Ijada, then. She is the only one I have trusted with everything I know so far. The others have only bits and pieces. She and I are bound together in this by more than"—his voice stumbled, choked—"more than affection. We have shared two waking visions. She can tell you more."

"Good. I will go to her discreetly as you advise, then."

"I am not sure if the gods and I seek the same ends. I am absolutely sure the gods and Wencel do not seek the same ends." His brow wrinkled. "Oswin said you shattered. In your dream. I did not understand what was meant."

"Neither do we."

"Would the gods use us to destruction?" She had not brought her children—for speed, for simplicity? Or for safety? *Theirs. Not hers.*

"Perhaps." Her voice was perfectly even, delivering this.

"You do not reassure me, Learned."

Some might call her return smile enigmatic, but Ingrey thought it more sardonic. He returned her a salute in the same mode and glanced out the wagon back for witnesses. He added over his shoulder, "If you go at once to Lewko, you might find your husband still there. And possibly a red-haired islander whose tongue is lubricated by either vile liquor or holy kisses from the Lady of Spring, or both."

"Ah-ha!" said Hallana, sitting up in sudden enthusiasm. "That is one part of my dream I should not object to finding prophetic. Is he as darling as he seemed?"

"I . . . don't think I can answer that," said Ingrey, after a bemused pause. He swung out of the wagon, slipped around its side, and took the shortcut up the alley toward the Horseriver mansion.

❧

The earl's porter admitted him with a murmured, "My lady and the prince-marshal await you in the Birch Chamber, Lord Ingrey."

Ingrey took the hint, nodded, and ascended the stairs at once. The room was the same in which he had surprised Fara on the first day of his so-called service—perhaps its quiet colors and sober furnishings made it a favorite refuge of hers.

He found the little company gathered there, Biast and Symark conversing over a tray of bread and cheeses, Fara half-reclining upon a settee while one of her women pressed a damp cloth to her forehead. The scent of lavender was cool and sharp upon the air.

Fara collected herself and sat up as Ingrey entered, regarding him with a worried glower. Her face was pale, the skin around her eyes a smudged gray, and he recalled Ijada's report of the princess's tendency to sick headaches.

"Lord Ingrey." Biast graciously gestured him to sit. "The learned divine kept you long."

Ingrey let this pass with a nod; he had no desire to explain Hallana.

Fara was not inclined to await a diplomatic lead-in. "What did he ask you? Did he ask you anything else about me?"

"He asked nothing further of you, my lady, nor of anything that happened at Boar's Head," Ingrey reassured her. She sat back in evident relief. "His questions were largely"—he hesitated—"theological."

Biast did not seem to share his sister's relief. His brows drew down in renewed concern. "Did they touch on our brother?"

"Only indirectly, my lord." There seemed no reason not to be frank with Biast about Oswin's inquiries, although Ingrey was not at all sure he wanted to reveal his other connections with the scholarly divine just yet. "He wished to know if I could cleanse Lady Ijada's soul of her leopard spirit, in the event of her death, as I had seemed to do for the late prince. I said I did not know."

Biast dragged one booted toe back and forth over the rug, frowned down and seemed to grow conscious of the tic, and stilled his foot. When he looked up, his voice had grown quieter. "Did you really see the god? Face-to-face?"

"He appeared to me as a young woodland lord of surpassing beauty. I did not get the sense . . ." Ingrey paused, uncertain how to express this. "You have seen children make shadow puppets upon a wall with their hands. The shadow is not the hand, though it is created by it. The young man I saw was, I think, the shadow of the god. Reduced to a simple outline that I could understand. As if there lay vastly more beyond that I could not see, that would have appeared nothing at all like the deceptive shadow if I could have taken it in without . . . shattering."

"Did He give you any directions for . . . for me?" Biast's tone of diffident hope robbed the question of hubris. He glanced over at his intently listening sister. "For any of the rest of us?"

"No, my lord. Are you feeling in need of some?"

Biast's lips huffed on a humorless laugh. "I reach for some certainty in an uncertain time, I suppose."

"Then you come to the wrong storehouse," said Ingrey bitterly. "The gods give me nothing but hints and riddles and maddening conundrums. As for my vision, I suppose I must call it, it was for Boleso's funeral. In that hour, the god attended to his soul alone. In our hours, we may receive the same undivided scrutiny."

Fara, rubbing her hand along one skirt-clad thigh in a tension not unlike her brother's, looked up. The vertical grooves between her thick eyebrows deepened, as she considered this dark consolation with the wariness of a burned child studying a fire.

"I spoke at some length last night with Learned Lewko," Biast began, and stopped. He squinted at his sister. "Fara, you really don't look well. Don't you think you had better go lie down for a while?"

The lady-in-waiting nodded endorsement to this idea. "We could draw the drapes in your chambers, my lady, and make it quite dark."

"That might be better." Fara leaned forward, only to sit staring down at her feet for a moment before allowing her waiting woman to pull her reluctantly upright. Biast rose also.

Ingrey seized the moment to conceal calculation in courtesy. "I am sorry you are so plagued, my lady. But if the inquest returns a verdict of self-defense, there might be no need for you to be so imposed upon again."

"I can do what I have to do," she replied coolly. But she looked as though a dismissal of charges was, for the moment, a newly attractive notion. She gave him a civil enough nod of farewell, though it caused her to raise one hand to her temple immediately thereafter. Biast's glance back at Ingrey was more curious. Ingrey wondered if he might, after all, remove the threat of a trial from Ijada by one strand of persuasion at a time, like a web, rather than in some more concentrated and dramatic manner: if so, well and good. The parallel with Wencel's preferred techniques of indirection did not escape him.

Biast saw his sister out, but then left her to her waiting woman; he looked up and down the corridor a moment before returning to the chamber, shutting the door firmly behind him. He frowned at his bannerman Symark and then at Ingrey, as though considering some comparison, though whether of physical threat or personal discretion, Ingrey could not guess. Symark was a few years older than his lord and a noted swordsman; perhaps Biast imagined him a sufficient defense from Ingrey, should the wolf-lord run mad and attack. Or Symark and Biast together so, at least. Ingrey did not seek to disabuse the prince-marshal of this comforting error.

"As I said, I had some conversation with Lewko," Biast continued. He sat again by the low table with the tray, gesturing for Ingrey to do likewise. Ingrey pulled his chair around and composed himself in close attention. "The Bastard's Order—which I take to mean, Lewko and a couple of forceful Temple sorcerers—have questioned Cumril in greater detail, at length."

"Good. I hope they held his feet to the fire."

"Something of a sort. I gather they dared not press him to the point of such disarray that his demon might reascend. That fear alone, Lewko assured me, was a greater goad to him than any threat to his body that any inquirer might make." His brow wrinkled doubtfully.

"I understand this."

"So you might." Biast sat back. "More disturbing to me was Cumril's assertion that my brother had indeed planned my assassination, as you guessed. How did you know?"

So that's why he had urged Fara out, that he might address these painful matters discreetly. Ingrey shrugged. "I am no seer. For anyone seeking the hallow kingship with less backing than you already have, it's a logical step."

"Yes, but not my own—" Biast stopped, bit his lip.

Ingrey grasped the chance to cast another thread. "So it seems Lady Ijada saved your life, as well as her own. And your brother's soul from a great sin and crime. Or your god did, through her."

Biast paused as though thinking uneasily about this, then began again. "I do not know how I earned my brother's hatred."

"I believe his mind was well and truly unhinged, toward the end. Boleso's fevered fancies, not any actions of yours, seem to me the springs of his behavior."

"I did not realize he was so—so lost. When that first dire incident with the manservant happened, I wrote my father I would come home, but he wrote back ordering me to stay at my post. Reducing one rebellious but ill-provisioned border castle and a few bandit camps seems to me now a less vital tutorial than what I might have been learning in the same time at Easthome. I suppose my father wished to insulate me from the scandal."

Or, perhaps, to protect him from worse and subtler things? Or was Biast's diversion to the border in this crisis engineered by other persuaders? Was the print of Horseriver's hoof anywhere in this?

Biast sighed. "In the fullness of time I expected to receive the crown from my father's own hands, in his lifetime, like every Stagthorne king before me. He'd had the election and coronation of my older brother Byza all planned out three years ago, before Byza's untimely death. Now I must grasp with my own hands, or let the crown fall."

"Byza's was a sudden illness, wasn't it?" Ingrey had been gone from Easthome on an early courier mission for Hetwar to the Low Ports, and had missed that royal funeral. Biast had received the prince-marshal's banner that had belonged to his brother before him only a few weeks later. Had Boleso dwelt too unhealthily upon the precedent?

"Lockjaw." Biast shuddered in memory. "I was in Byza's train at his naval camp near Helmharbor at the time. He was preparing some new ships for sea trials. Several men were stricken so. Five gods spare me from such a fate. It gave me an aversion to deathbeds that lingers still. My heart fails me at the thought of facing another. I pray five times a day for my father's recovery."

Ingrey had last seen the dying hallow king in person some weeks ago, just before his palsy stroke. He had been yellow-skinned, belly-swollen, and cheek-sunken even then, his movements heavy and voice low and slurred. "I think we must pray for other blessings for him, now."

Biast stared away, not disputing this. "The charge against Boleso, if it is not just Cumril's calumny, has left me wondering whom I can trust." His gaze, returning to Ingrey, made Ingrey feel rather odd.

"Each man according to his measure, I suppose."

"This presumes an ability justly to measure men, which begs the question. Have you taken the measure of my brother-in-law yet?"

"Not, um, entirely."

"Is he a danger like Boleso?"

"He's . . . smarter." And so, Ingrey was beginning to be convinced, was Biast. "No insult intended," Ingrey added, in a belated attempt at tact.

Biast grimaced. "At least, I trust, he is not so mad."

Silence.

"One does so trust—doesn't one?"

"I trust no one," Ingrey evaded.

"Not even the gods?"

"Them least of all."

"Mm." Biast rubbed his neck. "Well, the impending kingship does not give me joy, under the circumstances, but I am not at all inclined to hand it on, over my dead body, to monsters."

"Good, my lord," said Ingrey. "Hold to that."

Symark, who had been listening to this exchange with arms folded, rose and wandered to the window, evidently to check the clock of the sun, for he turned and gave his master an inquiring look. Biast nodded in return and stood with a tired grunt; Ingrey came to his feet likewise.

Biast ran a hand through his hair in a gesture copied or caught, Ingrey was fairly sure, from Hetwar. "Have you any other advice for me this day, Lord Ingrey?"

Ingrey was only a year or two older than Biast; surely the prince could not see him as an authority for that reason. "In all matters of policy, you are better advised by Hetwar, my lord."

"And other matters?"

Ingrey hesitated. "For Temple politics, Fritine is most informed, but beware his favor to his kin. For, ah, practical theology, see Lewko."

Biast appeared to muse for a moment over the unsettling implications of that *practical*. "Why?"

Ingrey's fingers stretched out, then tapped across the ball of his thumb in order, little finger to index. "Because the Thumb touches all four other fingers." The words seemed to fall out of his mouth from nowhere, and he almost jerked back, startled.

Biast too seemed to find the words fraught beyond their simplicity, for he gave Ingrey a peculiar stare, unconsciously clenching his hand. "I shall hold that in my mind. Guard my sister."

"I'll do my utmost, my lord."

Biast gave him a nod, gestured Symark ahead of him, and went out.

❧

Ingrey scouted the mansion to discover Fara laid down in her chambers and tended by her ladies as expected, and the earl gone out to the hallow king's hall. So what drew Wencel there that was more riveting than awaiting the news from the inquest? That he had not escorted his wife to the judges' bench was no surprise; Wencel quietly avoided Temple Hill, in such a routine fashion as to occasion no remark. But whatever menace the earl concealed, he'd been attending on his sick father-in-law for weeks without Ingrey's supervision. Ingrey hesitated to pursue him there. *Yet.*

The situation seemed to have more need for wits than a strong sword arm, and if the body was neglected, the brain flagged, too, so Ingrey took himself to the earl's kitchen to forage a meal, which was served to him along with certain oblique complaints. After that, he tracked down Tesko and bullied him into giving back to the scullions the money he'd won cheating at dice. His servant temporarily cowed, Ingrey then had him snip and extract the stitches from his scalp and rebandage his sword hand. The long and ragged tear in his discolored skin seemed closed, but still tender, and he pressed the gauze wrapping warily after Tesko tied it off. *This should have healed by now.*

Autumn dusk crept through the window embrasures as Ingrey sat on his new bed and meditated. The princess's impending bereavement curtailed the sort of society that had enlivened Hetwar's palace of an evening, or demanded Ingrey's services as an escort for its lord or lady. If Earl Horseriver chose to send him off on some untimely courier mission, how then could he carry out his princely mandate to guard Fara, or his self-imposed task to save Ijada? Get one of Hetwar's men to ride, and remain in Easthome sneaking about spying? The notion seemed stuffed with disastrous complications. His public duty to obey the earl was a pitfall waiting to swallow him, it seemed to Ingrey, and he was not sure Hetwar had quite thought it through.

Could he defy Horseriver? Each of them, it seemed, had been gifted with kindred powers. Horseriver was vastly more practiced, but was he stronger? And what did *strength* mean, in that boundless hallowed space where visions took seeming shape?

How, for that matter, did one practice, and upon what? Ingrey's battle-madness could not be rehearsed at all; it came only at need, and in deadly earnest. And the weirding voice—could its suggestions be resisted? Defied? Broken? Did they wear off in time, like Hallana's demon-sorcery had upon the be-pigged man? Ingrey could not imagine finding glad volunteers to test his talents upon. Though Hallana, he suddenly suspected, would be all for the trial, and Oswin would take careful notes. The image made him smile despite himself.

How old is my wolf? The question niggled him, suddenly. Warily, he turned his perceptions inward, and once more, the sensation was akin to trying to see his own eyes. The accumulated wolf souls seemed to meld together into a smooth unity, as though their boundaries were more permeable somehow; wolves became Wolf in a way that Earls Horseriver had failed to achieve in that tormented soul's cannibal descent through the generations of his human kin. Ingrey sifted the fragmentary lupine memories that had come to him, both in that first terrible initiation and in later dreams. The viewpoint was odd, and scents seemed more sharply remembered than sights. A sufficiently impoverished rural village of recent days was hardly to be distinguished from a forest town of the lost times.

But suddenly a most peculiar memory surfaced, of chewing with wolf-puppy teeth upon a piece of boiled leather armor, a cuirass almost bigger than he was. The chastisement when he'd been caught at it did not diminish the satisfaction to his sore mouth. The armor had been quite new, dragged to a corner of some dim and smoky hall. The design was distinctive, the breast decoration more so, a silhouette of a wolf's head with gaping jaws burned into the leather with hot iron. *My wolf is as old as the Old Weald, and then some.*

As old as Wencel's horse? Older, surely, in a sense, for his wolf had been abroad, repeatedly reincarnated, for four hundred extra years before being so bloodily harvested. Part of that time had been spent high up in the Cantons, judging by the pictures of cold peaks that lingered in his mind. A long happy period, several domesticated wolf-lives, in some tiny hamlet in a forgotten vale where seasons and generations turned in a slow wheel . . . The attrition of mischance might have cut short the accumulation of wolf souls, yet had not. Which suggested in turn that Someone with a long, long attention span might have been manipulating those chances. *Must have been,* his mirthless reason corrected this.

If he ever saw the god again, he could ask, Ingrey supposed. *I could ask now. I could pray.* He had no desire to; praying held all the appeal of thrusting his hand into the holy fire on the temple plinth and holding it there. Talking to the gods had been a much more comfortable proposition when there had seemed no danger of Their talking back.

He lay back and sought within himself for that millrace-current sense of Ijada. The quiet song of it calmed him instantly. She was not, at this moment, in pain, nor unduly fatigued, except for a tense piling-up of boredom. It did not follow that she was safe; the banal comfort of the narrow house was deceptive, that way. Horseriver had named this link the unintended relict of his murderous geas, and it might be so. Was not some good salvaged from evil, from time to time? He must contrive some way to see her again, secretly and soon. And to communicate. Could this subtle perception be made more explicit? *One yank for yes, two yanks for no.* Well, perhaps not that, but there must be *something.*

His brooding was interrupted by a page rapping on his door, bidding him to attend upon the earl. Ingrey armed himself, grabbed up his long court cloak, and descended to the entry hall, where he found Horseriver, who could only have come in a short time ago, preparing to go out again.

With some low-voiced instructions, the earl finished dispatching an anxious groom, then granted Ingrey a civil nod.

"Where away, my lord?"

"The hallow king's hall."

"Didn't you just come from there?"

Wencel nodded. "It is nearly time. I think the king will not last the night. There is a particular waxy look to the skin"—Wencel passed a hand over his face—"that is a very distinctive herald to these sorts of deaths."

And Horseriver ought to know. From both sides, Ingrey realized. They were briefly alone in the hall, the servants having been sent to hurry Fara; Ingrey lowered his voice. "Ought I to suspect you of some uncanny assassination?"

Wencel shook his head, apparently not the least offended by the suggestion. "His death comes quite without need of any man's assistance. At one time—long ago—I might have sought to speed it. Or, more vainly, to retard it. Now I just wait. A flicker of days, and it is done." He vented a long, quiet sigh.

Death, an old familiar, did not disturb Wencel, and yet his languid weariness seemed a mask, to Ingrey. He was tense with some hidden anticipation, revealed, barely, only when his eyes repeatedly checked the staircase for some sign of Fara. At length the princess appeared: pale, chill, cloaked in black.

Ingrey, bearing a lantern, led the way through the darkening streets of Kingstown; the sole retainer, he noted, called to this duty. The evening air was chill and damp—the cobbles would be slippery with dew by midnight—but overhead the first stars shone down from a rainless sky. Wencel escorted his wife on his arm with the unfailing cold courtesy that was his studied habit. Ingrey extended his senses—all of his senses—yet found no new threat looming in the shadows. *Indeed, no. We are the threats, Wencel and I.*

Torches in brackets lit the entrance to the hallow king's hall in a flickering glow. Only the name recalled the old forest architectures of timber and thatch, for it was as much a stone palace as any other Easthome noble pile built during the latter days of Darthacan glory. Guardsmen hurried to swing wide the wrought-iron gates and bow apprehensively to the princess and her husband. The sentries seemed faintly mortified by how useless all their pikes and blades were to protect their lord from what stalked him tonight. As distant as they still were from the king's bedchamber, the servants' voices were hushed and tremulous as they escorted the party along the dim and musty halls.

Ahead, lamplight spilled into the corridor and reflected off the polished floorboards. Ingrey took a steeling breath and turned to follow the earl and the princess within.

21

THE HALLOW KING'S BEDCHAMBER WAS LESS CROWDED than Ingrey had imagined it. One green-robed physician and his acolyte sat near the head of the canopied bed with an air of depressed quietude that acknowledged all their medical efforts now vain. A divine in the gray garb of the Father's Order waited also, in an inverse mood of stretched readiness not yet called upon. In a room beyond an antechamber, out of sight and, thankfully, muffled by the intervening walls, a five-voice chorus of Temple singers started a hymn. The quintet sounded hoarse and tired; perhaps they would take a rest soon.

Ingrey studied the king in the bed. He was not weighted by such dark intrusions as Ingrey's or Wencel's, not shaman, nor sorcerer, nor saint; he was but a man, if a riveting one even in this last hour. He was a long way now from the Stagthorne scion Hetwar nostalgically spoke of from his childhood, who had taken the prince-marshal's banner from his own father's kingly hand to earn early victory and reputation in a now half-forgotten border clash with Darthaca. When Ingrey had first returned to the Weald in Hetwar's train, the king had been hale and vigorous despite his graying head and all the sorrows of his life. The past months of creeping illness had aged him speedily, as if to make up for lost time.

Now his final sleep was upon him. Ingrey hoped Fara had exchanged whatever last words she wanted with her father earlier, for there would be no more tonight. The thin, spotted skin, an ugly yellow shade, indeed bore that waxy sheen Horseriver had named the harbinger of finality. More: the king's breathing was harsh and hesitant, each breath drawn in and released, followed by a pause that drew all eyes, until the chest heaved again, and the gazes dropped away.

Fara's face was ashy but composed; she signed the Five, placed a formal kiss on the king's slick brow, and stood back. The Father's divine dared to place a consoling hand upon her shoulder, and murmur, "He had a good life, my lady. Be not afraid."

The glance Fara cast him was equally devoid of both fear and consolation, or indeed, much expression at all. Ingrey was impressed that she did not snarl in return; if offered such a platitude in such a moment, *he* would have been tempted to draw steel and run the divine through. She merely murmured, "Where is my brother Biast? He should be here. And the archdivine."

"He was here earlier, my lady, for a good long time, and will return shortly. I expect the archdivine and my lord Hetwar will be accompanying him."

She nodded once and shrugged away from him. His hand hesitated in air, as if to offer another consolatory pawing, but fortunately he thought better of it, stepping away to leave the princess in her stolid sorrow.

Horseriver stood watching all this with his feet braced a little apart, the picture of a supporting spouse and lord. His face seemed no more stern than the occasion demanded. It was only to Ingrey's eye that he seemed crouched like a cat at a mousehole. What more was about to happen in this room than the long-expected death of an aged man, even if aged king? Horseriver had been hovering in Easthome for weeks. What did he await, besides the end of this vigil? And if his presence here was so vital to his schemes, how much had it maddened him to have to break away and tend to the untimely intrusion of Boleso's funeral?

There are two hallow kings in this room. How can there be two?

The question Ingrey had asked in Hetwar's chambers, to which he'd received no satisfactory reply, came back to him now. What made the hallow kingship hallowed? Ingrey could barely guess. Horseriver, he suspected, knew.

He became abruptly aware that Horseriver's spirit horse was no longer stopped down to a tight knot, but seemed flooded throughout his body, riding the river of his blood. It was quiescent—no—poised. Both Horseriver's tension and his patience seemed quite literally superhuman, in this moment.

Ingrey felt his own blood pulsing through his veins. He would have thought the piling up of his wolf's wolf-lives, and of Horseriver's stallion's horse-lives, would have made each more quintessentially wolf or horse, but it seemed not; it was as though all such wisdom-creatures converged on some common center, the denser and deeper they grew. *They are both a lot like each other,* Ijada had said. *Indeed.*

The hymn singers came to the end of their piece, and stopped; a faint shuffling suggested a recess. The Mother's acolyte had been dispatched down the corridor to watch out for Prince-marshal Biast. The divine had walked to the other side of the chamber and was helping himself to a glass of water. From the bed came a labored breath that was not followed by another.

Fara's face went stiffer, her eyes glassy with moisture that did not fall. Horseriver stepped briefly forward only to hand her a lace handkerchief, which she clutched with a spasm of her hand, then stepped back. The earl did not say anything foolish. He did not say anything at all.

He did shift back a pace, then rose almost on his toes, stretching his arms out like a falconer calling his bird to him.

Ingrey boiled up to full alertness, craning his neck and

straining his senses. Ingrey could not see souls, as saints were reputed to do. He discerned the departing essence only because something *unwound* from it in its passing, spooling off like some heady perfume spiraling through the air. Gods, he had more than felt before; only by that experience could he identify the vast *Presence* that raised his hackles like a breath in the dark. But this One was not to his address, and was gone with its prize before his pupils could widen in a futile effort to take it in.

The mysterious scent remained behind, cool and complex like a forest in spring: water, pine, musk, wet earth, sunlight—was *laughter* an odor? It roused and aroused him both, setting him all on edge, and his head lifted to it, eyes and nostrils widening in vain. He inhaled in utter bewilderment. What was he supposed to do? Knock Fara aside? Tackle Horseriver? He could not take his sword to the scent of a forest, carving the air like a madman. There seemed no evil in it: danger, yes, power, yes. *Glory. Yes.*

Ingrey caught the moment when Horseriver's head jerked back and breathed the kingship in. The earl staggered a little, as though a great eagle had landed upon those outstretched falconer's arms. His eyes squeezed shut, he folded his arms around himself, and he breathed out in a satisfied huff. When his eyes snapped open again, they blazed.

Holy fire, thought Ingrey. And, *So fast! What just happened?* Surely Horseriver had not—no, he had *not* waylaid the hallow king's departing soul and taken it in like another spirit animal atop the dark, distorted hoard he held already. And his spell for deathlessness captured body and soul both, leaving his own corpse behind like an emptied husk. Ingrey whispered in mystification to Wencel, "Have you stolen a blessing from the gods . . . ?"

Horseriver's faint mirth nearly melted his heart. "This"—the earl gestured down himself, barely breathing the words—"was never the gods'. We made it ourselves. It belongs *here*. It was wrenched from me two and a half centuries ago. Now it returns. For a little time."

The Father's divine, oblivious to all this, had hurried to the hallow king's bedside, where the physician was bent over making his final examination. They murmured together in grave consultation. The divine signed the corpse and himself, and began intoning a short prayer.

So. Wencel was revealed in another lie, or half-truth; Ingrey could not summon the least surprise anymore. There had not been two hallow kings in this room; there had been two partial kings, mutually crippled, each holding hostage the other's fulfillment. Now there was one, whole again. Ingrey shivered under the terrible weight of his sovereign smile.

"First things first," breathed Wencel, licked his thumb, and touched it to Ingrey's forehead. Ingrey jerked back, too late. He felt the *snap* of his connection with Ijada part like a physical thing, and he almost cried out in loss and outrage. Before he finished inhaling, the connection seated itself again, and instead of Ijada, he found himself mortally conscious of Horseriver. The kingly will mounted Ingrey's rising panic like an expert rider atop a green colt. The sensation nearly overwhelmed him, darkening his sight, unlocking his knees. Horseriver, brows pinching in, searched his face then nodded in satisfaction. "Yes . . ." The word floated out on a sigh. "That will do."

Fara turned to glance at her husband: her eyes widened and her breath drew in. If she saw one-tenth the towering glamour with her ordinary eyes that Ingrey sensed with his shaman's sight, he could not wonder at her sudden awe. Horseriver licked his thumb again and touched her brow, then moved to embrace her, leaning their foreheads together in a gesture one might mistake for comfort or blessing. Fara's eyes, when he drew back, were glazed and staring. Ingrey wondered if his own eyes looked just like that.

His arm around his wife's waist as if to support her, the earl turned to the Father's divine. "Tell my brother-in-law, when he arrives, that I have taken the princess home to lie down. All of this has brought on one of her debilitating headaches, I'm afraid."

The divine, suddenly very attentive to the earl, nodded eager understanding. "Of course, my lord. I am so sorry for your loss, my lady. But your father's soul is born now into a better world."

Horseriver's lips twisted. "Indeed, all men are born pregnant with their own deaths. The experienced eye can watch it quicken within them day by day."

The divine flinched at this disturbing metaphor, but plowed on sturdily. "I'm not sure that—"

Horseriver held up a restraining hand, and the man fell silent at once. "Peace. Tell the prince-marshal that we will meet with him in the morning. Late morning, probably. He may begin the arrangements as he wills."

"Yes, my lord." The divine bobbed a bow; on the other side of the bed, so did the physician.

"Ingrey . . ." Horseriver turned to his retainer, and his lips drew back on the most disquieting smile yet. His voice dropped to an eerie low register that vibrated through Ingrey's bones. *"Heel."*

Furious, fascinated, and frantic, Ingrey bowed and followed his master out.

Horseriver hustled his wife and Ingrey swiftly and alone through the darkened corridors of the hallow king's hall. Another murmur of Peace had the gate guards saluting them through without hindrance or question. They turned into the night streets, the air growing misty in the gathering chill. As they rounded the first corner, Ingrey looked back over his shoulder and saw a procession of swinging lanterns. Voices carried through the fog: Biast and a noble company hurrying back to his father's deathbed. Too late. Ingrey's ear picked out Hetwar's voice, replying to the prince-marshal. He wondered if Hetwar carried the hallow king's seal that was his charge in its oak box, together with the silver hammer to break it at the bedside.

Horseriver's party was lightless, black-cloaked, stepping softly; Ingrey doubted anyone from the prince-marshal's retinue saw them at all. They started down the hill. A few streets farther on, they did not turn aside to Horseriver's mansion as Ingrey expected, but continued till the stable mews loomed out of the darkness. The doors were open wide, and a few lanterns, hung from the rafters, burned softly within the redolent space.

A groom scrambled up from the bench by the outer wall and bowed fearfully as the earl approached. "All is ready, my lord. The clothes are in the tack room."

"Good. Stay a moment."

Horseriver ushered Fara and Ingrey ahead of him. Ingrey saw in the passing shadows of the box stalls on his left that Horseriver's big chestnut and the dappled gray named Wolf were saddled and bridled, with saddlebags tied on behind. A bay mare in a straight stall across from them was similarly accoutered. As they passed the box with the stag, it snorted and shook its antlers, sharp hooves thumping nervously in the thick straw.

Horseriver pointed to a lantern, which Ingrey reached up and retrieved, then led them through the open door of the tack room. Harness glowed on the wall pegs, with leather burnished and brightwork shining. Across some empty saddle racks, three piles of garments waited. Ingrey recognized his own riding leathers, together with his boots standing below. Another was a woman's riding habit in some wine-dark fabric picked out with gold thread. Horseriver gestured to the piles. "Clothe yourselves," he addressed Fara and Ingrey equally, "and make ready to ride."

Stone-faced, Fara dropped her voluminous cloak, which whispered to the wooden floor. "I must have help with the buttons, my lord," she said levelly.

"Ah, yes." Horseriver grimaced, and with practiced fingers undid the row of tiny pearl buttons down her back from their velvet loops. Ingrey stripped off court cloak, town shoes, and silver-stitched jerkin and had his leathers hiked up and fastened before Fara's dress and petticoats fell in a pool at her feet. He did not think either of them was prey to embarrassment at this unexpected intimacy. Exaltation, bewilderment, and terror left no room for lesser emotions. He slipped his boots on and straightened, then cinched up his belt for knife and scabbard. His unholy liege lord was still absorbed in the intricacies of his wife's garb.

As the earl raised his arms to help Fara into her jacket, Ingrey's eye caught the gleam of new leather from a knife sheath at his waist. New sheath; new knife? Quietly, he backed out of the tack room into the stable aisle. Could he defy Horseriver's entrancing will? If he could think resistance, surely he could act it? If he did not think too hard? *Ijada, what is happening to you now?* He could no longer tell. This moment was clearly well prepared for; with Ingrey securely leashed, had the earl readied some fatal assault on that narrow house, as well?

Still backing, he grabbed and drew the latch to the wise-stag's stall, dragging the door open. His fingers felt numb. *"Go,"* he whispered. The beast bounced twice in place, snorted like the crack of ice breaking, then bolted out past him, its hooves clattering and scraping on the colored pavement. It gathered itself and was gone into the outer darkness of the city in a near-hallucinatory flash of speed. Ingrey froze as Horseriver thrust his head out the tack room door and frowned. *"Stay,"* snapped the earl, and Ingrey perforce waited.

He was still standing there struggling . . . not so much to move, as to *want* to move, when the earl appeared again, his own town robes exchanged for leathers and boots, escorting Fara firmly with one hand clenched around her upper arm. Horseriver glanced aside at the empty stall and, to Ingrey's dismay, merely smiled sourly. "You almost frighten me," he remarked in passing. "That was inspired. So nearly right. Perhaps I should muzzle you, as well."

He said no more, but aimed Fara into the straight stall where Ijada's chestnut mare shifted uneasily.

"I'm afraid of that horse, my lord," Fara quavered.

"Not for much longer, I promise you," he murmured back. Ingrey could not see more over the boards and past the vine-decorated metal bars than the horse's flickering ears and the tops of Horseriver's blond and Fara's dark heads, but he heard a leathery whisper as of a knife being drawn. A low murmur from the earl in words he half recognized made his blood race and raised all the hairs on his arms. Then a meaty thunk, a truncated squeal, a jerk against a head rope that shook the walls—then a thudding of a heavy body collapsing, convulsing, and going still.

The two heads moved back into the aisle. Fara was leaning against Horseriver, shuddering fiercely. If blood spattered her riding costume, it did not show in the dark. "What have you *done* to me . . . ?" she moaned.

Within her, Ingrey's shaman senses saw, a powerful but frightened shadow plunged and strained.

"Sh," Horseriver soothed her. He touched her brow with his thumb again, renewing her glassy stare. The horseshadow, too, quieted, though seeming more benumbed than calmed. "It will be well. Come along, now."

The apprehensive groom had reappeared. "My lord? What was—"

"Fetch the horses."

The three saddled horses were marshaled in the darkened court before the mews. The groom and Horseriver between them boosted Fara aboard her bay mare; Horseriver himself checked her girths, adjusted her boots in her stirrups, smoothed her split skirts, closed her trembling gloved hands tightly over her reins.

"Mount up," Horseriver directed Ingrey, handing him the gray gelding's reins. Ingrey did so, though the horse skittered and hopped beneath him, trying to get its head down and buck. Horseriver glanced back and cast another *Peace!* over his shoulder in a voice of mild irritation, and Ingrey's mount settled down, if still uneasily. The earl closed the stable doors behind them.

The groom gave Horseriver a leg up, and the earl caught up his stirrups with the toes of his boots without looking, settling himself in his saddle. He reached down and laid a beneficent palm across the groom's forehead. *"Go home. Sleep. Forget."*

The groom's eyes went vague, and he turned away, yawning.

Horseriver raised a hand and called to Ingrey and Fara, *"Follow."* He wheeled his mount and led off at a walk into the foggy dark. Hooves scraped on the sloping cobbles, the sound echoing off the walls of the buildings as they wound down through the Kingstown streets.

As they passed through the empty market square, Horseriver leaned over the side of his saddle, pressed his hand to his stomach, and quietly retched. He spat something dark and wet upon the paving bricks. Ingrey, passing after, smelled not bile but blood. *Does he bleed for his weirding voice as I do for mine?* More discreetly, it seemed. And how much of that treasure had he misspent for Ingrey's murderous geas, that he named it *too much*?

The night guards at the southeast town gate let them exit at a simple order from Horseriver. He did not even seem to need the weirding voice to have them saluting him solicitously on his way. Once clear of the walls and the paved causeway, Horseriver pressed his mount into a trot. They turned left at the first village crossroad leading down toward the Stork. Along the rim of the hills behind them, overtaking its heralding pale glow in the sky, a fat gibbous moon broke free and cast their long dim shadows onto the road before them.

Where are we going? Why does he want us? What are we going to do when we get there?

Ingrey gritted his teeth in frustration that he'd had no chance to send a message. Or leave one . . . He tried to imagine what folk would make tomorrow morning of the mess left in the stables: three horses and the stag gone, one mare bloodily dead, an untidy pile of court dress left on the tack room floor. They had left Easthome swiftly and quietly, to be sure, but by no means in secret. For Fara's sake alone, there would surely be pursuit. *Then whatever Horseriver plans, he expects it to go quickly, before pursuit can arrive. Should I seek delay?*

It was Ingrey's charge to spy on Horseriver and guard Fara. So far the first was going swimmingly, in a way, but he was surely making a hash of the second, for all that he rode beside her seeming to guard her still. He'd made an effort with the stag that had proved sadly misdirected. His lurid fear that Horseriver might want his wife for some bizarre blood sacrifice did not stand up to reasonable examination. She could not be hanged from a tree as courier to the gods in her new horse-spirit-ridden state, nor was she virgin for all her barrenness. Nor did Ingrey think that Horseriver wanted to communicate with the gods, beyond obscene gestures of defiance. And where were They, in this night of inexplicable events?

Stags for the Stagthornes. *Horses for the Horserivers.* Fara was a Horseriver by marriage, however unsatisfactory the union had been for her, and there was a Horseriver bride or two up her Stagthorne family tree as well, and not too far up at that. The earl's sister-daughter-granddaughters all, they must have been in their day, Ingrey now realized. The loops in that family braid were staggering in their interlace, if one thought of the earl as one man and not a dozen. Kin. Kin. What of kin?

A hallow king's banner-carrier was traditionally a close kinsman. Symark was second cousin to Biast, and had been his elder brother Byza's bannerman before that. The late king's own longtime bannerman had died half a year before him, from natural causes, and the old man had delayed replacing him—anticipating his own end even then and scorning to set some latecomer in that treasured companion's place? Or had a new appointment been blocked by Horseriver, for arcane reasons? A hallow king needed a bannerman of his own high blood, to match his honor. Or bannerwoman? Ingrey glanced aside at Fara, clinging to her mount, her face pale and shadowed. She was an adequate horsewoman only. This night would test her endurance.

Hetwar would blister him for this. If he lived. If he lived, Ingrey decided, Hetwar could blister him to his heart's content. Better—if he and Fara lived, it would set an interesting conundrum for Ijada's judges. Any precedent of punishment or reprieve to Ijada for bearing her leopard must logically apply also to the princess and her new night-mare. *I think I could do something with this. And if I couldn't, I'll wager Oswin could.*

They neared the Stork and turned north along the main river road. The moonlight reflecting off the river's broad surface filtered in bright bursts through the trees lining the banks. Past the clip of hooves and creak of leather Ingrey could hear the faint rippling of the current, mixing with the whisper of falling leaves.

He kneed Wolf forward to match the big chestnut's long gait. "Sire, where are we going?"

Horseriver's head turned, and his teeth flashed briefly in the shadows at the honorific. "Can you not guess?"

North. They could be in flight to exile in the Cantons, but somehow Ingrey thought not. A two-day ride at a courier's pace would bring them to the edge of the Raven Range . . .

"The Wounded Woods. Bloodfield."

"Holytree that was. Very good, my wise wolfling."

Ingrey waited, but Horseriver added nothing else. After a moment, the earl urged his horse into a canter, and the other two mounts snorted and picked up the pace.

Ingrey's *reason* still worked, it seemed. It was his emotions that Horseriver's kingship had overwhelmed. What a strange geas—no, this was no mere spell. Not at all like the tight, self-contained parasite magic he had fought and defeated at Red Dike. This was something else, huge and old and strong. Older than Horseriver himself? Nor did it feel intrinsically evil, though all gifts turned to despair in Horseriver's age-blackened hands.

The terrible charisma of kings . . . men crept close, longing to bask in it, for something more than material reward. The lure of heroism, the benediction of action, might have only death for its prize, and yet men flocked to the king's banner. The seductive promise of perfection of self in service to this high bright-seeming thing?

Horseriver had not made his kingship out of himself alone, all those centuries ago. He had received it as heirloom—*time immemorial* was all too true a phrase for a tradition that knew no writing to bind the years in tame ranks, but the kin tribes had been on this ground so long they seemed as old as the great dark forest itself. Whatever royal magic they had made out of themselves, they had been making it for a very, very long time.

The old kinsmen, even by their own accounts, had been a collection of arrogant, stiff-necked, bloody-minded, and bloody-handed madmen. It would take something as intense as this burning glamour to bring them into any sort of line, however ragged. Fear of Audar had driven them, to be sure, in their late days, but fear was as likely to scatter efforts like leaves in a storm as to concentrate them. How much energy had Horseriver possessed, how much expended, to bring that great rite at Holytree even to a beginning, let alone to fruition? If this was his kingship's last dying gasp, what must it have been in its fierce prime?

The rising moon met the rising mists to turn the world into a seething sea of light. The hallow king raised and flung down his arm, and led his followers in a hard gallop up this straight flat glowing stretch of river road. They seemed to course the clouds, flying. Ingrey's eyes watered in the chill wind of their passage. His horse bounded effortlessly between his gripping legs, and Ingrey, his heart bursting, threw back his head and drank the rushing night. Failure lay behind, ruin, perhaps, ahead; but in this silver hour he was glorified.

22

BY THE TIME THE MOON WAS HIGH, THE LATHERED HORSES were flagging. They were miles beyond the point at which a royal courier would have stopped to change mounts, and Ingrey was beginning to wonder if Horseriver planned for them to ride the animals to death, when the earl finally allowed his big chestnut to drop to a weary walk. After a few more minutes, he pointed and led them off the road toward a farmhouse set alone in the trees toward the river. A lantern hung from its porch rafters, burning faint and red in the moon-blue dark.

Three horses were waiting, tied to the railing. As they dismounted a Horseriver groom scrambled up from a bedroll and set about transferring the tack. Horseriver allowed only enough time for Ingrey and Fara to consume some cheese wrapped in bread, swallow some ale, and visit the privy behind the house before mounting and taking to the road again. Fara was pale and strained, but the hallow king's will held her to her grim task of clinging to her fresh horse and galloping once more.

Even Ingrey was swaying in his saddle by the time they stopped again, at another old thatched farmhouse just over a hill from the main river road. They had passed no other riders in the deep night, and had swung quietly around the walled villages lying farther and farther and farther apart up the narrowing Stork. Fara fairly fell out of her saddle into her husband's arms.

"Surely she can ride no more tonight, sire," Ingrey murmured.

"It is just as well. Even you and I could not ride straight through without stopping. We'll take a rest here."

An arranged rest, clearly, for a daunted-looking farm girl appeared to take Fara in charge and lead her into the house. The earl followed another Horseriver groom, obviously stationed here for this duty, as he led the horses around behind the rambling house to a rickety shed. Wencel looked over the waiting remounts and grunted satisfaction. No farm nags, these, but more horses sent ahead from the earl's own stables.

This flight was well planned, it seemed. Pursuers might inquire at roadside inns and other public liveries where men in a hurry could rent remounts, yet find no trace of them, no witnesses, no abandoned horses. To stop and inquire at every farmhouse along the Stork between Easthome and the northern border would waste precious time, even for men with such resources as the prince-marshal and Hetwar. And they would have half a dozen other roads away from Easthome in all directions to search, as well.

To what degree can I resist this kingly geas? Ingrey wondered, in a sort of melted desperation. If he could but once gather the will and wits, that is. Would escape from the range of Wencel's voice break this false calm in which he seemed to float, would the trance falter if Wencel's attention was divided? Ingrey felt as hungry for that royal regard as a dog desiring a bone from its master or a boy a smile from his father. The dogged fawning merely made him grit his teeth, but that Horseriver should so casually pilfer a filial loyalty Lord Ingalef had never lived to enjoy sent a vein of molten rage through Ingrey's heart. Still he found himself creeping after his lord like a cold tired child huddling to a hearth.

Ingrey trailed Wencel to a seat on the floor of the farm-house porch, let his aching legs dangle over the edge, and stared with him out over the river valley at the descending moon. The groom brought plain fare again, bread and ham, though this time with a jug of new wine. The farm's vine-yard must have been fortunate in its sun and rain, for the wine was as sweet and smooth upon the tongue as liquid gold. Proximity to his master stirred a drunken elation in In-grey, anchored by his fatigue, like that lassitude wherein an inebriated man might be quite positive he could rise and walk away, if only he chose. Ingrey drank again.

"It is beautiful, my lord," Ingrey said, nodding to the light-frosted view.

Wencel's lips twitched in an odd little grimace. "I have seen enough moonsets." He added after a moment, "Enjoy it while you can."

A disturbingly ambiguous remark, Ingrey thought. "Why do we gallop? What foe do we outrace? Pursuit from Easthome?"

"That as well." Wencel stretched his back. "Time is not my friend. Thanks to the Stagthorne kin's shrewd habit of electing their sons hallow kings in their fathers' lifetimes, it has been more than a hundred and twenty years since the last interregnum. The effort of creating another such gap seems overwhelming to me, just now. I shall seize this one." His lips drew back. "*Or die trying* does not apply."

So, Hetwar's suspicions seemed sustained; Horseriver did covet the election, and had been manipulating the or-dainers. And possibly the lives and deaths of potential rival candidates, as well? "Is this all to make yourself hallow king again, then?"

Horseriver snorted. "I *am* hallow king. I need no further making."

He had needed *something*, however; some missing piece, spun off from the old Stagthorne king's departing soul. Some . . . half magic, or fragment of the Weald: but surely not political in its nature. "Hallow king in name and form, then. Publicly elected and acclaimed."

"If I had desired the name of king of this benighted land, I could have taken it years ago, Ingrey," Horseriver said mildly. "In a better body, too."

I have a better body, Ingrey could not help thinking. But indeed, if it was the election Wencel desired, they ought to be galloping toward Easthome, not away from it. He wanted something else, something more, then. Something stranger. Ingrey fought for clarity through the fog of fatigue, wine on an empty stomach, and Horseriver's arresting aura.

"If you don't want to win the election for yourself, what do you want?"

"To delay it."

Ingrey blinked grimy eyes. "Will this flight do that?"

"Well enough. The absence of one earl-ordainer"— Horseriver touched his chest—"alone would not be enough, but Biast will be distracted by Fara's disappearance on the eve of her father's funeral, once he discovers it. I have planted a few other disruptions. The multiple proxies I left for different candidates should be good for several days of argument all by themselves, when they surface." He grinned briefly and not especially humorously.

Ingrey hardly knew what to reply to that, although the term *interregnum* seemed to rumble in his mind, fraught with elusive weight. Through the mellow glow of his embezzled fealty, he gleaned his wits, and asked, "What was the stag for?"

"What, hadn't you guessed?"

"I thought you meant to invest it in Fara, to make her a spirit warrior, or to carry something away from her father. But then you chose the mare."

"When playing against the gods, sudden unexpected ploys sometimes work better than deep-laid plans. Even They cannot block every chance. The stag was a great beast in the making; four stag-lives it has accumulated since I began it. But the hallow king's death fell before the stag was ready. I don't know if They hastened the one or delayed the other."

"You meant to make a shaman of . . . of Fara? Or someone?"

"Someone. I had not yet decided whom. Were it not for securing you instead, I would have had to chance the unripe beast. Your wolf is surer, despite being less, ah, tame. Stronger. Better."

Ingrey declined to wag his tail at this pat, though it took effort. *Better for whom?* His exhausted mind struggled to put the pieces together. A shaman, a banner-carrier, a hallow king, and the sacred ground of Holytree. And blood, no doubt. There had to be blood in there somewhere. Assemble them and achieve . . . what? No mere material purpose, surely. What was Wencel about, that the gods themselves should struggle to invade the world of matter to oppose it? What could Wencel aspire to beyond his bedazzling kingship?

What was greater than a king? Had Wencel's aspirations outgrown matter altogether? Four had become Five once, in the legendary past; could Five become Six?

"What do you plan to make of yourself, then? A god, or demigod?"

Wencel choked on his wine. "Ah, youth! So ambitious! And you yourself have seen a god, you claim. Go to bed, Ingrey. You're driveling."

"What, then?" Ingrey asked stubbornly, although he did press himself to his feet.

"I told you what I wanted. You have forgotten."

I want my world back, Wencel had cried in fierce despair into Ingrey's face. He had not forgotten, and wasn't sure he could if he tried. "No. But it cannot be had."

"Just so. Go to bed. We ride at midmorning."

Ingrey staggered into the farmhouse to find the cot that had been prepared for him, then lay staring upward in the dark despite his weariness. Surely his thrall to Horseriver was not absolute, or it would not chafe him so. Wencel's glamour sat ill upon his crooked shoulders, like a king's gilded armor, made in the flush of his youth, put upon a wizened old man. A dissonance between the man and his kingship that even Ingrey could sense whispered through the fissures.

Even in its mis-fit, though, Ingrey felt the power of the thing like heat from a furnace on his face. On an Old Weald warrior of even ordinary merit, the kingship must have fallen like a mantle of light. Then he wondered what it had been like when it chanced to fall upon a man of extraordinary character: when soul melded to sacred trust in one continuous arc like a perfect bell casting. *Such a Voice might make the mountains march.* His mind shied from the vision.

His own present duties, to penetrate Horseriver's secrets and to defend Fara, both glued him to Horseriver's side perforce. Perhaps an effort to escape was premature. Better to lull his captor, watch, and wait his chance? Trust in the pursuit that his reason and private knowledge told him must follow? Pray?

He hadn't prayed before bed in his adult life. But sleep gave dreams and in dreams, gods sometimes walked. And talked. His dreams were no garden for Them to stroll in, as Hallana's were said to be, but in this remnant of night he prayed to be possessed.

❧

But whatever Ingrey dreamed vanished upon awakening. He shot up with a start when the groom shook his shoulder. Washbasin, food, and drink were thrust at him; Wencel had them on the road again within half the turning of a glass.

The rising land grew ever more rural and remote. There were other people and beasts on the road now in the broad day: farm wagons, pack trains, slower riders, sheep, cows, pigs. Wencel's gallop of last night gave way to a less conspicuous canter, alternated with trotting and walking where the road grew steep or, increasingly, bad. Nonetheless it was apparent that the pace was finely calculated to wring the maximum distance from their mounts in the minimum time. An hour after noon, another aging farmhouse yielded up another meal and change of horses.

Ingrey studied Fara. The past day that she had endured, beginning with the inquest, going on to her father's deathbed, then this forced flight, would have devastated any woman and most men. Her spirit animal, he suspected, was lending her a physical strength as surprising to her as it was to him. Other sorts of strength . . . she had, perhaps, not lacked in her own right.

Given the effect that Wencel's kingship had on him, it occurred to Ingrey to wonder what it would do to women. He watched Fara's response to Wencel, seeking his female mirror. She was dazzled, even astonished, when her eyes rested on her transformed husband, her lips parting in unconscious desire. But not happy. She already possessed what other women might vainly aspire to, and yet . . . not. Wencel's gaze in return offered nothing but cool evaluation, as though she were a mount of dubious soundness somehow foisted upon him, and she flinched under the disdain. Fara might not be brilliant or brave, but neither was she safe to betray. She had resisted Wencel's perceived infidelity before, if to disastrous consequence. Was she as entirely his chattel as he seemed to think?

Was Ingrey? Ingrey sought inward. His wolf and he were no longer divisible in this life, but it seemed to him that the uncanny part of himself was more fully and fawningly under Horseriver's spell than the rational. The part of him that thought in words remained more free. He had chained his wolf once, when he'd been younger and more frightened and bewildered than this. If the hallow king had leashed his wolf, did he truly control all there was of Ingrey?

He seeks speed. To resist, I should seek delay.

Horseriver slowed them to a walk again, looking leftward. At length, he turned toward the river upon a lesser road, and the horses slithered down a long bank through a thin screen of pine trees. Dirt gave way to stones; they faced not a rickety rural bridge, but a ford across the upper Stork. The Raven Range gave forth steady and abundant springs. The water here was not in so muddy a spate as the ford at which Boleso's cortege had so nearly come to grief, but the river was wide and deep despite the recent drought in this region that put a dusty autumn haze in the blue air.

The earl pushed his horse ahead, finding the way through the shallower sections. Fara followed obediently. *If I do not pause to think*—Ingrey pressed his horse upstream of Fara's, watched till the water came up to the beasts' bellies and half lifted them off their hooves, then spurred and jerked his mount sideways into hers.

Both horses stumbled, and Fara's went down. Ingrey had already kicked his feet free of his stirrups. He lunged out of his saddle, slid over the flanks of her plunging horse, and made a valiant grab for the princess.

She'd kept a grasp on one stirrup. Her wallowing mount might well have towed her to the far bank, but Ingrey's grip and weight yanked her away. She gave a brief cry ending in a gurgle as her head went under. Horseriver whipped around in time to see Ingrey trying to pull her back to the surface as they both were swept downstream.

"Stay!" the earl cried. Ingrey jerked in response, but though that uncanny voice might command man or beast, it had no effect on the heavy current. The water was chill but not bitterly so, and this time, Ingrey managed to avoid clouting his head on a boulder. But this time, he also discovered immediately, his partner could in truth not swim. He renewed his grip on the flailing woman and gasped as he in turn went under, and his struggle for breath grew as unfeigned as hers.

He still managed to push them back into the swiftest current three times, as his longer legs dragged the gravel, until at last the stream broadened and slowed in a pool so shallow that even Fara's feet could touch bottom. Sliding and floundering, they waded to shore.

Ingrey scanned the bank. They had passed some mighty tangles of brush, a stretch of high and rocky overhangs that had constricted the waters into a frighteningly speedy chute, and now, a clot of young willows growing thickly along the farther shore. Wencel, especially if he'd stopped to secure their abandoned mounts, would not soon catch up with them. Ingrey had a very clear idea of just how much delay such a sopping mishap might cause, and hoped to extend it even further.

Fara coughed. Her face was milk-colored with the cold, and she trembled in Ingrey's firm grip. She was, he thought, owed some tears by now, but to his intense secret relief she did not at once burst into a weeping fit. "You saved me!" she gasped.

It was not in Ingrey's present interests to clarify this. "My duty, my lady. And my fault—my horse stumbled into yours."

"I thought I—I thought we were both going to drown."

So did I. "No, my lady."

"Did we . . ." she hesitated, turning her dark eyes up at him. "Did we escape?"

Ingrey took a long breath, and let it out slowly. Distance from the hallow king was, as he'd hoped, sobering—but not enough. The unwanted sense of Wencel that had replaced his link with Ijada was still present, body deep. The earl was urgent, somewhere upstream. But not panicked. "I don't think so. But we may be able to delay."

"To what end?"

"We must be followed. *You* must be followed. Maybe more quickly than Wencel thinks. Biast will be frantic on your behalf." The earl might have pictured them not being missed till the next day, but Ijada would have known instantly. Would she have thought him killed? Would she have been able to communicate with anyone? Lewko, Hallana? Would Gesca have listened to her pleas to seek them, late last night? Once faintly guilty for intimidating Gesca on her behalf, Ingrey was now sorry he had not terrorized the lieutenant more. *Five gods help her. And us.*

And if They are as interested as They seemed, where are They now, curse Them?

Fara stood shivering in a patch of sunlight, her heavy sodden garments clinging to her solid form, hair knocked loose from its braiding tailing in wet, miserable strands down her face. Ingrey was in little better case, wet leathers squeaking irritatingly as he moved. He stepped apart, drew his blades, and made a futile effort to wipe them dry.

"Where is Wencel taking me?" she demanded, her voice quavering. "Do you know?"

"Holytree, that was. Bloodfield. The Wounded Woods that are."

"*Ijada's* woods? Her dower land?" She stared in astonishment. "Is this for her, somehow?"

"The other way around. It is the Woods that Wencel desires, not their heiress. They are old, old and accursed."

Fara's face pinched in, half-reassured, half–more alarmed. "Why? Why did he drag me from Papa's deathbed, what evil thing does he intend? Why did he defile me with this, this . . ." She turned in a circle, clawing at her breast as if she could so dig out her unwanted haunt.

Ingrey caught her clay-cold hands and held them. "Stop, lady. I do not know why you are wanted. Ijada thought I was destined to cleanse the ghosts of the Woods of their spirit animals, as I did for Prince Boleso. If this is what Wencel wants of me, I don't know why he doesn't just say so; it seems no improper charge."

She looked up at him eagerly. "Can you take this horrible animal thing out of me, as well? As you did for my brother? Now?"

"Not while you live. The Old Weald shamans cleansed their comrades' souls only after death, it appears."

"Then you had best outlive me," she said slowly.

"I don't know. I don't know what will happen."

Her face grew stonier. She grated, "I could make certain of it."

"No, lady!" His grip tightened. "We are not in such dire straits yet, though I will swear to you if you wish that I will try, if our deaths fall out that way."

She gripped him back, looking disturbingly possessive for an instant. "Perhaps. Perhaps." She released him and wrapped her arms around her torso, shoulders hunching.

It occurred to Ingrey that his conviction that Fara was disqualified as a courier sacrifice was more doubtful than he'd first thought, if he could indeed cleanse her soul after death as he had her brother's. Was that the use Wencel had dragged him along for? Did it make sense? Not much, but then, little about this did to him just now.

"Then you could not cleanse Wencel, alive, either," she continued, brows pinching in worry.

"Wencel, well, Wencel is not just infested with a simple spirit horse like yours. He is . . . possessed, I suppose is as good a word as any, by a spirit, a soul, a concatenation . . . he claims, anyway, to be the sundered ghost of the last hallow king of the Old Weald." *More than claims.* "Kept alive whether he will or nil by a great spell based in Bloodfield."

Her voice went hushed. "Do you think he has gone mad?"

"Yes." He added reluctantly, "But he's not lying. Not about that."

Fara stared at him for a long, long moment. He almost expected her to ask, *Do you think you have gone mad?* to which Ingrey did not know the answer, but instead she said, "I felt it when he changed. He *changed* last night, when Papa died."

"Yes. He reclaimed his kingship, or some missing part of it. Now he is . . . well, I'm not sure what he is. But he races time."

She shook her head. "Wencel always ignored time. He was maddening, that way."

"This thing in Wencel's body isn't really Wencel. I have to keep remembering that."

She rubbed her temples.

"Is your head bothering you?" Ingrey asked cautiously.

"No. It's very strange."

How should they delay further? Split up, so as to take

longer to find? A clever notion; he could get back in the water, which was immune to the hallow king's glamour, and let it carry him downstream for miles until Wencel overtook him. Ingrey tried to remember if they'd passed any waterfalls coming up. But no. He could not leave this woman alone, shivering in the wilderness, waiting for the uncanny chimera she'd married to find her. "Prince-marshal Biast commanded me to guard you. We cannot separate."

She nodded gratefully. "Please not, my lord!"

"Wencel will search first along the banks. Let us at least go a little more into the woods."

It would not be enough to elude Horseriver altogether; he could already feel the tug of their tie, growing tighter. But truth to tell, he was becoming wildly curious about Bloodfield. He wanted to see it, *needed* to see it. And the straightest way was to let Horseriver take him there. *But not too swiftly.* Wencel might have had all he required in Ingrey and Fara, but Ingrey didn't think he had all *he* needed. *I need Ijada. I'm sure of it.* Did Horseriver know it, to separate them so? *Trust in the gods, They will supply?* Hardly. He wondered suddenly if it was as hard for the gods to have faith in Ingrey as it was for him to have faith in Them, and a weird wild urge to show Them how it *should* be done swept him for a moment.

Whatever fey look had possessed him made Fara step back. "I will follow you," she said faintly.

They turned to scramble into the brush. Over rotting logs, up past the high-water mark of a second stony bank, into deeper shade. Out across a sunny meadow high with purple thistles and prickling weeds that laid a dotted trail of burrs on their damp clothes. Through scratching brambles into more shade, laced with fine spiderwebs that caught across their mouths. The hike did some good, he thought, if only to render them drier by the exercise.

But the crashing of a large animal sounded through the woods soon enough. There was nothing in this waste more dangerous than what sought them already, but it need not be *more dangerous* to be *dangerous enough*. Ingrey froze, hand on his hilt, and Fara cowered near him, until Horseriver's mount emerged from the blinking shadows, snorting displeasure at the clutching undergrowth that scraped its hide.

Wencel, sighting them in turn, breathed a long sigh seeming half anger and half relief. All desire to flee faded from Ingrey's heart, melting away in the heat of the king's proximity. He saluted courteously.

"Thank you, Lord Ingrey," Wencel said, riding up.

"Sire."

"My horse stumbled," said Fara, unasked. "I almost drowned. Lord Ingrey held me up."

Ingrey did not bother correcting that to *I clambered on top of Lord Ingrey*. A matter of viewpoint, he decided. His had been largely underwater.

"Aye, I saw," said Wencel

Not all, or you wouldn't be thanking me so sincerely. Wencel's look at Ingrey was searching but not unduly suspicious.

"Get her up," said Wencel, holding out his hand, and Ingrey cupped his hands for the princess's muddy foot and boosted her up behind her husband. He took up station after the horse, to let it trample down the trail and rake off the spiderwebs, and followed Wencel wearily back upstream.

It took upwards of an hour for them to find the road again, and then they turned back eastward for more than half a mile to the river where Wencel had left their horses tied. There, to Ingrey's silent satisfaction, they found that Fara's horse had strained a tendon in its fall. Wencel pulled its tack off and turned it loose, had Ingrey lash the spare gear behind his own mount's saddle, heaved Fara up behind him once more, and led off west at a much slower pace.

Four hours lost at least, perhaps more by the time they dragged in to their next stop. Not enough. *It's a start.*

Ingrey had added another two hours to his tally by the time they turned off the back road to a grubby and impoverished little settlement scarcely meriting the name of hamlet.

A rotting timber palisade provided bare defense from wild beasts and none from evil men. The sun was setting; Horseriver frowned at its yellow glint through the trees.

"We cannot go farther tonight. There will be no moon till midnight." His teeth set in a brief grimace. "And for the same reason, we will not be able to depart from the next change till the dawn after, if we are not to be then benighted in the trackless mountains. We are set back a full day. Well, take your rest. You'll need it."

Wencel was indifferent to a set of surroundings that made Fara recoil. She was so unnerved by the slatternly sallow woman with no teeth and a near-unintelligible dialect, drafted to serve her, that she made Ingrey act her maid instead. He himself ended up sleeping on a blanket across her doorway, screened with only a tattered curtain, which she took for courtly devotion; Ingrey didn't explain that it was excuse to avoid the infested straw pallet he'd been offered. If Wencel slept, Ingrey did not see where.

❧

Despite the poor and improvised bedding, both he and Fara rose late the following morning, drained by exhaustion of both body and heart. Without haste, but without undue delay, Wencel led them once more onto the rural road, in places hardly more than a track, which skirted the Raven Range now rising to their right.

The Ravens were rugged but not high; no snow, either early or late, clung to their green-and-brown heights, though here and there some sheer fall of rock, gleaming in the sun, gave the illusion of ice. Their deep folds were rucked up like a blanket, cut with sharp ravines and secret places. Autumn had turned their summer verdure to gold, brown, and in places splashes of scarlet like sword cuts, laced in turn by the dark green of pines and firs. Beyond the first line of slopes, seen through an occasional gap, the humped ranks swiftly receded into a hazy blue distance that blended imperceptibly with the horizon, as though these hills marched to some boundless otherworld.

Ingrey wondered how in five gods' names Great Audar had ever dragged an army through here, at speed. His respect for the old Darthacan grew despite all. Even though Audar had lacked the uncanny charisma of the hallow kings he opposed, his leadership must have been impassioned.

They were in Badgerbank country now, Ingrey was reminded when they swung around the mining town of Badgerbridge in a suddenly busy river valley that poked up into the hills like a green spearhead. Smoke rose both from the town and from sites farther up the valley, marking smelters, which thickened the autumn haze. He wondered where in this place Ijada's stepfamily lived. The five-sided temple, a big timber structure, stood out above the town walls, prominent in the distance.

For a little while, they joined a larger road until they crossed the river by the stone bridge just above the town. Under the arches, lashings of timber and some barrels moved down the rocky stream, attended by nimble men and boys with poles. They passed carts, trudging husbandmen with their beasts, pack trains of mules. Horseriver hurried them along here without pausing, turning upstream, ignoring a main crossroad, then once more striking west into the woodlands on a lesser track.

Horseriver marked the course of the sun and picked up the pace for a while, but as the track dwindled was forced to a more careful progress. The horses labored up and slid down the steepening slopes. More up than down, and finally they turned right onto a faint trail, heaved up a short slope, and descended into a hidden dell.

No hamlet or farmhouse awaited here, but a mere campsite. A pair of grooms jumped up as they approached and ran to take the horses. The usual three remounts were picketed among the trees: sturdy cobs, this time, rather than the long-striding hot-blooded coursers Horseriver had favored for the roads. Fara, exhausted, dismounted slowly and stiffly and stared in dismay at her next proposed abode, bedrolls sheltered in a stand of fir trees, less even than last night's dire hovel. If she had ever camped before on royal hunts, Ingrey was fairly sure her days had ended in silken pavilions attended by cooing handmaidens and all possible comforts. Here, every other consideration was clearly sacrificed to speed and efficiency. *We travel light now, and will not be here long.*

"Did you bring it?" Horseriver demanded of the older groom.

The man signed himself in respect, ducking his head. "Yes, my lord."

"Fetch it out."

"Aye, my lord."

Leaving the tired horses to his younger companion, the bowlegged groom trudged to the campsite and bent over a pile of packs. Horseriver, Fara, and Ingrey followed. The groom rose clutching a pole some seven feet long, wrapped about with ancient, brittle canvas tied with twine. Horseriver sighed in satisfaction as he took it, his hands wrapping about the canvas binding, and swung it upright, planting the butt by his boot. Briefly, he leaned his forehead against it and squeezed his eyes shut.

Ingrey led the weary Fara to one of the bedrolls and made sure she was able to sit down without falling. She stared up through shadowed eyes as he turned back to Horseriver. The groom trod away again to assist with the horse lines.

"What is that, sire?" Ingrey asked, nodding to the pole. It made his hairs stir, whatever it was.

Horseriver half grinned, though without mirth. "The true king must have his hallowed banner, Ingrey."

"That's not the royal banner you had at Bloodfield, surely."

"No, that one was broken and cut to shreds and buried with me. This is the one I carried when I last was king in name, if only to the remnant of the faithful kin who followed me, when I raided Audar's garrisons from across the fen borders. It was wrapped after my last death in battle and put away; and later delivered, it was thought, to my son and heir. Little comfort it brought me, but I was glad to have it nonetheless. I hid it in the rafters at Castle Horseriver. For three hundred years it has lain up there, preserved against some better day. Instead, it comes down to this day. But it comes."

Horseriver leaned it carefully against a great pine tree, propped up and sheltered by a couple of sweeping low branches, then stretched and dropped cross-legged to a bedroll. Ingrey followed suit, finding himself between Horseriver and the princess. Ingrey's eyes were drawn again to the bundle. "It gives me . . . it has some weirding upon it, sire." It gave him cold chills, if he was honest.

Horseriver licked his lips in something like satisfaction. "Good, my wise wolfling. Being so shrewd, have you realized yet what the *other* function of a banner-carrier was?"

"Eh?" said Ingrey. When Wencel wasn't deceiving him or terrorizing him, the earl also did a very good job of making him feel a fool, he reflected glumly.

"And yet you cleansed Boleso, no small task," Horseriver mused. "I do weary of trying to herd your wits, but last time pays for all." He glanced aside at Fara, as if to be certain she was listening, which caught Ingrey's attention, for Wencel had avoided looking at her or speaking to her beyond the most direct commands.

"The banner-carriers slit the throats of their comrades too wounded to carry from the field, you said," Ingrey put in. A ghastly enough duty, but Ingrey was suddenly sure there was more. Ghastly, *ghostly,* wait . . .

Horseriver took a breath. "Put it together. The soul of a slain spirit warrior had to be cleansed of its life-companion before it might go to the gods. But a warrior was likely to fall in battle, when there was not time for proper rites or sometimes even the chance to carry the body away. For when even the wounded must be abandoned, the dead fare no better. Nothing of spirit can exist in the world of matter without a being of matter to support it, I know you have been taught this orthodoxy. That a warrior's soul might not drift as a sundered revenant and be lost, it was the banner-carrier's task to bind it to him or her as a haunt, and carry it away to where it might at length be cleansed by his true kin shaman. Or whatever shaman might be had, in a pinch."

"Five gods," whispered Ingrey. "No wonder the banner-men were desperately defended by their comrades." And had Wencel's binding of Ijada to him been some variant of this ancient practice?

"Aye, for they carried their slain kinsmen's hopes of heaven away with them. And so every fighting cadre who were led by or contained spirit warriors had such a sacred banner-carrier.

"Now, the *hallow king's* bannerman . . ." Horseriver trailed off. He straightened his shoulders and began again. "He had this same duty to his lord's soul, should the hallow king bear a kin beast. Not all elected kings were so graced, though many were, especially in unsettled times. But whether his lord were spirit warrior or no, the hallow king's banner-carrier had another sacred task, and not only when his lord died in a battle going ill. Though you may take it that if the hallow king was slain on the field, that battle was generally going quite ill indeed. Water." Wencel licked dry lips, and stared into his lap, his back curving again.

Ingrey glanced to the pile of packs, spotted a flaccid waterskin, and brought it to the tale-teller. Wencel tilted his head back and drank deep, indifferent to the musty staleness of it. He then sighed and propped himself on one hand, as though the burden of this telling was slowly driving him into the earth.

"It was the *royal* banner-carrier's duty, upon the death of his lord, to capture and hold the hallow kingship itself, until time to transfer it back to the ordained heir. And so this greatest of native Wealding magics was passed down from generation to generation, from times lost in time until . . . now."

"Lord Stagthorne—the late king—had no banner-carrier when he died, day before yesterday," Ingrey observed suddenly. "Was this your doing?"

"One of several necessary yet not sufficient arrangements, yes," murmured Wencel. "If true interregnums were easy to come by, more would have occurred by chance ere now, I assure you. Or by design."

He grimaced and drew breath, continuing: "The *royal* banner-carrier, by tradition and profound necessity, had several qualities. He—or she"—his glance at Fara sharpened—"was usually of the same kin, close-tied by shared high blood, though not always the heir. Chosen by the king, bound to the task by the royal shaman—the king himself if he was one—acclaimed by the spirit warriors assembled in the kin meeting. And so we have all here that is needed to make another such, if in miniature. Though ceremony, likewise, shall be lacking. Not in song but in silence, shall the last royal banner-carrier of the Old Weald ride at her beloved lord's side." His side glance at Fara was blackly ironic.

Her gritted teeth shifted for speech, but Wencel raised a hand; his lips moved in an unvoiced Voice. This time, Ingrey could feel it when the geas wrapped itself around Fara like a gag, held knotted by her own fear and anger. Her lips moved, closed, pressed tight; but her eyes burned.

"To what purpose?" whispered Ingrey. *For he does not tutor us for no reason, of that I am certain.* Horseriver had been instructing him for days, he realized in retrospect.

Wencel crouched, hesitated, pushed himself up with a pained grunt. He turned his head and spat a gobbet of blood into the gloom. The iron tang smote Ingrey's nostrils. The earl stared into the gathering twilight where the grooms had finished with the horses and were diffidently approaching. "We must have a fire. And food, I suppose. I hope they brought enough. Purpose? You'll see soon enough."

"Should I expect to survive it?" Ingrey glanced at Fara. *Either of us?*

Wencel's lips curved, briefly. "You may." He walked off into the resin-scented shadows.

Ingrey wasn't sure if that last was meant as prediction or permission.

❧

Ingrey was awakened in the dark before dawn by Horseriver himself, tossing wood on the fire to build it up to a bright flare. They had all slept in yesterday's riding clothes, and the grooms, it seemed, were to be left to break camp and ride the spent horses home. So there was little for Ingrey or Fara to do to prepare beyond sitting up, pulling on their boots, and eating the stale bread, cheese, and blessedly hot drinks shoved into their hands.

The cobby horses were lightly burdened also, Ingrey noticed. Food for a day was packed into the saddlebags, including measures of grain for the mounts, but most of the spare clothing and amenities, largely for Fara, were stripped out; neither were the bedrolls or other camping gear added. The implication of these lacks disturbed Ingrey, an unease he did not confide to the voiceless princess.

Through the night fog that had risen from the forest, creating a dripping hush, gray light began to filter. Fara shivered in the cold and damp as Ingrey boosted her aboard her horse, a sturdy little black with a hogged mane and white socks. Horseriver disposed his banner pole rather awkwardly along his horse's off side, tied beneath the stirrup flap to ride under his leg. He mounted and motioned them forward with a wave of his arm: as he had promised, in silence. Ingrey glanced back at the grooms. The elder stood at attention, looking worried; the younger was already climbing back into an abandoned bedroll to steal some extra warmth and sleep.

Horseriver led them up into a gap in the hills, first on a trail, then on a path, then on deer paths. Ingrey, bringing up the rear, ducked swinging branches. Gray twigs scraped on his leathers like clawing fingernails as the way narrowed. The horses' hooves crunched through the fallen leaves, and slid, sometimes, on last year's black rot beneath the drifts, sending up a musty dank smell.

The brightening day drew up the soft curtain of mist, and the boles of the beeches stood out in sharp relief at last, as though the fog had clotted into firm gray bark. Then, beneath the pale blue bowl of sky, it grew hot. Biting black flies found the riders and their mounts, so that to the heave and plunge of the horses over the uneven terrain was added the occasional squeal and buck as the insects tormented them. When Horseriver led them into a ravine that ended in a cleft, with no way out but back the way they'd climbed in, Ingrey grew aware that however well Horseriver had known this land once, it had changed even beyond his recognition. *How long . . . ?* They backtracked and scrambled up an opposite ridge instead.

Horseriver pushed on slowly but relentlessly. Hours into the trek, with the sun high overhead, they stopped at a clear spring to feed, water, and rest the horses and themselves. Yellow leaves fluttered down in the filtered light like breaking promises to clutter the glassy surface of the pool. Not all the leaves had fallen yet, and the view around the site was still half-obscured; Horseriver climbed up to a higher point and stared out for a time. Whatever he saw apparently satisfied him, for he returned and commanded them aboard their horses once more.

We are in Ijada's country, Ingrey realized. He was not sure at what point they had crossed into her dower gift: possibly as far back as the campsite. The scene took on a sudden new interest, and he was almost prepared to forgive even the black flies. *Broad lands* did not precisely convey their mood, though if they could be rolled out flat, Ingrey thought, they would equal a small earldom. Instead they were crimped into something difficult, stony, and wild; beauty that arrested rather than soothed. *Yes, that is Ijada.*

He felt in his mind for her absence, like a tongue probing

the wounded socket of a drawn tooth. All he could find was the hot infection of Horseriver. *Alone together,* this taciturn royal procession of three seemed to him. *Godsforsaken.*

The sun was sinking toward the western horizon when they clambered up through another gap, angled left, and came out upon a sudden promontory. They pulled up their horses and stared.

Two steep-sided, undulating ridges embraced a valley about two miles wide and four miles long, then curved around again to enclose the far end like a wall. The valley floor was as flat as the surface of a lake. On the near end, beneath their feet, lay a stretch of dun grasses and yellowing reeds, a half-dried marsh. Beyond it, a few twisted oak trees stood out like sentinels, then a dark and dense oak wood crouched. Even with half the leaves down, backlit by the setting sun, its shadows were impenetrable to Ingrey's eye. His head jerked back at the miasma of woe that seemed, even from here, to arise from the trees.

He drew in his breath in sharp dismay, then tore his gaze away to find Horseriver looking at him.

"Feel it, do you?" the earl inquired, as if lightly.

"Aye." *What? What do I feel?* If Ingrey had possessed a back ridge, all the fur along it would be rising in a ragged line right now, he thought.

Horseriver dismounted and untied his banner pole from under his saddle flap. He stared briefly and without pleasure at his wife for a moment; Fara stared back wide-eyed, her shoulders bowing in, then dropped her gaze and shuddered. Horseriver shook his head in something that, had it more heart, would have been disgust, and strolled over and handed the pole to Ingrey.

"Bear this for a time. I don't want it dropped."

Ingrey's left stirrup included the small metal cup of a spear rest. He swung the pole up and seated it, and took up his reins with his right hand. His horse was far too tired by now to give him trouble. Horseriver remounted, swung his animal around, and motioned for them to follow.

They descended from the promontory in a zigzag through a thinning woods. At the bottom, Ingrey was compelled to dismount, hand the banner back to Horseriver, draw his sword, and hack a path for them all through a head-high hedge of brittle brambles that seemed not just thorny, but fanged. A few whipping backlashes pierced even his leathers, and the punctures and scratches bled flying drops as he fought his way in. On the other side, at the edge of the dried marsh, Horseriver dismounted again and unwrapped his banner at last.

The desiccated twine parted with faint puffs of powder as his knife touched it, and the brittle canvas cracked away. A discolored nettle-silk banner unfolded, bearing the device of his house, the running white stallion on a green field above three wavy blue lines; in the fading light, more gray stallion above gray lines on a gray field, disappearing into a fog. This time, he made Fara take it. He murmured words Ingrey could barely hear and still less understand, but Ingrey sensed it when a new, dark current sprang up between the two. The silent—*silenced*—Fara's backbone stiffened as though braced, and her chin came up; only in her eyes did pools of muted terror lurk.

Horseriver handed his mount's reins to Ingrey and took the bridle of Fara's black cob. He led off this time on foot, weaving his way oddly through the tussocks of yellow grasses. Ingrey saw why as they passed deceptive dark patches, sucking bogs lethal to a horse's heavy step. He took care to steer his mount precisely in the earl's wake. The day's warmth lingered in the air despite the dankness rising from the marsh. But then the shadow of the wood, cast long by the setting sun, crept out to meet them; when they passed into it, the sudden biting chill of it turned their exhalations to pale mist.

They approached the outlying oak tree, and the name of Wounded Woods seemed doubly earned to Ingrey. The tree was huge and old, but seemed blighted. The leaves still clinging to its withered branches were not crisp, brown, fluted curls, but limp, blackened, and misshapen. Trunk and branches seemed knotted and twisted far beyond the rule for oaks—wrung like rags—and tumorous burls wept sickly black ooze.

A warrior stepped from the tree. Not from under it, or beside it, or behind it: he stepped from the trunk itself as though passing through a curtain. His boiled leather armor was rotten with age. From the haft of his spear, upon which he leaned as though it was an old man's staff, an unidentifiable scrap of animal fur fluttered. His blond beard was crusted with dried blood, and he still bore the wounds of his death; an ear hacked away, ax gashes splitting the armor, a dismembered hand tied to his belt with a bit of rag. A badger pelt was attached by its skull to his rusty iron cap, peering through sightless dried eyes, and the black-and-white fur dangled down the back of his neck as he turned to slowly scrutinize each of the three before him.

Ingrey grew aware only then that sometime during the passage of the marsh they had stepped from the world he knew into another, where such sights were possible; its congruence with the world of matter filling his fleshly eyes was but a feint. Fara, too, was drawn into this vision; her body remained rigidly upright, her face blank, but from the corners of her eyes a faint gleam of moisture trickled downward. Ingrey decided not to draw Horseriver's attention to this, lest he subtract her tears as well as her voice.

The warrior straightened, and with his handless stump signed the Five, touching forehead, mouth, navel, groin, and heart—though he could not there spread his fingers. "Hallowed lord, you come at last," he said to Horseriver. His voice was a groaning of branches in a bitter wind. "We have waited long."

Horseriver's face could have been a carved wooden mask, but his eyes were like a night without end. "Aye," he breathed.

23

THE SENTINEL LED OFF, LIMPING, USING HIS SPEAR AS A walking stick. Horseriver continued to lead Fara. Her hand clutched the banner pole tightly, and its tremble and her horse's rocking were all that gave the limp flag motion in the breathless twilight. Ingrey's horse snorted and sidled, and the mount he led yanked at its bridle and dug in its heels, eyes rolling. Disliking the feel of both his hands encumbered, by his own horse's reins and by the other's, Ingrey dismounted and let the animals go free. They wheeled and skittered back past the tree, then, too weary to bolt farther, put their heads down and began nibbling the tough marsh grass. Ingrey turned and paced after the hallow king's banner.

As they entered the margins of the woods, more revenants stepped from the trees. They were as tattered as their sentry, or worse; most were decapitated, and carried their heads, sometimes still in helmets, variously: tied to belts by the hair or braids, tucked under their arms, over their shoulders in makeshift carrier bags made of rope or rags. It took Ingrey's disquieted gaze a few moments to wrench from their wounds and begin to take in other details of decoration, weaponry, or garb that told of their kin identities. Or personal identities. *See my things that I have chosen; by them you shall know me,* silently cried belts, loops of necklaces, and furs and skulls and pelt after pelt of the wisdom animals whose strength they'd hoped to inherit. Everywhere, faded stitchery peeked out, on collars, on baldrics, on the hems of cloaks, on embroidered armbands. *My wife made this, my daughter, my sister, my mother. See the intricacy, see the colors intertwined; I was beloved, once.*

A tall soldier, whose head still balanced upon a neck half–cut through and crusted with dark blood, sidled close to Ingrey. He bore a thick wolf pelt over his shoulders, and he stared at Ingrey in as great a wonder as if Ingrey had been a ghost and he a living man. He reached out a hand, and Ingrey first flinched away, but then set his teeth and endured the touch. More than a gust of air, less than flesh, it left a liquid chill in its wake across his skin.

Other wolf-skin-clad warriors clustered about Ingrey, and a woman as well, gray-haired, stout, her torn dress elaborated with twining strips of gray fur, her looping gold armbands tipped with elegant little wolf's heads with garnet eyes. *Some of these could be my own forefathers,* Ingrey realized, and not just on the Wolfcliff side; a dozen other kins' blood ran through his veins from foremothers as well, in a turbulent stream. It had disturbed him to think himself an intruder in a graveyard; it devastated him to suspect the fascination of the ghostly warriors with him was the excitement of grandparents seeing for the first time a child they'd never hoped to look upon. *Five gods help me, help me, help me . . . to do what?*

He blinked in astonishment when the growing parade was joined by half a dozen dark-haired hacked-about men wearing the tabards of Darthacan archers of Audar's day. They swung wide around Horseriver, but crept up to Ingrey's heels. The other revenants did not seem to mind their presence here; equal in death for four centuries, perhaps they had made their own soldier's peace. Audar, Ingrey had heard, had carried out his own dead rather than burying them in this accursed ground, sealed from men and gods, but the battle had been great, and conducted largely in the dark; it was no wonder a few had been missed.

The warriors flowed after the kingly banner like a muster of mourners; a river of sorrow; a whisper of supplication.

The bowl of the valley had turned shadowless with evening, but the sky above was still pale, and the oak branches overhead interlaced against it like crooked black webs. Horseriver seemed to be aiming generally toward the center of the wood, but not in a straight path; it was as though he searched for something. A faintly voiced *Ah* told Ingrey he had found it. The roof of branches thinned and drew back around a long low mound upon which no trees grew. Horseriver halted beside it, pulled Fara down from her wary cob, and helped her step up the bank and plant the banner pole by her boot.

Released, the horse sidled nervously away through the trees, somehow avoiding touching any of the gathering mob of curious revenants. More than curious, Ingrey realized; agitated. His blood seethed in the surf of their excitement. More and more came, crowding up thickly around them, and Ingrey began to feel in his marrow just how many four thousand murdered men were. He tried to count them, then count blocks and multiply, but lost his place and abandoned the attempt. It failed utterly to aid his sweating grip on reason anyway.

Horseriver knelt upon the mound, pushed aside a thin screen of sickly weeds, and ran his fingers through the dark soil. "This was the trench I was buried in," he remarked conversationally to Ingrey. "I and many others. Though I never actually spilled my blood at Holytree. Audar was careful about that. That shall be rectified." He climbed wearily to his feet. "All shall be rectified." He nodded to the ghosts, who stirred uneasily.

At the outer edges of the circle, late arrivals milled about; those few who could, craned their necks. It seemed they spoke to each other; to Ingrey, the voices were blurred and faint, like hearing from underwater men calling or arguing on a shore. Ingrey touched the dirty bandage on his right hand, hardly more than a rag wrapped about to keep knocks from paining the healing wound's tenderness. It wasn't bleeding again, at least. *Yet.*

With difficulty, Ingrey cleared his throat. "Sire, what do we do here?"

Horseriver smiled, faintly. "Finish it, Ingrey. If you hold to your task, and my banner-carrier holds to hers, that is. Finish it."

"Hadn't you better tell us how, then?"

"Yes," sighed Horseriver. "It is time." He glanced skyward. "With neither sun nor moon nor stars to witness, in an hour neither day nor night; what more befitting a moment than this? Long was the preparation, long and difficult, but the doing—ah. The doing is simple and quick." He drew his knife from his belt, the same he'd used to cut the throat of Ijada's mare, and Ingrey tensed. Kingly charisma or no, if Horseriver turned on Fara, Ingrey would have to try to . . . He made to lift his hand to his sword hilt, but found it heavy and unresponsive; his heart began to hammer in panic at the unexpected constraint.

But Horseriver instead pressed the haft into Fara's limp hand, then took the banner pole and ground it deeper into the soil so that it stood upright, if slightly tilted, on its own. "This will best be done kneeling, I think," he mused. "The woman is weak."

He turned again to Ingrey. "Fara"—he nodded to his wife, who stared back with eyes gone wide and black—"will shortly cut my throat for me. Being my banner-carrier, she will hold, for a little moment, my kingship and my soul here. You have until her grip fails, no more, to cleanse my spirit horse from me. If you do not succeed, you will have the full, but not unique, experience of becoming my heir. What will happen then, not even I can predict, but I am fairly certain it will be nothing good. And it will go on *forever*. So do not fail, my royal shaman."

Ingrey's pulse throbbed in his ears, and his stomach knotted. "I thought you could not die. You said the spell held you in the world."

"Follow it around, Ingrey. The trees, and all the living web of Holytree, are bound to the souls of my warriors, and support them in the world of matter. These"—he gestured broadly at the clustering revenants—"create my hallow kingship that binds them to me. My spirit horse"—he touched his breast—"my power as a shaman, binds the trees to the men. I told you that the hallow king was the hub of the spell for invincibility, I do remember that. Cut the link at any point, and the circle unwinds. This is the link you can reach."

And you cannot? No . . . he could not. Horseriver was bound up in his own spell, like a key locked inside its box. "That's what this has all been about, then? An elaborate suicide?" said Ingrey indignantly. He struggled once more to move, to jerk his physical body into motion, but achieved only a shudder.

"I suppose you could call it that."

"How many people did you actually kill to arrange this?" *As carelessly as you set me on Ijada?*

"Not as many as you'd think. They do die on their own." Horseriver's lips twisted. "And to say I would rather die than to have all this to do over again both sums and fails even to touch the truth."

Ingrey's mind lurched. "This will break the spell."

"It's all of a piece. Yes."

"What will happen to these, then?" Ingrey waved about at the crowding ghosts. "Will they go to the gods as well?"

"Gods, Ingrey? There are no gods here."

It is true, Ingrey realized. Was that part of what disturbed him so deeply about this ground? The interlocking boundaries of the spell, the will of this unholy hallow king, excluded Them. Had done so for centuries, it appeared. Horseriver's war with the gods had been in stalemate for that long, while his host had slowly become instead his hostages.

Horseriver pressed Fara to her knees and knelt in front of her, facing away. He pulled her knife hand round over his right shoulder and briefly kissed the white knuckles. A flash of memory washed over Ingrey, of his wolf licking his ear before he'd cut its throat.

The unmaking of this twisted spell, the long-delayed cleansing of Bloodfield, seemed no intrinsic sin, apart from Wencel's self-murder. Yet five gods had opposed this, and Ingrey could not see why. *Not till now.*

Once broken free from the misfortunes of the world of matter, the divines said, souls longed for their gods like lovers, save for those who turned their faces aside and chose slow solitary dissolution. And the gods longed back. But this was no mutual suicide pact between Horseriver and his spirit warriors. Even as his fortress fell, he meant to slay his immortal hostages along with him: eternal revenge, a death beyond death and a denial absolute.

"You will be sundered? Wait—you will *all* be sundered?"

"You ask too many questions."

Not enough. A very late one came to Ingrey then. Ijada, she had said, had given half her heart to these revenants. They held it still, somewhere here, somehow. What would happen to whatever piece of her soul she had pledged when these lost warriors went up in smoke? Could a woman live with half a heart? "Wait," said Ingrey, then, reaching deeper, *"wait!"*

A ripple ran through the revenants as if they swayed in an earth shock, and Fara looked up, gasping.

"And you *argue* too much," Horseriver added, and drew Fara's knife hand hard around his throat.

Blood spurted for three heartbeats while Horseriver stared ahead, his expression composed. Then his lips parted in relief, and he slumped forward out of Fara's grasp. She clutched the banner pole to keep from falling atop him, her lips moving in a soundless cry.

The world of magic peeled away from the world of matter then, ripping apart the congruence, and Ingrey found his vision doubled as it had been in Red Dike. Wencel's body lay facedown upon the mound, and Fara bent over it, half-fainting, the bloody knife fallen from her grasp. But upon the mound there arose . . .

A black stallion, black as pitch, as soot, as a moonless night in a storm. Its nostrils flared red, and orange sparks trailed from its mane and tail as it shifted. It pawed the mound, once, and a ring of fire shimmered out around its hoofprint, then faded. Upon its back a man-shaped shadow rode astride, and the figure's legs curved down into the horse's ribs and united with them.

This brutal, ancient power was not at all like Boleso's thin, miserable menagerie. *I don't know what to do with this, and I have no god on my side in this place.* Frenzy reverberated in Ingrey's belly. His beginning howl of terror transmuted in the voicing of it into a bellow of challenge. He leapt away from his frozen body, landing astonished on all four paws, heavy claws ripping up the dirt in clots. Completing a transformation he had only been half-able to effect, to mere man-wolf mixture, the time before.

The stallion snorted. Ingrey pulled back his black-edged lips along his long jaws, bared his sharp teeth, and snarled back. His tongue lolled out to taste a rank sizzle in the air, like burning rotted hair, and saliva spattered from his jaws as he shook the toxic tang from his mouth.

The stallion stepped off the mound and circled him, tracking little flames.

If I lose this fight, what returns to my body will not be me. It would be Horseriver re-formed. With such a prize, no wonder Wencel had not bothered to bespell him further in his cause. Ingrey was battling for more than his life.

So.

He circled the stallion in turn, head lowered, neck ruff rising, the earth cool and damp under his pads. Fallen leaves crackled like real leaves, and the sharpness of their musty scent amazed his nose. The stallion swirled, its hind legs lashing out.

Ingrey ducked, too late; one hoof connected with a heavy *thunk* to his furry side, and he rolled away, yelping. How could an illusion not be able to *breathe*? He would have to pay as implacable an attention as in any sword fight, but now he had to watch four weapons, not just one. *How do you kill a horse with your teeth?* He tried to remember dogfights he had witnessed, boar-baitings, the climaxes of hunts.

Any way you can.

He gathered himself on his haunches and launched himself at the horse's belly, twisting his open jaws at an awkward angle. He scored the skinless surface in a long slash, and barely made it away from a retaliating stamping. The—not blood—uncanny ichor, ink-black fluid, burned his mouth as the red snakes had, before. Worse. His jaws foamed madly in pained response.

The ghosts crowded around in a ring for all the world as though they *were* watching a boar-baiting. Which beast were they betting on, whom did they cheer? Not their lives but their souls had been wagered, and not by them. That Horseriver rode himself to oblivion, to sundering from the gods, was regrettable, but not even the gods could override a person's will in that matter. That his will overrode all these other wills seemed a blacker sin. *Ijada would surely weep,* Ingrey thought bleakly as he dodged the stallion's snapping teeth, swung round at the end of a suddenly snaky neck, ears back flat. And, *Five weapons. I have to watch five weapons.*

This is going badly. He was too small; the stallion was too large. Real wolves hunted prey this size in packs, not alone. *Where can I get more me?* Nothing of spirit could exist in the world of matter without . . . He eyed his standing human self, shivering mindlessly on his feet at the edge of the clearing. *Dolt. Dupe. Useless son.* All or nothing, then. All.

He pulled strength from his body, all he could. The emptied form swayed and collapsed onto a drift of leaves. Everything in the clearing slowed, and Ingrey's already-searing perceptions came ablaze. His wolf-body felt at once both dense as the past and weightless as the future. *Yes. I know this state. I have traveled this path before.*

He was, abruptly, half the size of the horse, and it shied back. But slowly, so slowly, as though it swam in oil. His mind sketched his strike at his leisure, measuring the arc of his leap. This looted strength could not last. *No time. Now.*

He plunged forward and sank his teeth into the horse's neck, shaking his head wildly. He could not flip it back and forth as a dog shook a rabbit, but it went down under his twisting weight, and something snapped and something spurted. Around them, the ghosts dodged back as though to avoid a splash from some tainted puddle.

The thing in his jaws stilled. Then melted away and ran down his lips like a bite from an icicle in winter. He spat and backed up. Horse-shape became shapeless, a mound, a puddle, a blackness soaking into the ground like a spilled barrel of ink. Gone.

Wencel stood up, freed from his dark mount. On two bowed legs. His shape was restored to humanity, but his face . . .

"I'm glad I didn't use that stag," he remarked from one of his mouths. "It would not have had the strength for this." Another mouth grinned. "Good dog, Ingrey."

Ingrey backed away, growling. Across Horseriver's skull, faces rippled, rising and sinking like corpses in a river. One succeeded another haphazardly, all the Earls Horseriver for four centuries and more. Young men, old men, angry men, sad; shaven, bearded, scarred. Mad. Young Wencel passed like a bewildered waif, his dumb gaze alighting on Ingrey in recognition and plea, though plea for what, Ingrey could not tell.

The body was worse. Cuts, scars, dreadful gaping wounds rose and fell from the surface of the skin, every death wound Horseriver had ever received. The burns were the most frightening, wide patches of red and weeping blisters, cooked and charred flesh. The stink of them wafted across Ingrey's sensitive wolf-nose, and he sneezed and backed away, whimpering for a moment and pawing his muzzle like a dog. This was Horseriver, turned inside out. This was what being Horseriver had been like, behind that smooth ironic mask, the brittle wit, the jerky rage, the apparent indifference. Every hour, every day, sunsets falling like trip-hammers, time without end.

The eyes were worst of all.

Ingrey stalked warily around the edge of the clearing, keeping his distance from the mound and the Horseriver-aggregate, until he came to his own collapsed body. It looked disturbingly more pale and dead than the headless ghosts gathered about looking on. He nosed it, pawed at it, and whined anxiously, but it did not stir. Did he even breathe? He could not tell. In this wolf-state, he realized, he had no voice—and, therefore, no weirding voice. A critical aspect of his powers seemed severed from him. Could he even get back in? *Five gods, what if I can't?*

Had Horseriver planned this? With his wolf and most of his own soul removed, Ingrey's silent husk was empty as an abandoned house, and as available for squatters to move into. If the undoing of his spell went awry, Horseriver might still have a body-heir, and now without the complications that had worried him earlier. Ingrey glanced up at the agonized thing that was Horseriver. No, that was not an end Horseriver desired, but if he indeed found himself with it *all to do over again,* well, he could. And judging by his level silence, watching Ingrey, he knew it. Ingrey shivered and pawed his unresponsive body again.

Hoofbeats and a frightened equine squeal sounded from the woods, and Ingrey whirled around. Could the haunt-horse have reanimated . . . ? No, this was a real horse; he could feel the thudding of its gait through the solid ground as he had not the fiery footfalls of the other. The hoofbeats stopped, shuffled about in the leaf drifts; then lighter footsteps rustled, running flat out.

The ghosts spun aside, opening an aisle, and many lifted their hands in clumsy salutes. And blessings, or troubled supplications; the fivefold sign wandered awkwardly, when forehead and lips were hung at a belt, and the hand moved only aside to navel and groin before rising to the unbeating heart. Wolf-Ingrey's head lifted and he sniffed in wild surmise. *I know that blissful smell, like sunlight in dry grass . . .*

Running through the gap between the ghosts, Ijada appeared. She wore her dark brown riding dress, the jacket sweat-stained, her split skirts splashed with mud, and all of it scored with little rips as though she'd galloped through a thorn hedge. Wisps of dark hair clung to her flushed face. She stopped short, and her gasping became a cry; then she staggered more slowly to where Ingrey's body lay and dropped to her knees beside it, her face draining white.

"No, oh, no . . ." She rolled his body over and gathered his head into her lap, and stared down in dismay at the lifeless features and pale lips. "Too late!"

She cannot see me, wolf-Ingrey realized. *She cannot see any of us.* Except for the very material Fara, still collapsed beside the throat-slashed body of Wencel. Ijada spared the couple a brief, appalled glance, clenching her teeth in distress, then turned back to Ingrey.

"Oh, love . . ." She lifted his face to her own teary one, and pressed her lips to his. Wolf-Ingrey danced around her in frustration, for he could not feel those warm lips or taste that wasted honeyed breath at all. Frantic, he pawed her sleeve, then licked her face.

Her breath drew in sharply, and she lifted her hand to her cheek and stared around. Had she felt some disturbing liquid chill, as he had from the ghost's hand? He licked her ear, and her breath huffed out in what might have been a laugh, under other circumstances; she scrubbed at the ear as though it had been tickled. She laid Ingrey's body out on his back, felt along it—*oh, if I might feel that touch*—and frowned. "Ingrey, what have they done to you . . . ?" His body bore no visible wounds, no crookedness of broken bones, but his rag-wrapped right hand, he saw, was soaked with blood, and his leather jerkin was smeared slippery with it. Ijada's frown deepened as she clutched the gory hand to her breast. *If I might only move those fingers* . . . "Or you to yourself?" she added more shrewdly. "You tried something brave and foolish, didn't you?" Her gaze rose once more to Wencel's corpse and Fara.

Horseriver snorted, and Ingrey spun around, growling. The face of the moment stared across at Ijada with a mixture of astonishment and revulsion. "You *do* keep turning up where you are not wanted, don't you, girl?" he remarked to the air, or perhaps to Ingrey. Ijada, in any case, did not seem to hear him. "Always in ignorance, but does that slow you? Taste the betrayal of the gods, then; I have dined on it for ages."

He turned away and looked across at the gathering of ghosts. "All here now," he breathed. Now the terrible eyes were distant, removed, implacably calmed. "But not for much longer, I swear to you, beloved ones."

The looks the revenants gave him in return were not loving, Ingrey thought, but wary and dismayed. A faint translucence hung about them, and Ingrey realized that they were already starting to fade. The ghost of a man fresh-killed, if he did not go at once to the gods through the gates of his death, might yet be redeemed from sundering during the god-touched rites of his funeral, as Boleso's had been. Up to a point. But the sundering soon grew irrevocable, the soul, in that last refusal, self-doomed to fade. That period of uncertain grace had been prolonged for these, not for days or weeks, but for centuries. With their link to the Wounded Woods now broken, they would not linger long, Ingrey thought. Hours? Minutes?

Ijada started to rise to go to Fara, but then gasped and sank back down. Her hand touched her left breast, then her forehead; her lips moved in surprise, then pinched in pain. Ingrey's whines redoubled.

The mob of ghosts shuffled aside once more, and a great-limbed warrior strode forward. He wore a broad gold belt, and bore a spearhead-tipped banner staff, its furled flag stippled in grass green, white, and blue. His head hung from the gold belt, tied on by its own grayed-yellow braids. The grizzled head's gaze flicked up to Horseriver, who started in surprised recognition, and raised his hand to return a salute that had not, in fact, been given; the gesture faded at the end as Horseriver belatedly realized this. The warrior knelt by Ijada, bending over her in concern, his hand touching her shoulder.

Ingrey danced anxiously around the pair, his wolf's head lowering to the warrior's eye level. The warrior stared across at him in some silent query. Ijada's spine bent, and her grip on Ingrey's bloody hand grew limp; it slipped from her grasp, and her own white hand fell atop it. *"Oh,"* she breathed, her eyes wide and dark. She was growing still more pale, almost greenish; when wolf-Ingrey licked her face now, she did not respond.

Ingrey backed away and looked up. Then rose on his hind limbs, resting one forepaw on the warrior's shoulder for balance, sniffing; the man stiffened to support him. Something was skewered up there on the narrow, willow-leaf-shaped spear point. A beating heart . . . no, half a heart. But its rhythm was slowing.

He bowed low, Ijada had said. *And placed my heart on a stone slab, and cut it in two with the hilt-shard of his broken sword. . . . The other half, they raised high upon a spear-point. I did not understand if it was pledge, or sacrifice, or ransom . . .*

All three, thought Ingrey. *All three.*

He did not know what, on this eerie ground, his actions all meant. But even with his voice muzzled, they were not without power. *He* was not without power. *I brought down Horseriver's horse, and it is gone. Maybe I can do more.* Horseriver plainly thought him spent, his task over, his use used up. Meant to just leave him, perhaps, in this disarray of body and spirit, to die alone upon the ground when the ghosts and all their magic drained away. And in and of himself, lone wolf, he did not think Horseriver was mistaken. *But I am not alone, am I? Not now. She said it, so it must be so. Truthsayer. How was it that I came to love the truth above all things?*

"Shall I die of love, then?" murmured Ijada, sinking onto Ingrey's chest. "I always thought that was a figure of speech. Together, then? No! My Lord of Autumn, in this Your season, help us . . . !"

There are no gods here.

But *Ingrey* was here. *Try something else. Try anything.* Maybe the revenant captain had some power here as well; he carried a banner, after all, Old Weald sacred sign of rescues beyond death and the death of all other hopes. Ingrey whined, danced around the man, scratched at his booted leg with one paw, then crouched and nudged his long nose repeatedly at the scabbard hung on the gold belt on the opposite side from his head. Would the revenant understand his plea? The man swiveled his hips to regard him, his sandy gray brows rising in surprise. He stood and drew the hilt shard. *Yes!* Ingrey nudged the hand some more, and turned to bite at his own side.

The man could not nod, but he half bowed. He knelt, and Ingrey lay down with his paws waving ridiculously in the air, his belly exposed. *If this can save her* . . . The sharp shard entered his chest in a long sweep.

Ijada didn't say this had hurt! Ingrey strangled a yelp and controlled a twisting jerk away. The ghostly hand descended into the gaping gash in his wolf-chest and emerged dripping red. The shard edge sliced across a slippery object in the warrior's palm, and then the warrior tossed something skyward. The bloody fist descended once more, and Ingrey's wolf-self seemed to breathe again as the hand withdrew emptied and the gash closed up in a long red line. Ingrey scrambled upright on his paws once more.

High on the spear tip, a whole heart beat, picking up the pulse.

Ijada inhaled sharply and sat up, blinking around. Her eyes met Ingrey's wolf-gaze, and widened in astonishment and recognition. "There you are!" Her head swiveled, as she took in the mob of agitated ghosts who had crowded up around this strange operation. "There you *all* are! You!" She struggled to her feet and curtseyed to the bannerman, signing the Five. "I was looking for you, my lord marshal, but I could not see."

The ghost bowed back in deep respect. Ijada's hand curled in Ingrey's neck ruff, clutching and stroking the thick fur. He pushed up into the caress. She looked down at him—not very far down, for his big head came nearly to her chest. "How came you to be all apart like this? What is happening here?" Her gaze traveled around the clearing till it caught on the multifaced Horseriver. "Oh." She flinched a little, but then her back straightened. "So that's what you look like, out of the shadow. What are you doing on my land?"

Horseriver had composed himself in an attitude of utter indifference, but this last jerked him into rage. "*Your* land! This is Holytree!"

"I know," said Ijada coolly. "It is my inheritance. For you are finished with it, are you not?"

The form of Horseriver stiffened, and the ironic mouth murmured, "Indeed, we go. Alas that you shall find your enjoyment of your legacy . . . brief." That mouth smiled nastily, and Ingrey growled in response. Ijada's hand tightened in his fur.

"And these?" Ijada glanced up at the gold-belted marshal, and gestured at the gathered revenants.

"I am their last true hallow king. Follow me, they must."

"Into oblivion?" she demanded indignantly. "Shall they die for you twice? What kind of king are you?"

"I owe you nothing. Not even explanation."

"You owe *them* everything!"

He could not, exactly, turn away, with the faces chasing each other around his skull, but he turned his shoulders from her. "It is done. It is long past done."

"It is *not*."

He whipped back, and snarled, "They will follow me down to darkness, and the gods who denied us will be denied in turn. Oblivion and revenge. They have made me, and you cannot unmake me."

"*I* cannot . . ." She hesitated, and gestured at the banner pole upon which the marshal-warrior now leaned, listening. Raising her face, she pointed to the mound where Wencel's body lay huddled and Fara knelt silent and staring. "You died, I think. Death lays a kingship down, along with all else a life accumulates in the world of matter. We go to the gods naked and equal, as in any other birth, but for our souls and what we've made of them. Then the kin meeting makes the king again." She stared around at the ghosts, challengingly. "Do you not?"

An odd rustle ran through the revenants. The marshal-warrior was watching with a most peculiar expression on his face, an amalgam of sorrow and unholy joy. It dawned on Ingrey then that this man must have been the very first Horseriver hallow king's royal banner-carrier, who had died by his lord's side at Bloodfield. His body was doubtless buried in this same pit, for Horseriver had said his banner had been broken and thrown in atop him. And this warrior would never have given it up alive. The royal bannerman should have received the hallow kingship in trust, to carry as steward to the next kin meeting, to be surrendered in turn to the new king—but for the great, disrupted spell, that had carried it instead into this far, unfriendly future.

"You died," insisted Ijada. "This is an Old Weald kin meeting, the last of all time. *They* can make another king, one who will not betray them beyond death."

Horseriver snorted. "There is no other."

The rustle grew, racing around the mob like fire, then back to the beginning. The marshal-warrior stood up straight, then saluted Ijada with that eccentric looping sign of the Five. The ghostly lips turned up in a smile. He let his banner pole fall out of his hand; Ijada's hand caught it and gripped it tight.

Wait, thought Ingrey, *we living ones cannot touch these ghostly things, they run through our fingers like water . . .*

Ijada grasped the pole with both hands and gave it a great yank. Above her head, the banner unfurled and snapped out in no breeze. The wolf's head badge of the Wolfcliffs snarled upon it, black on red.

Ingrey blinked up through his human eyes and wrenched to his feet, stunned. He was back in his body again, and it felt *astounding*. He inhaled. His wolf was gone . . . *No*. He clutched his heart. *It's right here.* Howling joyously through his veins. And something more . . . A line ran between him and Horseriver: the current between Ingrey and Ijada that Horseriver had made, broken, and bound again to his kingship. Tension seemed to reverberate back and forth along that line now, its power ascending. The pull between them was massive, straining.

Horseriver reached down and yanked Fara to her feet, and clasped her hands around his banner pole. *"Hold!"* She stared at him in terror and gripped as though her life depended on it. Grounded upon that mound of death and woe, the strength of the old kingship was vast.

Ingrey moistened his lips, cleared his throat. Found his weirding Voice. *"What do you have to say, Fara?"*

He could *feel* Horseriver's geas of silence fly away from around her face like a spring of metal released, spinning away in the air. Fara took a huge breath.

Horseriver turned to her, and Wencel's face rose fully to the surface for the first time. One hand reached out toward her. "Fara . . . ?" that young voice quavered. "My wife . . . ?"

Fara jerked as if shot with a crossbow bolt. Her eyes closed in pain. Opened. Glanced at Ijada, at Ingrey. At the ghastly revenant before her. "I tried to be your wife," she whispered. "You *never* tried to be my husband."

And she lowered the tip of the banner pole to the ground, the gray rag falling in a silky puddle, put her foot upon the dry wood, and snapped it in half.

24

HORSERIVER FELL BACK A PACE. HALF HIS FACES SEEMED contorted in rage. Others registered ironic resignation, disgust and self-disgust, and one sad visage an ageless, dignified endurance. His hands dropped to his sides, and the current between him and Ingrey faded away like sparks burning out in the dark. The unspeakably agonized eyes stared across at Ingrey, and almost all of his expressions melted into a bitter pity.

Ingrey found himself clinging to Ijada's banner pole lest he fall down. The immense flaring pressure of Horseriver's kingship was not *gone,* exactly, but it seemed to become dispersed, as if pouring in from all sides and not just from the one quarter. And then there came a moment of stillness, hushed hesitation, and the inward flow of the kingly current seemed to turn, becoming an outward urgency. And with that came a diffuse dread unlike any other he had experienced in these long hours filled with fierce shocks.

"You shall find," breathed Horseriver, "that a hallow kingship looks different from the inside. And my revenge shall be redoubled thereby. And oblivion . . . shall still be mine." His voice faded away in a sigh.

Though Horseriver did not move from his burial mound, he grew distanced, silenced at last, like a corpse seen underwater. Stripped of both his yoked powers—his great horse and his hallow kingship—he was reduced to one revenant among the many, except for his dire multiplicity, an extra denseness that lingered about him. *Yes,* thought Ingrey, *he, too, is a ghost of Bloodfield, who died on this sacred and accursed ground; he is no longer more, but he cannot become less.*

But what have I become?

He could feel the mystical kingship settle into place upon him, in him, through him. It did not make him feel as though he'd been stuffed with pride and power, replete and overflowing. It made him feel as though all his blood was being drawn out of him.

Ijada and Fara both, he realized, were staring at him with that same openmouthed awe tinged with physical desire that Horseriver had inspired. Such stares ought to make any man preen, surely. Instead, he felt as though they contemplated eating him alive.

No, not Ijada and Fara—*well, yes, them, too*—it was the ghosts that alarmed him now. They crowded up closer as if fascinated, reaching for him, touching him in chill liquid strokes that stole the warmth from his skin. They were growing unruly in their urgency, shouldering past and even climbing over one another, thicker and thicker about him. *Famished beggars.*

Nothing of spirit can exist in the world of matter without a being of matter to support it. The old catechism rang through his spinning head. Four thousand still-accursed spirits swarmed upon the ground of Bloodfield, upon it but no longer sustained by it. Instead, they were all now connected to . . .

Him.

"Ijada . . ." His voice came out a wail. "I cannot maintain them all, I cannot hold!"

He was growing colder and colder as the ghosts pawed

him. He grabbed for Ijada's outstretched hand like a drowning man, and for a moment live warmth, her warmth, flooded him. But she gasped as she, too, felt the unholy pull of the ghosts' insatiable hunger. *They will pull us both to shreds, drain us dry.* And when there was no more warmth left to give, his and Ijada's frozen corpses would be left upon the ground, fog steaming off them in the night air. And all trapped here would dwindle to oblivion in a last, starveling cry of abandonment, betrayal, and despair.

"Ijada . . . ! Let go!" He tried to draw his hand back from hers.

"No!" She gripped him tighter.

"You must let go! Take Fara and run, out of here, back through the marsh, quickly! The revenants will consume us both if you do not!"

"No, Ingrey! That's not what is meant! You must cleanse them as you cleansed Boleso, so that they may go to the gods! You *can,* that's what you were *made* for, I swear it!"

"I cannot! There are too many, I cannot hold, and *there are no gods here!*"

"They wait at the gate!"

"What?"

"They wait at the gate of thorns! For the master of the realm to admit them. Audar cursed and sealed this ground, and Horseriver held it against the gods ever after in his rage and black despair, but the old kings are gone, and the new king is acclaimed."

"I am only a king of ghosts and shadows, a king of the dead." *Soon to join my subjects.*

"Open your realm to the Five. Five mortals will bear Them across the ground, but you must admit Them—invite Them in." Shivering now almost as badly as he was, she eyed the thronging ghosts, and her voice went quavering up: "Ingrrreyyy, hurry!"

Terrified nearly to incoherence, he extended his senses. Yes, he could feel the boundaries of his blighted realm around him in the dark, an irregular circle encompassing most of the valley floor, saturated with all the ancient woe of this place. It extended past the marsh, all the way to the wall of brambles. Only now did he become aware that his first act as the last living shaman of the Old Weald this night had passed without his own notice, when he had taken his sword and hacked his way—*all of our ways*—through the towering thorns, breaking the boundaries of Bloodfield.

Outside the gate he'd made, a multiple *Presence* waited, impatiently as supplicants on a king's feast day. How did one admit Them? It seemed to call for hymns and hosannas, chants and invocations of great beauty and complexity, poets and musicians and scholars and soldiers and divines. *Instead, They must make do with me.* So be it.

"Come in," Ingrey whispered, his voice cracking, and then, *I can do better than that,* "*Come in!*"

The reverberation seemed to split the night in half, and a shiver of anticipation ran through the four thousand like a great wave crashing upon a disintegrating shore. Ingrey set himself again to endure, for all that he felt his strength pouring out in a cataract. The ghostly jostling settled, no less starveling, but with its desperation stemmed by astonished new hope.

It seemed forever before a human sound penetrated the dark woods, and a faint orange light drew near. A crackle and crash of brush; a thump and a muttered oath; some rolling argument cut short by Learned Hallana's crisp cry: "There, over there! Oswin, go left!"

What was to Ingrey's eye the most unexpected cavalcade imaginable blundered into the clearing. Learned Oswin rode a stumbling horse, with his wife riding pillion, clutching him around the waist with one arm and waving directions with the other. Prince Biast, a staggered look upon his face as he gawked at the milling ghosts, rode behind on another worn horse, and Learned Lewko and Prince Jokol brought up the rear on foot, Jokol holding a torch aloft. Lewko's once-white robes were mired to the thigh on one side, and all were sweat-stained, disheveled, and peppered with road dirt.

"Hallana!" Ijada waved thankfully, as if all was now well. "Come over here, quickly!"

"You were expecting *them*?" Ingrey asked her.

"We all came together, pell-mell down the road for the past two days. Five gods, what a journey. The prince-marshal commanded everything. I galloped ahead at the last—my heart was calling me to hasten, and I was desperately afraid."

Learned Lewko limped up to Ingrey and signed a hasty blessing. Jokol trod behind with the sort of breathless, maniacal grin upon his face that Ingrey imagined he'd have worn while facing a storm at sea, his boat climbing mountainous waves while all the sane men clung to the ropes and screamed.

"Ho! Ingorry!" he cried happily, saluting ghostly warriors right and left as though they were long-lost cousins. "This night will make some song!"

"Are you the mortal vessels for the gods, then?" Ingrey asked Lewko. "Are you all made saints?"

"I have been a saint," wheezed Lewko, "and it isn't this. If I had to guess . . ." His glare around the densely haunted clearing ended on a narrow-eyed look at Ingrey.

Oswin and Hallana abandoned their blown mount and came up, clutching each other by the arm over the uneven ground, staring at the ghostly warriors in wonder tinged with trepidation and, Ingrey would swear, a blazing scholarly curiosity not far removed, in its own way, from Jokol's appalling enthusiasm.

"If I had to guess, Oswin," Lewko continued to his colleague—Ingrey sensed the tail of a hot debate—"*I* think we are all made sacred funeral animals."

Oswin looked at first faintly offended, then thoughtful. Hallana *giggled*. The sound was overwrought but queerly joyous.

"Ingrey must cleanse my ghosts," Ijada said firmly. "I *told* you it would be so."

Two days of debate, Ingrey guessed, but in a company, however odd, fearsomely well equipped for it. *The gods have no hands in this world but ours.* Hand to hand to hand . . .

Biast spied his sister, now sitting slumped on the long mound not far from Wencel's body, and hurried to her, going to his knees and gathering her in his arms. Their heads bent together; they spoke hastily in low tones. He held her as she shuddered. She did not, yet, weep.

"Ijada," murmured Ingrey, "I don't think we had best delay, if this is to work." He looked around at the revenants, who had stopped milling and jostling and now stared back at him in yearning silence. *As if I were their last hope of heaven.* "How do I . . . what do I . . ." *What do I do?*

She grasped the wolf's head standard in both hands and set her shoulders. "You're the shaman-king. Do what seems right to you, and it will be." Beside her, the gold-belted marshal made a gesture of assent.

Four thousand, so many! *It matters less where I begin, as that I begin.*

Ingrey turned slowly around and caught sight of the tall warrior with the wolf cloak he'd seen earlier. He motioned the revenant forward and stared into his pale features. The ghost smiled and nodded kindly, as if to reassure him, fell to one knee before Ingrey, captured his left hand, and bowed his head. Fascinated, Ingrey extended his right index finger, down which a trickle of blood flowed from the soaked rag wrapping his reopened wound, and smeared a drop across the warrior's forehead. It disturbed Ingrey more than a little that the ghost felt solid to him now, not liquid as before, and he wondered what it bespoke of his own changed state.

"Come," Ingrey whispered, and the warrior's spirit wolf, so ancient and worn as to be hardly more than a dark smear, passed out through his fingers. The warrior rose and lifted his face to the watching divines, then extended his hand

toward Learned Oswin in a gesture half greeting, half plea. Oswin, with an anxious side glance at Hallana, who nodded vigorously at him, held out his hand to grasp the revenant's. The wolf warrior clasped it, smiled beatifically, and melted away.

"Oh," said Oswin, and his voice shook, tears starting in his eyes. "Oh, Hallana, I did not know . . ."

"Shh," she said. "It will be very well now, I think." She moistened her lips and gazed at Ingrey as though he were a cross between some famous work of Temple art she'd traveled days to see, and her favorite child.

Ingrey glanced around again, his eyes crammed with choices, and motioned another warrior to him. The man knelt and awkwardly, hopefully, presented his head held up between his two hands. Ingrey repeated the crimson unction upon the forehead, for whatever this last libation from the world of matter was worth, and released a dark hawk-spirit to fly into the night and vanish. The warrior reached for Oswin again, and this time Ingrey could see, just before he melted away, that the man was made whole. *The Father speed you on your journey, then.*

A woman revenant came forward, young-looking, carrying a banner that unfolded to display the ancient spitting-cat sigil of the Lynxlakes, a kin that had dwindled to extinction in the male line two centuries past. When Ingrey took her hand, he was startled to feel two other tattered souls clinging to her through her banner. Her lynx was sad and shabby, and the other two creatures so ragged as to be unidentifiable, in passing away. He signed her forehead in three parallel carmine strokes, which seemed to suffice, for she rose and strode to Jokol, who brightened and stood very straight, taking her hand to kiss it and murmuring something in her ear before she vanished. Ingrey swore he heard a faint low laugh, suddenly merry, linger for a moment in the air behind her. *Jokol for the Daughter, aye. The Lady of Spring gives notoriously abundant blessings.*

The next was a thin old man who went to Lewko, who

stood looking very reflective as the revenant passed through. *Lewko for the Bastard, naturally.*

"Prince Biast," called Ingrey softly. "I'm afraid I need you here." *Biast for the Son. Of course.*

"I suspect I will be least used, this night," murmured Hallana. She cast a shrewd glance toward the mound. "I will sit with poor Fara till you need me. I would guess she's had a time of it."

"Thank you, Learned, yes," said Ingrey. "She was treated most miserably from first to last. But in the end she remembered she was a princess."

Biast came forward to Ingrey's side, studying him warily. The entranced expression upon his face when he looked at Ingrey was laced with a thread of defiance. In an attempt at irony that faltered, he murmured, "Should I call you *sire,* here?"

"You need not call me anything, so long as you turn your hand to the task. Will Fara be all right?" Ingrey nodded across the clearing to where the princess sat huddled, watching grimly, as Hallana lowered herself beside her.

"I offered to take her to where Symark and the divines' servants wait, but she refused. She says she wants to bear witness."

"She has earned that." And it would make her the one person besides Ingrey who had seen all of Horseriver's actions from her father's death to . . . whatever the end of this night brought. If he survived, that could be important. *And if I don't survive, it could be even more important.*

"The most here will be yours, I suspect," Ingrey told Biast. "The old kings had two tasks: to lead their men to battle and to lead them home again. Horseriver lost sight of the second, I think, in his black madness and despair. These warriors of the Old Weald—their duty to their king is done; there remains only their king's duty to them. It's going to be"—Ingrey sighed—"a long night."

Biast swallowed, and nodded shortly. "Go on."

Ingrey looked around at the apprehensive revenants,

pressing close again, and raised his voice, though he was not sure he needed to; within the bounds of Bloodfield, his voice carried. "Fear no stinting, kinsmen! I will not end my watch till your long watch is done."

A blond-bearded young man knelt, first of a long string of such youths, many desperately mutilated. Ingrey released creature after creature: boar and bear, horse and wolf, stag and lynx, hawk and badger. Biast studied each man, as they passed through his hands, as though looking in some disquieting mirror.

It had taken a cadre of Audar's troops two days to slay all these here; Ingrey did not see how he was to release them all in a night, but something odd seemed to be happening to time in this woods. He was not sure if it was a variant upon what happened to his flow of perception in his battle madness—a shaman skill—or if the gods had lent some element of Their god-time, by which They attended to all souls in the world both simultaneously and equally. Ingrey only knew that each warrior was owed a moment at least of his hallow king's full regard; and if the debt had not been Ingrey's to contract, it had still fallen to him to pay. *Heir indeed.*

Then he wondered which he would come to the end of first, his warriors or himself. Perhaps they would end together, in perfect balance.

The Darthacan archers came forward midway through the night. Ingrey puzzled mightily over them, for they bore no spirit beasts for him to release. In what backwash of the uncanny their souls had been caught up, by what concatenation of disrupted magic, god-gift, night battle and bloody sacrifice they had been imprisoned here, he could not imagine. He signed them in his blood all the same, they thanked him with their eyes all the same, and he handed them off to their waiting gods, all the same.

The Wolfcliff woman with the gold wolf's head arm rings gave him a kiss upon the brow in return for his blessing of blood, then, apparently in a moment of pure self-indulgence, a kiss upon the lips, before she turned to Hallana. His lips stiffened with the chill of her mouth, but her lips warmed to a faint color, like a memory of happiness, so he thought it a fair trade.

It was in the dark before dawn, the stars and the waning half-moon shuttered behind deep clouds, when he came to the bitter end of his task. Some two dozen or so ghosts hung back, turning their wan faces from the gods.

Ingrey turned to Oswin. "Learned, what shall I do with these?" He gestured to the revenants: unable to flee him, unwilling to come to him.

Oswin took a deep breath and said reluctantly, as if reciting an old lesson, "Heaven weeps, but free will is sacred. The meaning of yes is created by the ability to say no. As a forced marriage is no marriage, but instead the crime of rape. The gods either will not or cannot rape our souls; in any case, They do not. To my knowledge," the meticulous scholar in him added.

These, too, died at Bloodfield; my duty to them does not change. All the same. Ingrey unlocked his voice and ordered each dark despairing revenant forward, and gave them their little gift of blood, and freed their spirit beasts. And let them go. Most unraveled, fading into utter nothingness, before they even reached the trees.

Two left now: the marshal-warrior, who had stood all night with Ijada and the royal Wolfcliff banner; and the being beside whom—for whom—he had once died at Bloodfield. It took most of Ingrey's remaining strength to compel Horseriver forward to face him; they both ended on their knees.

This one is not the same. Horseriver's spirit horse was gone, his kingship rescinded, but the concatenation of souls remained, generations of Horserivers still churning through his anguished form. Tentatively, Ingrey reached for the shreds of Wencel in the mass, and whispered, *"Come."* And, louder, *"Come!"* A shudder ran through the being in front of him, but no individual soul peeled out. Ingrey wondered if he'd made a tactical mistake; if he had attempted Horseriver first, before he'd been exhausted by this night, could he have taken apart what Horseriver's long curse had welded together? Or was this simply not within his earthly powers? He was almost certain it was not. Almost.

Some of Horseriver's faces, rising to the surface of that dreadful skull, looked longingly toward the gates of the gods, the five ill-assorted persons who now leaned on each other in a fatigue that nearly matched Ingrey's. Others looked away, with all of Horseriver's bitterness and rage and endless agony in their devastating eyes.

"What is your whole desire?" Ingrey asked it. "Lost centuries are not within my gift. The revenge of sundering these other souls from the gods I have denied you, for that was not the right of your hallow kingship, but its betrayal. What then is left? I would give you mercy if you would take it." *The gods would give you rivers of it.*

"Mercy," whispered some of the voices of Horseriver, looking to the gates, and "Mercy," whispered the rest, looking away. One word, encompassing opposite and exclusive boons. Could Ingrey, by any physical or magical strength, wrestle this divided being to any altar? Should he try?

Time had lingered for Ingrey this night, but time was running out. If dawn came without a decision, what would happen? And if he waited for dawn to carry the choice away from him, was that not itself the same decision? If Ingrey fell into his judgment out of sheer weariness, well, he would not be the first man or king to do so. He had thought leading men into battle against impossible odds to be the most fearsome task of a king, but this new impossibility enlightened him vastly. He stared at Horseriver and thought, *He must have been a great-souled man, once, for the gods to desire him still, here in his uttermost ruin.*

He looked around at the witnesses: three Temple divines, two princes, a princess, and the two royal banner-carriers, the quick and the dead. Biast's earlier little flash of princely jealousy was entirely drained from his face now. Not even he wanted the hallow kingship in this moment. The marshal-warrior's watching face was without expression.

Ingrey squeezed his aching right hand till the blood ran down his fingers, and dribbled a thick line all around the tortured revenant's head. And drew a long inhalation of the foggy night air, and breathed out, "Mercy." And let Horseriver go.

Slowly, like thick smoke rising up from a pyre, Horseriver dissipated, until soul-haze could not be told from the hanging fog. The marshal-warrior's dead eyes closed, for a moment, as if it would spare him the knowledge with the sight. Of all here, he was the only one Ingrey was sure understood the choice. All the choices. The clearing was very silent.

Ingrey tried to stand up, failed, and tried again. He stood a moment with his hands on his knees, dizzy and faint. He did not think he had lost enough blood this night to kill him, but the amount strewn about on the ground and down his leathers was impressive nonetheless. *It always looks like more when it's spread around like that.* Finally, he straightened his back and looked at the last revenant, and at Ijada, still holding up the wolf's head standard. High upon its steel point, a shadow-heart still pulsed.

He bowed to the marshal-warrior. "I would ask one gift of you in return, my lord bannerman. One moment more of your time."

The marshal-warrior opened a hand in curious permission. *All my time now is your gift, sire,* his eyes seemed to say.

Ingrey stepped forward and closed his hand around Ijada's shoulder; she smiled wearily at him, her face pale and dirt-streaked and luminous. Ingrey looked over the five of the sacred band. *Yes . . .* "Learned Oswin, Learned Hallana, would you come here a moment?"

They glanced at each other and trod near. "Yes, Ingrey?" said Hallana.

"Would you each take one end of this, and hold it level. Not too high."

A little apprehensively, they grasped the pole, as if uncertain at first if it would present a material grip to them, and stood apart. The Wolfcliff banner unfolded and hung down as though the great Wolf bowed its head to the ground.

Ingrey turned to Ijada. "Take my hand."

She touched his right hand uncertainly, careful of the damp red mess, but he squeezed her fingers in return, and then she gripped more tightly. He turned them both to face the horizontal staff.

"Jump over with me," he said, "if we shall be allies in such nights as this and lovers in all nights hereafter."

"Ingrey . . ." She peered doubtfully at him, sideways through escaped strands of hanging hair. "Are you asking me to marry you?"

More or less, he started to say, and thought the better of it. It was only *more.* "Yes. You should marry a king. This is your great chance." He looked around; Oswin's sober face had lightened in comprehension, and Hallana's had broken into a broad grin. "The company of witnesses could not be improved: three Temple divines of good character, two princes—one a poet who will doubtless immortalize this moment before we've made it halfway back to Easthome—"

Jokol, who had loomed closer to see and hear, nodded delightedly. "Ah, Ingorry, good work! Yes, jump, jump, Ijada! My beautiful Breiga would like this one, yes!"

"A princess . . ." Ingrey cast a half bow somewhat uncertainly at Fara, now sitting up somberly on the edge of the mound; she returned him a grave but not disapproving jerk of her chin. "And one other." Ingrey nodded to the marshalwarrior; Ingrey had not known ghosts could be bemused, but this one's surprised smile blessed him in advance for this unexpected last use of his long-defended emblem. "You can have other ceremonies later, if you like," Ingrey added to Ijada. "With better clothes or whatever. As many as you want. As long as they're with me," he added prudently.

"One or two is the usual limit," Oswin rumbled from his end of the pole, starting to smile.

Ingrey opened his mouth to persuade further, but Ijada extended two fingers and touched his lips to stillness. He wobbled a little, as his knees nearly gave way, and she glanced aside at him thoughtfully. She looked each way at Oswin and Hallana, reached out, and pressed the pole down; the two divines obediently bent to lower the barrier to something their somewhat pallid hallow king was sure to be able to clear.

Looking at each other, Ingrey and Ijada held hands and jumped.

Ingrey stumbled a little on the landing, as his head was swimming, but Ijada steadied him. They exchanged one kiss, which Ingrey began to make swift and promissory; Ijada captured his face between her hands and made it more thorough. *Yes,* Ingrey thought, pausing to feel the softness, the warmth, the faint hint of her teeth. *This is the only living Now.*

They parted, trading pensive smiles, and Ingrey retrieved the standard. The pulsing heart had vanished from the spearpoint. *But which of us received back which half?* He wasn't sure he knew.

The marshal-warrior knelt on one knee, undid his graying braids from his gold belt, and held his head up before him. Ingrey knelt, too, and shook down one last generous splash of blood to smear across the furrowed brow. The old spirit stallion he released was very worn, but Ingrey thought it must have been a fine fast beast in its time, for this night it flew.

The marshal-warrior rose whole: he rolled his shoulders as if in relief and nodded solemnly at Ingrey. He then turned and reached for Learned Oswin's hand, and, not looking back again, was gone.

The real darkness flowed in across Ingrey's eyes for the first time that night; only then did he become truly aware that he had been seeing, with unnatural clarity, by ghost-

light for most of the hours past. Jokol grunted and hurried to
stir up a small fire, unnoticed by Ingrey, that he had evidently built to warm Fara sometime during the night while
waiting for devotees of his Lady to present themselves. The
orange light licked up to gild the tired faces that now huddled around it.

Biast nodded cautiously to the Wolfcliff royal standard
which Ingrey still clutched, draped upon it for support.
"What are you going to do with that?"

What, indeed? He straightened up and stared at it, dis-
comfited. It felt as solid under his hand as the Horseriver
staff Fara had broken, but it had not come from the outer
world, and Ingrey doubted he could carry it back there, beyond the borders of the Wounded Woods. He was equally
doubtful that it would survive the dawn, presaged by a faint
gray tinge in the mists that drifted through the gnarled
trees. Ingrey's hallow kingship was more bounded by
space and time and need than Biast perhaps realized, or the
prince-marshal would not look so uneasily at him, Ingrey
thought.

He was disinclined to hand his standard humbly to Biast,
politically prudent as that might seem. It was Wolfcliff not
Stagthorne, it was a thing of the night not the day, and anyway, anyway . . . *Let him earn his own.*

"In the Old Weald," said Ingrey, "the royal banner-carrier
guarded the standard from the death of the old king to the in-
vestment of the new." *And now I know why.* "Then it was
broken, and the pieces burned on the pyre of the dead king,
if events made such ceremony possible." And if not, he
began to suspect, someone had made it up as best he could
out of inspiration, urgency, and whatever came to hand. He
looked around a little vaguely. "Ijada, we must cleanse this
ground as well, before we leave this place. With fire, I think.
And we must go soon."

"Before the sun rises?" she asked.

"That feels right."

"You should know."

"I do."

She followed his gaze around. "My stepfather's forester said these trees were diseased. He wanted to fire the woods then, but I wouldn't let him."

"Will you allow me?"

"It is your realm."

"Only till dawn. Tomorrow it is yours again." He glanced aside at Biast, to see if he took the hint.

"Perhaps it is as well," sighed Ijada. "Perhaps it is necessary. Perhaps it is . . . time. What, um," she moistened her lips, "what of Wencel's body?"

Learned Lewko said uneasily, "I don't think we can carry it out with us now. Our beasts were used hard yesterday, and will have burden enough getting us back to the main roads. Someone will have to be sent back for it. Should we build a little cairn, to protect it from the wild beasts and birds till then?"

"The last Horseriver king never had his warrior's pyre," Ingrey said. "No one here did, except for a few trapped in burning huts that night, I suppose. I don't know if burying them all in pits was a theological act of Audar's, or part of his magic and curse, or just military efficiency. The more I learn of Bloodfield, the more I think no one really knew, even at the time. It is late; it is the last hour. We will fire the woods." For Wencel. *For all of them.*

Ijada moistened a cautious finger and held it in the air. "The wind's a little in the east, such as it is. It should do even if the rain doesn't come on."

Ingrey nodded. "Biast, gentlemen, can you help Fara get out? Can someone collect the horses?"

"I can do that!" said Hallana brightly, and took everyone but Oswin aback by stepping up onto the mound, turning to the four quarters, and calling loudly and rather maternally through her cupped hands, "Horses! Horses!"

Oswin looked a trifle pained, but appeared not in the least surprised when after a few minutes a crashing and crunching through the undergrowth announced the arrival of their several abandoned mounts, trailing reins and snorting anxiously. Jokol and Lewko, at Ingrey's nod, had quietly collected more dry deadfall from the margins of the clearing and discreetly piled it around Wencel's body. Lewko took charge of Wencel's purse, rings, and other items of interest to his future heirs at law. Ijada tucked the broken pieces of the Horseriver banner atop the pile. Hallana helped the widowed princess mount her horse. The company straggled into the foggy shadows in the direction of the marsh. Fara never looked back.

Biast did, wheeling his horse about to watch as Ingrey poked up the fire with a stick. "Will you two be all right?"

"Yes," said Ingrey. "Make for the gate of thorns. We will catch you up."

Gravely, Ijada took the standard, backed a few paces, and held the black-and-red banner in the fire till it caught alight. She handed the staff to Ingrey. Ingrey gripped it tightly in both hands, closed his eyes, and heaved it skyward. He opened his eyes again, grabbed Ijada's hand, and prepared to dodge whatever fell back. If anything.

Instead, the staff spun up and burst into a hundred burning shards, which rained down all around.

"Oh," said Ijada in a tone of surprise. "I thought we would have to walk through the woods with torches for a while, finding dry brush piles . . ."

"I think not," said Ingrey, and began to tow her toward Biast, who was staring back wide-eyed in the growing yellow light. "But it's time to go. Yes, definitely." Somewhere in the woods behind them, something very, very dry went up with a roar and a fountain of sparks. "Briskly, even."

Biast's horse jittered despite its weariness, but the prince-marshal kept pace with them as they wound through the misshapen trees back toward the marsh. He eyed Ingrey and Ijada as if trying to decide which of them to pull up behind him on his horse and gallop for it, if the wind shifted. Happily, in Ingrey's view, because he did not have the energy for another argument tonight, the faint breeze didn't shift, and the ring of fire crept out from its center at no more than a walking pace. They reached the edge of the woods if not well in advance of the flames' steady destruction, sufficiently so.

Ijada supported Ingrey as far as the gate of thorns. Then Biast, watching him stumble, climbed down off his horse and boosted Ingrey aboard instead, and led the beast. They needed no other lantern than the distant burning to climb the zigzag path up the wall of the valley. They reached the open promontory to find that all the others had gathered at a meager campsite prepared by Symark, Ottovin, Bernan, and Hergi.

Lewko helped Ingrey down from Biast's horse. Ingrey was shivering badly now, in the dawn cold. Seeing Lewko draw Ingrey's arm over his shoulders to escort him to the campfire, Hallana abandoned Fara, who was being hovered over by Hergi as well, and hurried to them. Ingrey found her low mutter of *Dratsab!* more alarming than his own weakness.

She frowned medically. "Get him hot drinks and hot food, swiftly," she ordered Bernan and Oswin. "And whatever blankets and cloaks we have."

Ingrey sank down on a saddle pad, because standing was no longer quite feasible.

"Has he spent too much blood?" Ijada asked her in worry.

Hallana replied, a little too indirectly, "He'll be all right if we can get him warmed up and fed."

Hergi appeared with her leather case, and Ingrey endured yet another washing and rebandaging of his crusted right hand, though the wound was closed—again—and the bruises green and fading. Others bustled about with what seemed to him needless excitement, scavenging food and blankets and building up the fire. Ingrey was tired, breathless, and dizzy, and his chilled shaking threatened to spill the odd-tasting herb tea from his cup before he could get it to his numb lips, but Ijada plied him repeatedly with refills and what bits of fare the camp could supply. Better still, she huddled under his blankets with him to share the warmth of her own body, warming his hands with hers. Eventually the shudders stopped, and then he was merely very, very tired.

"How did you come here?" Ingrey asked Learned Lewko, who sat down to keep him company and share a bit of dried fruit someone had produced from a saddlebag. "I could not send a message, after we left the king's deathbed, though I wanted to. Horseriver held both Fara and me in thrall."

"I had escorted Hallana to interrogate Ijada that night. We were talking together when Ijada became most upset, insisting something dire must have just befallen you."

"I could not feel you anymore," Ijada put in. "I feared you had been killed." She would have inched closer, but they were out of inches already; her arm around him tightened instead.

"Horseriver stole our bond."

"Ah!" she breathed.

Lewko raised a curious eyebrow at this, but elected to go on with his narrative. "Lady Ijada insisted we go investigate. Hallana agreed. I . . . decided not to argue. Your Rider Gesca also decided not to argue, at least not with Hallana, though he followed along for the sake of his warden's duty. We all four walked up to Horseriver's palace, where they told us you had gone to the hallow king's bedside. Then up to the hallow king's hall, where we found Biast at his father's deathbed saying you had all gone back to the earl's. We knew we had not missed you in the dark. Hallana got, well, the way she gets sometimes, and led us to the earl's stables."

"That must have been quite a scene," Ingrey remarked.

"To say the least. Biast had been unconvinced of anything untoward beyond his sister's usual illness, till then. From that point on, no one could have been more urgent in pursuit. Hallana hurried off to fetch Oswin and Bernan and their wagon, and found Prince Jokol talking to Oswin—he still wants a divine to carry back to his island—and she brought everyone. I was uncertain about taking this unruly mob upon the road, but, well, I can count to five. At least"—Lewko sighed—"Jokol didn't bring his ice bear."

"Did he want to?" Ingrey asked, bemused.

"Yes," said Ijada. "But I talked him out of it. He is a very sweet man."

Ingrey chose to let that pass without remark.

Lewko continued, "That was the point at which I decided the gods must be on our side—how does one say *five gods help Them* when it *is* the gods?—just imagine this same jaunt *with* the ice bear." He shuddered. "Fafa would have had to ride in the wagon, I suppose, although the beast is big enough *to* ride." He blinked for a moment, looking reflective. "I wonder . . . do you suppose this whole quest for a divine was a ploy on the beautiful Breiga's part to get rid of the bear before it ended up sleeping at the foot of her marriage bed?"

Ijada's eyes lit, and she giggled. "Or worse, on it. Possibly. She sounds a determined lady. For pity's sake, don't suggest that in Jokol's hearing."

"I wouldn't dream of it." Lewko rubbed the grin from his mouth and continued, "Biast thrust everything in Easthome onto Hetwar's shoulders, which I think are sturdy enough to hold them. We were on the river road pelting north not four hours after you three had left Easthome. After that it was all commandeering Temple courier horses and royal mail station remounts, and taking turns resting in the wagon, all the way to Badgerbridge."

"You took the main road straight there?" said Ingrey, considering a mental map. "That would have saved some time. We took a lesser track when we turned west, for secrecy I think."

"Yes. There appeared never to be any doubt about where we were going. Such a deluge of dreams! I did not see why, until . . . well. I have now seen why. We traded the wagon for fresh mounts and outraced the prince-marshal's escort out of Badgerbridge; they may yet catch us up, if they have not lost themselves in Ijada's forest, here."

Ijada nodded thoughtfully, as she considered this possibility. "The forester is with them; they will find their way eventually, maybe by another pass." She glanced out over the valley. "The smoke must draw them, if nothing else."

Hallana motioned to Ijada from across the camp, and Ijada rose to see what she wanted. Ingrey stretched and, finally warmed to comfort despite a headache, clambered up to wander to the edge of the promontory and gaze out over the bowl of Holytree–Bloodfield–The Wounded Woods. *My kingdom of All-That-Was.*

He unclutched the blanket from around his neck and sat on it, his arms wound about his knees, and stared into the graying gulf of mist and smoke. The earlier hot bright yellow that had seared the dark was dying down to a sullen red ring, black in the growing middle. The bloody light reflected off the undersides of the charcoal-colored clouds; far off, Ingrey heard a faint rumble of thunder reverberate through the serried hills, and the heavy scent of the coming rain mixed in his nostrils with the stink of smoke. He wondered if the morning after the original massacre had looked and smelled like this, and if Audar himself had also paused upon this spot to reflect on what clashing kings had wrought.

Biast strolled over to stand beside him, his arms crossed, staring out likewise, as if sociably. The prince-marshal was a little too drawn to bring off the illusion, but Ingrey spread his hand in invitation nonetheless, and Biast sank down next to him. Biast's tired sigh was not feigned.

"What will you do now?" Biast inquired of him.

"Sleep, I hope. Before we must ride."

"I meant more generally."

I know you did. Ingrey sighed, then a small smile turned his mouth. "After that, I shall pursue a courtier's supreme ambition—"

He made the slightest of pauses, to give Biast time to tense.

"—and marry a rich heiress, and retire to a life of ease on her country estates." He waved about at the enclosing hills.

"Ease? In this waste?"

"Well, she may find a task or two to which to turn my hand."

"She may," said Biast, surprised into a chuckle.

"If she is not hanged."

Biast grimaced and waved away this concern. "That will not happen. Not after this. If you do not trust in me and Hetwar, well, I do think Oswin and Lewko will have a thing or two to say about it. Among such a fellowship, some sensible path to justice must be found. And"—his voice grew hesitant not in doubt, but in a kind of shyness—"mercy."

"Good," Ingrey sighed.

"Thank you for saving Fara's life. More than once, if she tells me true. Making you her guard wolf was one of my luckier decisions, if luck it was."

Ingrey shrugged. "I did no more than my duty to you, nor less than any man's duty to his conscience."

"*Any man* could not have done what I saw you do last night." Biast stared at his feet, not meeting Ingrey's eyes. "If you chose to be more now—to reach for my father's seat— I do not know who could stand against you. Wolf king." *Not I,* his bowed shoulders seemed to add.

Now he comes to it. Ingrey pointed outward. "My kingdom measured two miles by four, its population included not one breathing soul, and my whole reign ran from one dusk to one dawn. The dead did but lend my kingship to me, and in the end I handed it back. As any king must do; your father, for one." Although not Horseriver: one root of the problem had lain in that, to be sure. "You, too, prince, come your turn."

Upon consideration, Ingrey's geography lacked a dimension, he decided. Eight square miles by four centuries—or more, for all of the history of the Old Weald had surely concentrated itself upon this patch of ground that fatal night, to be so thoroughly dislocated thereafter. Like the abyss beneath the deceptive surface of a lake that this valley floor resembled, time went down unimaginably far beneath this ground—*all the way down. My domain is larger than it looks.* He decided not to trouble Biast with these reflections, but said only, "If any kingship lingers on me, this little realm will content it."

Biast's shoulders relaxed visibly, and his face lightened, at this oblique assurance that the wolf-lord of alarming powers desired no more exalted part in Easthome politics. He scanned the horizon, perhaps looking for signs of his bedraggled escort making their way down one of the other gaps, found none, then picked up a few pebbles and tossed them meditatively over the edge.

"Tell me true, Lord Ingrey," said Biast suddenly. He turned to look Ingrey full in the face for almost the first time. "What makes the hallow kingship hallowed?"

Ingrey hesitated so long in answering, Biast began to turn away again in disappointment, when Ingrey blurted, "Faith." And at the puzzled pinch of Biast's brows, clarified: "Keeping it."

Biast's lips made an unvoiced O, as though something sharp had pierced him through the heart. He sank back wordlessly. He said nothing for a rather long time. They sat together in more companionable silence as the glimmering fires crept across the ground below, in the last deconsecration of Holytree and Bloodfield's belated pyre.

Epilogue

INGREY LEFT IJADA'S FOREST THAT AFTERNOON CLINGING dizzily to his saddle, his horse towed by one of Biast's late-arriving guardsmen. He spent most of the following week flat on his back in Ijada's stepparents' house in Badger-bridge. But as soon as he could stand up without blacking out, he and Ijada were married—or married again—in the house's parlor, and then he had her fair company by night as well as day in his convalescent chamber. Some things one didn't need to get out of bed to accomplish.

Prince Biast and his retinue had hurried back to Easthome and the prince's duties there; news of his election as hallow king arrived the day after the wedding. Prince Jokol and Ottovin lingered just long enough to enliven the wedding party, and to amaze the town of Badgerbridge, then took horse on the southern road to return to their ship.

Hallana, too, with her loyal servants, returned immediately to her children at Suttleaf, but Learned Oswin waited with Learned Lewko to escort Ijada, still technically under arrest, back to Easthome. Even with their support, the wheels of the Temple and King's Bench ground slowly, and it was some days thereafter before the inquest returned its final verdict of self-defense. Oswin adroitly put the pleas for dispensation for Ijada's and Princess Fara's spirit animals together in one document, with identical arguments; whatever arm wrestling went on behind the scenes that made Learned Lewko smile wryly, the dual dispensation was forthcoming shortly after the verdict.

Fara settled swiftly into a very private widowhood, under her brother's protection. If her spirit horse rendered her less a prize for some new political marriage, she seemed more grimly pleased than regretful. Her sick headaches did not recur.

Just exactly how Lewko and Oswin between them produced a divine for Prince Jokol, Ingrey never found out, but he and Ijada did come down to the docks to bid the island prince and his comrades farewell. The young divine looked nervous and clung to the ship's rail as though he expected to get seasick going downriver, but seemed very brave and determined. Fafa the ice bear, in a move of swift wit on someone's part, was gifted to King Biast as an ordination present, and took up residence on a nearby farm, with his own pond to swim in.

Withal, snow was flying by the time Ingrey and Ijada rode out of Easthome free, on the southeastern road toward the Lure Valley, with Learned Lewko's expert company. Ingrey spurred them all onward despite the cold. That he was too late about this business was all too probable—but that he might be *just too late* seemed unendurable. They came to the confluence of the Lure and the Birchbeck on the winter solstice, the Father's Day, an accident of timing that gave Ingrey's heart hope despite his reason and the learned saint's advice.

❦

"I fear it is a fool's errand, cousin," opined Islin kin Wolfcliff, castlemaster of Birchgrove. "In all the ten years I have lived here, I've never seen or heard tell of ghosts in this citadel. But you are certainly welcome to make yourself free of the place to hunt them." Islin eyed Ingrey and his two companions uneasily, and yawned behind his hand. "When you tire of casting about in the dark and cold, warm feather beds await you. Mine calls to me; pray excuse me."

"Of course," said Ingrey, with a polite nod. Islin returned the courtesy and took himself out of the great hall.

Ingrey glanced around. A couple of good beeswax candles in silvered sconces cast a warm honeyed flicker over the chamber; a fire burning low in the stone fireplace drove back some of the chill. Beyond the window slits, only midnight darkness lurked, though the gurgle of the fast-flowing Birchbeck, not yet frozen over though its banks were rimed with ice, came up faintly through them. The room was much the same as on the fateful day he and his father had received their wolf sacrifices here, and yet . . . not. *It is smaller and more rustic than I remembered. How can a stone-walled room grow smaller?*

Ijada said in a worried voice, "Your cousin seemed very reserved all through dinner. Do you think our spirit animals disturb him?"

Ingrey's lips twitched up in a brief, unfelt smile. "Perhaps a little. But I think mostly he's wondering if I mean to use my new influence at court to take back his patrimony." Islin was only a little older than Ingrey, and had inherited his seat from Ingrey's uncle some three years past.

"Would you wish to?" Ijada asked curiously.

Ingrey's brows bent. "No. Too many bad memories haunt this place; they overtop my good ones and sink them. I would rather leave them all behind. Save for one."

Ijada nodded to Lewko. "So, saint. What does your holy sight reveal? Is Islin right? Are there no ghosts here?"

Lewko, who had been doing his accustomed imitation of a simple, humble, and nearly invisible ordinary divine since they'd arrived that afternoon, shook his head and smiled. "In an edifice this old, large, and long occupied, it would be more a wonder if there were not a few. What do your shaman senses tell you, Ingrey?"

Ingrey lifted his head, closed his eyes, and sniffed. "From time to time, it seems I smell an odd little dankness in the air. But at this time of year, that's no surprise." He opened his eyes again. "Ijada?"

"I am too untutored to be certain, I'm afraid. Learned?"

Lewko shrugged. "If the god will touch me tonight, any ghosts nearby will be attracted to the aura. Not by any spell of mine, you understand; it just happens. I will pray for my second sight to be shared. The gods are in your debt, Ingrey, Ijada; if only you can receive, I think They will give. Compose yourselves to quietude, and we shall see." Lewko signed himself, closed his eyes, and clasped his hands loosely before him. He seemed to settle into himself; his lips moved, barely, on his silent prayer.

Ingrey did his best to quell all desire, will, and fear in his own mind; he wondered if just being very, very tired would be enough, instead.

At length Lewko opened his eyes again, stepped forward, and wordlessly kissed first Ijada, then Ingrey on their foreheads. His lips were cool, but Ingrey felt a strange welcome warmth flush through him. He blinked.

"Oh!" said Ijada, looking with interest around the chamber. "Learned, is that one?" She pointed; Ingrey saw a faint pale blob floating past, circling in toward Lewko, scarcely more substantial than a puff of breath in frosty moonlight.

"Aye," said Lewko, following her gaze. "There is nothing to fear, mind you, though much to pity. That soul is long sundered, fading and powerless."

To imply that Ijada, who had shared the terror and triumph at Bloodfield, might fear a ghost seemed absurd to Ingrey. His own fears lay on another level. "Learned, could it be my father?"

"Do you sense his wolf, as you sensed the spirit animals within the others?"

"No," Ingrey admitted.

"Then it is some other, long lost. Dying beyond death." Lewko signed the Five at it, and it drifted back into the walls.

"Why would the god lend us this sight, if there was nothing to see?" said Ingrey. "It makes no sense. There must be more."

Lewko looked around the now-empty chamber. "Let us make a little patrol around the castle, then, and see what turns up. But Ingrey—don't hope too hard. The ghosts of Bloodfield had great spells and all the life of that dire ground to sustain them beyond their time. Lord Ingalef, I fear, had none of that."

"He had his wolf," said Ingrey stubbornly. "It might have made some difference." At his tone, Ijada's hand found his, and squeezed; they left the chamber arm in arm, and took the opposite direction in the corridor from Lewko, the better to quarter the castle while this gift of second sight lasted.

In the bleak winter darkness the castle was cold and dank even without ghosts, but Ingrey found his night sight keener than heretofore. They paced the corridors and chambers, Ijada trailing her hand over the walls. Exiting the main keep, they circled the buildings along the inner bailey wall; in the shadows of the stable, warm with the breath and bodies of the horses, Ijada whispered, "Look, another!"

The pale mist circled them both as if in anxiety, but then faded again.

"Was it . . . ?" asked Ijada.

"I think not. It was simple like the first. Let us go on."

As they trod across the snow in the narrow courtyard, Ingrey muttered, "I am too late. I should have come earlier."

Ijada's hand, gripping his forearm, gave it a little shake. "None of that, now. You did not know. And even if you'd known, you had not yet come to your powers."

"But it rides me to know that there might have once been a time for rescue, and it slipped through my hands. I scarcely know whether to blame myself, or my uncle, or the Temple, or the gods . . ."

"Blame none, then. My mother and father both died before their times. Yes, they went to their gods, which was some consolation to me, but—not enough. Never enough. Death is not a performance to rate ourselves upon, or berate ourselves upon either."

He squeezed her hand in return and bent to kiss her hair in the moonlight.

They made their way up the inner steps of the wall and along the sentry walk to the battlement's highest point, above the river, and paused to look out across the steep valley of the Birchbeck. The water of the stream rippled like black silk between the steel sheen of the spreading ice along its banks. The snow cover on the slopes caught the light of the westering moon in a pale blue glow, webbed with the bare tree branches like charcoal strokes, save where stands of black fir marked the rises, or clusters of holly made mystery in the dells. The bare boles of the birches blended with the snow and shadows, eluding the eye.

They stood for a time, gazing out. Ijada shivered despite her woolens, and Ingrey wrapped himself around her like a cloak. She smiled gratefully over her shoulder. *You warm me just as much as I warm you, love . . .*

For once, Ingrey sensed the revenant before Ijada, although she felt him stiffen and instantly turned her head to follow his glance. A few paces away floated a shape like mist in the moonlight, denser than the others had been, elongated, almost a man length. Within it, another shadow lurked, like smoke shrouded by fog.

Ingrey's arms spasmed around Ijada, then released her. "Fetch Learned Lewko, hurry!"

She nodded and sped away.

Ingrey stood silent, scarcely daring to breathe, lest this image fade or flee like the others. A head end it seemed to have, and feet, but he could not discern any features. His imagination tried to paint it with his father's face, but a chilled realization came over him that he no longer remembered exactly what Lord Ingalef had looked like. His father's appearance had never greatly mattered to Ingrey; it was his solid presence that had warmed, and his rumbling voice, resonating in a chest to which a child-ear pressed, that had promised safety.

The illusion of safety. *I might now become a father in my turn, and I cannot give such perfect safety. It was always an illusion. Will my own children forgive me, when they find out?*

Rapid footsteps scrunching through the snow and heavy breathing heralded the return of Ijada with the divine, making their way up the steep steps to this high point. Lewko paused at the top, gazing past Ingrey at the smoky revenant. "Ingrey, is it . . . ?

"I . . ." Ingrey started to say, *I think so,* but changed it to, "Yes. I am sure of it. Learned, what should I do? I wanted to ask a thousand questions, but it has no mouth. I don't think it can speak. I don't even know if it can hear me."

"I believe you're right. The time for questions and answers seems past. You can only cleanse it, and release it. That is what a shaman does, it seems."

"And when he's cleansed and released, will the Father of Winter take him up? Or is he sundered beyond recall? Are there no rites you can offer to help him?"

"He had his funeral rites long ago, Ingrey. You can do what you can do, which is cleanse him; I can pray. But if it has been too long, there will not be enough of him left to assent to the god, and then not even the god can do more. It may be that all you can do is release him from this thrall."

"To nothingness."

"Aye."

"Like Horseriver." Horseriver's hatred of irrevocable time made more sense to Ingrey now.

"Somewhat."

"What is the use of me, if I can send four thousand stranger-souls to their proper gods, but not the four-thousand-first that matters most to me?"

"I do not know."

"And that is the sum of Temple wisdom?"

"It is the sum of my wisdom, and all the truth I know."

Was Temple wisdom like a father's safety, then, an illu-

sion? And it always had been? *Would you rather Lewko told
you comforting lies?* Ingrey could not walk back through
that veil of time and experience to a child's sight again, and
wasn't sure he would if he could. Ijada stepped forward and
laid a hand upon his shoulder, lending the comfort of her
presence, if not the comfort of some more desirable answer.
He let himself absorb the warmth of her body against his for
a moment, then touched her hand for release and stepped
forward.

From a pouch on his belt he fumbled out a fine new
penknife, purchased in Easthome for this moment. The thin
blade reflected the face of the moon in a brief blink. Ijada gritted her teeth along with Ingrey as he took it in his left hand
and pressed the edge into his right index finger. He squeezed
his fist and raised his hand to the top of the fog-shape.

The drops fell through onto the trampled snow in a spatter of small black circles.

Ingrey's breath drew in, and he clutched the knife harder.
Lewko barely caught his arm as he made to stab his hand
more deeply.

"No, Ingrey," Lewko whispered. "If a drop will not bless
it, neither will a bucketful."

Ingrey exhaled slowly as Lewko let go again, and tucked
the knife back in the pouch. Whatever of his hallow kingship
lingered in his blood, it seemed it had no power over this. *I
had to try.*

He took a long, slow, last look, wondering what to say.
Fare well seemed a mockery, *be at peace* little better. He
moistened his lips in the frosty, luminous air.

"Whatever you thought you were about, the thing you
began here is finished, and done well. Your sacrifice was not
in vain." He thought of adding *I forgive you,* then thought
better of it. Fatuous, foolish, hardly to the point now. After a
moment he merely said, "I love you, Father." And, after another, *"Come."*

The dark wolf-smoke spun out from the pale fog and
through his fingers, and away.

More slowly, the frost-fog dissipated as well, with a last faint blue sparkle.

"The god did not take him up," Ingrey whispered.

"He would if He could have," Lewko murmured back. "The Father of Winter, too, weeps at this loss."

Ingrey was not weeping, yet, although little trembles ran through his body. He could feel the second sight fading from his eyes, the gift returned. Ijada came to him again and tied a strip of clean linen around his finger. They wound their arms around each other.

"Well . . ." Learned Lewko signed them both. "It is finished." His voice grew more gentle. "Will you not come in out of the cold, my lord and lady?"

"Soon," sighed Ingrey. "Moonset over the Birchbeck is worth a shiver or two."

"If you say so." Lewko smiled and, with a nod of farewell, clutched his coat about himself and made his way down the steps, careful now on the ice.

Ingrey stepped behind Ijada and rested his chin on her shoulder, the both of them staring out over the valley.

"I know this was not what you'd hoped, with Lord Ingalef," said Ijada after a time. "I'm sorry."

"No, it wasn't. But it was better than nothing, and vastly better than never knowing. At least all is concluded, here. I can go and not look back."

"This was your childhood home."

"It was. But I am not a child anymore." He hugged her a little fiercely, squeezing a breath of a laugh from her belly. "My home has a new name, and she is called Ijada. There will I abide."

Her warm laugh now was voiced, enough to make moonmist before her lips.

"Besides," he said, "I expect Badgerbridge is warmer in the winter than Birchgrove, am I not right?"

"In the valleys, yes. There is snow enough on the upper slopes, should you miss it."

"Very good."

After a dozen slowing breaths, he added, "He did not seem to be in any great pain or torment. So. I have seen my fate. I will not fear it."

Ijada said thoughtfully, "Mine and Fara's, too, if you do not outlive us to cleanse our souls in turn."

"I scarcely know which order dismays me more." He turned her to face him, and stared in worry into her eyes, wide and dark with a faint amber rim in the blue shadows. "I must pray I may go last, mourning and unmourned. I don't know how I'll bear it."

"Ingrey." She placed her chilled hands on either side of his face, and brought it directly before her intent gaze. "A year ago, could you even have imagined, let alone predicted, standing here being what you now are?"

"No."

"Neither could I have imagined me. So perhaps we should not be so sure of our future fate, either. What we don't know of it is vastly larger than what we do, and will surely not stop surprising us."

His thoughts sped back to that night in Oxmeade, where the black fit had come upon him and he had so nearly cut his own throat. He still was not sure if that had been Horseriver's doing, or all his own. *I would have missed all this.* "I met four thousand unexpected souls who would agree with you, banner-carrier."

"Then let their vote rule your mind in this, as well."

"Ah." The bleak midnight mood was losing its hold upon him, in favor of her wool-wrapped warmth.

She added, "It is premature to call yourself the last shaman, too, I think. You yourself could make more great beasts and spirit mages."

"I would not send any other into this state unless I knew they could find a way out again."

"Indeed. And do you think the Temple must always oppose the old forest magics? If they came in some fresh version, reformed to our new days?"

"That would take much thought. Five gods know we've seen the troubles the old ways can cause."

"Yet the Temple manages its sorcerers, and not perfectly. Look at poor Cumril, for one. But they manage well enough to go on with. And we both know divines who are capable of much thought, now."

"Huh." His eyes narrowed in a hint of hope.

"You are very arrogant, wolf-lord." Her hands gave his head a tiny, reproving shake.

"Ah? What now, sweet cat?"

"How can you say that multitudes yet unborn shall not mourn you greatly? It is not yours to dictate their hearts."

"Do you prophesy, lady?" he inquired lightly, but even as he spoke a shiver ran through his belly, as though he had heard a weirding voice.

She shrugged. "Let us agree to endure our fates, and find out."

Her lips were warm, like rising sunlight chasing an icy moon. She rubbed her face against his, sighing contentedly. But then added, "Your nose is cold, wolfling. You are not so hairy that I take this as a sign of health in you. If we are ever to be ancestors and not just descendants, perhaps we should return to that feather bed your cousin promised us."

He snickered and released her. "Aye, to bed then, for the sake of our posterity!"

"And I can thaw my feet on your back," she added practically.

Ingrey yipped in mock-dismay, and was graced with her fairest laugh yet. The sound lifted his heart like a promise of dawn, in this longest night of the year.

Arm in arm, they descended the snowy steps.

Turn the page for a sneak preview of Lois McMaster
Bujold's next fantasy novel

THE SHARING KNIFE
Volume One: Beguilement

Follow the adventures of Fawn Bluefield, a young
farmer girl running away from home, and Dag
Redwing Hickory, a rather weary patroller from a
race of mages called Lakewalkers, on a desperate
quest to return a magical knife belonging to Dag that
Fawn has unintentionally and mystically altered . . .

Available in hardcover from Eos,
October 2006

FAWN CAME TO THE WELL-HOUSE A LITTLE BEFORE NOON. More than a farmstead, less than an inn, it sat close to the straight road she'd been trudging down for two days. The farmyard lay open to travelers, bounded by a semi-circle of old log outbuildings, with the promised covered well in the middle. To resolve all doubt, somebody had nailed a sign picturing the well itself to one of the support posts, and below the painting a long list of goods the farm might sell, with the prices. Each painstakingly printed line had a little picture below it, and colored circles of coins lined up in rows beyond, for those who could not read the words and numbers themselves. Fawn could, and keep accounts as well, skills her mother had taught her along with a hundred other household tasks. She frowned at the unbidden thought: *So if I'm so clever, what am I doing in this fix?*

She set her teeth and felt in her skirt pocket for her coin purse. It was not heavy, but she might certainly buy some bread. Bread would be bland. The dried mutton from her pack that she'd tried to eat this morning had made her sick, again, but she needed something to fight the horrible fatigue that slowed her steps to a plod, or she'd never make it to

Glassforge. She glanced around the unpeopled yard and at the iron bell hung from the post with a pull cord dangling invitingly, then lifted her eyes to the rolling fields beyond the buildings. On a distant sunlit slope, a dozen or so people were haying. Uncertainly, she went around to the farm-house's kitchen door and knocked.

A striped cat perching on the step eyed her without getting up. The cat's plump calm reassured Fawn, together with the good repair of the house's faded shingles and fieldstone foundation, so that when a comfortably middle-aged farmwife opened the door, Fawn's heart was hardly pounding at all.

"Yes, child?" said the woman.

I'm not a child, I'm just short, Fawn bit back; given the crinkles at the corners of the woman's friendly eyes, maybe Fawn's basket of years would still seem scant to her. "You sell bread?"

The farmwife's glance around took in her aloneness. "Aye; step in."

A broad hearth at one end of the room heated it beyond summer, and was crowded with pots hanging from iron hooks. Delectable smells of ham and beans, corn and bread and cooking fruit mingled in the moist air, noon meal in the making for the gang of hay cutters. The farmwife folded back a cloth from a lumpy row on a side table, fresh loaves from a workday that had doubtless started before dawn. Despite her nausea Fawn's mouth watered, and she picked out a loaf that the woman told her was rolled inside with crystal honey and hickory nuts. Fawn fished out a coin, wrapped the loaf in her kerchief, and took it back outside. The woman walked along with her.

"The water's clean and free, but you have to draw it yourself," the woman told her, as Fawn tore off a corner of the loaf and nibbled. "Ladle's on the hook. Which way were you heading, child?"

"To Glassforge."

"By yourself?" The woman frowned. "Do you have people there?"

"Yes," Fawn lied.

"Shame on them, then. Word is there's a pack of robbers on the road near Glassforge. They shouldn't have sent you out by yourself."

"South or north of town?" asked Fawn in worry.

"A ways south, I heard, but there's no saying they'll stay put."

"I'm only going as far south as Glassforge." Fawn set the bread on the bench beside her pack, freed the latch for the crank, and let the bucket fall till a splash echoed back up the well's cool stone sides, then began turning.

Robbers did not sound good. Still, they were a frank hazard. Any fool would know enough not to go near them. When Fawn had started on this miserable journey six days ago, she had cadged rides from wagons at every chance as soon as she'd walked far enough from home not to risk encountering someone who knew her. Which had been fine until that one fellow who'd said stupid things that made her very uncomfortable, and followed up with a grab and a grope. Fawn had broken away, and the man had not been willing to abandon his rig and restive team to chase her down, but she might have been less lucky. After that, she'd hidden discreetly in the verge from the occasional passing carts until she was sure there was a woman or a family aboard.

The few bites of bread were helping settle her stomach already. She hoisted the bucket onto the bench and took the wooden dipper the woman handed down to her. The water tasted of iron and old eggs, but was clear and cold. Better. She would rest a while on this bench in the shade, and perhaps this afternoon she would make better time.

From the road to the north, hoof beats and a jingle of harness sounded. No creak or rattle of wheels, but quite a *lot* of hooves. The farmwife glanced up, her eyes narrowing, and her hand rose to the cord on the bell clapper.

"Child," she said, "see those old apple trees at the side of the yard? Why don't you just go skin up one and stay quiet, till we see what this is, eh?"

Fawn thought of several responses, but settled on, "Yes'm." She started across the yard, turned back and grabbed her loaf, then trotted to the small grove. The closest tree had a set of boards nailed to the side like a ladder, and she scrambled up quickly through branches thick with leaves and hard little green apples. Her dress was dyed dull blue, her jacket brown; she would blend with the shadows here as well as she had on the road verge, likely. She braced herself along a branch, tucked in her pale hands and lowered her face, shook her head, and peered out through the cascade of black curls falling over her forehead.

The mob of riders turned into the yard, and the farmwife came off her tense toes, shoulders relaxing. She released the bell cord. There must have been a dozen and a half horses, of many colors, but all rangy and long-legged. The riders wore mostly dark clothing, had saddlebags and bedrolls tied behind their cantles, and—Fawn's breath caught—long knives and swords hanging from their belts. Many also bore bows, unstrung athwart their backs, and quivers full of arrows.

No, not all men. A woman rode out of the pack, slid from her horse, and nodded to the farmwife. She was dressed much as the rest, in riding trousers and boots and a long leather vest, and had iron-gray hair braided and tied in a tight knot at her nape. The men wore their hair long too: some braided back or tied in queues with decorations of glass beads or bright metal or colored threads twisted in, some knotted tight and plain like the woman's.

Lakewalkers. A whole patrol of them, apparently. Fawn had seen their kind only once before, when she'd come with her parents and brothers to Lumpton Market to buy special seed, glass jars, rock oil and wax, and dyes. Not a patrol, that time, but a clan of traders from the wilderness up around the Dead Lake, who had brought fine furs and leathers and odd woodland produce and clever metalwork and more secret items: medicines, or maybe subtle poisons. The Lakewalkers were rumored to practice black sorcery.

Other, less unlikely rumors abounded. Lakewalker kinfolk did not settle in one place, but moved about from camp to camp depending on the needs of the season. No man among them owned his own land, carefully parceling it out amongst his heirs, but considered the vast wild tracts to be held in common by all his kin. A man owned only the clothes he stood in, his weapons, and the catches of his hunts. When they married, a woman did not become mistress of her husband's house, obliged to the care of his aging parents; instead a man moved into the tents of his bride's mother, and became as a son to her family. There were also whispers of strange bed customs among them which, maddeningly, no one would confide to Fawn.

On one thing, the farmers were clear. If you suffered an incursion by a blight bogle, you called in the Lakewalkers. And you did not cheat them of their pay, once they had removed the menace.

Fawn was not entirely sure she believed in blight bogles. For all the tall tales, she had never encountered one in her life, no, nor known anyone else who had, either. They seemed like ghost stories, got up to thrill the shrewd listeners and frighten the gullible ones. She had been gulled by her snickering older brothers far too many times to rise readily to the bait any more.

She froze again when she realized that one of the patrollers was walking toward her tree. He looked different than the others, and it took her a moment to realize that his dark hair was not long and neatly braided, but cut short to an untidy tousle. He was alarmingly tall, though, and very lean. He yawned and stretched, and something glinted on his left hand. At first Fawn thought it was a knife, then realized with a slight chill that the man had no left hand. The glint was from some sort of hook or clamp, but how it was fastened to his wrist beneath his long sleeve, she could not see. To her dismay, he ambled into the shade directly below her, there to lower his long body, prop his back comfortably against her tree trunk, and close his eyes.

Fawn jerked and nearly fell out of the tree when the farmwife reached up and rang her bell after all. Two loud clanks and three, repeated: evidently a signal or call, not an alarm, for she was talking all the time in an animated way with the patroller woman. Now that Fawn's eye had time to sort them out in their strange garb, she could see three or four more women among the men. A couple of men busied themselves at the well, hauling up the bucket to slosh the water into the wooden trough on the side opposite the bench; others led their horses in turn to drink. A boy loped around the outbuildings in answer to the bell, and the farmwife sent him with several more of the patrollers into the barn. Two of the younger women followed the farmwife into her house, and came out in a while with packets wrapped in cloth— more of the good farm food, obviously. The others emerged from the barn lugging sacks of what Fawn supposed must be grain for their horses.

They all met again by the well, where a brief, vigorous conversation ensued between the farmwife and the gray-haired patroller woman. It ended with a counting over of sacks and packets in return for coins and some small items from the patroller saddlebags that Fawn could not make out, to the apparent satisfaction of both sides. The patrol broke up into small groups to seek shade around the yard and share food.

The patrol leader walked over to Fawn's tree and sat down cross-legged beside the tall man. "You have the right idea, Dag."

A grunt. If the man opened his eyes, Fawn could not tell; her leaf-obstructed view was now of two ovals, one smooth and gray, the other ruffled and dark. And a lot of booted leg, stretched out.

"So what did your old friend have to say?" asked the man. His low voice sounded tired, or maybe it was just naturally raspy. "Malice confirmed, or not?"

"Rumors of bandits only, so far, but a lot of disappearances around Glassforge. With no bodies found."

"Mm."

"Here, eat." She handed him something, ham wrapped in bread judging by the enticing aroma that rose to Fawn. The woman lowered her voice. "You feel anything yet?"

"You have better groundsense than I do," he mumbled around a mouthful. "If you don't, I surely won't."

"Experience, Dag. I've been in on maybe nine kills in my life. You'e done what—fifteen? Twenty?"

"More, but the rest were just little ones. Lucky finds."

"Lucky ha, and little ones count just the same. They'd have been big ones by the next year." She took a bite of her own food, chewed, and sighed. "The children are excited."

"Noticed. They're going to start setting each other off if they get wound up much tighter."

A snort, presumably of agreement.

The raspy voice grew suddenly urgent. "If we do find the malice's lair, put the youngsters to the back."

"Can't. They need the experience, just as we did."

A mutter: "Some experiences, no one needs."

The woman ignored this, and said, "I thought I'd pair Saun with you."

"Spare me. Unless I'm pulling camp guard duty. Again."

"Not this time. The Glassforge folk are offering a passel of men to help."

"Ah, spare us all. Clumsy farmers, worse than the children."

"It's their folk being lost. They've a right."

"Doubt they could even take out *real* bandits." He added after a moment, "Or they would have by now." And after another, "If they are real bandits."

"Thought I'd stick the Glassforgers with holding the horses, mostly. If it is a malice, and if it's grown as big as Chato fears, we'll need every pair of our hands to the front."

A short silence. "Poor word choice, Mari."

"Bucket's over there. Soak your head, Dag. You know what I meant."

The right hand waved. "Yeah, yeah."

With an *oof,* the woman rose to her feet. "Eat. That's an order, if you like."

"*I'm* not nervy."

"No," the woman sighed, "no, you are not that." She strode off.

The man settled back again. *Go away, you,* Fawn thought down at him resentfully. *I have to pee.*

But in a few minutes, just before she was driven by her body's needs into entirely unwelcome bravery, the man got up and wandered after the patrol leader. His steps were un-hurried but long, and he was across the yard before the leader gave a vague wave of her hand and a side-glance. Fawn could not see how it could be an order, yet somehow, everyone in the patrol was suddenly up and in motion, sad-dlebags re-packed, girths tightened. The whole lot of them were mounted and on their way in five minutes.

Fawn slipped down the tree trunk and peered around it. The one-handed man—riding rear guard?—was looking back over his shoulder. She ducked out of sight again till the hoof beats faded, then unclutched the apple tree and went to seek the farmwife. Her pack, she was relieved to see in pass-ing, lay untouched on the bench.

Dag glanced back, wondering anew about the little farm girl who'd been hiding shyly up the apple tree. There, now—down she slid, but he still gained no clear look at her. Not that a few leaves and branches could hide a life-spark so bright from his groundsense at *that* range.

His mind's eye sketched a picture of her tidy farm raided by a malice's mud-men, all its cheerful routine turned to ash and blood and charnel smoke. Or worse—and not imagina-tion but memory supplied the vision—a ruination like the Western Levels beyond the Gray River, not six hundred miles west of here. Not so far away to him, who had ridden or walked the distance a dozen times, yet altogether beyond these local people's horizons. Endless miles of open flat, so devastated that even rocks could not hold their shape and slumped into gray dust. To cross that vast blight leached the ground from one's body as a desert parched the mouth, and it was just as potentially lethal to linger there. A thousand years of sparse rains had only begun to sculpt the Levels into something resembling a landscape again. To see this farm girl's green rolling lands laid low like that . . .

Not if I can help it, Little Spark.

He doubted they would meet again, or that she would ever know what her—mother's?—strange customers today sought to do on her behalf and their own. Still he could not begrudge her his weariness in this endless task. The country people who gained even a partial understanding of the methods called it black necromancy, and sidled away from patrollers in the street. But they accepted their gift of safety all the same. *So yet again, one more time anew, we will buy the death of this malice with one of our own.*

But not more than one, not if he could make it so.

Dag clapped his heels to his horse's sides and cantered after his patrol.

The farmwife watched thoughtfully as Fawn packed up her bedroll, straightened the straps, and hitched it over her shoulder once more. "It's near a day's ride to Glassforge from here," she remarked. "Longer, walking. You're like to be benighted on the road."

"It's all right," said Fawn. "I've not had trouble finding a place to sleep." Which was true enough. It was easy to find a cranny to curl up in out of sight of the road, and bedtime was a simple routine when all you did was spread a blanket and lie down, unwashed and unbrushed, in your clothes. The only pests that had found her in the dark were the mosquitoes and ticks.

"You could sleep in the barn. Start off early tomorrow." Shading her eyes, the woman stared down the road where the patrollers had vanished a while ago. "I'd not charge you for it, child."

Her honest concern for Fawn's safety stood clear in her face. Fawn was torn between unjust anger and a desire to burst into tears, equally uncomfortable lumps in her stomach and throat. *I'm not twelve, woman.* She thought of saying so, and more. She had to start practicing it sooner or later: *I'm twenty. I'm a widow.* The phrases did not rise readily to her lips as yet.

Still . . . the farmwife's offer beguiled her mind. Stay a day, do a chore or two or six and show how useful she could be, stay another day, and another . . . farms always needed more hands, and Fawn knew how to keep hers busy. Her first planned act when she reached Glassforge was to look for work. Plenty of work right here—familiar tasks, not scary and strange.

But Glassforge had been the goal of her imagination for weeks, now. It seemed like quitting to stop short. And wouldn't a town offer better privacy? *Not necessarily,* she realized with a sigh. Wherever she went, folks would get to know her sooner or later. Maybe it was all the same, no new horizons anywhere, really.

She mustered her flagging determination. "Thanks, but I'm expected. Folk'll worry if I'm late."

The woman gave a little headshake, a combination of conceding the argument and farewell. "Take care, then." She turned back to her house and her own onslaught of tasks, duties that probably kept her running from before dawn to after dark.

A life I would have taken up, except for Sunny Sawman, Fawn thought gloomily, climbing back up to the straight road once more. *I'd have taken it up for the* sake *of Sunny Sawman, and never thought of another.*

Well, I've thought of another now, and I'm not going to go and un-think it. Let's go see Glassforge.

One more time, she called up her wearied fury with Sunny, the low, stupid, nasty . . . stupid fool, and let it stiffen her spine. Nice to know he had a use after all, of a sort. She faced south and began marching.